Melissa Hibbert

Tananarive Due teaches Black horror and Afrofuturism at UCLA, and her most recent novel, *The Reformatory,* won the *Los Angeles Times* Book Prize for science fiction, fantasy, and speculative fiction. Her stories have been featured on *LeVar Burton Reads* and *Realm*, and she is an executive producer on Shudder's documentary *Horror Noire: A History of Black Horror.* Due and her husband/collaborator, Steven Barnes, wrote for Jordan Peele's *The Twilight Zone* and for Shudder's anthology film *Horror Noire.* They also cowrote the Black Horror graphic novel *The Keeper,* illustrated by Marco Finnegan. Due and Barnes cohost a podcast, *Lifewriting: Write for Your Life!*

cracker of a collection . . . Like its predecessor, it covers a wide range of genres and subgenres—dystopian, Afrofuturism, horror, Southern gothic, fantasy/ supernatural—and highlights the best of what Due can do . . . It would make a great introduction to her body of work for new fans especially. Due is the queen of horror noir, and she is in fine form in this collection."   —*Locus Magazine*

"One of the great torchbearers of Afrofuturism and Black horror . . . For Due, horror is situational and philosophical, a bubbling cauldron of terrible irony, systemic breakdowns, and worldwide devastation . . . The title tract in *Wishing Pool*, meanwhile, is a pitch-perfect, careful-what-you-wish-for tale that leaves readers pondering memory, identity, and the meaning of happiness."   —*Philadelphia Inquirer*

"One of Due's skills is authentic dialogue and a smooth, easy, acceptable narrative. It's easy to slip right into the story and lose all sense of time and place . . . During my read through this entire collection, I had an overwhelming sense of what a treasure short stories are: bite-sized works of fiction we can consume a little or a lot of depending on what our heart needs . . . This is a treasure!"   —*The Lineup*

"*The Wishing Pool* is the first book in seven years from the horror and Afrofuturism boss Tananarive Due. It's a collection of short stories that are just as smart as they are scary."   —*The Root*

"Threads of connection weave throughout Due's new collection, which will leave readers wanting more . . . Though the stories include a wide range of supernatural and more earthbound horrors, racism and anti-Blackness shadow all of the characters and drive much of the volume's terror."   —*Booklist*

for *Blood Colony*

"*Blood Colony* will steal your breath on every impossible-to-put-down page. Due is masterful in crafting this thrill-ride of a tale that was truly worth the wait!"
              —L.A. Banks, author of the Vampire Huntress Legend Series

"An elegant, scary, richly exciting tale—all that we've come to expect from Tananarive Due."   —Greg Bear, author of *The Unfinished Land*

for *Joplin's Ghost: A Novel*

"Due shows herself true to her own powerful gift."
                                        —*Publishers Weekly* (starred review)

"[M]ore than just a ghost story is Due's sense of musical and cultural history . . . Even while she brings to life Scott Joplin the man, Due makes us appreciate Scott Joplin the icon, the symbol. This understanding gives *Joplin's Ghost* its haunting power." —*Washington Post*

"In this ambitious and action-packed novel, Tananarive Due blurs genre boundaries as adroitly as her ghost walks through walls. Part love story, part ghost story, part historical fiction, part contemporary adult drama, this book is difficult to categorize—and impossible to put down."
—Valerie Boyd, author of *Wrapped in Rainbows*

for *The Good House*

"A subtle tale of terror. Tananarive Due is a powerful storyteller with a rich social agenda."
—Graham Joyce, author of *Ghost in the Electric Blue Suit*

"Long one of the reigning icons of suspense, with *The Good House* Tananarive completes the near impossible: she outdoes even herself. [She] delivers a novel that is as haunting as it is humanistic. Long time fans can look forward to a welcome return. New readers are in for a great beginning." —John Ridley, author of the Black Panther comics

"Shiveringly good. Due has an unflinching way with the terrors that can beset the nuclear family, and with the love and honesty, can heal it."
—Nalo Hopkinson, author of *Skin Folk*

"When it comes to suspense, Tananarive Due has no equal. *The Good House* is as packed with thrills as it is well-written . . . another winner!"
—Valerie Wilson Wesley, author of the Tamara Hayle mysteries

for *The Living Blood*

"Tananarive Due continues to thrill, intrigue, and frighten us with her special brand of fiction. No one else can capture the particular hum and beat of her vision, which extends from South Florida to South Africa. Tananarive Due is creating classics." —Tina McElroy Ansa

"Stunning . . . an event of sustained power and energy . . . This novel should set a standard for supernatural thrillers of the new millennium."
—*Publishers Weekly* (starred review)

"One of the best and most significant novelists of her generation."
—Peter Straub

THE
WISHING
POOL

THE
WISHING
POOL

and Other Stories

TANANARIVE DUE

BROOKLYN, NEW YORK

Published by Akashic Books
©2023, 2024 Tananarive Due

ISBN: 978-1-63614-179-4
Library of Congress Control Number: 2022947055

Akashic Books
Brooklyn, New York
Instagram, X, Facebook: AkashicBooks
info@akashicbooks.com
www.akashicbooks.com

For my father, John Dorsey Due, Jr.

TABLE OF CONTENTS

Introduction

I *love* writing short stories. I've been publishing novels since 1995 and writing screenplays for twenty years, but in many ways short stories feel like my purest fiction.

Several of these stories feature young protagonists, as in my previous collection, *Ghost Summer*. I enjoy writing children in horror in particular, perhaps because childhood has so many harrowing moments that haunt us throughout our lives. I also learn so much from young protagonists about how to accept new realities and confront them with imagination and courage. But a thread of aging and mortality is also woven through this volume, starting with the titular story, "The Wishing Pool."

When I first began publishing horror, I had not yet experienced the worst traumas of my life—losing my mother and grandmother. As of this writing, my father, "Freedom Lawyer" John Due, is eighty-seven years old and experiencing dementia. I wrote the story "The Wishing Pool" in the wake of the COVID-19 pandemic, when I was about to see him for the first time in nearly two years and I was bracing for signs of his decline. I asked myself what was more important to me: the former trappings of our relationship or his own happiness? It's a question I still wrestle with, but writing this story helped prepare me emotionally for that visit. (In real life, my visit with my father went much better than Joy's visit with hers.)

I'm sure that most of the characters in these stories, like Joy, are different versions of me. Or I'm bringing my fears to life in fantastic, impossible ways. Or I'm conjuring answers to questions I can only confront through stories.

Of course, every attempt doesn't work. Sometimes I'll sketch a few lines, or a couple of pages, and somehow the ember isn't strong enough to forge a full story: the premise isn't interesting enough, or the world never comes into focus for me. "The Biographer" is based on a premise I toyed with as an unpublished writer with a day job as a reporter at the *Miami Herald* and dreams of becoming an author. Back then, I remember feeling so frustrated that some ideas were too big for my life experience—but the time for "The Biographer" is finally right.

Several of the pandemic stories in this collection were written before COVID, including "Attachment Disorder" and "Ghost Ship." But like my protagonist in "The Biographer," I suppose I thought it was possible that a pandemic would strike—or it represented one of my worst nightmares.

"Last Stop on Route 9" is a title I borrowed from a story I wrote while I was an undergraduate at Northwestern University. In my original story, a white traveler stops at a gas station reeling from an unidentified illness. That was pretty much the whole story. In those days as a creative writing student learning from the "canon," I lost sight of myself as I began writing contemporary realism about white male protagonists having epiphanies.

Not genre. Not Black women. (The first short story I sold right after college, "Amusement," also featured a white male protagonist.)

Gloria Naylor's *Mama Day* taught me that a Black woman could be respected writing Black characters and the metaphysical; a chance telephone interview with Anne Rice for the *Miami Herald* in 1992 taught me to lean into horror with pride. My rewritten version of "Last Stop on Route 9" is a racism-as-the-monster story that feels like a reclamation of my voice.

Times are also very different now than when I first began

testing my skills as a writer. With the growing respect for the late Octavia E. Butler, the rise of Jordan Peele, and a slew of talented writers of all races and ethnicities, no speculative fiction syllabus would be complete without a much broader spectrum of voices.

I didn't discover Butler's work until after the publication of my first novel, *The Between* (1995), so writing that story was an act of faith that I could find an audience that would appreciate Black Horror. Now, young writers of all kinds can see themselves reflected in genre fiction, yet the rise of Afrofuturism in particular—science fiction, fantasy, horror, comics, and magical realism in fiction—has opened a whole new world of opportunities.

I feel so fortunate to share these stories with you as a member of a growing community of writers who need to add a dash of magic and mayhem to their stories. Whether they take place in the future, the past, or the present, my most authentic voice—usually horror, sometimes a dash of science fiction too—is present in every single one.

PART I

Wishes

The Wishing Pool

oy nearly got lost on the root-knotted red dirt path off Highway 99, losing sight of the gaps between the live oaks and Spanish moss that fanned across her hood and windows like fingertips. Driving back to her family's cabin twenty years later reminded her that the woods had rarely been restful for her. Once, Dad had made her play outside instead of sitting on the couch with her Virginia Hamilton books, and she'd stepped in an anthill up to her shin. She howled so loudly from the vicious stinging that Dad and Mom heard her all the way from the lake, and when they reached her they expected to find her half dead. She'd never forgotten that wild, frightened look in their eyes. No, Joy did not like the woods.

If she'd started her trip closer to dark, she would have had to turn around and wait out the night at the overpriced Hampton Inn off I-10. (Like her father, she didn't want to sleep alone at her parents' main house in the ashes of her childhood ten miles back toward civilization.) But her father's old Bronco finally appeared in the glare of orange dusk light fighting through the treetops, parked in front of the cabin.

And the cabin looked so, so small—much smaller than she remembered. The trees and wildly growing ferns dwarfed it, with no obvious path to the door from the red-brown dirt driveway. She'd imagined that she and her brother might fix the cabin up as a rental one day, but in real life it was puny and weather-beaten and sad, more relic than residence. Their great-grandfather built this cabin in the 1920s to hide from lynch mobs roused by their envy that a Negro businessman could afford a shiny new Ford Model T.

Every inch of the cabin was sagging a hundred years later, weary of standing. The slanted roof had collected a thick blanket of dead leaves at the heart of the L shape that separated the cabin's main room from its single bedroom. The bathroom her parents had added in the rear in the nineties wasn't in great shape, Jesse had warned, but it was better than the outhouse she still saw a few yards beyond the cabin, its wood blackened with age.

How had Dad been living there alone for two months? Maybe longer, if her brother's theory was true: that he'd moved into the cabin soon after Mom's funeral a year ago. Almost to the day.

"How?" she said aloud.

Gaps between the walls' wooden slats gaped like missing teeth, so the cabin probably had no insulation just when the weather was getting cold. Joy was wearing a jacket and it wasn't dark yet. North Florida wasn't New York, where she lived now, but it wasn't South Florida either. The temperature was dipping to the forties at night. Jesse had warned her to bring extra blankets to supplement the coal stove, which was still the main heating source.

The cabin looked abandoned. But dim light bled through the threadbare curtains she recognized in the window, the ones with patterns of fish Mom had found at a garage sale with Joy a million years ago. Or yesterday. Time was a mystery and a lie since Mom had died.

Joy was glad that Dad wasn't waiting outside, since she might have forgotten to prepare herself to see him look smaller too. Thinner. More frail. Grayer. Jesse had warned her what to expect after his visit a week ago—the reason she was here—but she might have forgotten if the cabin had looked anything like she remembered it.

Joy checked her cell phone: *NO SIGNAL*.

Shit. No wonder Dad never picked up his cell phone. Jesse said he'd made an appointment to install a landline, but the technician couldn't come for another thirty days. She wished she could call Jesse now; she was a year older, but he was a better fit for this job. He'd been deployed in Afghanistan most of Mom's last year with cancer, so Joy was the one who had cleaned and fed her and raged at negligent nurses. They both knew it was Jesse's turn now. She could not have faced another round of nursing home applications and medical assessments on her own, not so soon. Jesse had already taken Dad to a neurologist in Jacksonville to confirm the dementia they already suspected before Mom died.

But Jesse's last visit had worried him so much that he'd promised Joy he would drive from Jacksonville to stay with Dad in the cabin every weekend. He just wanted to be sure she didn't think Dad needed more than that. All he'd asked from Joy was *one* weekend.

"Stay there in the cabin with him a couple nights," he'd said. "Observe his life. Let's compare notes on what we think we should do."

Then Jesse had held her forearm and stared her in the eye. "But he loves it out there, Joy. He really wants to be in that cabin. That's the only thing that makes him happy."

If she'd realized what Jesse really meant, she would not have come alone.

Joy heard her father's terrible cough before she reached the door.

For a couple of years, Joy had a friend during their family visits to the cabin. It turned out that a white family lived in a lake house only a quarter mile away, an easy walk if you knew where to look. The two kids were miraculously close to their ages: a daughter, Natalie, who was ten like Joy, and a son, Nate, who was only a year older than Jesse. For two summers and two winters, Joy and Natalie had tried every way they knew to entertain themselves in the woods. Collecting tadpoles. Tracking butterflies. Kicking over ant mounds in vengeance. Whittling figures from fat twigs. Smoking cigarettes Natalie stole from her mother. Anything that wasn't fishing.

Natalie was the one who told her about the Wishing Pool, which was midway between their properties, nestled between two ancient live oaks that bent toward each other as if to hug. It was more like a puddle than a pool, Joy had always thought, maybe six feet across, so shallow that the green-brown water only reached their knees—although Natalie cautioned against ever touching the water.

"It's for wishes," Natalie said. "Touching the water ruins them."

For their first wish, they kept it simple. They wished for a dog.

They didn't think it through, exactly. They didn't live together or even see each other outside of short visits, so they didn't have a clear picture of what that joint dog ownership would look like. But the next morning, when Joy was arguing with her brother over who had to wash the dishes piled in the cabin's tiny sink, she heard a happy bark outside. She rushed to the window and saw Natalie with a grin that filled her face. A black-and-white dog, coat a bit muddied (as if, just *maybe*, it had crawled out of the Wishing Pool), was running in circles around Natalie. Just like that, they had their dog.

Dad said it looked like a terrier mix of some kind, 100 percent pure mutt, and filthy at that, but they were ecstatic. No collar identified an owner who might be looking for him, so the dog was theirs. They named him Lucky because—well, the obvious. Lucky fetched sticks no matter how far they threw them, helped them sniff out rabbit holes, barked protectively at any strange rustlings, and generally made everything they did ten times more fun. They washed, combed, and groomed him until he looked like he belonged on TV.

They worked out a joint custody arrangement with their parents: Natalie would keep Lucky until the Christmas visit to the cabin, and then Joy could take him until summer.

But none of that happened. The day Joy was scheduled to go home, Natalie knocked on the cabin door teary-eyed and said Lucky had crawled out of her house and wouldn't come when she called. From the moment she heard, Joy knew the dog was gone. She wasn't surprised to learn, on her next visit, that Natalie had never seen Lucky again. She decided their wish had not been specific enough: they should have said they wanted a dog to *keep*.

Natalie had changed in the six months Joy had been away, a bit thinner, not smiling as much, bored with tadpoles and butterflies. The Wishing Pool had shrunk too, only half its previous size, the water more brown than green. Joy assumed they would wish to bring Lucky back, but Natalie just shrugged and said she didn't want a dog anymore.

"My wish is for my parents to get a divorce," Natalie said.

That wish was unimaginable to Joy, but Natalie said her parents fought so much that she'd rather they split up and get separate houses. She'd mapped it all out: two Christmases, two summer vacations, guilt presents. So Natalie threw the shiny penny in the pool, closed her eyes, and said, "Please let my parents split up." Joy was both scandalized and thrilled. The secret felt better than smoking. But the wish didn't come true. At least not right away.

The next summer, when Joy knocked on Natalie's door, a tenant answered and said they had sold the house after the owner was killed by a drunk driver. "Natalie?" Joy had said, hardly able to speak. The tenant soothed her: "No, honey, the little girl and her mom are fine. They lost the daddy, though."

Please let my parents split up, Natalie had said.

As an adult, Joy told the story often with a breezy air, never confessing how she'd walked far out of her way to avoid the Wishing Pool ever since. How maybe it was the Wishing Pool, not the boredom of fishing, that had soured her on visiting the cabin with her parents after she graduated from high school. How the Wishing Pool had ended her childhood.

"Joya!" Dad said, the nickname he'd made up for her. He grinned, his teeth unchanged, stripping thirty years from his face. That would be her happiest memory of this visit: his eyes bright with surprise and delight when he called her by the name that belonged to him alone.

Then another cough came, terrible, swaying him until he steadied himself against the doorframe. He sounded winded despite the cannulas in his nostrils, tubes snaking to rest heavy in a pocket of his robe. He was wearing piss-stained long underwear and a threadbare robe.

Joy wanted to burst into tears. Somehow, she didn't, leaning in for a casual hug. She was relieved that the nape of his neck smelled the same. She clung to every grace.

"Surprise, Dad!" She hadn't realized how good an actress she was.

Jesse hadn't told her the most important thing: Dad was dying. Maybe Jesse was hiding it from himself. She'd seen plenty of death up close with Mom, so she knew it when she saw it. The shriveled frame. The dark shadows beneath his eyes. That cough. How could Jesse have left Dad like this even for a day?

If she'd had a phone, she would have called for an ambulance already.

"Well, why the heck didn't you call when you got to town?" Dad said. "I'm a mess. I would've . . ." he surveyed himself, ". . . done better, pumpkin." He coughed a river of phlegm.

She took his arm—so thin!—and led him back inside, nudging the door closed with her heel so no heat would escape. The coal stove glowed golden orange through the grate, but it must be burning embers. The front room was cold, so his bedroom must be frigid. She wanted to take out a notebook and start making a list of the urgent things he needed.

Heat.

Clothes.

Medicine.

Chronicling it in her head dispassionately kept her lip from trembling.

"I'll help you put a few clothes in your bag. Then I need to take you to a doctor."

Dad waved an impatient hand over his shoulder before he opened the stove's door and stirred the dying coals. "I'm not gonna talk about that." Joy's silence finally wore him down. They had always had a kind of telepathy, weathering Mom's and Jesse's emotional storms with telling glances. "I've already seen the doctors, Joya. There's nothing I can do. It just has to play out. That's that. Ask your brother. We're not gonna talk about it."

So Jesse *did* know more, probably had heard a diagnosis. She'd fought so hard not to be irritated at Jesse, but now she was furious. Jesse was doing it again. He was hiding behind her.

Dad's hands had been waving above the coal bin so long that she realized he had forgotten his task. "Let me light that," Joy said. "It's *freezing* in here, Dad."

She'd sounded scolding, like Mom would have. They both heard it. The enormity of Mom's absence rocked through them.

Dad looked down at the coal, hiding misty eyes, and shrugged. "Not cold to me. But do what you want. Jesse was always cold too. Jesse was just here, you know. Few days ago."

"He told me." That was almost *all* he'd told her.

"Anything you want to know, ask him. Jesse's got it . . . under control." He coughed with a mighty struggle for breath.

"Dad, don't talk. You're wearing yourself out." She helped

him sit down in the wobbly wooden chair at the table, cupping his elbow. The ritual evoked a vivid image of helping Mom sit down to eat her last meal before they took her to the hospital she never came home from.

Joy's hands shook less when she dug into the coal bin and savored the rough texture of the coal, which was running low. The puzzle of finding the matches. The miracle of flame.

A thought made her nearly gasp with hope. "Is the phone hooked up?"

Dad reached into the pocket of his robe to pull out his cell phone, as shiny as new.

"Not your cell, Dad. Jesse said he called the phone company."

"Don't know . . . anything about that," Dad wheezed.

"I'm sorry—don't try to talk."

She checked his cell anyway, but it was dead. She wondered when he'd last charged it and decided it was probably ages ago—because her father had dementia. Hope, once spent, had exhausted her. Her situation flared into harsh focus again.

"Okay," she said in a down-to-business tone that made her own ears prick, eager to hear the plan. "First we need to warm it up in here. Then I'm gonna bring in my bag." Dad had a stack of newspapers piled on one end of the sofa, but she could clear it to sleep. She'd forgotten to bring extra blankets, though she could probably find some. If she meditated, she might be able to sleep. Eventually.

"You're staying?"

"Tonight, yes."

That was the simplest thing. His coughing had stopped, so it might not be the emergency she'd feared. The cabin was cold, but not frigid. The gaps in the planks had been patched with drywall; Jesse's work, she guessed. A kettle and saucepan were on the stove and she saw a stack of soup cans in the cabinet, ordered by type with military precision. Jesse again. She always traveled with a bag of protein bars, so she had plenty for breakfast and lunch, enough to share. Maybe Jesse really did have it under control.

The idea of a night's sleep, putting off tomorrow, elated her.

Then she saw the tears shining in her father's brown eyes. "Dad? What's wrong?"

He shook his head, staring at the bright orange glow of the stove. She waited, so he finally said, "I'm forgetting her. Your mother."

"You'll never forget Mom," she said before she could think, and the look he gave her was a lashing, as if she had betrayed his honesty with lies. "Some part of you will always—"

"Horseshit," he said. "I can't remember a thing. If I took my meds. If I *ate*." He spoke the final word painfully. "Have I bathed? I could take all of that, but . . . now it's Patricia I'm forgetting. I can't remember your mother's middle name." The confession wrenched him.

"Jesse probably doesn't know it either."

"That's different," he said. "He didn't know her since she was sixteen. He didn't grow up down the street from her. He's not one of the only ones left who *should* know."

Dad was so upset that he was shaking. His trembling loosed a coughing fit that made her doubt her plan to let him stay the night. His cough sounded like it needed a hospital.

"Her middle name is Rose," Joy said—*is*, not *was*—and Dad closed his eyes like the name was a devotion. She rubbed his back—his bones felt so frail!—and his coughing eventually stopped. She was glad to see that the tiny kitchen's faucet still worked. The well water tasted fresh when she tested a sip before handing him the glass.

"Yes, *Rose*," he wheezed when he could speak. "Patricia. Rose. Bryant." Mom's name before she got married. He repeated it several times. He found a pad on his table and wrote with the pen tied to it with a rubber band: *Patricia Rose Bryant* in jittery script. She saw other words and phrases he'd written:

Jaden and Jordan, Jesse's children. *10-2-32*, his birthdate.

She flipped the page and saw he'd filled the other side with his reminders. And the next page. He was harvesting his memories, collecting them one by one. Catching them while he could. Had he filled the entire notebook?

"Dad," Joy said gently, "do you know that sometimes people die of a broken heart? It's bad enough that we lost her, but you can't do this to yourself every time you can't think of something right away. Can you let yourself heal a little bit?"

"Heal." He spat the word.

"You're torturing yourself," she said. "You can't live like this. You've turned Mom into a kind of ghost haunting you. She wouldn't want that. It's alright to let some of it go."

"Sometimes," Dad said, "I can't remember her smile, Joya."

Then he buried his face in his arms on the tabletop and sobbed. Which led to a spate of coughing so severe that she was ready to carry him to her car if she had to. But then it stopped, and Dad went to his bed to sleep propped up on a mound of pillows, sitting up. Yet he slept.

Her cell phone told her it wasn't even seven o'clock. The sky had not darkened yet.

Joy remembered the Wishing Pool.

She found herself looking for the trail with the powerful flashlight she kept in her emergency pack in the trunk of her car. Much of the woods were overgrown and unrecognizable years later, though she knew to veer right after the outhouse, so she waded through the underbrush and tried to find any hints of the trail.

She never did. But she did see the twin live oaks, still standing, eerily unchanged, their trunks colored bright gold in the waning daylight. A beacon calling to her, almost.

When she reached the trees, she was sure the Wishing Pool would have dried up. But it hadn't. It barely looked like a puddle anymore, covered in leaves, but dark brown water still peeked through in that spot and *only* that spot. Joy wanted to test its depth with her foot, but she remembered what Natalie had said about tainting it with touch. So she didn't.

Thinking about Natalie was almost enough to change her mind. But not quite.

Joy reached into her back pocket for the change she'd shoved there after she broke a twenty at a McDonald's on the road. A shiny penny gleamed in her flashlight beam. She pressed it between her fingertips until the copper was warm, her heart speeding up.

The last time she had stood in this spot, Mom had been alive, back in the cabin with Dad. How could this physical place still exist when the life it was tied to was gone?

"Please," she said aloud to the night woods, "just let my father be healthy and happy."

She tossed her penny into the murky water just beyond the edge of a drowned leaf and watched until it sank out of sight. She waited for the surge of certainty she'd felt as a child that magic was humming around her. Instead, while crickets whirred in a fever, she could only remember Natalie's dead father and his salt-and-pepper beard. She wondered if Natalie had blamed herself for his death and felt certain she *had*. Joy wanted to plunge her hand into the puddle and retrieve her penny, but she told herself she was being silly, since wishes weren't real.

Or she might ruin her wish if she touched the water.

Or both.

The short walk back to the cabin was harrowing because it had gotten dark so fast, but Joy was grateful to return to a warming room and the sound of her father snoring safely in his bed. No coughing. She touched his forehead. No fever. Could the wish that couldn't possibly work be working already? She didn't believe it—though *wanting* to believe made her smile at herself.

Smiling made everything easier. She cleared off the sofa, found fresh blankets in the cedar-scented trunk at the foot of Dad's bed (beside two large oxygen tanks she tried not to notice), and chanced upon a package of Almond M&M's she didn't know she had in her purse. She was asleep as soon as she rested her head. The cold room only made her sleep harder, and she dreamed a kaleidoscope of her childhood: lively meals and talent shows and beach days. She woke up in the daylight feeling better rested than she had in weeks, swaddled under a mound of blankets.

The first thing she heard was the silence. No snoring. No coughing. No sound at all.

She kicked off her blankets and jumped up to look into the bedroom's open doorway. Dad's bed was empty, his blankets on the floor. She barely squeezed out the thought *Where the hell is*—

And then she heard a chopping sound outside, an axe splitting wood. She'd forgotten how Dad used to chop piles of wood, more than they needed since coal burned long. He said swinging his axe made him feel like John Henry. But *now*?

Joy ran outside barefoot, ignoring her cold toes and the prickling and poking against her bare soles. A pine cone stabbed her foot so sharply that she was sure it drew blood. She hopped the rest of the distance to find Dad in the shadow of the outhouse, the axe raised high above his head, his back turned. He arced his swing and cleaved the wood chunk in half.

Then he *laughed*. Not his polite chuckle he forced out to put her at ease—a deep belly laugh she was sure would make him cough. But it didn't. He heaved in a breath before he swung the axe again, and his lungs sounded strong and clear. *Healthy*. He laughed again. *Happy*.

Adrenaline tingled Joy's skin.

"Be careful!" she said. "Should you be exerting yourself like that?"

Dad whirled around, startled. His smile withered when he saw her. He stared, eyes flat.

"Help you?" he said.

"Very funny."

But his eyes stayed flat. His smile stayed gone. Joy's stomach cramped.

"It's . . . Joy. Joya."

When he heard his nickname for her, recognition flared in his eyes, but oh-so-tepid. He studied her features the way he would a painting in a museum. Mildly curious.

"Joya," he said. He nodded. He took one step closer to her. Another. He spoke directly into her eyes: "Pleased to meet you. You remind me of someone."

His smile returned, perhaps the one he'd flashed for her mother when he spotted her raking leaves in her yard that day he passed on his bicycle when they were both sixteen and he had just moved to her street. Or, perhaps it was the smile he'd worn the first day he held Joy in his arms, still slick from Mom's womb. Soon, Joy couldn't see his smile for her tears.

She only heard the sharp *CHOP* of the wood and her father's strong huff of breath as his laughter and liberation rang in the treetops.

Haint in the Window

They walked in with a gale of authority, the bells on the door jangling with a ferocity that made you jump and feel guilty even if you'd only spent the morning arranging to rent chairs for next week's Terry McMillan book signing. Darryl noted their flanking formation—one on one side, one on the other—as they eased inside the bookstore, their hands never far from their waistbands. Fingers never far from their triggers. Maybe that was how they had moved when they served in Afghanistan, or wherever else they had moved on the lookout for targets.

Darryl had noticed the uniforms through the window long before the door opened, but he kept his eyes down on his seating chart just the same, as if they hadn't shaken those bells loud enough to wake the dead. Fucking security guards. A salt-and-pepper team like *Lethal Weapon*. Or *48 Hrs*. In *his* store with such an imperious air. (His store except on the deed, anyway.)

"Sir?"

When Darryl looked up, the Black security guard, who was closest, smiled an irritated smile, worse than a frown. The white one kept a distance as if he were waiting for Darryl to pull out a sawed-off from underneath his counter: his head tilted slightly down, eyes angled upward. Meant to look scary, maybe, but he was only five eight, so Darryl, who was six feet, wasn't scared. They looked like they were serving a warrant. Darryl had to remind himself they weren't really cops. And that he'd never been served a warrant in his life. He managed a damn bookstore.

"Yeah," Darryl finally answered when he figured they had waited long enough.

"A couple was mugged down at the intersection today."

Darryl waited for the part that had something to do with him.

The white security guard went on, trying to enlist Darryl's indignation: "New residents at the Gardens?" *The Gardens.* Darryl almost laughed at the nickname for the former eyesore he'd walked past his whole life. Residents had been begging for a new paint job for twenty years, but new paint only came with the reopening. The evictions.

"We're keeping an eye out for a Black male," the white one said.

I'll let you know if I see him. It took all of Darryl's restraint not to say it aloud. He did say it with his eyes, though. The Black security guard glanced away, getting the joke.

The song "Fuck the Security Guards" from Rusty Cundieff's *Fear of a Black Hat* was in Darryl's Friday-night mix, which he played late when there were fewer children in the store. It would be so easy to punch on the sound system and let it blast. Security guards were cops without the training or even imaginary ideals, and a whole gang of them had been hired to patrol the shopping center where Sankofa was nestled since the renovated apartment building across the street began leasing at three times the price. Leimert Gardens, the landlord called the complex now, although it had no garden and the bougainvillea flowers wrapped around the fence had turned brown and died years ago. Darryl had seen these two rent-a-cops before through his picture window at the counter, their necks swiveling as they marched up and down the strip like the street was under occupation. Darryl hoped the sun was burning them up in those black uniforms that made them look like SS.

"About your height and weight," the white security guard said without irony. The brother still didn't meet Darryl's eyes. "If you see anyone—"

"If I see *me*?" Darryl said. "Sure. I'll give you a call. You got a card?" He held out his hand. The white security guard was confused by his juxtaposition of sarcasm and willingness. He finally reached into his front pocket, behind his badge, and pulled out a business card: *South LA Security—established 2016.* But now his minor irritation had bloomed to anger that turned his earlobes red. When he leaned forward, he stared into Darryl's eyes almost like a lover—and that was when Darryl *knew*.

Darryl's grandmother had called it his Third Eye, claiming it was his birthright. Darryl knew things that were unspoken sometimes, whispers of premonitions. His stomach always knotted when he brushed against knowledge that was none of his business, but he'd learned to use the feeling to avoid problems when he interviewed job candidates or suffered through first dates that wouldn't lead anywhere except where he'd already been. This time, the feeling was even stronger: the knotting, but also a *burning*.

This guy was bad news, a violent bully. Okay, maybe he didn't need a premonition to guess that, but Darryl knew this particular man—*RICK*, his name tag said, no last name offered—was a security guard because he couldn't qualify for LAPD, which was a true testament to his instability. And he deeply craved an excuse to hurt a smart-ass like Darryl Martin Jones. To kill someone, if he could get away with it—just to see what it might feel like. Even his smile looked like a trap ready to spring. Darryl pulled his hand back, hesitating to take the card. He wanted no ties to Rick.

"You've got a great view of the street here," the Black one said. "Maybe you'll see someone you don't know? Someone who doesn't belong?"

The door jangled again, and this time a white couple walked

inside, maybe in their late twenties, both in hiking sandals and cargo shorts, their toes bare. On an adventure together. They hesitated at the sight of the security guards, but after a quick assessment they decided the space was safe. Darryl noticed how the woman drew her arms around her oversized purse.

"Do you have any children's books?" she asked Darryl. "Picture books?"

Darryl pointed to the colorful corner display at the front of the store with the child-sized plastic play table. Bright red. Truly impossible to miss. But because his desk was so prominent across from the door, he was the concierge from the moment customers walked inside—no need to look for themselves. "Picture books up front. Most young adult books are near the back. Let me know if you're looking for something specific."

"Great!" the woman chirped. She seemed to notice how tightly she was clutching her bag and let it fall limp to her hip. "Just looking for something for my niece for Black History Month. This is a beautiful store."

"Thank you," Darryl said, his eyes back on the white security guard. He realized he had never taken the business card, which the guard still held out within his reach. He hated the part of himself that felt more at ease with white witnesses nearby. He even put on a show for them. "And we serve beautiful customers. In a beautiful neighborhood."

Darryl took the security guard's card. From Rick's icy smile, he hadn't liked waiting.

Darryl hoped they wouldn't come by the store again. But the knot in his stomach, still stewing, told him they probably would—Rick would, at least. Darryl was pretty sure of that.

A less watchful manager might not have noticed, but that wasn't Darryl, so he saw right away: two books were face out in Protest & Revolution. Instead of the newly published books by UCLA professors he was trying to promote, the two books facing out were Franz Fanon's *The Wretched of the Earth* and *The Autobiography of Malcolm X*. He had read both of them in high school, his first and favorites. Truthfully, they usually *were* facing out—but not today. Except they *were*. He hadn't seen a customer in that section in the hour since he'd propped up the other books, so no one else could have done it. And the two books he'd chosen were on the floor. Facedown. As if the two books in their place had popped out on their own and knocked down the upstart competition.

Darryl wasn't a haint-believing kind of brother, so that's not where his head went first. He told himself that he must not have noticed one of the customers rearrange his shelf for whatever entitled reason—maybe a *"well, actually"* commentary on which books deserved to be in the section and which didn't—and Darryl was muttering about it under his breath for the rest of the day because *the fucking nerve*. The thing was, the only customers who had been in his store since he arranged those shelves were two white dudes who had gone straight to Biography and then ambled over to the *New York Times* best sellers, and then the new section at the front where he kept most of his books by white authors, decorated with big enough posters to be seen from the store window: Colson Whitehead, yes, but also the usual suspects: Stephen King, James Patterson, John Grisham, and Gillian Flynn. Whitenip for casual passersby who weren't drawn to the kente cloth and *Essence* best sellers that took up most of the window space.

For the first year after the Gardens opened up, newly renovated, three times the price for a one-bedroom, he'd delayed stocking anything except Black and brown authors as usual. But he had to admit that his sales had gone up almost 20 percent since he added the new section. Maybe more, if he was honest. His old customers were moving on and out, and his new customers wanted to treat him like a Barnes & Noble despite the sign clearly marked *Sankofa Books & Gifts* outside. Even if they didn't speak any languages from Ghana, where Sankofa meant to go back and retrieve what was lost, they should be able to tell it meant *Black*.

Darryl had studied enough sales trends to predict that if he had a time machine, he might not recognize Sankofa in five years—assuming it was still here—just like he already didn't recognize the rest of the street. The books and shelves might still be here, but the spirit of the place could be gone.

Like everything. Like everyone.

Darryl never planned to run a bookstore. He'd noticed how hard Mrs. Richardson worked as he strolled the aisles and vowed that he would never be seduced by a love so fickle. Too many empty seats when the visiting author deserved a stadium. Hardcover books too expensive for customers to afford. He promised himself he would not be swayed by the whine of Coltrane's sax hypnotizing him from the speaker in the top corner of the east wall. Not by boxes of greeting cards adorned with the blazing colors of Harlem Renaissance artists: Jacob Lawrence. Romare Bearden. Loïs Mailou Jones. Not by hand-painted placards posted to announce the myriad sections, each more glorious than the last: Protest & Revolution and Biographies, of course, but also Science Fiction. Mystery & Thriller. Romance. Comics & Graphic Novels. Each aisle a world unto itself, his mother's favorite weekend spot, God rest her soul. *Lemme take you to school so you'll see what they won't teach you*, Mama used to say, and they would each disappear into Sankofa as the hours passed outside. Sankofa was the sun on its venerated street in South Central and everything else was in its orbit. Or so Darryl thought.

Sankofa was not only a fortress from erasure, it had been a citadel during the fires. In 1992, when a jury in Los Angeles proclaimed that a Black man's plight was worth less than a dog's (since his neighbor had gotten jail time for beating his dog, unlike those cops who beat Rodney King for the world to see), the strip mall across the street had gone up in flames while Mrs. Richardson opened her doors to anyone who needed to sob or rant, or both, behind the safety of her bookshelves. Fruit of Islam guarded the doors, but even if they hadn't, Darryl's father and his Uncle Boo—both high school football coaches— would have joined any dozen other men or women to protect Sankofa and its treasures. Smoke rose east, west, north, and south of Sankofa, but not a single page in the bookstore burned.

When Mrs. Richardson offered Darryl a job after school when he was fifteen, it seemed harmless enough. Why not earn his movie and comic book money organizing the boxes, stacking books on shelves, and—after a couple of months of building trust—running the register when Mrs. Richardson had more than one customer, so she could hover and make suggestions? He'd imagined himself becoming a writer, so a bookstore felt like a natural incubator. If he were honest with himself—and honesty was harder to come by now that he was nearly forty— his days working at Sankofa had been some of the happiest of his life.

The problem was, he'd fixed the store, the street, the neighborhood, in time, as if they would always be the way he remembered. But in the Afrofuturism section, Octavia E. Butler had written, "The only lasting truth is Change" in *Parable of the Sower* for all the world to see, so that fallacious thinking was nobody's fault but his. *Everything* changed. The South Central LA he'd grown up in had been different in his grandmother's time, when it was mostly white. His grandfather used to say that the coyotes and mountain lions and bears that sometimes ventured from the hills were only a reminder that this land had never belonged to humans, period.

The Only Lasting Truth indeed.

Darryl first thought the word *ghost* the day the boxes tumbled down in the storeroom. The store was empty when he heard the noise, and the cramped storeroom, which housed the bathroom, didn't have a door to outside. (How many times had the more celebrated authors complained that there was no rear door to sneak into past the crowd?) This was about a week after the wrong book covers had been turned out, which he'd pretty much forgotten, even when the other strange things started happening. Always when he was alone.

On Tuesday, the blinds over the picture window unfurled even though no one touched the pull string. The right half fell until it nearly touched the floor, but the left half got caught midway up, a leering eye. *That* was a first. Then the Barack Obama book cover he'd hung on the wall was on the floor when he opened the store Wednesday morning, the plastic frame cracked, Obama's face grinning sideways at him. By then, it was three strange occurrences in as many days, and he'd begun to wonder if someone was sabotaging him on purpose. Low-key.

Then the storeroom. Darryl had part-time helpers who came in after school like he had—although, frankly, they lacked both drive and pride in their work—so Darryl checked the stability of every box himself even if he didn't stack them. Hardcovers could get bent up in the box, and returning them was a hassle, so he ran a tight storeroom. When he heard the crash, he thought a vagrant had snuck in to find a quiet place to sleep . . . and instead, he found all six boxes from the top of the wire shelf on the east wall tumbled down to the concrete, one of them bashed open and spilling Stephen King paperbacks.

"Hey! Who's back here?" he called out with extra bass in his voice, picking up his broom, because, again, he wasn't a "ghosty" kind of brother and the only hauntings he'd heard about were in old houses. Grudgingly, he remembered the security guards' visit and talk of a local mugger, so he thought maybe his store was a target: he couldn't guess the angle of knocking down boxes in the storeroom, but it *could* be a ploy to get him away from the register. He tried to keep one eye on his desk through the doorway, but the storeroom had a lot of narrow aisles to cover, so eventually his desk was no longer in sight as he peeked around corners.

No one. The storeroom was empty. He was about to try to figure out what else could have made the boxes fall when the bathroom door slammed itself shut. The slam was a loud *CRACK* like a gunshot that made him jump inside his clothes. The doorknob rattled like it might fall off, then abruptly fell still.

"Hey!" Darryl called with far less bass this time, more like a petulant child. "Get your ass out here and get the hell out of my store!"

The door didn't move. The doorknob didn't so much as tremble.

Darryl never kept a gun in his store. He had his dad's old Glock at home, a memento more than protection, but it wasn't with him now. The notion of an armed bookseller didn't sit well with him, felt like an oxymoron, so all he had in his shaking hand was a broom handle as he approached the bathroom door. "Come on. No one's gonna hurt you!" he said, trying to sound folksy and empathetic. Sometimes desperate people only wanted five dollars, or a sandwich. "You need somethin' I can get you, brother?" (Sexist to assume it was a man, he knew, but whoever it was would have to be pretty tall to reach those boxes on the top shelf. And strong enough to pull them down.)

Stillness and silence.

Darryl knew that most store owners would call the police, but not on his damn watch. And he wouldn't call those security guards either. He used the hashtag *#abolitionnow* on his Twitter, so this was how a world without policing would look like. People would need to deal with their own damn problems instead of expecting somebody to come help them.

"Alright, then. One . . . two . . ."

He didn't wait for *three*. He turned the knob and kicked the door open so hard that he tore a foot-sized hole in the wood, which apparently was hollow inside. *Shit.*

No one was in the bathroom, which was only as big as a broom closet, with no windows, so its emptiness sat in plain view. One gray-white toilet, water low as usual. A sink with a rust trail in the basin from the faucet left dripping over the years. The mirror with a triangular crack in one corner. An old *Devil in a Blue Dress* movie poster featuring Denzel. Empty.

"What . . ." Darryl said aloud to his reflection in the mirror, ". . . the fuck?"

That was the first time the word came to his mind: *I've got a damn ghost.* His grandfather would have called it a haint or a spook. Whatever the word for it, his experiences in the past couple of days finally made sense.

"Well, I'll be damned," he said.

And just maybe, he thought, he was.

The Spirituality section gave him clues but no real answers. Yet he'd pieced together enough from ghost stories and horror movies to figure out that any haint going to the trouble of being noticed by human eyes must have a message. But what? And, more importantly, *whose* message?

He thought first of Mrs. Richardson's husband, Calvin, who had died of a heart attack behind this very desk back in 2005, but why would he bother coming back after all these years? (All he'd talked about was getting *away* from the burdens of Sankofa, so it was hard to imagine him returning now.) Same for Calvin Jr., who had never shown much interest in the store before he'd OD'd on painkillers in 2010. Documentary filmmaker St. Clair Bourne had spent hours at a time visiting Sankofa before he died after brain surgery in 2007, but wouldn't he be more likely to haunt a movie theater, his beloved medium? Muhammad Ali had done a signing and called the store "the greatest" years ago, though believing it was Ali's ghost was plain wishful thinking. Like, damn, Ali could haunt anywhere in the world. Same with so many of the others: Prince had surprised him one day and bought a couple hundred dollars' worth of music biographies, but wouldn't Prince haunt a recording studio instead? Or, better yet, a keyboard? Could it be E. Lynn Harris, gone so soon in 2009? Or Eric Jerome Dickey, who'd broken his readers' hearts when he passed away in 2021?

And sister Octavia. Octavia E. Butler had done a book signing for *Fledgling* only months before she died, on Halloween night, no less. He'd almost sprung for an overflow space but decided to let the customers sit close to each other for the experience. They'd been shoulder to shoulder, beyond standing room only. Some had sat on the floor. Every time Octavia spoke with her deep, wise timbre, the room had been so silent it might as well be empty. Her books might be grim, yet she'd smiled all through that night. Octavia *might* be haunting the store, he thought, so he put an asterisk by her name. She just might.

But how many other customers had died since Darryl started working here when he was fifteen, their hair graying, walk slowing, persistent coughs shaking stooping shoulders, breaths wheezing under the weight of cigarettes, heart conditions, and diabetes? Three dozen, easily. And those were just the ones whose names he remembered, whose faces had graced the aisles with laughter and smiles and "What you got for me today?" That wasn't counting the ones who had just moved away, and that was a kind of death too, so why not?

The more Darryl tried to think of whose ghost might be haunting Sankofa, the more he realized it was a long-ass list. His parents were gone, killed by a drunk driver on Crenshaw when he was thirty. His mother might be the haunting type, but she would never intentionally knock over boxes of books; that was sacrilege. And why nearly twenty years later? His Aunt Lucy and Uncle Boo. His cousin Ray. Dead, all of them. They were ghosts haunting him even when they didn't make themselves known. But would they follow him to Sankofa?

All he knew was that this haunting felt deeply personal. The haint *knew* him, and well. The *Autobiography of Malcolm X* could have been a good guess, but Fanon too? When he'd read them the same year, back to back? No way that was random. Only his father knew that—maybe. But his father would never have knocked down the Obama poster, not enough to hurt it. They'd had long arguments over what Obama was and wasn't doing for Black people, and his father had been Obama to the bone. If anything, Dad would have sat the poster in Darryl's office chair.

Darryl wrote down as many names as he remembered. Tried calling out a few. But no answer came, not even the sound of a flapping page. The more names he called out to the silence, the more a cold loneliness wrapped itself around Darryl's chest, the feeling he sometimes tried to drink away with half a bottle of wine after work, when there was nothing else for his hands and mind to do except remember that, once upon a time, he'd planned a bigger life. He couldn't remember the last time he'd even pretended to write.

Old folks called dead people who came back *haints*, but what was the word for those, like him, who had been left behind?

Darryl was close to telling himself he'd imagined everything when he saw the haint in the window. He?—She?—was standing just below the giant golden script of the backward *S* in *Sankofa* on the glass. At first he thought it was someone standing outside, obscured in a blaze of sunlight, but it was a reflection as if someone was standing *inside* the store. No one else was with him, not on a Tuesday afternoon when it wasn't Black History Month. About six feet tall. Dark skin. Darryl couldn't make out the facial features, but the figure's bulk standing there looked as real as the life-sized Michelle Obama cutout posed beside his desk.

Darryl couldn't read the expression on the blurry face, though the eyes were staring straight at him. The stare felt ominous, so dispassionate and yet . . . so urgent. All moisture left Darryl's mouth. For the first time in his life, he rubbed his eyes like people do in movies to make sure they're not hallucinating. He wasn't. The haint was still in the window when he opened his eyes.

"Who . . ." Darryl cleared his throat, since the word was buried in nervous phlegm. "Who are you? What's your name? What do you want?" The questions running through his mind for days spilled from his mouth.

The haint only stared from the window, reflecting . . . no one.

"Why are you here? Tell me what you want me to—"

Bells jangled, and for one glorious, endless breath, Darryl was sure the haint was communicating in a musical language from another plane—until the front door opened and a customer wandered in. (Only the door chimes! The disappointment was *real*.) She was a blond-haired white woman in a sundress and wide-brimmed hat like a Hollywood starlet. A tourist, obviously. Her nose was sunburned bright red.

"Excuse me . . . can you recommend a good beach read?" She pointed to the new names in his window display. "How about Stephen King?"

Darryl had glanced away for only an instant, yet of course the haint was gone the next time he looked. Rage coursed through him, but he swallowed it away. Would rage bring the haint back? Bridge the gulf between the living and the dead? The present and the past?

For horror fans, Darryl usually recommended Victor La-Valle instead, or Octavia's *Fledgling*, or that anthology *Sycorax's Daughters* with horror by all of those fierce sisters, but instead he only said blandly, "Which one? I think I've got 'em all."

"Right?" she laughed. Her laugh was a knife twist, though he didn't have time to explain the long story about how San-kofa was supposed to be.

He pointed her toward his *New York Times* Best Sellers section. She bought two King books and didn't blink at the price. At the register, she chatted about how she was staying in an Airbnb at the Gardens after flying in from Phoenix for a pitch meeting and how the neighborhood was *so* convenient to everything in LA. Darryl barely heard her. He was thinking about how Mrs. Richardson rarely visited in person after she broke her hip last December, and how she would barely recognize her own store now. And how maybe it was time for him to find another job. Another city, even. Another life.

Darryl stared at the window looking for his haint the rest of the day.

The next morning, every book from the shelves lay across the floor in a sea. Darryl stood in the doorway staring at the spectacle for a full two minutes, nearly in tears. Then he went inside, locked the door, and kept the CLOSED sign turned out. He definitely wouldn't be selling any of Stephen King's books today. Or anyone else's.

He almost called the security service—the card was still propped by his register as an inside joke to himself—but he didn't want to invite those two assholes near him again, especially not that itchy one. Besides, the more he looked around, the more he realized it couldn't be the work of vandals.

The evidence was all around him. The door had been locked. No windows broken. Nothing taken from the register. It was as if Sankofa had suffered its own private earthquake, the books shaken away while everything else was left upright. No part of it looked natural.

And the scene felt angry. An attack. A taunt. For the first time, Darryl felt afraid of the haint. (But he definitely didn't want the haint to know that.)

"Oh yeah?" Darryl said. "*Fuck you.* This is my store, not yours. What else you got?"

His knees were tense, ready to spring him under his desk in case the haint *did* have something else. (As he thought about it, a haint might have a hell of a lot else.) Yet the store was still and silent, just like the storeroom before the door slammed.

"You want me to leave? Is that it?" Darryl said. "*You're* the one who needs to leave. Get out of here! I better not see you again. Leave me alone!"

Darryl didn't go to many horror movies because the characters could be so dumb, though he wondered why more people in movies didn't just tell the ghost to fuck off. *Because that would be a short-ass movie*, he decided. But that was his plan. And if establishing dominance wasn't enough, he'd bring in that new tarot reader from down the street to make the banishing more official. "Mess up *my* store like this?" he said as he went shelf by shelf, replacing the fallen books one at a time, setting the ones with bent covers aside, a growing pile. "You just fucked *all* the way up."

He impressed himself with his tough talk, decided he wasn't scared, but then a soul food cookbook teetering on a shelf behind him fell to the floor, and he screamed like a high school girl. And then laughed at himself. And then . . . yeah, maybe he cried a little too. Or a lot. All of those Black books scattered in disarray on the floor, the bare shelves looking eager for a new adventure, made Darryl want to curl up in a corner. The store felt closer to the truth today than it had in a long time. Mrs. Richardson said she could barely make rent over the past couple of years. How long before he would be packing up Sankofa anyway? Should he even bother reshelving the books?

Yet over time, as he filled the shelves aisle by aisle, the despairing feeling was replaced by resolve. Excitement, even. He'd always wanted to move the Science Fiction section closer to the Mystery & Thiller section, and add a dedicated Horror section, and suddenly he had the freedom to recreate the store the way he'd wanted to, no longer bound by Mrs. Richardson's years of habit. By the end of the day, he'd filled all of the shelves except the *New York Times* Best Sellers section. No way he'd put those back. Now he finally had room for the Young Adult section he'd been dreaming of: rows of Black and brown boys and girls who were wizards. Vampires. Basketball champions. They were anything they damn well pleased.

What was that line from the baseball movie? *If you build it, they will come.*

The tourists could buy Rivers Solomon and Nnedi Okorafor and Attica Locke and Steven Barnes and Nikki Giovanni and Toni Morrison too. They just had to learn. Someone could stay behind and teach them. Then mail orders, which were picking up since he'd hired someone to update the store's website, could take care of the rest.

Maybe that was what the haint was trying to tell him. Make the store *his*.

Darryl was so excited that he climbed inside the window display to start ripping down the posters and signs he had put up to try to catch the newcomers' eyes. More than he remembered, actually—an entire side of the display, including the prime corner. Gillian Flynn was dope, but why was she in the window at Sankofa when she could be celebrated anywhere?

Darryl didn't hear the commotion until it was practically in his ear, the shout of a woman who sounded like Big Hat with the sun-broiled nose. "Maybe he went that way?" More of a question than a comment, and Darryl heard stampeding feet from around the corner.

When his attention slipped, his foot followed. He landed against the plate glass hard enough to make him think he might fall through and be shredded. But only a small shard of glass in the center fell out, a sparkling diamond in fading sunlight, and the spiderweb of cracks seemed to cradle him as he tried to straighten himself up.

The white security guard was amped up on imagination and anger when he turned the corner, his gun already drawn, looking for something to shoot. Darryl winced as soon as he saw him, expecting a gunfire blast. But it didn't come at first.

The security guard squinted against the window's glaring dusk light to glance inside the window at the *New York Times* best sellers still scattered across the floor. He noted the *CLOSED* sign on the door. Then his eyes came back to the man who'd broken the glass—still standing inside the store window. Darryl saw him decide what to do.

"Freeze!" the security guard yelled, probably because he'd seen it on TV so often, but he didn't wait for Darryl to freeze. Didn't seem to care that Darryl's only motion was raising his hands.

Just before the gunshot, the first one, Darryl noticed a figure reflected in the glass, too far away to be him—and yet, it *was* him. The same eyes he'd seen from behind his desk now stared at him up close with an expression that seemed to say: *Do you get it now, brother?*

Grandmama had always said he had a touch of the psychic. He'd had a feeling about this security guard from the moment he saw him. And he still hadn't read the signs.

"Well, I'll be goddamned—" Darryl started to say.

Then the bullets came. One. Two. Three.

"He works there!" a woman's voice screamed from somewhere far away.

Before the brief flash of pain turned to a silent soup, Darryl had time to vow that he would haunt the fuck out of whatever they built where Sankofa used to be.

Just you wait.

Incident at Bear Creek Lodge

The last time I saw my grandmother was at her lodge in '73. It was also nearly the first time I'd seen her, unless you counted when I was a baby and then another time when I was about four, but all I remembered was long, glittery nails. She and my mother weren't what you'd call tight, meaning they barely talked to each other. So I was shocked when Mom started selling me on staying at Grandmother's for a few days that fall, saying I could miss a couple days of school and sleep in a cabin and meet Grandmother's famous friends. Their whole relationship was birthday and Christmas boxes, swathed in bright, pretty wrapping. But that was it.

"You can see *snow*," Mom said, which was tempting for someone who'd never lived anywhere except Miami. But then she sealed it: "She says Diahann Carroll will be there."

"You're lying." I loved the old TV show *Julia*. Diahann Carroll was my first crush. I knew I was too young to marry her, but I was jealous of that kid playing Corey because he got to see her every single day. In person.

Mom glanced over a letter she'd kept taking in and out of her pocket. I glimpsed the lined paper, both sides crammed with slanted, jittery handwriting that felt urgent. Desperate.

"Diahann Carroll. Lena Horne. Maybe Joe Louis, if he's up to it. He's been having some health issues. Her lodge used to be like a resort in the forties and fifties."

"You. Are. Lying."

I didn't care about the other names, only Diahann Carroll. I was trying to make sense of how someone I watched on TV could be hanging out at my grandmother's house in Colorado.

"You know Mother was an actress, Johnny," Mom said wearily. She said *actress* like our Cuban neighbor would say shit-eater: *comemierda*. Mom folded the letter and slid it back into her pocket with more force this time, as if she wanted it to disappear.

"Why don't you want to come too?"

"I've already seen snow," Mom said, ignoring the obvious question. So I ignored it too. Sometimes I wondered if she hated Grandmother; her voice changed when she talked about her, small and soft. "You just spend a few days there, get to know her for yourself—understand a few things better. You're old enough now." Since I'd turned thirteen, Mom acted like I was ready for the draft.

"By myself?"

"Of course not. You and Uncle Ricky will share a cabin. I can arrange it."

Uncle Ricky lived in Amarillo, Texas, and knew how to ride horses, which basically made him a cowboy to me. Seeing him would *almost* be as great as meeting Diahann Carroll.

Mom fumbled in her pocket for the letter again. "So what should I tell her?"

That's how I ended up on my first solo airplane ride, which should have been the scariest part of my trip. I was terrified to use the bathroom because the plane was shaking so much. (I tried to focus on my comics, but even Spider-Man can't fix everything.) When the plane landed, the misty mountain range through my window was so pink and gold and surreal that I wondered if I'd crashed and gone to heaven.

Uncle Ricky was waiting at the gate in a thrift-store army

jacket that made him look like he'd just come back from the war, but his big, toothy grin assured you that he'd never killed anyone or been shot at. His bad knee from an accident in high school had kept him out of Vietnam, Mom said. Uncle Ricky gave me a soul shake I messed up all the way through, but he only winked and rubbed my head instead of razzing me.

"Ready to hobnob with the bourgeoisie?" he said.

Whatever *that* meant.

"Is Diahann Carroll here yet?"

Uncle Ricky looked down with sad eyes. "Mother just got her letter, kid. She's shooting a movie in New York. She thought she was done, but she got called back to the set."

"What movie?" I said, challenging his story. Praying it wasn't true. "What's it called?"

"*Claudia. Claudine.* Somethin' with a C."

The name of the movie, however vague, made it real. I almost cried on the spot, and he could tell. He squeezed my shoulder. "Listen, you'd better learn it now: people in show business ain't shit. They'll disappoint you every time. You hear? That goes for your grandmother too. She ain't the peppermint candy and gimme-some-sugar type. But I'm here to look out for you. Don't you even worry about it."

Thinking back, I wonder why I didn't ask why I needed to be looked out for with Grandmother. Maybe I'd stuffed that question away with my questions about why Mom didn't want to come too. Or why she and her mother spoke so rarely. Maybe I didn't want to know.

"Where's the snow?" I said. Denver asphalt looked no different than Miami's, except for the mountains in the distance.

"Not at this altitude," he said. "Just wait till we get higher. You'll see so much snow, you'll never want to see snow again."

He was right about that part, at least.

I climbed into the passenger seat of Uncle Ricky's powder-blue Volkswagen Beetle, which he'd driven from Texas and had the Burger King wrappers to prove it. My feet were cushioned by the pile of Black Panther newsletters he'd told me to push from my seat to the floor. I tried to smile at his jokes about Nixon as he toked on a joint and the smoke blew back in my face from his cracked-open window.

But as far as I was concerned, snow or no snow, my trip was already ruined.

I'd fallen asleep to the rhythmic coughing of Uncle Ricky's engine as it climbed the steep road, so by the time I woke up we were in the woods. I jolted awake when his tires skidded on the packed gray slush. At first, I thought I was back on the plane.

Snow! I sat up, electrified. Every window in the car was filled with the sight of white clumps of snow: draped across craggy branches of fir trees, piled in what looked like hills on either side. A few flakes were lies hitting the windshield like pale butterflies before the wipers washed them away. Uncle Ricky was grinning again too, infected by my excitement.

"Pretty when it first falls down, ain't it?" he said.

"Can I get out and touch it? Please?"

He turned on his blinking yellow hazards and let me jump out of the car to catch snow on my tongue and kick at the snowdrifts to watch them scatter. It was a fairyland. My clothes were soaked by the time I got back in the car, but Uncle Ricky turned up his heater and let me sip warm coffee from a thermos—I didn't care how bitter it was because at least it was warm—and my heart was full of excitement for the next twenty minutes at least. And I was with family, which was no small thing, since my father lived in Jacksonville and my mom's family lived in Texas, California, and Germany, so I didn't see any of them often. Mom blamed the distance on "bad memories," but they weren't *my* bad memories.

The drive was the good part. The best part.

"Here it is," Uncle Ricky said, slowing the car.

I only saw snow at first, a sheet of white, so I wiped away the condensation on the windshield. We were approaching wooden cattle fencing topped with snow, the sagging gate hanging open. As the car crawled past, I made out a tall, rusted insignia discarded against the side of the fence rails, written in fancy script: *The Lazy M*. I almost asked Uncle Ricky about it, since Mom always called Grandmother's place Bear Creek Lodge.

I wish I had. If I had, the whole incident might never have happened.

Twenty yards ahead, as we drove past the low-drooping fir branches, a long wooden porch came into view, light shining from behind the curtains. I felt my second big disappointment: Mom had called Grandmother's lodge "a resort for Negroes during segregation," but it looked just like a regular old two-story house, only made of wood. The cedar was an uneven gray from age, not pretty at all. Three or four shiny visitors' cars parked by the side of the house were the only evidence that anything inside was worth seeing.

Two lights stared down in golden yellow from twin second-story windows. Below, the porch wrapped around the house like a ragged grin, gapped from missing porch rails. I tried to conjure a way to convince Uncle Ricky to drive me back to the airport, but no excuse I thought up could change the fact that my ticket wouldn't be good for another three days. I was stuck. The house looked dangerous for reasons I couldn't explain even to myself.

"Are there bears here?" I looked for a clue in its name.

Uncle Ricky laughed. "No more'n anywhere else in the woods. We don't see killer grizzlies this far south, just black bears. Don't feed 'em and you'll be fine. Doubt you'll see none anyway. Bear Creek doesn't have bears just like Atlanta doesn't have peach trees. Every other street is Peachtree down there, ain't it? I bet every street in Miami is named for the ocean."

I shrugged, annoyed by his small talk about Miami when

Mom always complained that he never came to visit. He was a plumber by trade and made good money, she always said, so why didn't he come see her more? Then he'd know all about Miami's street names.

"Listen . . ." he went on, voice assuring. "Some years back, Mother got her feelings hurt by Hollywood and holed up here by herself. For five years, she wouldn't see nobody. And I mean *nobody*. If *she* made it alone, you'll do fine with all of us here."

"Got her feelings hurt how?"

"Folks decided she was too old-fashioned, that's all. Times changed. They treat her like a curse, like she sold her soul. Half the folks who'll talk to her only have their hand out."

Uncle Ricky parked, careful to keep several feet between him and the mile-long shiny red Caddy closest to his space. Beside that Caddy, Uncle Ricky's car looked like it belonged in the junkyard on *Sanford and Son*. Uncle Ricky kept his hands on his steering wheel, staring at a door on the side of the house with frilly white curtains. Like the house had put him in a trance.

I was in my own trance, staring beyond the three steps leading to that back door, trying to understand the snow. A small mound rested there, soft and white, not like the grimy snow ground into the road. A few flakes puffed out as if the mound had sneezed. Was it settling? Mr. Ramos, my science teacher, said we should consider the world with a curious mind, so I tried to figure it out without asking Uncle Ricky. I waited two seconds, and the snow puffed again; this time, a dark hole appeared at the center of the mound. Could a cat or small dog be buried there?

The snow itself seemed to come to life, shivering flakes free, and then the entire mound moved in a shimmy, undulating away from the porch, snakelike. A twig snapped beneath its motion; I thought I might be imagining it. Then the mound fell flat. No cat or dog emerged to explain it. The snow just settled to stillness.

I slowed down my heart by telling myself this must be a normal thing, that it was childish to be scared of snow. But I think I knew better even then.

Uncle Ricky slapped his palms against the steering wheel, making me jump. "Well?"

I realized I was holding my breath. My socks were still damp, so my toes felt tingly. I wondered if I'd only dreamed any fun, just as maybe I'd dreamed the dancing, breathing snow.

"Well what?"

"Ready to go in and see Mother?" He could have been talking to me, or to himself.

I nodded, shivering.

It was a bold-faced lie.

The side door led to the kitchen. A piece of luck. Old-timey band music and loud laughter were floating from another part of the house, though I didn't hear any children, as I'd been promised when Mom said, "I'm sure somebody else's grandkids will be there too, baby." There was a party, but it wasn't a party for *me*. You couldn't call it a party if they were playing some old horn section in an orchestra instead of the Jackson 5.

Although it was empty, the kitchen was a party all its own, the tile counter lined with an array of casserole dishes under loose aluminum foil. Uncle Ricky grabbed a plate from the stack right away, so I did too. Each surprise under the foil was better than the last: Roast chicken legs. Macaroni and cheese. Greens with turkey necks. Peach cobbler. I hadn't realized how hungry I was until I used one hand to hold the chicken leg I was stripping with my teeth while I spooned cobbler onto my plate with the other.

"Slow down, boy. Your mom'll never forgive me if you choke to death on my watch."

By silent agreement, we stood hunched over the counter to eat instead of joining the party right away. Mom would have been mortified that I wasn't sitting at a table with a proper place setting: salad fork, dinner fork, butter knife, the whole nine, like Grandmother had taught her. I couldn't even eat a bowl of cereal at home without a napkin in my lap. But we just lived in a two-bedroom apartment near her job at Miami Jackson High, not in a big house in Baldwin Hills ("the Black Beverly Hills") like the one Mom had been raised in. I was glad Uncle Ricky didn't care about greasy fingers.

Uncle Ricky finally slapped cornbread crumbs from his palms and filled a water glass from the sink to wash down his meal. The pipe under the sink whined like it was in pain.

"I'll have to take a look at that," he said, mostly to himself. "All you gotta do is nod and smile and be impressed with everything they say. And don't call my mother anything except Grandmother—not Granny, not Grandmama especially. She'd hate that. She needs everything a certain way."

"Okay."

He studied me closely, frowning a bit at my faded sweater and jeans. He took off his army jacket and hung it on a hook. Underneath, he'd dressed in a black sweater and slacks, instant formality. He glanced down at his cowboy boots and meticulously wiped mud from the tips with a napkin. He patted down his 'fro. Then he took a breath, jouncing his shoulders like he was about to run out onto a football field.

"Let's do it," he said.

Uncle Ricky pushed past the wooden swinging door from the kitchen and we followed the music and laughter down a narrow wood-paneled hall. For the first time I noticed his limp, how he slightly favored one leg.

The lodge was more impressive inside because of the decorations on the walls: rows of signed old photographs, some of them with Grandmother as a young woman in a ball gown posing with other well-dressed people, some close-ups of almost every famous person I could think of. Duke Ellington.

Bob Hope. Lena Horne. I stopped in front of Diahann Carroll's photo: her head thrown back, smile wide and full of joy. I wanted to cry again.

"Well, *there* he is!" a woman's voice said ahead, and I realized that Uncle Ricky had left me alone in the hall.

The laughter stopped. Someone turned the music down.

"Goodness gracious, what have you done with your *hair*?" the same woman said.

"That's how they wear it now, ma'am."

"Well, if everyone jumped off a bridge, would you jump off behind them? Imagine if we'd been running around with these bushes on our heads."

I was glad that Mom had trimmed my hair short before the trip. I took a few tentative steps and saw Uncle Ricky face-to-face with Grandmother: she was tall for a woman, reaching his nose, in a sequined dress that could be in one of the photos. Her hair was black and straight, hanging loose in a girlish fashion, but the dark color looked like dye. Grandmother was in her seventies, although you couldn't tell from her smooth brown skin. I'd never seen anyone so thin. Those same long, long fingernails sparkled in the room's light.

Uncle Ricky looked like he might want to hug her, but Grandmother wouldn't come close enough. "Sadie's boy is here," Uncle Ricky said instead, motioning to me.

The living room was just as elegant, with a white baby grand near the double doors and a lively fireplace big enough to warm the house. Three other people were there: one man and two women, all of them Grandmother's age or a bit younger. The man was husky, sitting in a chair as wide as he was. His face was familiar, though I couldn't place it right off. The women were fashionably dressed, one in a fur wrap, but Grandmother was the queen of the room.

I walked toward the queen, trying to remember to smile. I don't know why I was so nervous with everyone looking at me, but I could barely keep my head raised. She took a small step back, so I stopped short of her like Uncle Ricky had.

Grandmother did not smile at me. "Spitting image," she said to the room instead.

"Isn't it spooky?" one of the women agreed.

"Where's your mama, boy?" the man called out.

"Had to work," I mumbled, then raised my voice to project it like Mom was always telling me. "Grading papers. She teaches English in high school."

The others seemed impressed, but Grandmother frowned. "She'll barely make a living on a teacher's wages. I told her to keep up her voice lessons. I could have given that girl the world."

Grandmother suddenly glared at me like I was everything that had let her down in life, her eyes so angry that my skin prickled. Then her face softened to a mask: not a smile, but less severe. The transformation was so fast and convincing that I had to remind myself that Grandmother had been a famous actress, after all. Her eyes were as flat as the settled snow.

"How old are you now?" she said. "Ten? Eleven?"

I winced, insulted. "Thirteen."

"Thirteen! You're small for your age. Your mother needs to put some meat on your bones. And I'll bet she coddles you like mad. We'll have to get to know each other, Johnny. I need to teach you a few things about the world."

Uncle Ricky's hand landed firmly on my shoulder. It felt like a prompt, so I said, "I'd like that, Grandmother."

"I'll be getting to know him too," Uncle Ricky said. "Out in the cabin."

"No, I don't want him out with you in that drafty cabin," Grandmother said, floating away toward her friends gathered on the plush twin sofas near the fireplace. "You stay out there and smoke. He'll stay in the main house. My old powder room has a bed."

I glanced up at Uncle Ricky. He looked actually *scared*. But he didn't say a word.

"Ain't you gonna come over, or you too grown now?" the man teased Uncle Ricky.

"Nah, Uncle Joe. You're lookin' good, man."

The fear was gone from Uncle Ricky's face and his voice. But it was too late: I'd seen it.

Someone had one of the new Polaroid cameras that took color photos on the spot, so I posed with everyone in the room like I was long-lost family. Uncle Ricky called all of Grandmother's friends "Aunt" this or "Uncle" that. I learned later that "Uncle Joe" was the legendary boxer Joe Louis, so that photo would become one of my most prized mementos on the days when I could forget about the rest.

But I didn't know who he was yet. And in my only photo with him, I wasn't smiling.

"You need anything, I'm right across the way," Uncle Ricky said, pointing vaguely as he walked me to my room. "Right outside. Head out the kitchen door and keep walking straight."

I couldn't imagine anything that would tempt me to walk past that snow pile beside the steps, especially at night, but I nodded.

Uncle Ricky handed me a heavy flashlight. "For seeing in the dark," he said. "*True* dark. Trust me, you don't know nothin' about that."

The closed door at the end of the hall was Grandmother's room, he told me. The narrow powder room door, also closed, was at a right angle. A small silver star shined from a nail.

"If there ain't enough room in here, lemme know and I'll see what I can do."

The main light switch didn't work, so he stepped in and flipped on the lights on the mirror and vanity table that took up most of the space. This room was all tile instead of wood, so the bright mirror lights made the room look like noontime. Three or four of the bulbs were missing, leaving a few darkened spots in the reflection. I saw myself standing there puny beside Uncle Ricky, my face lost in a shadow.

"Not much of a bed," Uncle Ricky said. He quickly began hauling piles of fashion magazines to the vanity table, uncovering folded blankets and a cot underneath. "We used to have to sleep in here if we were on punishment. It's a little claustrophobic, but it's alright. Mostly it was the *idea* of being on punishment that made it bad. Know what I mean?"

The windowless space looked more like a cell than a bedroom: of course it was a punishment room. It was only slightly larger than a walk-in closet in a slight L shape, leading to a second closed door painted white.

"Where does that go?" I asked.

"That's her bathroom. Don't go in there. You need to pee in the night, run to that other little bathroom at the end of the hall. When you need a bath, use the one upstairs."

The idea of being that close to where my grandmother would be sitting on a toilet—or taking a bath!—made me want to puke. "Can't I sleep in the cabin?"

"Lady's house, lady's rules. Remember what I said about how to find me. Use your flashlight instead of turning on a bunch of lights. She don't like you burning up her electricity."

When he turned to go, he was already patting his pocket for his lighter. If the car ride was any indication, he couldn't wait to light up another joint. And now he would have the cabin to himself. When he hugged me good night, I could see how relieved he was to go.

As soon as I was alone, I wanted to cry again. The lodge didn't have a telephone, so I couldn't even talk to Mom. Uncle Ricky had promised to drive me to town to talk to her sometime, but my real life already seemed far away and long ago. Mom always said action made her feel better, so I dug into my backpack for my stack of comics and my cassette player from Christmas, my survival plan. Six new comic books, most of my best cassettes, and headphones to make my music my own business.

The cot was stiff even with three blankets beneath me, but I managed to get comfortable enough. I turned off the bright lights and read my comics by flashlight with "ABC" playing on my headphones. Soon I forgot where I was, lost in Peter Parker's adventures.

When the vanity lights flared on, I gasped and nearly fell out of my cot. Craggy tree branches were only Grandmother's nails before she snatched the headphones from my head.

"Get some sleep, Johnny," she said in a honeyed voice. "You have these turned up so loud, you didn't hear me knocking. You'll hurt your ears. Rest up so you'll be fresh tomorrow."

I was stunned, but I thought fast enough to push *stop* so the music wouldn't come blaring into the room when she yanked the headphone cord free, because then she would have taken the cassette player too. And maybe the cassettes. It was clear on sight that no one was supposed to have any fun in this room. I nudged my flashlight under the blanket so she would forget about it now that the too-bright vanity lights were screaming.

"Yes ma'am," I said, mimicking Uncle Ricky. "I'm sorry I didn't hear you."

The flashlight made a tiny clicking sound when I turned it off. I hoped she hadn't heard it.

"Don't forget your prayers," Grandmother said.

When she turned off the light and closed the door behind her, I realized my earlobe was stinging from where her nail had caught my skin. When I touched it, I felt a spot of damp blood.

I woke in a tomb. My room was cold despite the blankets, and the darkness made it impossible to tell what time it was even though my glow-in-the-dark Timex said it was seven thirty in the morning.

But my watch was wrong, I realized when I crept into the hallway from my room. The sun had barely risen outside, casting gray light. It took a couple of sleepy, confused moments to remember that Colorado was in a different time zone, an hour behind. The quiet house was a mercy, freedom I hadn't expected. I rushed to dress, ate leftover peach cobbler from the kitchen counter for breakfast, and ran out of the kitchen door. The cold slapped my face and made me miss the down jacket Mom had bought me, but I didn't dare go back inside.

The snow piled near the steps looked different in new light. Ordinary. Light snowfall had buried any signs of the original mound I'd seen, and evidence of movement. I even poked at the spot with a stick. Nothing. Feeling silly, I tossed the stick away.

I surveyed the property, which was easier to see in rising daylight. The fence ring seemed huge the night before, but her property wasn't much more than five acres. The main house sat at the end of a snow-covered driveway, and three small cabins lay beyond it, blending in with the stand of fir trees. The two rear cabins looked like shacks, with boarded-up windows and part of one roof under a tarp. But the closest cabin seemed okay, with a shiny axe standing beside the door and a nearby pile of wood that appeared freshly chopped. I admit I tried to peek into that cabin's window, but the thick curtains were pulled closed except for a tiny slit that only revealed a small wooden table with Uncle Ricky's thermos.

Still, I knew where he was now. And compared to the powder room, Uncle Ricky's cabin looked like a palace. I wondered if I could get on Grandmother's good side so she would let me sleep there, but my sore ear told me she might not be the type to change her mind.

I tried not to let my sneakers sink too deeply into snow as I walked inside the fence, reveling in the sight of small animal tracks and frozen spiderwebs and knotted tree trunks shaped like open mouths. At the end of the driveway, I came back to that large metal insignia, *The Lazy M*, nearly as tall as I was, leaning on the fence. It was now obvious that this had once been posted on the driveway gate, though maybe it had fallen. Maybe that was one more thing Uncle Ricky would need to fix.

I didn't notice the red droplets on the snow just beyond the *Lazy M* sign until I saw the dead thing. Actually, it was a dead thing's *head*.

I was so startled that I fell backward, landing my butt in the snow. But I jumped right back up again to get a better look at the matted fur, open black eye, and bloody mess where its head had once been attached to its now-severed neck. Maybe it was a raccoon, though hardly enough was left to tell, especially to a boy from Liberty City.

Yet I knew it was dead. And I noticed from a pinkish trail in the snow that it had been *dragged* to that spot. Parts of the trail had been covered by snow and sometimes disappeared, but I kept following until it took me back to the kitchen steps, beside the Caddy. A sound like shifting sand behind me spun me around fast, panting like I'd been running. My eyes looked for movement everywhere, and finally I saw something under the snow slither around a tree trunk, out of my sight except for a few loose flakes spraying away. *Fast.* I ran to where I thought I'd seen it, but all of the snow was flat again. The one mound I kicked was only a buried tree trunk.

I went back to the Caddy. The trail didn't originate exactly where I thought I'd first seen the snow move, though close enough. I picked up the stick I'd thrown away and scattered the snow beside the steps until I uncovered a blood-soaked center, maybe as big as a car tire. The blood spot was almost purple.

The way I stood there staring, I might have been frozen solid. I wasn't sure myself.

A thump on the kitchen window made me look up. Grandmother was standing there, her hair covered by a bonnet, which made her seem much older. She cracked open the kitchen door.

"Johnny, come inside!" she said. "Get out of that cold without a coat. What's wrong with you? You'll catch your death out there."

That was something Mom said a lot too, so now I knew where she'd gotten the saying about catching death. But this was the first time it sounded real. I threw my stick away and hurried to do as I'd been told. Yet as I walked back to those kitchen steps, I was sure something was slithering under the snow behind me. On my heels.

Tracking me.

"What kind of animals move under the snow?" I asked Uncle Ricky when I cornered him to myself. I'd spent most of the day like a mascot for the ongoing party, answering prying questions about Mom and Dad that I was pretty sure Mom would *not* have wanted me discussing with Joe Louis or his wife or anyone else. (I figured out part of the rift between Mom and Grandmother had to do with Mom having a baby—me.) The rest of the time I'd sat stiffly trying to pretend I wasn't bored, and I was afraid Grandmother would confiscate my comic book if she saw me reading one. I was deep in my head, wondering about what I'd seen outside.

Uncle Ricky reeked of grass when he finally emerged from his cabin. Inside the house, he gave me a red-eyed stare. "Oh, like mice?" he said. "That's all that was. You'll see all kinds of mouse tunnels out there. That's how they hide from foxes and such."

"Bigger than a mouse."

"Foxes too," he said, and my heart sped up. "They'll sleep in the snow sometimes."

I was both intrigued and relieved. Now it was making sense. But I wanted to be sure.

"Did you . . ." I lowered my voice, ". . . chop off a racoon's head with your axe?" I was sorry as soon as I asked, since he looked at me like I was smoking grass too. I went on: "So . . . that was probably a fox, then. Right? Hunting under the snow? Moving like a snake?"

Uncle Ricky shook his head. "That's not how foxes hunt. They leap up and dive—"

Laughter swallowed whatever he'd been about to say. The group was moving toward the card table in the corner. "Come on over here, Ricky," called a woman whose name I still don't remember, but she was an opera singer. "You be on my team so Joe and Martha don't clean our asses out." She winked at me. "'Scuse my French, Johnny."

"Two people you never wanted to play cards with . . ." Grandmother began, and everyone fell silent, evidently eager for one of her stories. "Billie Holiday, rest her sweet soul. And Clark Gable, that cheap SOB. I had to tell him, *You know you're getting paid more for this picture than I am, don't you?*"

Everyone laughed, so I did too.

"Were y'all *just* playing cards?" the opera singer teased, and Grandmother swatted her.

"You should write a book, M," Joe Louis's wife said. "We keep telling you. You should have your own star on the Hollywood Walk of Fame. It's long overdue."

Grandmother made a motion to dismiss the thought, though her eyes twinkled with pleasure.

"Spades or bid whist?" Uncle Ricky said.

An argument ensued over which game to play while Grandmother fussed with her stereo console, fanning through a pile of records. Seeing her with her music reminded me that she'd taken my headphones. I sidled behind Uncle Ricky and whispered in his ear, "Can you ask her to give me my headphones back?"

"She'll give 'em back when she's ready." He sounded sorry, but not enough to help.

I glanced up at Grandmother to see if she'd heard us, and

she was staring right at me. Smiling, for a change. Her smile was cruelty, not comfort. Oh yes, she had heard.

"How about Sam Cooke?" she called out. "I can't stand this new music today. Just sounds like plain old noise."

Her friends agreed that Sam Cooke would be a wonderful choice. While Cooke sang "A Change Is Gonna Come" and the card game was in full swing, I escaped to my room.

The powder room wasn't big enough to pace in, so I explored. Uncle Ricky had warned me not to open Grandmother's bathroom door, but he hadn't told me not to open the cabinet built into the wall under the vanity table. The tiny door was paint stuck, so I had to tug on it for a couple of moments before it gave way and opened with a belch of musty air. Even the vanity lights couldn't brighten it, so I grabbed my flashlight, crawling halfway in, which was as far as I could get. Three large filing crates were piled on each other, filled with yellowing pages. I skated my flashlight beam past those, looking for something more promising.

I found it staring right back at me: a framed movie poster against the far wall. My grandmother's name was in large red type: *Mazelle Washington*. From the size of the type, bigger than anyone else's, she could have been as big as Barbra Streisand. A true movie star!

I shifted the light to see the faces: not photos like the modern movie posters I saw at the theater, but realistic drawings. The only Black face on the poster was a young woman encircled by a white man and two white women who were laughing against the backdrop of the Empire State Building. But the Black woman wasn't laughing—her mouth was in a wide-open O, her hands clapped to her ears in exaggerated shock.

It took me a long while to realize that the woman in the sketch was Grandmother. She was Mama's age, and she wasn't in a ball gown like I'd seen her in every other photo, she was wearing a frumpy black dress and white apron, a maid's uniform. Her hair was in short, thick braids with bows flying out in every direction, a crown of spikes on her head. If it wasn't for the way the artist had captured her eyes and sharp chin, I'd never have recognized her.

The movie title was just above her hair: *Lazy Mazy Goes to New York*.

My surge of pride upon noticing her name wilted when I saw the whole poster, sinking to a dull throb in my stomach. I didn't understand everything then, but I knew that Grandmother wouldn't have hidden the poster in the darkest cubby in her darkest room if she ever wanted to see it again. She would have hung it on her wall.

I'd found a true secret. And it felt like power.

I scooted out of the crawl space as fast as I could and jammed the door closed again, hoping she would never notice that I had opened it. Between the mysteries in the snow and the treasure in my own room—which I planned to dig into more late at night, when everyone in the house was sleeping—I was starting to think the visit to Grandmother's house wasn't so bad.

Then I turned back my blankets.

My cassette player was gone.

"Excuse me," I said, and the card game came to a halt. Uncle Ricky looked at me with one eyebrow raised, on alert.

"We've got a game goin', Johnny," Uncle Ricky said with a note of caution.

"Can I please talk to you alone, Grandmother?"

She took her time turning her head to acknowledge me, and this time she didn't disguise her simmering eyes. I'd embarrassed her, and she was enraged. I might have been more afraid of her if I hadn't found her secret.

"Have you ever heard the saying that children should be

seen and not heard?" Her voice was still sweet, a show for her friends. "You can see the adults here are busy."

"It's alright, M . . ." the opera singer said, though it didn't soften Grandmother's eyes.

Uncle Ricky tapped on my foot so hard with his boot that it hurt.

"Some stuff is missing from my room," I told Grandmother. "My tape player my mom gave me for Christmas. And most of my tapes. Can you give them back, please?" After frantic searching, I had learned that my Sly & the Family Stone and Ohio Players were gone too, along with the Jackson 5 tape still in my player.

"Did your mother buy you those?" Grandmother said. "Has she listened to those lyrics? Those lyrics aren't for children. Half those band members are out of their minds on drugs. Did she tell you that? None of that so-called music you like is worth a damn. I'll teach you better. You need to learn about Ella Fitzgerald and Billie Holiday. Louis Armstrong. *That's* music."

I don't know what Uncle Ricky saw in my face to make him jump up from the table to grab me by the arm, but I couldn't remember ever being so mad. A *stranger* had stolen from me, was lecturing me. Was saying I had a bad mother.

"I'll talk to 'im," Uncle Ricky said, and he pulled me toward the kitchen.

"You'd better," Grandmother responded with bland menace. "Marching in here like . . ."

"Just hush," Uncle Ricky said when I complained about his tight grip. He steered me past the kitchen and out the door, to the steps. He closed the door carefully behind us, his breath hanging in clouds. "What are you doing? You don't talk to my mother like that. *Ever*. No one does."

"Somebody should," I said, defiant. "She doesn't have any right to—"

"She has the right to make up whatever rules she wants in

her house, and *never* forget that. When you go back in, you apologize."

"Why are y'all so scared of her?"

Uncle Ricky looked away from me, out toward the gate. He and Mom had that in common, at least. Neither of them wanted to talk about Grandmother.

"Look . . ." he said, sighing a fog of breath. "We'll stop at a record store on the way to the airport. I'll grab you a new player, whatever you want. Cool? Just . . . smile. Get along."

"You mean pretend."

"What the hell you think?" he said. "You're gonna spend every goddamn day of your life pretending. Get good at it. She's doing you a favor. *Shit*. What do you think this world is?"

He went back toward the kitchen door. I thought he might slam it, but he didn't. He slipped back inside, leaving me to my anger.

I glanced down toward the bloody spot I'd uncovered, or where I thought it had been. My own circling footprints were there, and my stick, but the purplish blood ring was gone.

Buried again.

That night, Grandmother brought out her film projector to show off for her friends. I thought we might see one of her movies, but instead she showed interviews of famous people talking about her. Someone must have collected every nice thing anyone had said about her, as if preparing for her funeral. A tall white actor in a tuxedo who was in that movie about a flying car I'd seen with Mom said, "I'll tell ya . . . if you want to learn about comedic timing, find the work of the greats like Mazy Washington." A white woman with short orange hair was on *The Tonight Show* and said to Johnny Carson, "I grew up loving Mazy and those terrific pratfalls, so it never occurred to me that a woman couldn't be funny." Last, Muhammad Ali was ringside in boxing trunks when he said to Howard Cosell,

"Get in the ring with me, you must be crazy. I'll dance and I'll jab and I'll dodge you like Mazy."

Everyone laughed and applauded, Joe Louis loudest of all. "That boy still talks smack."

"He can back it up," Uncle Ricky said. Everyone laughed again. Uncle Ricky looked back at me: "Uncle Joe helps train Ali, you know." He winked at the way my mouth fell open.

"But we're not here to talk about me," the retired boxer said. He raised his glass in a toast. "To Mazelle Washington—one of the greats."

"And fuck anyone, Negro or white, who doesn't think so," the opera singer muttered, though I don't think anyone else heard her except me.

Everyone toasted Grandmother with champagne flutes while I drank apple juice. When Grandmother put on her old-timey Duke Ellington, I let the opera singer lead me in a dance. I was smiling so much that I fooled myself into thinking I was having a good time. I was blood kin to one of the greats, after all. Grandmother's seizure of my music didn't seem as upsetting anymore. Maybe any grandmother would have done it.

Besides, I wouldn't need my music that night. I had the cubbyhole to explore.

Once again, I excused myself early to be alone. Grandmother stepped in front of me just when I was almost clear of the room. Her approach felt like a performance.

"We need to know each other better," she said. "Tomorrow we'll walk in the yard."

"Yes ma'am."

She patted my arm, the most affection she had shown me. I missed the way Mom hugged me like she didn't want to let go. Maybe that was another way Mom made sure she wasn't too much like her mother.

"Sadie says he does well in school . . ." Grandmother bragged to her friends, which sounded like another performance. I thought about asking if I could sleep in the cabin with Uncle Ricky while she had an audience. But I wanted to see what was in her files.

I read my comics until all of the noises in the house were gone: the footsteps from guests trudging upstairs, the shower running in Grandmother's bathroom, her toilet flushing for the last time. When the house was still, I climbed back into the cubbyhole and pulled out the first case of files to scour with my flashlight. Most of them were notices about Lazy Mazy, and photos of her with that same hairdo and oh-shit expression, or some with a grin so wide that it seemed too big for her face. One headline from 1935 said: *What Has Lazy Mazy Gone and Done Now?* Beneath the stack of articles, I found reels of film. The true treasure. Since she'd already set up her projector in the living room, it felt like fate instead of prying.

I had to see for myself.

I moved quietly and made sure the projector volume was turned all the way down before I flicked it on. At first, I threaded the film wrong and it spun with a flapping racket I was sure would wake the whole house, but nobody came out while I fixed it.

Lazy Mazy Goes to New York began to play.

The film opened with Lazy Mazy asleep at a kitchen table, slowly stirring a mixing bowl while she dozed. A white man in too much makeup walked in wearing his work clothes, and I didn't need the sound on to know he was mad to find her sleeping. Lazy Mazy fell back in her chair and rolled to her feet like a gymnast. The bowl she'd been stirring had ended up on her head somehow, dripping batter on her face. That only made the white man more mad, and he spanked her butt as she ran away.

I tried to be quiet, but I laughed. Her eyes were so big, nothing like Grandmother's. The expressions on her face! The way she could contort her body in unexpected ways. Every moment on the big living room screen was a revelation. *This* was Mom's mother? My grandmother?

I'd been watching the film for maybe ten minutes, laughing louder than I should have, when I realized someone was standing behind me. I felt a presence before I turned around, the same way I had in the snow. I hoped it was the opera singer, or Uncle Ricky.

But it was Grandmother, framed in the living room entryway's blue light from the projector in a fancy robe with her straight hair loose, spread across her shoulders. She'd been pressing her hair; she was holding a hot comb. Instead of looking at me, she was staring at herself on the screen.

"Grandma!" I blurted. "You're Lazy Mazy! Is that what *The Lazy M* means—"

That was all I had time to say before her robe's sleeves fanned out like a night creature's wings as she swooped toward me.

"*How dare you,*" she hissed in my ear before she grabbed my arm with shocking strength.

And then I was in the worst pain of my life. I had to look down to realize she'd pressed the hot comb into my upper arm *hard*, applying more pressure the more I tried to pull away. It wasn't orange-hot, but it was hot enough to stick to my skin and make me yowl. Hot enough to leave a scar I would carry into adulthood.

"Stop! It hurts!" I yelled, and wrenched my arm away.

She was standing in front of the screen now, the film playing across her face, the ghost of her forty-year-old grin mocking from her forehead while she stared at me with tearful loathing.

"I'm sorry," I said. To this day, I don't know what I was apologizing for. She was the one who'd hurt me, yes, but I'd hurt her too. Scarred her too. It was as if I'd dug up a dead body and dragged it into her living room the way our cat brought us dead mice. I saw it in her eyes.

I ran as fast as I could to the kitchen door and outside, to the snow.

* * *

"It'll be fine," Uncle Ricky said after he'd dressed my burn with a cold, damp cloth from his cabin's tiny bathroom. "Stay out here tonight."

The burn had turned an ugly red, with a rising bubble on my skin I'd never had before.

"I wanna go home." I'd stopped crying, but the tears were still in my voice.

Uncle Ricky sighed, then nodded. "Okay. We'll figure it out tomorrow. But I don't drive out on these roads in the dark."

"Did she ever do that to you?"

"Not that, exactly." I thought he would leave the story unspoken, but after a moment he went on. "One time I was about fourteen and I gave her some lip at the store. When we got home, she pulled a tire iron out of the trunk and whacked my leg good a couple times. I had to stop playing football after that . . . but it kept Uncle Sam off me."

His story was so much worse that I almost felt better. Almost.

"What about Mom?"

"I tried to protect her. But when you get home . . . ask."

"How can you not hate your mom?" I said. "She's the worst person I've ever met."

Uncle Ricky sucked in a long breath. "I used to. I guess your mom still does. But nobody's born like that, Johnny. One day I realized . . . everything has a price. A burden. So I just started feeling sorry instead. There but for the grace of God. You know?"

I didn't know. And I hoped I never would. As I nursed my arm, I was mad at all of them.

Uncle Ricky went right to sleep on the bottom bunk of the cabin's bunk bed, and I stared through the curtains toward the house, the kitchen door. I expected her to come after me.

About an hour after Uncle Ricky fell asleep, as I'd feared, the kitchen light went on and the door opened with a shaft of light. Instinct made me crouch low in the cabin window.

Grandmother was still in her robe, carrying an aluminum tray of food. She looked like she was taking out the trash. But instead, she sat on the frigid steps with the tray on her lap. She looked so sad and alone that I almost felt sorry for her. She could catch her death out there.

She opened the tray and tossed a chicken leg onto the snow. And another.

The snow near the meat *moved* . . . and something popped out, showing itself as it shook off a layer of frost.

It wasn't a fox. It wasn't a dog or a cat. It was white but didn't seem to have fur, just pale skin cleaved to a frame that looked more like an insect's than a mammal's despite a bony tail lashing from side to side. Long, too-sharp teeth chomped at the offered meal, grinding meat and bone alike. I gasped with each snatch of its powerful jaws.

The terrible, nameless thing slid closer to Grandmother, ready to keep feeding. She didn't run. She didn't even flinch. As the hideous creature burrowed its snout in the tray in her lap, she let out childish laughter, her cheeks puffed wide with Lazy Mazy's mindless grin.

Return to Bear Creek Lodge

December 26, 1974

In Johnny's dream, he is running in white, snowy woods. He hears music—distant, tinny-sounding trumpet fanfare from the Duke Ellington Orchestra—before he sees the light. The vague glow is brighter with every step, until darkness parts to reveal the wooden rail fence of his grandmother's lodge. One rotting rail has fallen out of place, leaving a breach he can easily run through.

But he doesn't. He stops short, staring at the lodge. And the back porch.

And the woman sitting there.

In his dreams, Grandmother doesn't look the way she did the last time he actually saw her, when she was already emaciated and sharp-jawed from illness. This is Mazelle Washington the way she has immortalized herself in her photos framed all over her house: hair hanging long and loose (*straightened*, of course), in radiant makeup, shoulders nestled in the fur collar of her shiny silk bathrobe, the kind of garment only movie royalty would wear. She shines so brightly that the light seems to glow from her.

Something rustles just beneath her on the porch steps, snow flung aside by a long neck and then a head with a snout the size of a long weasel, white fur almost camouflaged by the snow. It rises between Grandmother's knees . . . as if she is giving birth.

Grandmother's face snaps into focus—but her eyes are the

color of blue ice. She opens her mouth, and her jaw hinges beyond any human length, revealing rows of long, sharp teeth.

He screams as—

"Wake up, hon. We're here."

Johnny's mother's voice coaxed him to open his eyes, and his dream had come to life. Snow. The wooden fence rails. Grandmother's lodge. The back porch. He tried to rub it out of his eyes, but the nightmare was real this time. Mom had parked the rental car they'd picked up in Denver in Grandmother's snow-dusted driveway after driving up the mountain. He'd fallen asleep to static-filled AM radio, which was all the car offered. *Shit. We're actually here.*

Grandmother's lodge would seem like an ordinary two-story wood-frame house if it weren't so secluded in the Rocky Mountains woods. Its isolation alone made it seem luxurious to have electricity lighting the windows, or a fence claiming five or six acres. Thirty yards from the main house, three small cabins stood in a perfect triangle as relics of a time when Bear Creek Lodge had provided dignity to Black celebrities lucky enough to get an invitation. In those days, fine hotels nationwide did not accept them, no matter who they were. Once, he'd been told, Grandmother had her own ski lift for her guests.

But all of that had been a long time ago.

"My stomach hurts," Johnny said. He had learned that his mother wrapped herself in silence like warm clothing, but he vowed he would never be like her. "This place already gives me nightmares, Mom. I want to leave."

"I know, baby. And I understand."

"But you don't care."

"Of course I do. If I could've left you somewhere else, I would have. I didn't want you here either. I don't want to be here my own self."

"Then why?" Johnny's voice hitched, but he would *not* cry.

"Because she owes us." *There. She finally said it.* "She owes *you*. She's got a college fund set aside for you. If I just . . . say goodbye this weekend. Two days. Her last Christmas. I haven't seen her at Christmastime since I wasn't much older than you."

Mom was thirty-one, although her face was still round and girlish. With a scarf wrapped around her Afro—probably hiding it from Grandmother—Mama reminded him of Aretha Franklin. Johnny had always assumed she ran away from home at seventeen because she was pregnant with him.

Uncle Ricky's blue VW Bug was already parked beside them in the lodge's driveway, a reminder that his uncle kept coming back although he had good reason never to speak to his mother again either, much less stay with her in the woods.

Based on his own short visit last year, Johnny could hardly imagine the horror of growing up in a house raised by Grandmother. His mother and uncle had lived in a mansion in Los Angeles, but Johnny would choose his two-bedroom apartment in Miami with Mom anytime, even with the flying cockroaches that kept coming back no matter how much she sprayed.

"I don't care about her money," Johnny said. "She can keep it."

Mom blinked as if he'd struck her. If she'd convinced herself they were making this trip for his sake, he had just stolen that lie away. Good. Johnny wondered what other ways Mom had been lying to herself, or to him. He could never trust her again, not the way he had before. That idea, worse than his nightmare, cramped his stomach once more.

"You'll be in one of the cabins, like I said," Mom told him. "You won't even have to see her. She stays in bed in her room. Rick's been here looking after her, and a nurse comes in the mornings. This is our burden, not yours—okay?"

None of it was okay, and never would be. At fourteen, Johnny was already certain of this. His birthright was soiled to the core; not just Grandmother, but Mom and Uncle Ricky too.

But he nodded, a lie. Mom looked relieved, choosing to believe him. Or to pretend she did.

"All money ain't good money," Mom said, "but bad money can be put to good use."

When she got out of the car, she headed straight for the back porch that haunted him. And the small mounds of snow beside the three back steps.

"Can we go in through the front, please?" Johnny hated being afraid that a dream might come to life, but if he stared at the snow long enough, he thought he might see it move from something buried underneath. His mother cast him a confused look over her shoulder, though she changed course to walk around to the front double doors.

Inside, the smell of Grandmother's dying was everywhere. The smell froze him in the open doorway. Mom, behind him, patted his shoulder.

"You don't have to go in her room," Mom reminded him. Her whisper smelled like the peppermint candy she'd used to mask her cigarette smoke; she was still apparently afraid of what Grandmother might say if she caught her smoking. She cupped his chin in the way she used to when he was younger. "I'm still so mad at your Uncle Rick for not watching you like I told him to. And you heard me cuss Mama's ass out on the phone last year, didn't you? What she did to you is *not* okay, cancer or no cancer. "

No one had said the word *cancer* before now. But Johnny swore he knew from the smell.

It was all in place: the white grand piano, the oversized fireplace with gleaming stones, grinning celebrity photos framed on the wood-plank walls, even the film projector where she'd caught him playing her old reels from the 1930s movies that filled her with shame. "You shouldn't have gone in Mother's things," Uncle Ricky had told him during the drive to the airport to go home last year, nudging blame back toward him after a night of consolation.

Nothing in the living room had changed in the year since

Grandmother had burned leering teeth into his arm from her steel hot comb, scarring him with dark marks that would never go away.

Uncle Ricky had gained at least ten pounds in the past year, his hair cut marine short. He had trouble meeting Johnny's eyes—maybe because Uncle Ricky's eyes were so red from smoking grass every chance he got. The smell of grass baked from his uncle's clothes as he hugged him. Johnny saw his mother's lips tighten as she glared at Uncle Ricky. For an uneasy instant, Grandmother's rage was reborn in his mother's eyes.

"Good to see you, lil' man," Uncle Ricky said, speaking as quietly as he would in a hospital. "Front cabin's all yours. Star treatment all the way. Nothing but the best for—"

"Oh, hush," Mom said. "Nobody wants to hear all that."

Uncle Ricky was still in trouble with Mom, so after saying hello, Johnny escaped to his cabin.

The cabin was decades past any elegance, but it was a good size, with a bunk bed, sofa, and a table near the front picture window. A too-large crack beneath the door couldn't keep out a bold breeze and traces of snow that melted in a pale ring on the floor. The air near the door felt ten degrees cooler too. At least. The space heater's coils stank of roasting dust when he turned it on and they glowed bright orange.

Johnny pulled aside the fading curtains to stare out at the snow-covered woods beyond Grandmother's wood-rail fence. He'd been excited to see flurries for the first time last year, but now snow was the backdrop to his nightmares. *You saw something in the snow*, his mind whispered, a reminder. *Or did you?*

All he knew for sure was that he kept having the same dream, where *something* popped up from the snow, its head appearing between Grandmother's knees. A pointy nose, so pink it was almost red. Long, active whiskers near its mouth. And white fur so tight across its frame that it seemed bony instead of soft. Not quite a reptile, not quite a mammal. In the year since, he had decided that maybe his waking mind had conjured a creature that mirrored Grandmother's true self—a vision for the casual monstrosity she hid from everyone except her own family.

The door to the back porch opened abruptly. He expected to see Grandmother glide outside in her fur-lined robe, staring straight at him. The thought raked the back of his neck with icy pinpricks. But Mom and Uncle Ricky came out instead, neither of them wearing a coat, and Mom was hugging herself tightly as she leaned close to her brother. They were trying to keep their voices down, their argument spilling outside from the kitchen.

Johnny knew they were talking about him.

"... All I asked you to do was watch him in the goddamned cabin," Mom was saying. "*Never* let him be alone with her. I haven't asked either of you for shit his whole life, and that's all I asked. *That's all*, Rick."

"Sadie, she said—"

"Damn what she said! You were supposed to stand up to her for once. You're a grown man! How's a sick old woman gonna make you do shit? You want the Baldwin Hills house that bad? Is that what's got you so cowed that you couldn't do one simple thing? You *knew* better."

Uncle Ricky didn't have an answer for that, hanging his head. He listened in that childlike pose for some time, a big man made small. Mom's words knit his face until he finally said, "You acting like I'm the one who burned him! You know who you really need to be mad at. I wish I'd done more, but I ain't the one who did it."

At last, Mom had nothing else to say. She went back inside, slamming the door.

"What's all that noise?" he heard another voice call, perhaps through a cracked-open window. Reed-thin, but he heard it. The dying woman was awake.

Johnny stepped away from his window. Even if the cabin

was cold and only a short walk from the back door, at least he wasn't in the same house with her.

"Coming, Mother!" he heard his mom call as if she were a child again too. Johnny braved another peek through his window.

Uncle Ricky didn't go inside behind Mom. Instead, he sighed a cloud of breath and walked carefully down the stairs, nursing the knee his mother had hurt when he was young. He glanced up at Johnny's cabin as he passed on his way to his own and waved. But he didn't smile. Johnny did the same, running his fingertip across the raised bump of the dark keloid scar on his upper arm. His mother told him it would never go away unless he got plastic surgery—which meant they might as well find a doctor on Mars. A scar for life. More like a brand.

"How could she do that?" he'd asked his mother, tearful, when he came home with the fresh scar and its story.

Mom had met his tears with her own and said, "I don't know, baby. My grandmother told me she changed after she started working in pictures. Playing Lazy Mazy turned her into somebody else. I swear, I used to think she sold her soul."

Mom insisted that he come inside to eat at the long dining table with her and Uncle Ricky, and that part wasn't bad. She served heated-up leftover ham, macaroni and cheese, and greens from Christmas she'd carried in Tupperware on the plane from Miami. Then she lit a candle, explaining that she hadn't had room to bring the kinara from home, but she reminded him that the first principle of Kwanzaa was Umoja, which meant *Unity*. She squeezed his hand on one side and Uncle Ricky's on the other.

"So I'm glad we're all together," she said. She wanted to say more, but shook her head in a way that told Johnny she was trying not to cry.

Uncle Ricky said he had a surprise for Johnny and put the Jackson Five's "Dancing Machine" on Grandmother's console—oh so softly, if music could whisper—a peace offering like sage, since Grandmother had confiscated his cassettes and tape player last year. After venting at Uncle Ricky on the back porch, the anger had left Mom's eyes and she was already smiling and twisting to the music in her seat, especially after her second glass of wine. She and Uncle Ricky toasted "getting rid of that asshole Nixon," both of them tossing their heads back to drink. Mom's empty wineglass slipped from her grip, shattering on the wooden floor, and they both froze and waited to hear their mother call out, as they no doubt did as children, terrified of making her mad. When she didn't make a sound, Mom and Uncle Ricky smothered giggles. Johnny didn't like it when his mother drank, but it was good to hear her laugh.

Johnny was taking his empty plate to the kitchen, in the hallway just behind the kitchen doorway, when he saw, in a slant of shadow, Grandmother's partly open door at the far end of the hall. His heart batted his throat at the sight of the space beyond her open door, a dim light shining out. Was she awake? Johnny ducked into the kitchen at the thought that she might be about to walk out of her room. He closed the swinging kitchen door behind him, breathing fast. He threw his plate into the sink so hard that dishwater splashed on the floor.

Why don't you go see if she's awake, chickenshit? Pussy. Mama's boy. Sissy. Lil' bitch.

Johnny thought of every name he'd been called at school, shouted across the PE field, or whispered through a bathroom-stall door. And didn't all those names fit? Wasn't he scared of a sick old woman, trapped under the same hex as Mom and Uncle Ricky?

Johnny's breath tickled the roof of his mouth as he walked closer to the sickroom, touching his feet down lightly until he was standing just beyond her doorway. Through the slit he saw a bed table and the side of her bed frame—not the fairy-tale princess bed with a canopy she'd slept in before, but a curving metal rail like a hospital bed.

A low *hisssss* floated from the room, the sound of a giant snake close enough to touch him. Johnny jumped back, startled. A mechanized click made him realize that the sound was coming from an oxygen machine somewhere near the bed. This time, he used the rhythmic *hisssss* to hide the sound of his movement as he cracked the door open wider to peek in. The sole tea lamp on the bed table offered the room's only light, patterns of green in panels of stained glass. Most of her furniture had been pushed aside, though he recognized the fur collar of her fancy bathrobe hanging on a hook beside the door.

Grandmother's bare brown arm lay straight at her side, the flesh at her elbow a mass of jellied wrinkles. She had lost weight, and her frame had already been slight and bony in her clothes a year ago. Her face was hidden from him by the lamp. Her sheet rose up and down with her breathing; maybe she wasn't quite awake, not quite asleep.

"*I hate you,*" he whispered loudly enough to be heard over the hissing, but not loudly enough to escape the hallway. "I hope you die."

The words exploded inside of him, a shock to his own ears. His knees felt unsteady, so he leaned against the doorframe with a small pant. Was she awake? Had she heard?

He waited three seconds, four, five, to catch any response other than measured hissing. With each thin breath, his fear gave way to triumph. A celebration rose in him that he wished he could share with Mom and Uncle Ricky. *You'll never believe what I just said to that old—*

A chair across the room tipped so wildly that it almost fell over, rocking back and forth. A scrabbling shook the window above the chair, and for the first time he noticed it was open nearly six inches. (Had it always been open?) Something had bumped the chair and was crawling—snaking?—back outside through the narrow gap.

The creature from his nightmares with a long snout looked

back at him, white whiskers sweeping back and forth across the pane like a dog's wagging tail. Two ice-blue eyes glittered at him. The creature's odd chittering filled the room.

It's real, he thought. *It's real and it's here.*

Johnny had not imagined how a demon might look until he saw the thing at the window. Maybe it had possessed Grandmother. Maybe that was what had brought out the meanness in her. But these thoughts didn't come to Johnny in the doorway: they would only come later. In that instant, all thought had vanished. His body was stone except for his savagely blinking eyes.

The thing at the window rattled the frame, and a mouth yawned open, revealing a row of top fangs so long and sharp that they gleamed in the moonlight. A white fox-worm from hell.

"Johnny? That you?" *WAS IT TALKING TO HIM?*

The demon smacked against the window . . . and then it was gone. Outside, its slithering scattered the snow as it raced away in an erratic pattern, here and there almost simultaneously, moving *fast*. Impossibly fast

"Johnny?" Grandmother's voice was louder, recognizable despite its deep hoarseness. Not the demon's voice, then. He was torn about which frightened him more—the demon in the window or Grandmother calling for him. She might have heard the terrible thing he'd said, the words he was certain had conjured that thing. What if she got up and staggered toward him . . . ?

"I'm sorry," Johnny whispered, just like he had as she burned him that night, senseless with surprise and pain. He closed her door and ran back to the kitchen, where he helped his mother and uncle dry the dishes, trying to hide his shaking hands.

He didn't tell them about the cracked-open window. Or the demon. He didn't say a word.

That night, Johnny didn't sleep as he sat sentry fogging up his cabin's window, watching the back door and snowy patch of yard, reciting the Lord's Prayer like a record needle caught in a groove. He held a snow shovel in his hands, the only weapon he'd found in his cabin. Even with only the moonlight to guide his vision, he recognized the path the creature had left in its wake, a sinuous pattern of burrowed snow from Grand-mother's window, between the cabins, toward the gate and the woods beyond. He might not have seen it if he didn't know it was there. All night he jumped at falling clumps of snow from the treetops, or rustling in the dried brush, believing the crea-ture had come back for him. His fingers shivered, but not from the cold.

He only realized he'd fallen asleep by the window, slumped over the cabin's rude wooden table, when a knock at the door scared him so much that he fell to the floor.

"Hey, J!" Uncle Ricky's voice called. "You up? Said I'd take you rabbit hunting, right? Gotta get 'em early if we're gonna get 'em."

Johnny's head felt blurry. Then he remembered Grand-mother's room, the thing at the window, and he leaped to his feet to unlock the flimsy pin and open his cabin door. He'd tried keeping the secret, but silence was burning a hole in him. He would have to confess, that was all. He would have to tell Uncle Ricky what he'd summoned from the snow. But how could he make Uncle Ricky believe him?

"You're already dressed, huh?" Uncle Ricky said. Johnny stared down and realized he was still wearing his jeans and aqua-blue Miami Dolphins sweatshirt from dinner. He felt a strong certainty that he must be dreaming, that maybe he wasn't at Grandmother's property at Bear Creek at all. "Grab your coat and gloves. Cold as a witch's tits out here today."

Outside. He'd tell him while they were outside. He'd show Uncle Ricky the—

"Uh-oh," Uncle Ricky said from the cabin doorway as he

surveyed the snow, tipping back his black-suede cowboy hat. He walked a few paces and squatted, staring down.

Johnny ran outside, still pulling on his coat. Of course! As a hunter, Uncle Ricky had seen the creature's tracks right away. And Uncle Ricky had a gun! Now they could—

"Lookie here!" Uncle Ricky said, grinning up at him. He was squatting in the middle of the fox-thing's swishes in the snow, but he was pointing to much smaller tracks in an un-threatening, predictable pattern just beyond them. "The rabbits are out, see? Told you. You can always tell rabbit tracks cuz they land with their hind legs first, up front. They're bigger. And that's the front legs behind them, kinda off-center . . . see?"

Johnny didn't see, or want to see. He only saw the evidence the fox-thing had left behind, a trail like a broom pushed by a madman. He was bewildered that his uncle was missing what was right in front of him.

"They don't like to come out in the open, so I'm surprised to see tracks here," Uncle Ricky said. He leaned on his rifle stock to straighten to his full height and shook out his bad knee as if to wake it up, or quiet it down. "Let's go out in the woods where there's some brush. They like bushes, pine stands. Places they can hide."

Johnny swallowed back his disappointment that Uncle Ricky didn't know, that he must explain it all. And time was wasting. Who knew how far the thing had traveled overnight?

"This way," Johnny said, pointing toward the fence and the old-growth forest of pine and spruce trees beyond it.

Following the fox-thing's trail.

They waded through snow so deep that Johnny wished he had cowboy boots like Uncle Ricky instead of the new Converse sneakers Mom had given him for Christmas. Fighting through a dreamlike feeling after so little sleep, he realized that he and Uncle Ricky hadn't talked about rabbit hunting at all on this trip; the proposed hunting lesson last year had been one more thing cut short by the burning.

Johnny never let his eyes veer from the wild flourishes of the fox-thing's path in the snow. Uncle Ricky seemed content to let Johnny lead, though he was studiously ignoring the creature's trail. Instead, Uncle Ricky pointed out places where he'd found rabbits.

Then . . . the trail was gone, as if the thing had burrowed more deeply underground and never resurfaced. Or vanished outright. Johnny stopped walking, panicked that the hidden beast might yank him by his feet and drag him away. He didn't know what he'd expected on the outing, but the lost possibility, once within reach, crushed him. They were beneath a towering old cottonwood tree with a dark gap, like a doorway. A mound of snow in front of the tree looked undisturbed, but who knew what it was hiding?

And were those blue eyes glowing from the folds of the dark? Instead of moving toward the shadowed hole, Johnny stepped away. He hadn't wanted to trade familiar terror for a worse one, sharpening the claws of his nightmares. With Uncle Ricky beside him, he hadn't felt scared until he lost the trail.

The morning woods were not quiet. Bear Creek was east of them, the babbling of water of its stony bed suddenly loud, although most of the creek must be frozen. To the west, a coyote's far-off yipping startled him. He looked toward every noise . . . then back at the old tree.

"What's wrong, youngblood?" It might have been the first time Uncle Ricky had looked him dead in the face since he'd knocked on his door. Uncle Ricky's eyes were an invitation to tell. And his eyes weren't red from grass, for a change. He had come to hunt with a clear head.

"I did something," Johnny whispered.

Uncle Ricky and his sober eyes waited.

"I . . . said something to your mom last night. Outside her

door. But I didn't go in." He added the last part in case a respectful distance somehow made it better. He tried to bring the words he'd said to his mouth, but they seemed worse in daylight. "I said something bad."

"What'd you say?" Uncle Ricky's voice was only curious. No judgment.

Still, Johnny shook his head. He couldn't tell him. He would never tell anyone.

Uncle Ricky chuckled. "Listen—I'm sure you didn't say nothin' me and your mom didn't think up first. And she probably didn't even hear you. That what's got you all freaked out?"

"When I said it . . ." He wanted to say, *a demon came.* That explained it best, yet it would sound the worst. ". . . something climbed out of her window. It was in her room."

Now silence draped the woods. Uncle Ricky's eyes moved away, scanning the landscape. Beyond the cottonwood, they were at the base of a steep incline knotted with fir trees. Finally, Uncle Ricky stared toward the old cottonwood and its large gap before turning back to Johnny.

"Did you see it?"

Johnny nodded. "Kind of. It moved fast. But . . . I saw the teeth."

Uncle Ricky grabbed Johnny's shoulder, his fingers tight through his thick coat. "Did it hurt you?" For the first time, he sounded worried.

"No. It ran. It doesn't go straight, it goes like . . ." Johnny scraped his shoe in the snow in a zigzag to show him. His toes were so cold inside of his sneakers that they burned. ". . . here . . . and then there. It doesn't go in a straight line. The tracks are right outside her house. They come out here . . . and then they stop."

Johnny pointed at the spot in the snow where the tracks ended a few yards in front of the cottonwood tree and the mass of snow that might be a perfect hiding place. He wanted Uncle

Ricky to jack a cartridge into his rifle's chamber and say, *Let's go see where it went.* Instead, a stormy uncertainty grew on Uncle Ricky's face. He tipped up his hat to run his hand across his forehead, fretting.

"What kinda animal did it look like?" Uncle Ricky finally asked.

"Didn't look like *any* animal! It looked like a demon that crawled out of the ground." There. He'd finally said it. He expected Uncle Ricky to laugh at him . . . but he didn't.

"Then you shouldn't try to go chasin' after things you don't understand." Uncle Ricky's voice was sharp with scolding. "Should you?"

The change in Uncle Ricky was troubling in an entirely different way. Johnny's ears rang as if his uncle had shouted at him.

"You already know about it. Don't you?"

"Don't ask me that." Uncle Ricky stared at the ground like when Mom told him off.

"Because it's a secret?"

Uncle Ricky's jaw flexed so tightly that Johnny was afraid his uncle would slap him. "Hardheaded, ain't you? What'd I just say? You listen to me good: we ain't gonna talk about it. You're not gonna say nothin' to your mama, neither. What you saw is just between me and you."

"But you believe me," Johnny said, testing him. His heart was pounding in his chest so hard that his lungs barely found room to breathe.

Uncle Ricky half shrugged and half nodded, the way he would if they were talking about when it might snow next. Or if Grandmother's private nurse might be late on the icy road.

"Say it," Johnny said. "Say you believe me."

Uncle Ricky nodded. Close enough. The pressure in Johnny's chest eased, though he was shivering despite his coat and gloves.

"I told you!" Johnny said. "I told you I saw something last year!"

"Yep, sorry." He didn't *sound* apologetic. "And you don't yell when you're hunting."

Despite his anger and a dizzy feeling from doubting everything he thought he knew about the world, Johnny obediently lowered his voice. "Well, why—"

"Come on," Uncle Ricky said, and walked toward less steep ground, away from the cottonwood tree and its yawning maw. "Let's get us a hare."

WHAT. THE. HELL. Johnny came as close as he ever had to cussing out an adult. He breathed in angry puffs, struggling to keep pace in the deep snow. The creek burbled ahead.

"You know what a nervous breakdown is?" Uncle Ricky said.

"I'm not crazy," Johnny responded, still quiet. "I know what I saw."

"Not you—my mom. Remember I told you how she had to step away from Hollywood and spend some time by herself? They were forgetting her, or worse: calling her a *coon*. Oh, she hated that word. That grinnin' and foolishness she did to make all that money off white folks in those old movies came back on her after times changed. When I tried to visit to see after her, she just fussed and hollered and sent me away. Hell, she threatened to shoot me once. For five whole years, it was just her out here in these woods."

Johnny sensed that his uncle was winding to the point—*the creature?!*—so he tried to slow his breathing and hear past the pounding of blood in his ears. Uncle Ricky held up his hand: *Stop.* Johnny stopped abruptly, nearly stumbling into him.

"Snow hares are brown in summer, but in winter their fur turns white." Uncle Ricky nodded toward an arrangement of stones a few yards from them. Something moved, barely visible against the gray rocks—but it was small, not the creature in

Grandmother's window. As Johnny stared, a form took shape: a white-haired rabbit was standing against the rocks, rubbing its face with its paws. Johnny couldn't help thinking of the hare from *Alice's Adventures in Wonderland*, as if it might pull out a pocket watch next. That wouldn't be any stranger than what he'd already seen.

To Johnny's surprise, Uncle Ricky slipped his hunting rifle into Johnny's hands, guiding him to raise it high with the stock beneath his chin. The gun wasn't as heavy as Johnny had expected, given its deadly power. Still, his arms trembled beneath its weight.

"So . . ." Uncle Ricky said, his voice low in Johnny's ear, "one time I came out here, just like you, and I saw it's not just rabbits and ermines out here with white fur." He gently moved Johnny's arms to reposition the rifle slightly. "You see 'im?"

Johnny looked all around for the fox-demon, but Uncle Ricky was only pointing toward the hare. "Get 'im in your sight. You ain't even lookin'." Uncle Ricky pointed out the nub of the rifle's front sight and used his palm to push gently on the back of Johnny's head so he would lower it to a proper hunting stance.

The rabbit changed position only slightly, unaware that they were so close, favoring the other side of his face for cleaning.

"Where did you see it?" Johnny whispered.

Uncle Ricky chuckled. "I was sittin' outside in my old truck tryin' to figure how to talk sense into her . . . and that thing came runnin' out the back door."

"It opened the door?" Johnny remembered Grandmother's cracked-open window.

"*She* opened it," Uncle Ricky said. "Let it out like it was her pet pooch. And then . . . *boom*. It was gone in a flash, just like you said. She saw me too. That was the night she threatened to shoot me. She said to get the hell away from her and never come back."

THE WISHING POOL AND OTHER STORIES

A sound from closer to the creek made the hare stick its head up high, alert.

"Hurry," Uncle Ricky whispered. "Don't miss the shot."

But Johnny could barely remember who and where he was, imagining Grandmother feeding the fox-demon. It *hadn't* been a dream. He had seen with his own eyes and then in his dreams. His mind whirled with the dizzy feeling again.

By the time his wooziness passed, the hare was gone, only a pile of stones left behind.

"Damnit," Uncle Ricky said.

"What is it? I thought I made a demon come. Like . . . saying something so bad was praying to it."

Uncle Ricky didn't seem to hear him, staring with longing at the spot where the hare had been. "I got no goddamn idea, but it's no demon," he finally said. "All I know is, it's been out here with her, the two of them hiding from the world, I guess. She's been feeding it, and it's been here a long time. It was smaller when I saw it. Maybe it thinks she's its mama."

"So . . . what will happen when . . ."

For the first time, Johnny noticed that his uncle's eyes were red after all. And moist. "When the time comes . . . I suppose I'll have to come out here and take care of it. So it won't hurt nobody. Whatever it is . . . it ain't natural. Is it?"

Johnny shook his head. The cold hadn't been as bad when they were walking, but now that they were still, the frigid breeze was slicing into his bare cheeks and ears.

"Don't feel bad about whatever you said to Mother," Uncle Ricky said. "She brought it on herself. Besides, there's worse. Way worse. If I tell you something, will you keep it a secret? Never let your mama know I told you?"

Something yelled inside of Johnny that he should say no, that his mother would never want him to make that promise. It was bad enough he couldn't say anything to her about the odd creature—not that she would probably believe him. Maybe secrets, and silence, were a part of the key to becoming an adult, but they also took something away.

"Okay," Johnny said despite himself.

"It's hard, watching somebody dying," Uncle Ricky said. For a while, Johnny thought that was the end of the secret. "You know what bedsores are?"

Johnny shook his head.

"Believe me, you don't *want* to know. A body laying in bed a long time gets . . . holes in it. Big ones. *Sore* ain't even the right word. I could fit an orange in one. The nurse comes in and cleans her up, but . . . it hurts a lot. So anyway, last night your mama and I stayed up late talking about whether we should mash up some pills and . . . let her rest. Put a stop to her pain."

The world's axis tilted again, but this time Johnny fought the dizziness, staring into Uncle Ricky's eyes to make sure he understood: *They had talked about killing her.*

A tear escaped the side of Uncle Ricky's eye, and he didn't wipe it away. "Only thing that stopped us? We couldn't be sure if we wanted to do it out of love. Your mama's mad as hell about that burn, and killing out of hate's a sin. Neither of us wants that demon on our backs. But it could be a worse sin to let her suffer. If she was a dog, we would've put her down a long time ago."

Uncle Ricky's confession sat heavy in the morning air, how he and Mom had weighed whether or not they loved their mother enough to kill her. Or if they hated her so much that they must let her live. Johnny wished he could unhear all of it. The confession felt like a curse that would follow him. One day his mother would get old too, and she might get bedsores big enough to put his fist into.

"I'm cold," Johnny whispered.

Uncle Ricky nodded and took back the rifle Johnny had forgotten he was still holding. "Yeah. We better head back and make sure the nurse made it on that road. Always take your shot, Johnny. Now I gotta drive to town or we're gonna eat leftover ham for dinner. Again."

While Uncle Ricky walked ahead, Johnny noticed how his limp was worse in the cold; Grandmother's lasting gift to him in her moment of rage with a tire iron that had ruined his chance to play football when he was in high school, or anywhere. A year ago, Johnny thought it was the worst story he had ever heard. But not anymore.

Johnny landed his feet inside his uncle's deep footprints, hopping from one to the next, trying to keep the snow from burying his new shoes.

The nurse, a white woman, jounced up the driveway in an old blue station wagon with snow chains, but Johnny never saw her except through his cabin window. He slept leaning in his cabin's hardback chair much of the day undisturbed, except when Mom brought him a ham sandwich for lunch. Her smile was so sweet that it made his stomach ache again. His secrets stewed inside of him while he mumbled his thank-you, trying to pretend he didn't know what he knew. This trip had ruined more than Christmas and Kwanzaa; he couldn't even reclaim joy from his mother's smile. His groggy mind kept flashing him the creature's sharp teeth.

He was nodding off at the table again when he heard the scream.

Johnny's hands tightened around the waiting snow shovel as he jumped up to stare out of his window. He saw the back door ripped away, the windows shattered, a bloody heap quivering in the driveway from a sudden attack—but all of that was his imagination, vanishing when he blinked. Uncle Ricky's VW Bug was gone, leaving only the nurse's station wagon and Mom's rental car parked near the back door, but there were no new tracks. No blood. A bright light from Grandmother's bedroom shined through her window, which was now firmly closed. Last night's swishes from the retreating creature were unchanged because no new snow had fallen yet.

Another scream clawed through the stillness. He was sure it must be from Grandmother's room. Was Mom alone with her? Had the nurse gone on an errand with Uncle Ricky? A well of panic swallowed Johnny as he imagined his mother as a knife-wielding killer like in *Black Christmas*, which he had snuck into a theater to see while Mom was at work a week ago.

"Shhhh . . . it's alright . . ." Mom's muffled voice soothed, a plea nearly as sad as the screaming. "Emma's almost done . . . Please hold still. It's alright, Mother."

Mom wasn't alone! *The bedsores*, he remembered. That was why his grandmother was yelling: the nurse was doing her difficult work. Maybe Uncle Ricky hadn't left just to find something else for dinner; the suffering might have driven him away.

Another scream. Even muffled, the sound made him drop the shovel and mash his palms against his ears so hard that it hurt. He had never heard a person in so much pain. Sick people in movies and on TV didn't wail like wounded animals. Was *this* how people died? And last night he had heaped his horrible words on top of her suffering. Johnny could barely catch his breath.

Why had Mom brought him here for this morbid ritual? Why had Uncle Ricky told him a secret he would be forced to remember with every scream?

As he stared outside, Johnny glimpsed Uncle Ricky's hunting rifle leaning unattended against his cabin door on the other side of the yard. *Always take your shot, Johnny*, he had said.

As soon as Johnny saw the rifle, he rushed to put on his coat and sneakers, which he had dried in front of his space heater. Several facts fell into place: He had a gun. The creature's tracks were visible. He still had the chance to conquer his nightmares.

He had missed his chance to fire at the hare, but he would not hesitate to pull the trigger again.

The tracks had ended right near that big old cottonwood tree, and the hollow in the trunk looked just like a doorway, didn't it? That thing in the woods was dangerous, or else Uncle Ricky's eyes wouldn't have widened so much when Johnny told him he'd seen its teeth.

Somebody had to do what needed to be done, even if nothing could be done for Grandmother. Anything was better than waiting. Johnny grabbed the rifle, ducking under his grandmother's wood-rail fence to run into the graying woods.

Farther behind him with every step, Grandmother was still screaming.

His feet, it seemed, remembered every dip and crevice as he followed the slashing, senseless trail between the firs and pines. This time, the creature's passage was accompanied by Uncle Ricky's boot tracks and Johnny's smaller ones beside his, sometimes intersecting, sometimes roughly parallel. Johnny panted with his mouth open as he ran, his breath charging in bursts from his lips. He held the rifle like a bayonet, ready to strike.

Fear made his legs heavy, yet he pushed through until he was sweating despite the cold, until he could see the large tree ahead, dwarfing the surrounding conifers with a massive canopy of feathery branches made ominous without their leaves.

Yes, this was the place. He had no doubt. The tracks stopped abruptly, but at the end of the creature's trail was a small heap, a sign of burrowing for sure. When he nudged the heap with his foot—jumping quickly away, of course—lumpy snow fell away into a hole as wide as a basketball. And the cottonwood stood only yards from the creature's tunnel.

Upon his second visit, the mound of snow in front of the tree seemed like a wall, and the gap itself looked bigger; an archway of inky blackness against the snowdrift.

"Come out! *I'm not afraid of you!*"

In that moment, it didn't feel like a lie because his terror only felt like rage. He was enraged with his mother for bringing him on such a horrible trip. Enraged with Uncle Ricky for the secrets he kept, and the one he had shared. Enraged with himself for cursing Grandmother to die and then pitying her and for feeling anything for her after everything she had done. His rage poured out of him as tears, and his throat grew clotted, but he yelled again, "*Come on out!*"

He had never wanted to kill a thing, but he did now with a ferocity that felt primal. If he could turn back time, he would shoot that hare until his rifle clicked empty. Maybe this creature had no more to do with poisoning his family than the hare, but he hoped that killing it would help him sleep without nightmares.

The silence infuriated him. Johnny picked up a stone and threw it at the dead cottonwood tree, missing the cavity by two inches. The second stone he threw flew inside and vanished in the blackness with a *THUNK*.

The chittering he had heard in Grandmother's room floated from the gap, though much louder than before. Agitated. Rising in pitch. A slithering sound echoed from inside the tree trunk, something moving fast, perhaps racing in a circle. Would it come outside?

Always take your shot, Johnny.

The rifle snapped into place beneath his chin, the perfect shooting stance. Johnny's sight was aimed directly into the dark crater, barely wavering despite his heaving breaths. Nothing else in the woods existed except the inky maw and his breathing.

Two ice-blue eyes emerged from the darkness. Moving toward daylight. Toward him.

Johnny's breathing stopped. The world stopped. For a moment, neither of them moved. The urge to kill, so consuming before, withered. *Maybe it thinks she's its mama*, Uncle Ricky had said.

"Don't come back!" Johnny said, although phlegm tried to strangle his voice. "You hear me? She's dying, so stay away!"

More chittering, but it seemed softer this time. Plaintive, even. Could it understand?

A large twig cracking from the creature's motion in the darkness sounded like a gunshot, snapping Johnny awake from his fugue state. Without realizing it, he dropped Uncle Ricky's gun when he turned and stumbled to run away.

His own scream was bottled in his throat, ringing between his ears.

When Johnny made it back to the lodge, the nurse's car was gone.

Mom was bundled up in her coat and scarf on the back porch, bent over with her head wrapped between her arms; the same spot where Grandmother was always sitting in his dream. He had never seen his mother look so weary and sad.

He thought Grandmother might be dead until he heard a soft moan through her window.

Mom sobbed so loudly that Johnny thought about sneaking back into his cabin unseen. But he decided to go to her instead.

Mom heard his feet crunching toward her and looked up with a smile she tried to paste in place to greet him. When she saw his face, her smile died unborn. Wildness was playing in his mother's eyes, and he suspected she saw the same wildness in his.

"This is no kind of Christmas for you, Johnny," she said. "I'm sorry."

"You neither. I'm sorry too."

He sat beside her, so she scooted to make room on the narrow stair. The part of him that wanted to tell her everything quieted, obsolete, when she hugged him close. And he hugged her, comforting, not merely comforted—different than when he'd been younger—something new.

Johnny knew then that he would never tell his mother about Grandmother's strange creature in the woods, perhaps the only one of her children she had not scarred for life.

Three weeks after their trip to Bear Creek, Grandmother died at a Denver hospital. Neither Mom nor Uncle Ricky gave her the pills to end her misery, although Johnny could never forget that only their fear of hating her had stopped them. Her lodge sat empty for a year, but then Uncle Ricky moved in. He and Mom split the proceeds from the sale of their childhood home, and Mom bought a three-bedroom house in North Miami with a yard full of mango and avocado trees. It was the best place Johnny had ever lived, though that didn't stop the bad dreams.

Five years after Grandmother died, Uncle Ricky vanished on a hunting trip near the lodge. His mother, of course, was devastated. By then, Johnny was in college in lily-white Iowa on a full academic scholarship, never needing a cent from Grandmother's estate—and the story of his uncle's disappearance didn't sit right. Uncle Ricky had been a seasoned hunter, and he knew those woods well.

Johnny called the local sheriff's office to find out more, since a Black man missing in the woods surely wasn't their top priority. But the deputy who picked up the phone told him he drank beer with Uncle Ricky on Friday nights and had been a part of the search party. He didn't need to pull up a report to share the facts: a set of footprints they thought held promise had simply stopped cold in a clearing. The dogs sniffed Uncle Ricky to that spot and no farther.

"In front of an old tree?" Johnny said. Beyond his doorway, music blared from an impromptu dance party erupting in his dorm to celebrate the weekend. Metal rock. Johnny and his classmates were in two different worlds, yet again.

Come to think of it, a deputy said, there *had* been an old

husk of a tree near where the tracks disappeared. The dogs had whined and circled, and one of them had started digging.

But all they found was snow.

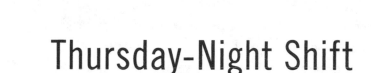

Thursday-Night Shift

April 1968

For as long as she could remember, Shana had been teaching herself to be content in the dark. She'd discovered her gift for night sight during frequent trips to the bathroom that dogged her even now that she was thirteen and no longer wet her bed. She was careful not to wake her younger sister, Missy, since their bedroom was directly beside their parents', and nobody would have a good morning if Daddy didn't get his sleep. Shana had taught herself to move mouse-like through the dark room when she needed to climb in and out of her bed, guided only by the faint blue-white glow of the moonlight through her window.

Shana's phantom vision had become so sharp over time that she could swear she saw better with her eyes *closed*, relying on other senses rather than fighting the dark. The rounded curve of her mattress, her globe-shaped bedpost, the crumpled sheets— all seemed in perfect view when she touched them. That was one more odd thing about herself she could never explain to anyone, not even Missy. *No one can see with their eyes closed*, Missy would say—but Shana would almost swear on a Bible she *could*.

Even before the box arrived, Shana had begun to wonder about small ways she no longer felt quite like herself. She didn't feel quite like a regular human being—maybe she never had, as if she had accidentally found herself in a world where brown skin and white skin held unusual importance and it was considered abnormal to see in the dark.

So, the box.

From the sight of it, the package from Aunt Priscilla might have been from the president of Mali himself. Slightly bigger than a shoebox, it arrived in the mail after school Wednesday, decorated with colorful international stickers and official red and blue stripes. *République du Mali*, the stamp said; it bore the image of an odd black beetle with spiny legs. Mama had set it down on the table before she called to her, as if to give her privacy with it. The package was inscribed to Shana alone— her aunt *always* included her middle name to remind her of her namesake—Miss Shana Priscilla Jackson, 500 Lauderdale Street, Memphis, Tennessee, 38126.

Two smaller boxes lay inside the first box, an immediate disappointment as Shana's imagination shrank to scale. Was it jewelry? A lion's tooth? The final box, padded on all sides, was burnished metal. The latch clicked open without a key. A typed letter lay neatly folded into a thick square. When Shana lifted the letter, she found the glistening black stone beneath, an exact fit in the palm of her hand. Maybe the box had been sitting out in the sun; the stone was warm.

Sweet Shana—I thought of you when I came across this lovely stone. I know you have loved exotic rocks since you were a baby. I was traveling with friends in the Dogon region, it's of fantastic historical importance, so you'll have to work on your French and come with me one day. The Dogon culture is quite astronomically advanced here, you know, which your American teachers will never tell you. It's a shame how they're cutting down the forests, but I found this stone near an excavation site, and I've never seen one quite like it. The geology grad students from university were very jealous of me and frantic to have it, but I hid it to send to you. If you ever tire of this, promise me you'll give it back to me when you come visit. Otherwise, keep it as my gift—and remember you come from great people who used their own science to navigate the stars.

Aunt Priscilla always wrote as if Shana's future relied on knowing history from a continent across the ocean. And what did she mean by "navigate the stars"? Surely Aunt Priscilla didn't think Africans were exploring space like John Glenn had orbited the earth. The space flights were Shana's most fixed memories, and in some ways she felt as if she were watching the rocket's violent departure from the earth's atmosphere all the time in her mind. Outer space was far from Memphis. Far from a country that did not love her. Unbound by gravity. Perfect.

Shana didn't often get excited about presents, but she was so happy with her mysterious new stone that she slept with it wrapped in the palm of her hand.

She was sure she saw the stone's luxuriant velvet glow even with her eyes closed.

By morning, her palm was empty. An oval-shaped shadow remained, faintly painting her palm's crevices. She patted her mattress for the stone and finally realized it was nestled in her armpit, as smooth as her own skin. To yank it free, she tugged harder than she'd thought she should have to. Removing it stung a bit, so she immediately slid it back.

"What's that?" Missy said, bounding to the foot of Shana's bed.

As Shana stared at her sister's face upturned to hers, she saw her anew: eyes starving for adventure, for relief from the constant hum about the marches and the beatings and how Larry Payne got shot. The night before, Missy had asked her,

"How come they hate us so much?" and Shana couldn't find an answer. She'd told Missy to ask Mama.

Now Shana wanted to tell Missy about the stone and the stain on her palm—as a big sister, she felt a *duty* to tell her. But she could not make herself say it. The words stayed coiled in her throat.

"Come on—what is it?" Missy pressed.

"Get off my bed!" Shana said, more angrily than she'd meant to. "Leave me alone! Why are you always bothering me?" She spoke all the words she knew Missy hated the most.

But Missy didn't storm with the anger Shana expected. Instead, tears came to Missy's eyes and her bottom lip shook.

"Why are you so mean?" she said, and walked out of the room. Shana thought she heard her sob, and her own throat hurt. She was near sobbing too. But not a bit of that mattered. Shana swallowed her sob and forgot it.

The stone had lost some of its coloring, so it appeared lighter than it had been when she went to sleep. *It bled*, she thought. That was when it started: her ability to understand. Shana instantly knew that she must keep the stone with her at all times and safeguard it while she slept. She must not let anyone else see it: Mama had barely given it a glance. Papa would never lay eyes on it. (How had Aunt Priscilla negotiated her way to it? Hidden it? It was remarkable.)

And she'd slept with it in her hand! She could never be that foolish again.

Her armpit was the perfect place to carry the stone—as if the crevice of warm skin were designed for the task. The long sleeves on her dress obscured the stone's bulk, and it felt so natural that Shana had to pat the spot to remember it was there. She sat with it under her arm at breakfast, where Missy sulked and wouldn't look at her. Shana was staring at her scrambled eggs thinking the word *incubation* at the moment she realized the stone's warmth matched her body temperature exactly. And the kitchen's aqua blue seemed unusually bright: the stove, the refrigerator, the sink's basin. Colors leaped at her.

Papa had a smile for them at breakfast, and smiles were rare since the strike. He'd gone to Mason Temple to hear the speech yesterday, and then he'd gone straight to bed.

"Did the reverend give a speech, Papa?" Missy said.

Papa nodded, shoveling scrambled eggs in his mouth. He always ate in a hurry. Said he'd grown up poor with eight siblings, and if you didn't eat fast, you didn't eat.

"What'd he say?"

"Same old same old," Papa said. "Tellin' us what we already know."

"Reverend's staying at the motel, Shana, not the Holiday Inn like usual," Mama said, trying to sound casual so Papa wouldn't accuse her of worship. "So the Baileys, they want everything right to show what a Negro business can provide. Mr. Bailey asked me to put in extra hours tonight, and I want you to come help me so I'll finish by a decent hour."

Daddy was a trash collector who had never gone to college, and Aunt Priscilla thought it was scandalous that Mama was "training" Shana to be a maid; Mama being a maid was one of the things they argued about. Mama said she didn't mind cleaning when it was for Negroes, and the Baileys' motel was nicely kept up with modern décor and a colorful lighted neon sign that pointed up at the sky. The owners had named it after the song "Sweet Lorraine."

And Mama met so many people there: actors, musicians, writers. Papa complained that Mama acted like she needed to breathe the same air famous people breathed or she didn't get enough oxygen. She was the maid supervisor and sometimes worked behind the desk, and all the famous people who came knew her by name, so Mama was not going to leave her job at the Baileys' motel anytime soon. One day Shana had passed a room and heard loud guitar licks and singing that stayed in her mind for weeks. Later, when the song "Midnight Hour" came on the radio and she knew it already, Mama only laughed and said she'd probably heard Wilson Pickett making it up through the walls. The motel was that kind of place, with music and laughing and Negroes dressed in ties and long skirts.

Still, of course, Shana didn't want to clean motel rooms after school. But she noticed the dark splotches under Mama's eyes and her gingerly movement as she walked from the counter to the table with the coffee pot to refill Papa's mug. Mama often hissed quietly when she bent over, or hummed a phrase from a freedom song to keep herself from groaning. While she'd lain curled on the ground during a sit-in in Nashville with Aunt Priscilla, a police officer had kicked them both. He'd kicked Mama's lower back, and she'd never felt right since. Having the stone helped Shana see the polished black shoe as it swung down to kick her mother with all the force the cop who wore it could muster. That was when Aunt Priscilla had left the country, and Mama had never forgiven her.

"Okay, Mama," Shana said.

"I want to go too!" Missy said. "I want to meet him."

"Just a man," Papa said. "Why make such a fuss over a regular man? He's no better'n me or you. Should have seen him sweating at the podium. He's just as scared as anyone else."

"I only need Shana, Missy," Mama said. "Bad enough for us two to be out tonight."

The curfew had been lifted Monday, but police still harassed Negroes they saw out at night. With the soldiers and the shooting, Memphis looked like the newscasts from Vietnam. Larry Payne, who'd been shot by police at the reverend's march last week, was only sixteen—three years older than Shana. Papa had gone to his funeral.

"Papa, can I go too?" Missy said. "Please?"

Papa shook his head. "Just Shana." Then he turned his grave eyes up to Mama. "And don't be out late."

* * *

Shana's heart thumped with excitement as soon as she stepped outside to walk with Missy to school. Nothing was different—rows of redbrick homes, neighbors climbing into their cars or walking to the bus stop, dogs barking, piles of debris on the street—but it looked new somehow. *All* of it. The stone under her arm seemed to vibrate as the expanse of the sky unfolded above her, feeding from sunlight through her skin. Blue, again: she felt like she could see through the sky. Tonight, she promised her stone, she would sleep outside.

Shana hadn't realized she'd been standing fixed on the street staring at the sky until some time had passed. She looked around, remembering herself, and saw that Missy had kept walking without her across the street to the next block. The part of her that was still Shana remembered that she had hurt her sister's feelings, and most of her still cared enough to run to catch up to her and try to say something to make amends.

She decided to talk about the things Missy was afraid of.

"I know why white folks don't treat us right," Shana said.

Despite herself, Missy was interested. The question *why* was on everyone's lips. Everyone knew how Echol Cole and Robert Walker had been crushed in the broken garbage truck, proof enough the conditions weren't fit for workers. And everyone from Thomas Jefferson to President Johnson had said all men were created equal. Everyone else knew what was right.

"They're afraid," Shana said, simplifying it as best she could. "They don't want to be under us like we're under them."

"That's stupid. Ain't nobody tryin' to be over them." She and Missy said *ain't* only when Mama wasn't within hearing, thrilling with the forbidden slang. "We just don't want to be treated so mean. Like dogs. Worse than dogs."

"If it was the other way," Shana said, "we'd be the same."

"Nah-uh. That's stupid."

"Yes," Shana said, knowing. "We would."

"Quit trying to act like you know everything. We wouldn't never be like that. *I* wouldn't." Shana barely heard Missy, as if her sister were speaking far below her, because she could see time unlayering, unfolding—an unwrapping and redoing of things—that proved her right: that Missy's twin in that other time could be standing on the curb shouting rage as white marchers passed quietly with signs: *I AM A MAN*, which could be reduced to *I AM*. Which could be reduced to *I*. Someone very much like Missy would cheer as police officers beat them and snatched their signs away. But she would never convince Missy of what she saw.

The street's stench was stronger today. The low, sour odor that had wrapped itself around the city was unmistakable even in the morning cold. Shana's nose was separating the scents into organic, metallic, and acidic, studying them with great interest, cataloging them. (Or the stone was, anyway.) She could tell which scents were from a liquor store and which were from a butcher shop and which were from a house with a newborn or an invalid who soiled diapers or sheets beyond cleaning. If not for Missy, Shana would have stood stock-still on the sidewalk with her nose turned up high to take in the smells.

Stillness felt like Shana's natural position now. To walk felt awkward, although the part of her that was Shana remembered movement fine. She more consciously monitored her movements: her steps, her breathing, her hands, her fingers. All fascinating.

And she kept noticing a number everywhere—on mailboxes, on passing buses, on car license plates: 306. The number was important somehow.

"Stinks today," Missy said. "Good. I hope nobody ever picks up the trash in this whole city. That's what they deserve."

One of the first things Shana learned about her stone was that it had a kind of unspoken language—if she squeezed her arm a certain way, or for a certain duration, she could communicate with it. This happened as Mrs. Harris called her to write on the chalkboard during math—that number 306 came up again—and although Shana was right-handed, she'd foolishly chosen her right armpit to secure her stone. Wouldn't the stone fall as soon as she lifted her arm? She stammered and lied to say she didn't know how to solve the equation—but Mrs. Harris commanded her to the board. As it turned out, she shouldn't have worried: the stone burrowed so deeply in its cavern that it seemed to disappear, not moving at all when she raised her arm.

Shana perfected her language with it throughout the day: short bursts for instant clarity, a long squeeze for energy when she felt sleepy (carrying the stone *did* seem to drain her), and subtle shifts when she was curious about things that were about to happen. For instance, her sight blurred and she thought she saw Assistant Principal Gandy walk into the room to whisper in her teacher's ear—but his broad stomach did not actually appear in the doorway until seconds later.

Like Mr. Spock always said on *Star Trek*, the stone was *fascinating*.

In English, instead of copying vocabulary words from the chalkboard, Shana began documenting her new knowledge of the stone's history: *Landed three hundred years ago as a piece of a larger mass shattered by contact with the outer atmosphere. Attracted to the Dogon region. Never touched by human hands before the forests were cut down. Remembers everything it touches. Has gathered volumes of data on ants, insects, small mammals, and primates. I am its first true human incubation.* That powerful word again—*I*.

Shana stopped writing when her English teacher, Mrs. Hayward, rapped a ruler on her desk and snatched away her notes. Shana had a foreign impulse to take the notes back to keep the stone's secrets, yet her Shana part remembered that she must not disrespect her teacher. Mrs. Hayward read the notes silently with her forehead wrinkled in a frown, but she gave the paper back. The stone helped Shana realize her teacher was actually amused—even impressed by Shana's imagination. "Write only what's on the board and stop wasting your time with silly stories," she said, and Shana said, "Yes ma'am," as she was expected.

Then Mrs. Hayward turned to the class and asked for everyone's attention. Shana only half listened, because she had resumed writing her notes: *I will share my human data and it will teach me how to see the layers.* "Layers" wasn't the right word, exactly, but Shana was writing too quickly to be choosy. The notes were only meant to occupy her racing mind. She would not need notes. She would remember everything she learned from the stone. She would *be* the stone.

"Shana!" Mrs. Hayward scolded, and Shana laid her pen down flat. Once Shana's eyes looked up, Mrs. Hayward went on: "Now, I've heard a rumor some of you may be planning to skip school again Friday, that there might be another march planned? If that's true, please raise your hand."

No hands went up. Shana sensed the hum of emotions around her—defiance, shyness, secretiveness, sadness. If there *was* a march, many would go. But the only plan she had overheard from Daddy was that the reverend would lead a march on Monday.

Mrs. Hayward pursed her lips to a thin line. "Now you all listen to me," she said in a funeral director's voice. "I know everyone is excited. But you need to stay away from the marches now, hear? Some of those teenagers feel too hopeless to think straight. And soldiers would just as soon shoot you as look at you, like this is a Tet Offensive here in Memphis. We don't want anyone else getting killed. We have a national spotlight now. We don't want the world to look at Memphis and say, *Look how they act. They cuss at police and set fires.*"

Many students nodded obediently, but they were only wearing masks like Shana, pretending she was the same Shana and nothing more. She remembered what Papa had said about the reverend being scared. He had reason to be scared. People only set fires and cussed out police when they were scared.

Mrs. Hayward knew her students were keeping their true thoughts silent, so she only shook her head when the bell rang. "Don't forget: we have a quiz," she said. "See you Friday."

But she would not see them Friday. Her quiz would not matter. Everyone in the class seemed to know it, though Shana knew better than anyone.

Papa had driven the Buick to work and Missy had stayed at their cousins' house after school, so Shana and Mama took the Mississippi Boulevard bus to the Patterson bus and walked the remaining blocks to the motel past decaying storefronts and boardinghouses. From some distance, on Beale Street, Shana could hear raucous ghosts from years past and future. Aretha Franklin's "Chain of Fools" poured from a passing car window, and Shana nearly forgot how to walk because the music was startling: deepest grief, but also a celebration. The stone beneath her armpit burned. (Had the stone never heard music before?)

Shana patted her crease where she was carrying the stone, and it was smaller now. Shrinking. If she examined herself in her bathroom mirror later that night—if she ever looked in a mirror again—she would see a large dark spot like the one on her palm as the stone bled into her. Bled into *them*. After today, there would be no "I."

"We're just gonna tidy the rooms where the guests checked out late and get on home," a voice said from close by. *Mama.*

Shana waded out of the music's web and saw the street again, the sky's stunning light. Her mother's pearl-handled clutch purse with flower patterns swung beside her. Shana didn't dare look up at Mama's face just then because she might change her mind and fling the stone away. No one would miss her more than Mama. But Shana could never let her stone go, because it would be like letting go of a part of herself. It was too late now.

When they reached Mulberry Street, a National Guard truck rumbled by, driving slowly as if to avoid attention. The bayonets did not show like at the marches, but the truck screamed violence. A dozen soldiers watched, bored by the sight of them. They weren't much older than she was, glad to be on US soil and not in a jungle. Shana noticed *306* painted at the end of a long string of numbers on the side of the truck. The stoplight blurred at the crosswalk: Shana saw the light change from red to green 2.6 seconds before her vision sharpened and the light *actually* changed.

When they reached the motel at five thirty, the parking lot was filling up as always at the dinner hour, but most of the curtains were drawn. Shana admired the shiny white Cadillac and, beside it, an older Dodge Royal with majestic green fins. Cars fit for a king. A choir was rehearsing in one of the rooms nearby, muffled. Dazzling.

Mr. Bailey was on the phone and barely had time to speak when Mama peeked into the front office to say hello. He cupped his hand over the receiver. "Second floor," he said. "But don't bother 306." As an afterthought, he greeted Shana: "Hello, sweetheart."

"Hello, Mr. Bailey," she said, as she always did. No differently.

The cart was waiting at the top of the stairs, with its mop and broom and bucket and cleansers. Mr. Bailey didn't like the cart exposed on the balcony, where anyone could see from the parking lot and street. Quickly, Mama pushed the cart past room 306. Laughter came from inside when a man said, "I know *your* wife ain't gonna cook. She's too pretty."

They went to a room two rooms past, curtains wide open to expose the mess. Inside the room they cleaned, Shana was so distracted by the stone's explorations that Mama had to keep saying, "Hurry up," or, "Go hang that up," or, "Put that down," sounding more and more weary and annoyed, and Shana forced herself to forget the things the stone was studying—the temperatures and textures and scents and layers. The stale odor of cigarettes helped Shana fix herself in Now as she emptied a heap of ashes and cigarette butts into her trash bag.

She was still *Shana* enough to want to enjoy her last night with Mama, anyway.

But tonight, when her family was sleeping, she and the stone would leave the house and find a quiet place to become Shana-Stone. They would find their position to analyze and observe this world and its layers, buried somewhere in darkness, perhaps under the ground. Shana felt sadness again, but not as sharply as when she'd heard the music. She would miss her family, but not as much as she would have missed them yesterday. Or even that morning.

"Why can't grown folks remember to flush the toilet?" Mama called from the bathroom. The sound of flushing roared an echo against the wall.

"I don't know, Mama," Shana made herself say. Talking aloud was suddenly a chore.

The room was in such poor shape that cleaning it took nearly half an hour. Mama fretted over how late they would get home as she rolled the cart back outside, where the daylight was waning in a furious orange fireball to the west. A ruckus raged in the parking lot below, the sound of milling and preparation. A few voices still sang, practicing spirituals in harmony.

Behind them, a man on the balcony was laughing. The stone was especially intrigued by laughter, so Shana turned and saw that the door to 306 yawned wide open. She knew the face of the man standing outside of the room near the railing. He was wearing a suit and tie, as if he were already dressed for a funeral.

It was the reverend. His face was familiar from the news even if she'd had no stone to tell her. The burning in her armpit flared, and Shana allowed herself to see the layers that were always present, the different versions of Now: she and her stone were witnesses, as her stone had witnessed for hundreds of years before she'd been born.

"Doc!" a voice called from downstairs. "You remember Ben? Ben Branch?"

The reverend grinned and waved to the parking lot below. "Hey—how are you?" Excitement lighted his face as he leaned over the railing. "Tonight, be sure you play 'Precious Lord, Take My Hand.' Do it real pretty, now."

Downstairs, more laughter. "I will, Doc. I will."

As Shana and her stone—the Shana-Stone—studied the layers, the balcony blurred. Shana-Stone heard the gunshot 3.2 seconds before the gunman down the street squeezed the trigger. They heard before Mrs. Bailey would hear it and fall, shocked to the point of having a stroke. They heard before anyone would duck for cover or point out where the fearsome sound had been born. The layers unfolded in a blizzard.

"It's cold tonight!" another man called up. "Don't y'all forget your coats."

The gunshot had not yet come. Mrs. Bailey was on her feet and the city wasn't burning and the reverend was still smiling. Downstairs, a girl who sounded Missy's age giggled wildly.

The part of Shana that was still Shana called out: "Reverend!"

Her voice was loud. Mama's hand tightened on Shana's shoulder, warning her to hush and not be a bother. The reverend's head moved one and three-quarters of an inch to the right when he turned to her. His widening smile at her was cut short by the gunshot.

As they remembered everything, Shana-Stone would never forget the look of resignation on the reverend's face when the window to room 306 shattered behind him, or how his shoulders hunched high as he waited for a second shot to come. Or the way he crouched back against the wall like a child, his arms wrapped over his head amid the shouting and screaming. Or his panting voice as men scrambled from the room to see after him: "I'm okay. I'm okay."

Shana-Stone could see the layers: others would try to kill him. Violence was the humans' tradition, and the end of one Now led to another. The reverend had confessed to Daddy and everyone else gathered at Mason Temple last night that he knew his time had come. Daddy never told them at the breakfast table, but he'd cried himself to sleep after the speech.

For the briefest instant, Shana-Stone wondered if calling out to the reverend had been a mistake—because *their* way, Shana-Stone, was stillness. They were witnesses.

But until her final shift, a piece of Shana-Stone was only Shana. Human. And humans were never still—they were always in motion, even in their sleep.

That was one of the first things the stone had learned about Shana.

Dancing

I t began at her grandmother's funeral.

Grand-mère had been ninety-six years old, that was the thing. She'd done a lot of living in those years, mother to ten children between four marriages, three ending in divorce, the last cut short by widowhood. So when it was time for tributes at the feedback-ridden microphone, the first three speakers all called her by different names, Mrs. Bassett and then Mrs. DuPont and so on, and by the end of the third speech Monique was shaking with giggles fighting through her layers of sorrow.

Monique saw herself as ridiculous in the crowded pew: grief clawing her insides when Grand-mère had been only four years shy of one hundred, the very antithesis of *Too Soon*. Yet her absence had flayed Monique from the instant the old woman's chest never rose for her next breath while Tchaikovsky played on her CD player.

Why hadn't she spent more time preparing herself? "I thought we would have more time," Monique had whispered to Grand-mère's cooling ear.

More time! Outrageous. Another laugh shook Monique's shoulders. She had been caring for Grand-mère, sharing her apartment, for twenty years—half of her life. She'd moved in during her last year at Xavier to save expenses and never moved out, as Grand-mère had more trouble walking and needed help cleaning her house and running her errands. When they realized

Grand-mère's situation was "handled," her aunts, uncles, and cousins visited less and less, and Monique had entered middle age without truly living a life on her own.

Her laughter turned to tears; grief and self-loathing and, well, a dash of the root laughter, and she was caught in a terrible loop. She could only bark out noises she hoped sounded like sobs. In the end, she stopped her demon laughter by forcing a memory of how her mother, dying of cancer when Monique was a college freshman, had asked her to take her favorite blue dress. Monique had carelessly told her that she didn't have any more room in her closet and she didn't look good in blue anyway, answering her mother's realness with bullshit she'd never had a chance to make up for. By the time Monique had stewed herself in guilt, she was wailing for real and her cousins behind her were patting her back, saying, "Let it out." (But what more could she let out? Her throat was already raw.)

Monique had family in name, but as she watched Grand-mère's casket sink out of sight, she felt erased from the world. Grand-mère had always been ready to commiserate over gossip and headlines ("Evil asshole," she'd whispered while she watched CNN with her the night before she died), and now all of her cussing and complaining were over, along with her gap-toothed smiles and gentle birdlike hands braiding Monique's hair.

Everything felt wrong. The world. The air. Her body. Everything.

She found herself trapped in the line for fruit punch at the repast in the church basement where Grand-mère had never missed a Sunday meal (until just six months ago), with Monique dutifully pushing her wheelchair. She was only a yard from the stacked plastic cups and punch bowl when she couldn't stand the wait and began pacing the old wood-plank floor instead. Her feet could not stay rooted anywhere, tracing the wheelchair's phantom tracks around the room. Standing still made her cramp up, so her only relief was to pace, or to shift her weight from side to side. She stood on her tippy toes until it was uncomfortable, then started pacing again. She had never felt so restless in her skin.

Because the only music was sad flourishes from the new organ upstairs stabbing through the age-old planks, she wasn't aware at first that her body's unpredictable movements were *dancing*. She didn't hear imaginary music in her head to stir her, not even Grand-mère's favorite, James Brown. She might never be able to listen to "I Got the Feelin'" without imagining bedsores and shit-stained sheets, so James Brown was probably ruined for her now.

While she tried to think of an excuse so she could leave early, a thrumming bass beat from a car parked outside found her ear, from someone on one of the surrounding streets Pastor Moss referred to as "The Forsaken." The music was too far away to fully penetrate even half-open windows, but the beat was untouched, unmuffled. Pristine.

Monique's feet shuffled to the music, one-two, back and forth. Then her hips joined in, swaying from side to side, gently at first, then with surprising abandon. Her cramps vanished, replaced by a feeling like floating. Flying, even! The more she moved, the lighter she felt in body and spirit.

Monique let out a small gasp of happy startlement.

When she looked up, everyone was staring at her.

The dancing felt divine at first. Beyond divine. Mourners lined up to watch while she boogied out of church to the parking lot and the 1990 Mercedes she had inherited from Grand-mère, all cares of death lifted while her body celebrated life and motion. When she could no longer hear the music, her body swayed instead to honking cars and clattering construction and barking dogs and any rhythm she could find while she unlocked her car door. Particularly dramatic sounds propelled her to leap into the air, a remnant of the ballet lessons Grand-mère had paid for and insisted she attend when she was ten, until Monique begged to stop going because she hated the girlie costumes and slippers.

The liberation was indescribable. Her first day of dancing was her finest. Until the moment she died, she would remember it as the best feeling of her life.

But Monique couldn't stop.

As she started the car, her knees bumped against the steering wheel in spasms and her foot would not stay steady on the pedal. *Lord Jesus, what's wrong with me?* The thought came for the first time, halfway between a prayer and a curse.

She wondered if she should be more alarmed, even terrified, but she was so relieved to be freed from her grief that she rationalized her movements as a stress response and decided to walk the mile back to her apartment—which wasn't such a bad walk, she told herself, although she was sweating within half a block. No matter how she tried to disguise her motions as gliding or skipping or jogging, the dancing made her a spectacle. Strangers raised their camera phones to chronicle the sight of her. Small children waved, laughed, and mimicked her until she seemed to be leading a conga line to Grand-mère's faded green-gray building.

Once the darkened first-floor window came into view, the impromptu Pied Piper street party was over. Back at home, grief was inescapable, dancing or not. As she shimmied through the doorway, the stitch beneath her rib cage on the left side felt like a yawning wound. She touched herself to make sure she wasn't bleeding while her hips rolled and swayed to the rhythm of her panting.

"Please . . ." she whispered to her relentless muscles, or to the hidden puppet master who'd taken hold of them somehow, ". . . let it stop."

It did not stop. The terror she'd denied herself began taking hold as every item in sight that reminded her of Grand-mère made her dancing more frenzied: the old CD player, with Tchaikovsky still queued up; the woven straw basket from South Africa her Uncle Roy had sent when he was in the Peace Corps; Grand-mère's voter registration card from 1954 framed on her wall, which she'd won after breezing through the civics quiz designed to deny Negro voters their rights, a story Monique had heard a dozen more times in the last few weeks of Grand-mère's life because Grand-mère wanted her to remember it.

A muffled *crack* stiffened Monique's lower back as her hips tried to twerk. She let out her first cry of real pain. Her body was at war with itself, her shoulders trying to wrench her one way, hips another, knees fighting to keep steady, ankles steering her with dizzying speed. The more she smelled signs of Grand-mère in the room—her peppermint tea in the kitchen, the faint remnants of urine absorbed by the sofa cushions, her Zest soap in the bathroom—the faster and harder Monique whirled.

She thought actual music might give her dancing more order, at least, so she turned on the CD player and tried to tame her movements with the O'Jays, the Temptations, Earth, Wind & Fire, and, yes, James Brown, but Grand-mère's favorite music only sharpened her grief, fueling her wild gyrations with sobs.

I can't go on like this, Monique thought, just before the room went dark.

When she woke up, new gray daylight was peeking through Grand-mère's flower-patterned curtains that had been unchanged since the 1970s. She was lying on the living room floor, the back of her head still throbbing because she had collapsed just beyond the edge of Grand-mère's old shag rug and banged her head on the wooden floor. Every muscle hurt, so she did not move, savoring stillness.

Thank you, Lord, she thought. *It's over—*

But it wasn't.

* * *

Monique trained herself to stand with her laptop on the kitchen counter and slide only a few inches side to side so she could do Internet searches for any clues about what the hell was going on with her. She studied diseases and disorders with tics and spasms, but nothing came close to capturing her movements: rhythmic and complex and sometimes with jazz hands. She also scanned countless articles on delusions and hysteria, though nothing she read made sense of her dancing.

She finally called her freshman-year roommate, Rose, who was now a school board member in Chicago with a wealth-manager husband and three teenage children. Life had torn her and Rose farther apart over the years as Monique's dreams shrank while Rose's blossomed one after the other, but Rose was the first person she'd told when her mother died, and when she lost her virginity (the two happening in such close succession that Monique had rarely had sex since, out of superstition), so she trusted Rose to at least listen. Until now, she hadn't mentioned to hardly any of her friends that Grand-mère had died, postponing the telling.

"You're free now," Rose said, overly chipper.

"What?"

"Girl, I'm sorry you lost her, bless her spirit, but now you can live *your* life." After Monique's stunned silence, Rose elaborated: "Remember last year? I offered to *pay* to fly you to Hawaii for my fortieth, and you were all like—"

"Grand-mère had that appointment." Grand-mère's feet had been swelling from her congestive heart failure and they had waited for weeks for an appointment with her specialist. Her decline had begun in earnest during those months.

"She always had an appointment, Mo. That big family she had and no one else could help? It always had to be *you*? I tried to tell you."

Monique blinked away her rage. She reminded herself that Rose always had a touch of that affliction when people didn't know the right thing to say, so she ignored the celebratory high five her friend was trying to give her so soon after her grandmother's funeral. You could never take what Rose said seriously—although her words stirred a sick feeling in the pit of Monique's stomach that felt far too close to *Yes, thank goodness she's finally gone.*

"That's not even the real reason I called," Monique said. Her swaying hip bumped the counter when she shifted position. "I can't stop . . ."

"Crying? You just need to—"

"Dancing," Monique whispered. "I can't stop *dancing.*"

She described everything that had happened to her since the funeral, including collapsing on the floor from exhaustion. And how the dancing had started again before she could stand up that morning, her body flopping on the floor like a catfish.

"Number one," Rose said with the air of authority she'd adopted since they realized she was six months older than Monique, "you had too much to drink at the repast. You never could hold a drink. That's why you passed out."

"I didn't—"

"And number two," Rose said, "what did I just tell you? You're *free.* Of course you're dancing! Just let it out."

Let it out. The advice was as useless now as it had been at Grand-mère's funeral. "It hurts, Rose. Every part of my body is—"

"All passages hurt, Mo. You'll be alright."

Monique already knew she would *not* be alright. She had not been alright since Mom died, and maybe her destiny was never to be alright. What did that word even mean? "Alright" was a great anthem by Kendrick Lamar, but it was mostly a lazy word for a temporary designation—more like a delusion—so how could it matter? It was like trying to clutch a puff of smoke in her hand, as futile as trying to will Grand-mère to breathe.

"You keep on dancing, girl," Rose said. "There's no shame in it."

As if Monique could help it.

As if shame meant anything compared to the pain.

Monique tried taking a shower in the hope that hot water beating across her skin might soothe her strained muscles, but her heels' squeaky movements against the slippery tub floor stole her balance, and she banged her elbows against the tiles. A bath was no better, since her gyrations splashed everywhere and made her head slip underwater, where soapy residue from Grand-mère's Zest stung her nostrils.

Monique had never suffered childbirth, though she couldn't imagine how it could be worse than her uncontrollable limbs. By the time she managed to climb out of the bathtub, she was sure that since the funeral, she had dislocated at least one shoulder, perhaps both, and pulled muscles in her calf and her side, or even cracked a rib or two. In the mirror, her brown skin was mottled with ugly bruises inflicted from within.

Was she being punished? Was it a hex? Monique had never had patience for Grand-mère's candles and powders, yet she lit every candle she could find (knocking a few over with her frenetic motions, quickly stamping out the flames) and tried to pray—although, honestly, the pointed silence she'd met during her prayers over Grand-mère in the past six months made it feel like a useless exercise.

Naked and shuddering, still damp from the tub, she bounce-walked to Grand-mère's closet and washed herself in her grandmother's scent, rubbing her face across Grand-mère's favorite French robe. She slipped the silk across her shoulders, wincing when her body jerked to and fro.

Was Grand-mère trying to dance *through* her?

Yes, she realized. *Yes, of course.*

She finally remembered the story.

* * *

1937

That day had begun as the greatest adventure of Nadine Moreau's life.

Nadine's mother surprised her with a quarter to start dance lessons when she was ten. The studio was in the basement of a row house six long blocks from her home. The lessons were after school, at three o'clock sharp, so she made a litany of promises about her behavior and common sense to win the privilege of walking alone, since her parents both worked for a rich white family in the Garden District until after dark. They did not want Nadine to ride a railcar even if they could have afforded it.

From the moment she had seen photographs of *Swan Lake* in *Life* magazine, Nadine had hounded her parents for dance lessons. She practiced twirls and leaps in a cracked shaving mirror she mounted on a stool (and got a spanking for breaking), and eventually could stand on her toes for eight seconds straight, even without special shoes.

Mme. Pinede, Dance Instruction

The sign on the door made her breath catch. All day at school, she'd been afraid it would not be real—but it was! The studio might have been shabby to someone else's eyes, but to Nadine the large mirror on the wall made it look as grand as a mansion. Madame Pinede was Maman's age, two shades shy of passing for white, and pleasant. She took the quarter without asking for a penny more. The lesson was off to such a wonderful start that Nadine was bouncing on the soles of her feet.

"Let's get your shoes," Madame Pinede said. "I think I have your size."

Nadine practiced standing on her toes while Madame

Pinede turned a corner into a small office, but she was too nervous to stay up.

Then, the shoes. Madame Pinede returned with an offering in outstretched hands. Instead of ballet shoes, the woman held very plain brown, scuffed shoes with frayed shoelaces.

"These aren't for ballet," Nadine said.

"*Chéri*," Madame Pinede said, "what would you do with ballet slippers?"

"I'm going to dance ballet," Nadine responded. "*Swan Lake*. See?" She propped herself up on her toes, realizing this might be an audition: of *course* she would have to audition! She was amazed as she counted off the seconds, *one, two, three,* and then *seven, eight, nine,* and she still did not fall.

"Oh my!" Madame Pinede said. "Isn't that lovely?"

Nadine grinned up at her, thinking she must have passed the audition, but Madame Pinede met her grin with sagging cheeks. A smile tried to peek out, although it was the wrong kind of smile.

"Nadine," Madame Pinede said, her voice hushed and stripped of anything to remind Nadine that one of them was an adult and one was a child, the way her mother might talk to her auntie, "no ballet company will take a Negro girl."

Nadine thought about *Life* magazine and how rarely she'd seen a Negro face except for a photograph Maman had spread on the table like a lace cloth: Negro men, women, and children lined up for food beneath a massive billboard of a sunny white family and the words, *There's no way like the American Way.* She remembered how the words mismatched the image. Wasn't *Swan Lake* a part of her American Way too?

"You should study a kind of dancing where you'll have a future, Nadine," Madame Pinede said. "Your folks can't afford flights of fancy. Let's see how it goes with your lessons, and maybe you can dance in pictures one day. But not ballet."

Slowly, the woman turned the shoes over until the soles

faced upward, glinting in the late-afternoon light from her narrow basement window. Metal plates shone at the toes and heels. "Tap shoes," she said, answering the confusion on the girl's face.

Nadine had been delighted by boys dancing for pennies on street corners, their feet in furious motion. But these shoes didn't hold the promise of leaping high in the air like the ladies with impossibly long legs on the magazine pages. Only now did she remember that all of those ladies in *Life* had been white.

Nadine's lip tremored. She'd never felt like such a fool.

"Maybe one day, *chéri*," Madame Pinede said. "But not today."

Years later, long after her dancing dreams were ash, after she'd fled from marriage to marriage searching for the joy she'd lost, after she'd fortified her heart and driven most of her family away, she had heard about the Dance Theatre of Harlem. And Anne Benna Simms, who would become the first Black dancer in the American Ballet Theatre long decades later, in 1978. In her last years, she thought about Madame Pinede when she saw Misty Copeland standing on her toes on the cover of *Time* magazine in 2015.

But she remembered only for an instant, a flick of a match, before her muddy mind swallowed it away.

After all, Grand-mère had not been that little girl for more than eighty years. Grand-mère had lived to be ninety-six, but that little dancing girl had died long before.

A buried dream could be reborn like a curse in the wake of the dead, it seemed. Monique had not known you could love someone so much, and want to hold on to them with such fervor, that you could swallow them inside of you—even their dead dreams. And that those dreams could eat you in return.

Still wearing Grand-mère's robe, Monique was trying to stand on her toes, counting *one, two, three*—

She screamed when her untrained ankle folded beneath her weight. This was not the first bone her dancing had broken, yet the pain of the fracture cascaded up and down her leg. She fell against the wall so hard that her head snapped back with a *crack*.

Finally, stillness. Her pain, gone.

Monique exhaled in an unsteady stream as she realized she had damaged herself so badly that she could not move, could barely breathe. The missing pain was only a lack of *any* sensation. Had she broken her neck?

Smoke. The haziness she thought was only in her mind was real. She strained her eyes to see as far as she could behind her without moving her neck and glimpsed flames climbing Grand-mère's bedspread, greedy and gorging. She had knocked over another candle, and this time the fire was spreading fast, fueled by Grand-mère's stacks of old newspapers and *Life* magazines piled under her bed.

She almost laughed at herself. Almost. What a ludicrous sight she was, contorted like a snake half-naked on Grand-mère's floor. Would anyone find her? Would anyone except Rose ever know how she had danced? Would she ever have the chance to tell anyone about Grand-mère's lost dream?

Even before she felt the heat, the growing fire turned the room a brilliant, angry gold color until smoke leeched her vision gray.

I thought I would have more time.

Her body, so untamed since the funeral, lay immobile except for her right index finger tapping to the rhythm of the crackling flames.

PART II

The Gracetown Stories

Last Stop on Route 9

"I thought you said you wouldn't get lost," Kai said.

Charlotte's teeth tightened to match the pressure of her hands on the rented Toyota's steering wheel. They were already a half hour late to the luncheon after her grandmother's funeral in Tallahassee, a drive her navigator said should have taken an hour and five minutes heading west on the I-10. She'd been doing fine until they got off the freeway and passed the collection of quaint shops on Main Street in the throwback town, but the last few turns had plunged them more deeply into the swampy woods bordering each side of a two-lane road.

No other cars were in sight. No houses. No anything.

"We're not lost," she said.

Kai glared.

Thin pines and oaks with branches draped in hanging moss choked the road, which the clay soil had ground red, as much dirt as asphalt. Mud from earlier rainfall was slick enough to splash the tires. The air conditioner was on full blast, but the sun burned her skin through her sleeveless black funeral dress. The burr of insects around them was loud enough to penetrate the closed windows. Her car sped past a derelict shack wrapped in weeds, its wooden walls gaping from missing planks. The rusted tin roof made Charlotte wonder if it had been a sharecropper's shack. Or a relic from slavery.

Charlotte's twelve-year-old cousin could have joined his parents and older aunts in the limousine after the burial, but since Charlotte had to drive anyway because the "stretch" wasn't as big as they'd expected, she'd asked Kai to ride with her to escape the limousine's sadness, and he'd happily agreed. ("I only met her a couple times," he'd shrugged to Charlotte privately.) Until now, he'd been bobbing his head to his ear-buds, his face stoic beneath limp braids, his tie loosened with the knot at midchest. *Like a noose,* she couldn't help thinking.

Charlotte hated the South. Her mother had fled Florida at her first chance, never coming back to Gracetown after she'd gone to UCLA as a freshman, just like Kai's dad, her Uncle Harry, who had joined the army the day he graduated from high school. Uncle Harry loathed the town. He had spent six months in Gracetown's notorious reformatory when he was Kai's age, and he had blamed his parents for his imprisonment.

It wasn't surprising that his son didn't feel much warmth for the recently buried Sadie Myrtle Jones Williams. Charlotte's parents had swapped Christmases between Oakland and Grace-town, but Uncle Harry's seat at the table always sat empty. His four sisters had taken bets on whether he'd show up for the funeral—and he had, sobbing worse than the rest. "I thought I'd have more time," he'd cried out in the church, although Grandmama had been six days shy of eighty. Still, he had re-fused to set foot in Gracetown for a luncheon at the home of Grandmama's childhood friend. Kai was more a novelty than family to Charlotte, one reason she had been glad to give him a ride. She'd only seen the kid three or four times, and the last time he'd been only nine. Twelve was a different story: he was almost as tall as she was and—

"Shit, we're in the middle of fucking nowhere," Kai said.

"Hey!" Charlotte said. "Watch that mouth."

"You're not my mom. You don't tell me what to do."

She stared at him so long that she nearly veered off into one of the ditches that yawned open on either side of the road. He'd been so quiet until now that his sudden rebellion surprised her.

Her voice was ice. "Don't start with me, baby boy. This is not the time."

His tone softened. "I'm just saying—nobody wants to be driving around in the middle of nowhere. Dang."

He had a point, but although she was only twenty-two, she felt obligated to sound parental. "Watch your mouth around me—or you can walk," she said, and threw in, "Hear?" Grandmama had always said that: *Hear?* Charlotte heard Grandmama's voice in her ear, sharp as a whip. Her throat pinched tight with a smothered sob. This awful day had no end in sight.

Kai looked away toward the unbroken forest and its tangle of trees and said, "My dad got locked up here. He told me that place was just a bunch of rednecks who hurt kids for fun. And he said Gracetown is haunted as shit."

His voice trembled. For the first time, Charlotte realized he was cursing because he was genuinely afraid. What kinds of stories had Uncle Harry filled his son's head with? Grandmama had always said Uncle Harry should see a therapist, although she'd said it more like an insult than a recommendation. Her aunts said he'd never been the same since the reformatory, and maybe Grandmama had been in denial because she hadn't fought harder to get him out. (To hear Uncle Harry tell it, his parents' attitude had been, *Maybe it'll be a good wake-up call for him.*) Charlotte's mom had superstitions about ghosts too, but nothing like Uncle Harry's.

"That was a long time ago," Charlotte said. "That place is closed now."

"Whatever," Kai mumbled.

But again, Kai was right: they were alone. Charlotte hadn't seen another car in ten minutes, maybe longer. A thick fog bank sat across the road ahead like a wall, and Charlotte felt a strong urge to stop the car and turn around. She checked the navigator: *SATELLITE UNAVAILABLE.* The map showed the dot of their car surrounded by a sea of nothing. She and Kai had

THE WISHING POOL AND OTHER STORIES

given up on getting a cell phone signal soon as they passed the county line. It never failed: whenever one thing went wrong, everything else joined in a chorus. She'd had her first car accident two years ago, when she swerved to avoid hitting a dog on her way home from getting her wisdom teeth pulled.

Today felt as cursed as that one. Worse. She'd just buried a grandmother she'd barely bothered to get to know, so both of her grandmothers were gone. She'd had a much closer relationship with her father's more cosmopolitan mother in Oakland, who ran a bookstore and hadn't been nearly as hard to understand beneath a thick country accent and old-school rules.

"Fuck," she said under her breath, and drove through the fog. It was so thick, she braced for the car to shudder, holding her breath while all of the windows went gray.

"I can't see!" Kai said.

But as soon as he said it, they passed through to the hot sun again, everything in bright focus. Only then, she allowed herself to ponder it: Fog in the middle of the day? During the summer? The oddness skittered across her mind, though she shut down the part of her that wanted to panic. Like Kai had said—whatever.

Evidence of civilization emerged ahead, a small billboard nearly covered by the trees with large red letters: *LAST STOP ON ROUTE 9—1/2 MILE—GAS—FOOD*. All of the paint was cracking in rivulets across the weathered wood.

"Yes!" Kai said, at the same time she'd been thinking, *Thank fucking goodness.*

She kept deities' names from mind to avoid blasphemy so close to where Grandmama had lived, as if Grandmama might still hear her. Or maybe, just maybe, cussing alongside God's name really was a sin.

"Listen . . ." Charlotte began slowly, wondering if she'd been too harsh on Kai by threatening to make him walk. "It sounds like your dad's said some stuff to you that's pretty confusing.

And . . . raw. Maybe he should have waited until you're older."

"Dad says you're never too young to know the truth." Kai recited it like a mantra.

That sounded like Uncle Harry, alright. Every conversation was a speech. Yet he'd never told her about his time at the Gracetown Reformatory. Not that she'd asked.

"What did he say happened to him when he was locked up, Kai?"

Kai parted his lips as if to answer, then changed his mind. He stared at the road ahead, eyes searching for the promised gas and food. He looked hungry enough to eat a wrinkled gas station hot dog. Or two. She'd been anticipating the feast after the funeral.

"Well, whatever it is . . ." she went on, "it's not happening now. It won't happen to you."

"What if we get pulled over? And I get locked up for no reason like him?" His pitch grew higher with his agitation. "And then . . . then . . ."

"Who's gonna pull us over—a racoon?" she said. "Nobody's out here. Right?"

Kai surveyed the empty road and both sides of the thick woods and nodded, smiling a bit at her joke. Poor kid! Charlotte needed to talk with Uncle Harry and let him know to ease back on his Gracetown horror stories. Uncle Harry was the oldest of the siblings and Kai was a son he'd had from his third marriage, late in life. He and his son were from two different worlds. When would Uncle Harry have been locked up? The late 1960s? Black drivers in the South could just disappear in those days. Times weren't perfect, but they weren't still like that, at least.

The gas station appeared. And Charlotte's stomach knotted. *Shit.*

This building was an artifact, shuttered with planks across its windows. She could barely read the faded sign above the door: *HANDEE GAS*. It was an old-fashioned station with only two bright red pumps long out of service, their hoses emptied on the ground like oversized snakes in a blanket of pine needles.

"What the hell?" Kai said, exactly what she was thinking.

As Charlotte slowed, hoping the gas station would morph into an AM/PM like in California, she noticed a light in the woods to the left. A driveway from the road led to a second structure behind the gas station, a wood-paneled house hardly bigger than a cabin. But a light was on behind sheer white curtains, and a vintage round-hooded pickup truck was parked in the driveway, white paint also fading.

Charlotte turned into the driveway at the last second, her tires skidding on mud.

"What are you doing?" Kai said.

"There's a house. I'm just going to knock on the door and ask for directions."

"That's crazy!" Kai said. "Haven't you ever seen *Deliverance*?"

Again, Charlotte looked at him with surprise. She'd seen the film in college, and once was enough. The banjo theme played in her head, cryptic. "Your father let you watch—"

"He says Gracetown is like *Deliverance*. I've never seen it. Don't *want* to either."

"Kai, stop freaking yourself out. Just stay in the car."

Charlotte rarely missed a hashtag, so she knew that sometimes when Black people knocked on strangers' doors, they'd be met by gunfire. She remembered one Black woman's name in particular: Renisha McBride. And there were others. But she also wasn't going to let fear rule her life. It was broad daylight. She was lost. She was dressed for church. She would be fine.

Charlotte didn't want to block the cabin's driveway, so she veered slightly to the right of it a few yards from the house's door, parking beneath an oak tree that looked a century old. Something crunched beneath her tires, the sound of bad news.

Damnit! Had she damaged the car? She turned off the engine, and the insects' songs grew louder.

As Charlotte opened her car door, Kai grabbed her wrist. "Wait! Don't you feel it?"

"Feel what, sweetie?"

He stared at her, earnest, trying to choose his words. His grip was a vise. "It . . . it feels . . . *mad*. Like, everything is pissed off." When she squinted, trying to make sense of what he'd said, Kai sighed and let her go. "I can't explain. My dad says you can't always explain."

"Lock up after I get out. I'll be right back."

When Charlotte closed her car door behind her, Kai hit the electric lock right away. The humidity felt soupy, and her armpits pricked with sweat as soon as she stepped outside. In a way, maybe the air *did* feel pissed off. She wanted to laugh at Kai, but she couldn't. And it was smart to leave Kai in the car, she remembered. He was a Black male, too tall to be considered "cute" by many strangers; instead, he looked like the national boogeyman since *The Birth of a Nation* and before. Kai was wearing a dress shirt and tie, but still.

Charlotte glanced at the gas station behind them. Someone had made a junkyard of the station's side wall, not as visible from the street: rusted old cars, discarded gas cans, an old road sign advertising Fatima cigarettes, which she'd never heard of. Maybe this was what Kai had meant too: these items were pissed off because they were old and forgotten. Like she had so often forgotten Grandmama.

Music was playing faintly from the house. Elvis? It was impossible to mistake the voice, though the music was gospel, not rock and roll. She recognized the song, "Peace in the Valley," from the handful of times she'd attended church with Grandmama at Christmas.

Charlotte did not go to the little house's sagging front porch as she'd planned. She stared, thinking it over.

The plants on the porch, even in the hanging basket, were dead. Only a screen door was closed across the doorway, and despite the light she'd thought she'd seen from the road, the house was dark now. It was hard to imagine that light had ever shined from this house, much less a moment before. A hidden hinge squealed lazily back and forth. At the edge of the wooden awning, she saw the chain from a ruined porch swing rocking in the mild breeze. Somewhere behind the house, a dog was barking. It might not be big, but it wasn't small. Maybe it was on a chain, maybe it wasn't.

Then Charlotte noticed the Confederate flag on the bumper sticker on the oversized truck parked near the porch. The words printed beside it had faded, but the crossed blue stripes and white stars still showed. Charlotte's heart thumped her breast-bone. She'd known a girl at UCLA who defended the flag as "heritage" and insisted it wasn't racist despite the way racists loved it, and now Kai's words came back: *Everything is pissed off.* How hadn't she noticed it right away?

None of it felt right. Instead of stepping toward the house, Charlotte stepped away.

She looked back at Kai, and he was watching her wide-eyed, his nose pressed to the window on the driver's side. She gestured toward the house dismissively: *Never mind.* And he nodded, agreeing wholeheartedly. He motioned for her to come back.

Charlotte walked back toward her car—but then she remembered the crunching sound when she'd parked. It would drive her crazy wondering if she'd damaged a tire, so she leaned over to take a peek.

Her left front tire had knocked over a mound of large, sharp-edged stones, alongside a silver cross, tarnished black. *Shit!* She kicked the closest tire to make sure it wasn't punctured, then kneeled to see if the stones had left any marks on the bumper the rental guy in Tallahassee would notice. The car was fine. But broken glass was scattered across the soil from a cracked picture frame near the cross. She picked up the frame and saw a decades-old photo, the image splotched by rain and time. Vaguely, she could make out a white man's long gray beard.

"*Desecration*!" a woman's voice screeched from somewhere. From everywhere.

Charlotte dropped the photo frame, gasping. She was so startled, she had to hold the car's warm hood for balance, her neck yanking around too hard to see who had spoken. A woman was standing behind the house's screen door, features hidden by the mesh. All Charlotte could see was a powder-blue housedress, maybe a floral pattern. The woman's face was in shadow.

Had she damaged a memorial site, or even a grave? The word charged Charlotte's thoughts, so violent that it felt imposed: *DESECRATION*. The insects' buzzing seemed to flurry *between* her ears rather than beyond them. Kai was thumping on his window.

"Let's go!" she heard him call, muffled through the thick buzzing.

Unsteady with fright, Charlotte stumbled back toward her car door. She tried to raise her voice so the woman could hear her apology. "I'm . . . so sorry. I won't . . . disturb you." She raised her hands slightly in case the woman was armed. She expected a gunshot.

Although the woman's features were fuzzy, Charlotte thought she saw her mouth and jaw open into an impossibly long O, stretched beyond the boundaries of where her face should be. The woman let out a shriek too loud to be human. The sound echoed through the woods, rattling the metal and glass in the gas station's debris. Birds flocked from the treetops, shrieking and calling in response. The unseen dog barked in a frenzy. Charlotte's limbs locked, her mind emptied of thought.

Then came an eerie, sudden silence, all sound stripped, even the dog's. Charlotte's hand fumbled with the door handle two or three times before she remembered the car was locked. She slapped at the window. *Let me in*, she tried to say, but her mouth was parched mute.

The click from the car door came at last, breaking the un-natural quiet, and Charlotte jumped back into her seat, banging her knee hard against the steering wheel. Kai was sitting on the passenger-side floor, his face wet with tears. He pulled his hand away from the electric lock and rocked himself like a toddler, arms wrapped around his knees.

"It's okay," she said, absurdly. She was lying to both of them.

Just go. Just go. Just go. Her thumping heart had learned language, preaching to her.

When she turned the key, she expected the ignition to ignore her—a waiting tide of grief and terror she did not know how she could withstand—but the engine roared with fiery life. *That's a great car, that one*, the rental guy had said. The memory of his gaudy yellow blazer was her mind's anchor to the world she knew. Charlotte threw the car into reverse and swerved back so far that she almost hit the truck before she shifted to plow back toward the road. Her heart was thunder. How had Kai known to keep away from this house on sight? How had he sensed the rage boiling just behind the screen door?

She made a frantic turn to the road, back toward the fog, the way they'd come—the only way she knew—so sharply that one of the tires plunged halfway into the roadside ditch, but she quickly righted it. Mud sprayed the underside before the car was back on solid ground.

"What was that?" Kai said.

Charlotte could only shake her head. Her existence had shrunk to her beating heart, its rhythm pulsing to her hands tight on the steering wheel and her foot pressing the gas pedal. Since the too-loud screeching, her muscles felt drained. Emptied out.

The radio came on with loud squeals and pops. Charlotte glanced at the glowing dial, hoping to see Kai's hand near it, but he was still hugging himself tight. He stared at the radio too, then back at her with the same plea in his teary eyes. His jaw trembled.

"I wanna go home . . ." Kai whimpered.

The radio answered him with the same woman's reedy tremolo voice filling the car's front and rear speakers: "*THE DESECRATION IS YOU. I CURSE YOU BOTH TO HELL. I CURSE YOUR PARENTS. I CURSE YOUR TAR-BLACK BABIES—*"

Frantic to banish the voice, Charlotte looked away from the road to the radio dial. She jammed at the power button with her palm—once, twice, three times—until the terrible voice was gone. By then, Kai was sobbing.

"It's okay . . ." she started to say again.

But it wasn't.

As soon as Charlotte looked back to the road, a sun-reddened white man with a pea-green hunting jacket and an unkempt gray beard appeared in her windshield—he hadn't *walked* there, he wasn't *standing* there, he simply *was*—and she only had time to scream and hit her brakes so hard that the car skewed sideways after a horrible *THUNK* beneath her floorboard. She felt the unmistakable bump of rolling over a mass on the road. The car shook from end to end, flinging Kai so hard that he slammed his head on the glove compartment as his arms flailed to hold on to something.

The vehicle lurched to a stop as if it had been yanked back by invisible wires. Kai was wailing more loudly than she was, but not by much.

In the long aftermath with nothing moving, Charlotte stopped yelling as her thoughts unscrambled. The yellow blazer. She had to get back to the rental guy in the yellow blazer. And Kai was her cousin; if she let anything happen to him, the family would tell the story for generations. She would be reliving this day on her deathbed in a loop, the way Grandma Bernadine couldn't stop talking about a lightning storm that had set her rooftop in Port-au-Prince on fire when she was a child. The fire that had killed her baby sister.

"Are you okay?" Charlotte didn't know why she was whispering, but she was sure whispering was the right thing to do, even if it wasn't nearly enough. She needed to do far more. Kai shook his head *NO*, his braids whipping his face.

"We hit someone, Kai." The firmness in her voice surprised her.

"We didn't!" Kai screamed at her. "Someone hit *us*!"

"Kai . . . calm down. Breathe."

He did, taking heaving breaths that began to fog the windshield. Charlotte wiped away the condensation with a crumpled napkin she snatched from the cup holder: she didn't want any blind spots. Outside the windows, the stillness was unnerving. She waited for the man she'd run over to pop up and try to scare the actual life out of them, but he didn't appear. Nothing moved.

"I know something is messed up, alright?" Charlotte told Kai, and he nodded, his eyes flooding with grateful tears that he didn't have to shoulder reality alone. "I can't explain what happened back at that house. But we ran over a man with the car—*I* ran over a man. I have to check on him. That's the law, Kai. I can't leave an old man in the road."

Kai's gratitude vanished, replaced by bitter fright. "You still don't get it!"

"I need you to stay in the car—"

"Don't leave me! You better not leave me—"

"—and I'm just going to check on him. To see if he's alive."

"*Alive*? Alive don't just—just—"

"Breathe, Kai. Breathe. Or you'll pass out. I'm serious. Look at my eyes and breathe."

She held out her hand, and he took it and squeezed hard. He

forced himself to breathe more slowly, keeping his eyes fixed on hers, desperate to believe in her.

Still, nothing moved outside. No corpse popped up like a jack-in-the-box. In the quiet, it was easier to forget the woman's unnaturally loud screech at the house and worry more about the dead man who lay beneath her car. Never mind going to law school one day after her break from classrooms: she would go to prison for manslaughter. She and Kai had been so shocked by the sight of the man that they'd fooled their eyes, making him a phantom.

I probably killed someone. Her stomach curdled at the thought. If she'd had food in the past few hours, she would have spit it up. *Put on your big-girl panties*, Grandmama used to say.

Somehow, Charlotte navigated the lock and door handle with hands like jelly. She eased the door open, touched her foot to the road. Pressed down to feel its solidness. She prayed as hard as she knew how that the man was alright. When she stood, adrenaline cascaded down her legs.

At least no limbs protruded from the bottom of the car as she'd feared, like Dorothy killing the wicked witch with her house. Both the front and rear tires were flat on the driver's side, the rubber clawed to strips. The sick feeling in her stomach turned rigid, twisting. Were the other tires flat too? They wouldn't get far with even two flats. She was afraid to check right away and learn that they were stranded.

Charlotte lowered herself to her knees to peek beneath the car, expecting to see the pea-green jacket. But no man was under there—only a scattered pile of large, sharp stones like the ones beneath the tree. Back at the house. At the makeshift grave site. Charlotte drew a long breath, sucking in air. The road seemed to shake with her heartbeat.

"I can't see you!" Kai shouted.

Charlotte pulled herself to her feet, looking away from the impossible sight, but not before she noticed that the other two tires also had been ravaged by the stones, rims shining through. *Damn, damn, damn.*

As she straightened up, Charlotte's mind tried to make sense of it: Had the car sent him flying into a ditch? She hadn't seen any stones in the road, though she'd looked away at the radio. That many stones hadn't appeared from nowhere—had they?

"There's no one under there!" she called to Kai.

"I told you!" He wasn't surprised at all. He *knew*. "Come back in!"

"I have to see if he got thrown."

Kai thumped his fist against the window, so scared and frustrated she thought he might break the glass or his hand, or both. "Just come back!"

"Stop that, Kai. I'll be right there. He could be only injured." She said it although she didn't believe it—she wouldn't find a man sprawled in the ditch, and if she did he would be dead. But she had to be sure she wasn't just in denial, trading an evening-news brand of horror for something else. Police would ask if she had looked.

But no one was in the ditch on either side. While Kai kept thumping the window, she walked up and down in her clicking heels searching for the man's coat, or his beard, or blood. Beyond the drainage ditches, she saw nothing but untended woods growing wild. She felt a vibration shiver beneath her feet and held her breath until the trembly sensation was gone.

Kai honked the horn, pressing it for a long, unbroken tone. It sounded like sacrilege.

She waved back at him. "*Shhhh.* Don't do that!"

Kai was pointing toward the road behind her. "Look!"

A car was coming from the direction they'd just left, taking its sweet time. Not a car, she realized—a truck. A white truck with its oversized hood and cab. Like the one parked back at the house. Somewhere in the woods, a dog was barking.

"The radio's on again!" Kai yelled, panicked. She heard Elvis sing reverently about no sadness, no sorrow, no trouble, no pain, the volume too loud inside the car. Kai was covering his ears. "Charlotte!"

She ran to the car. Each time she glanced back at the truck over her shoulder, it had gained an alarming distance. There might be both a driver and a passenger in the cab. She had to grab Kai and pop the trunk to see if she could find a weapon. Maybe she'd find a tire iron.

"We have to run," Charlotte said, breathless. She reached for the door handle the instant she heard the click of the locks. But Kai's hands were still plugging his ears. He hadn't locked the doors, yet the door wouldn't budge. "Kai! Unlock the door!"

She could see for herself that he was now trying, reaching across to the driver's door, pushing every button he could. Panic had dried his tears. "It won't open!" he said. "Get me out!"

Charlotte kneeled to find the biggest stone she could. One just beyond the mangled front tire weighed at least five pounds. "Get in the backseat in a ball—hurry! Cover your eyes."

As she raised the stone high, she glanced back at the truck. It was close enough now that if it sped up, they would have no time to outrun it. She could see that the driver was a woman by the outline of her frizzy hair. The truck rambled on at its slow, steady speed.

Charlotte heaved the stone at the windshield with all of her strength. A thin line of a crack appeared, but the glass didn't break. The second time she hit it, the stone made a spiderweb in glass that would not yield. Instead, the stone broke in two. Charlotte let out a frustrated yell, kneeling to search for another stone.

"Do the side window! I'll fit!" Kai said. He was watching the truck's approach and knew she didn't have time to keep trying.

None of the stones remaining under the car were as big as the first, but she found a slightly smaller one that she smashed into the driver's-side window—and the glass shattered, falling away. Though not enough. She and Kai were still batting at the remaining glass when they heard the guttural engine's purr as the truck pulled up beside them, crunching smaller stones beneath it. She could not leave Kai. She reached for him as he squeezed through the jagged exit. A fixed glass shard dug into his shoulder, leaving flecks of blood on his white dress shirt.

Two women laughed from the truck. The sound chilled Charlotte and tried to make her run, but she held on to Kai while he pulled his leg through. She glanced at the driver sitting high in the cab—

—and saw a Black woman with honeyed skin and spiky plaits. Beside her sat a white woman with wild auburn hair; a young woman who did not look like the one she'd seen through the screen door. Both women grinned at them with badly yellowed teeth.

"You're not fixin' to run, I hope!" the Black woman said. "Don't you hear the dogs?"

Charlotte did hear dogs then: a chorus of barking from the woods. Two dozen or more dogs might be waiting in the brush. Kai tried to run right away, but Charlotte held him back with her arm hooked around his neck. "Dogs," she whispered.

"I don't care," he said, wriggling like a fish against her grip.

"We're not the ones you ought to be afraid of," the Black woman said. She tapped her horn, and Kai went limp at the strangled sound. "*Hey*. Look at me—I said you don't need to be 'fraid of us. Aunt Sally's the one who hexed you."

"Meanest woman who ever lived or died—that's Aunt Sally for you," the white woman said. She was fanning herself with a *Life* magazine. "By the way, I'm Rose. That's Malindy."

"I was named from a poem," the Black woman said with pride. "My mama liked it."

Charlotte didn't answer. She couldn't stop blinking to test if the women were real.

"I'm sick to death," the white woman, Rose, said. "Sick of Aunt Sally hexing and swallowing folks up in the ground. Then they're gone and their kin never know where they went. I say people are people. That's what I say. Look at us—oh, she hates how we're cousins."

"Just leave us alone!" Charlotte said, finding her voice. She was too afraid to move. All the while the women chatted, the truck idled, ready to run her and Kai over with the slightest lunge. "Just—please—go back where you came from."

"Where you headed? Into that fog?" Malindy said.

Charlotte nodded, hating herself for trusting this stranger—far worse than a stranger—with the truth only because her skin color felt like a promise.

"That's the way you'd better go, alright," Malindy said.

"But she'll swallow you up on the road," Rose said. "See?" She pointed toward Charlotte's feet.

The asphalt beneath her black pumps had crumbled, as if she were forcing a great weight upon it. A gap near her big toe was already two inches across. Startled, Charlotte stepped back. More ruptures webbed the road.

"That just gets worse and worse till it swallows you whole," Rose said.

"And the woods, they ain't no better," Malindy said, and she pointed too: at the tree line, a large brown dog as big as a wolf stood with its front legs perched on a log, watching them. The sight of the beast was a worse fear at a distance than the truck up close. "She'll set dogs on anybody Negro. Old, young, woman, child. Makes her no never mind. All this fuss ain't over Johnny," Malindy went on, and cackled to herself. "He shot himself cleaning his shotgun, dumb as the day is long. Sally just loves chasin' coloreds, still mad 'cause Johnny was my papa in secret. Everybody knew it but her. I call her Aunt Sally because I don't have another name for her."

"Uncle Johnny was better'n some," Rose told Malindy. "I

think she still loved him in a way, or wouldn't she have shot him herself?" They spoke to each other as if they were alone.

The dog at the roadside growled, stepping tentatively closer. Kai tried to lunge away again, but Charlotte held on. A dog that size would maul him to death, and there were others.

The women seemed to remember them again. "Way we see it . . ." Malindy began.

". . . Y'all better hop in back of the truck," Rose finished. "We can drive you back to the edge of the fog. We can't drive through it, but we can get you that far."

"What you doin' way out here anyways?" Malindy asked. "No one takes Route 9 unless they want to get lost."

"Real lost," Rose said, and giggled.

"They drove right over Johnny's grave," Malindy said to Rose, and they laughed again. "This one here did everything but lindy-hop over his bones."

Their chatter, and the impossible choices, made Charlotte dizzy. A low cracking sound rumbled beneath her, and the two-inch gap in the asphalt widened to half a foot. Kai whimpered, stepping away. The dog barked again, more insistent.

"Let's go with them," Kai whispered.

Charlotte looked at him, surprised. The same thought had been teasing her, but she'd been sure he wouldn't dare. He looked calmer than he'd been since before they passed through the fog. "Do you . . . feel something? Like at the house?"

His eyes fervent, Kai nodded. "Yes. Let's go."

He was right. She was sure of it. No matter how much she hated the idea, and she wasn't close to understanding why, the truck was their best chance.

Charlotte grabbed Kai's hand, and they ran together. They both climbed into the truck's bed with a leap, and the vintage vehicle sped forward as they were still pulling their legs into the prickly bed of pine cones, painful against her bare legs and palms. The truck was moving faster now than it had on its approach, pitching them against each other until they held on to the rusted sides, where the paint flaked off beneath Charlotte's sweating palm.

Dogs chased the truck, pouring onto the road from the woods. German shepherds, hounds, and oversized creatures that looked half wolf sprinted after the truck, barking their loathing as spittle flew between their teeth. Only five or six were close enough for Charlotte to see their glowing eyes, but a dozen more trailed farther behind, with more appearing from the woods. Some of the dogs stumbled in the widening gaps in the road. Wherever the truck drove, the road gave way beneath it, trying its best to eat them. The women in front laughed while the vehicle swerved around gaps and cracks, as if they'd never had such a merry time.

Charlotte was staring at the dogs, so she didn't see the fog bank until they were in the heart of it, wreathed in gray-white mist. The truck stopped on whining brakes. The house was only half a mile from the fog, she remembered. Only half a mile, yet so much farther.

"I can't take you past here," Malindy called back to them.

"Keep ahead of those dogs," Rose said. "They're all hers. All mean just like her."

Charlotte didn't need to hear any more. She grabbed Kai's hand again and they climbed out. She had lost her shoes somewhere in her terror. Her stocking foot slipped on the chrome bumper, but she barely felt her knee and elbow scrape when she fell. The barking was still behind them, enraged and determined.

Clinging to Kai's hand, Charlotte ran barefoot into the soupy gray.

Within her first three steps, the fog was gone. And so was the barking, and the laughter. When she turned the other way, the fog was gone too. She had known it would be. Some part of her had always known the fog wasn't real in the way her skin and beating heart were real. The fog wasn't as real as her memory of everything that had happened on the road.

A modern gas station and convenience store stood a hundred yards ahead, with a large sign on a highway pole. She knew they had driven past no such place, but that didn't matter—it was there now.

She peered at a highway sign as they walked toward the gas station, which of course said *Highway 46* instead of *Route 9*. If she asked someone at the gas station ahead, they would tell her there hadn't been a Route 9 in Gracetown as long as anyone could remember, maybe as far back as the 1960s or 1950s. Maybe long before then. She was certain of it.

She had left her car beyond the fog. She would have to explain that somehow.

"We'll say we got carjacked," Charlotte said. "When we asked a guy for directions."

Kai nodded. "The guy with the beard. We'll say it was him. And . . . it's true."

Charlotte tried to remember if she'd bought the rental car insurance. She thought about her purse and cell phone she'd left behind. Then she wondered how long this family had been in the land of the dead. And how long Aunt Sally had stood hidden behind her screen door ready to vent her hatred.

"I'm telling my dad," Kai said. "But just him."

Charlotte was still trying to sort through it all without feeling dizzy again. "Tell him . . . what? He won't believe you."

"Yeah, he will," Kai responded. They walked in silence for a moment, then he said, "I'm never going to another funeral."

But he would, she knew. They both would. Their grandparents were gone now, so they would bury their parents next, and all their stories and secrets. Charlotte stared at their feet walking together on the unbroken road: hers bare, still pedicured, his with black shoes, still shiny. This road felt no more real than the cracking one they had fled, and the only evidence of their shared ordeal was their breathing, too hard and fast.

Kai's father must have felt this way when he'd been released from the reformatory. He'd gathered stories while in that place that even his parents would never fully grasp, a wall of fog between him and the world, hoping the nightmares wouldn't last. But they had. And now his son would have them too. But at least Kai and his father had someone to tell.

Charlotte vowed she would never go to Gracetown again.

Suppertime

Summer 1909

A mother's scream pierced through the barn planks, near-human enough to bring hot tears to Mat's eyes. And Mat hated to cry, especially in front of her father. The lamb wriggling on the straw-dusted floor bleated with pathetic agitation, and his mother wailed outside as if she knew how sharp Mat's father's blade was. And what Mama wanted for Sunday supper.

"Firm hand, Mat. Don't let 'im suffer."

Mat tightened her gloved grip on the struggling lamb's legs, still powerful despite being tied, wishing she could let him run free. He must weigh seventy-five pounds—the biggest autumn lamb they had left, one she'd secretly named Buster. "It's alright," Mat told Buster in her sweetest voice, close to his ear. "Don't be scared."

Buster believed her lie and quieted. His thrashing stopped. Then came a barely audible, expert slicing sound and gurgling. Mat swallowed back a sob as she felt the creature's life seep from her fingertips. Against her will, she imagined herself feeding him hay from her hand when he was small. His mother's scream outside grew more terrible.

Papa looked down at her with pride. "Good girl," he said. "You did better with it than your brother. Go wash. I'll hang him up."

Mat looked down at her clothes: blood had sprayed her

shirt beyond the borders of the leather apron she'd worn. And her trouser cuffs. She would need to wash the blood out quickly or Mama would put her in a dress all day tomorrow, not just for supper. Confound it!

But Pa's approval gave her walk to the house a bounce. *You did better with it than your brother.* Now she would have something else to tease Calvin about when he came home from Howard for the summer on Sunday. Mat's tears had not yet dried, but a smile found her lips as she hurried down the dirt path through the stand of thin Florida pines to the two-story wood-plank farmhouse Papa and a crew had built two years ago, when Mat was eleven. The oak planks remained richly dark, not sun-faded, and some corners of the house still smelled like sap. Mama said some ladies from church were so envious of her roomy two-story house with a water closet instead of an outhouse that they hadn't spoken to her since they moved in. And Pa said some white men were so jealous of his prize hogs that he sat by the window with his rifle most nights to make sure no one would try to steal them, or burn his new house down from spite.

The kitchen was hot from Mama's stew pot, and the baby carriage hinges squeaked as Mat's young siblings whined with complaints that reminded her of the lamb. Booker had just turned a year old and Harriet was two; both identically insufferable. Mat knew she should relieve Mama of the babies, but Booker and Harriet were squalling in the carriage and a glimpse of Mama's huge belly pulling her housedress taut made Mat back away instead, toward the stairs. And freedom.

Another baby on the way! Mama had been only fifteen when she had Calvin, twenty-three when she had her. Thirty-four when she had Harriet, and thirty-five with Booker—when Mat heard her swear to Papa that her days of carrying babies were over. But she was with child *again*, and every time Mat thought about the new baby she felt a combination of pity and rage for

Mama. How could Mama stretch and twist her body time after time with such terrible agony, tying herself more firmly to her stove and sewing machine?

Sunday, she'd teased Mat with remarks about how one of the Stephens boys was asking how old her daughter was because she was so tall, and how Mat would be sixteen in three years, a fit age for marriage. *Marriage!* What made Mama think marriage was anywhere in her heart? Did she want to punish her because she dressed as she pleased and Papa relied on her just as much as he'd ever relied on Calvin? (Or more, since Calvin could not stand the sight of blood.)

Mat would go to college like her brother. Calvin had promised to help pay her way, since he got a good stipend from the aging writer whose memoir he was typing. Mama was old-fashioned and didn't believe girls needed schooling, though Papa had said to wait and see if she could keep up her grades. That wouldn't be hard: she could read and figure better than her teacher, for what that was worth.

The biggest godsend in the new house was her own bedroom, so Mat fled there and closed her door as if a bear had chased her. The oak wasn't sturdy enough to completely mute the whining of her brother and sister, but it helped. A surge of guilt replaced her anxiousness. Mama was standing over a hot stove almost ready to give birth, and Mat should have rolled the carriage out to the "parlor," as Mama now called their front room. (Booker and Harriet stopped fussing when she played happy music on the Victrola.) *You care more about sheep and goats than your brother and sister*, Mama always said. *But after this baby comes, they'll be your responsibility. Who knows how long it'll be 'fore I'm back on my feet. Better start learning now.* Mama's weary desperation had chilled Mat to her toes.

Her precious stereoscope goggles were waiting on her desk where she'd left them. After lighting her lamp, Mat pressed the velvet-lined mask to the bridge of her nose. Just like that, the narrow room around her melted and she was *inside* the slide glowing to life in her lamp's flame. The Palace of Electricity—a night view of a regal mansion draped in strings of stars, lit up from corner to corner, as if it might burn off her eyelids if she got too close. The Palace of Electricity seemed as far from Gracetown as the sun itself, yet the magical pictures from the '05 World's Fair reminded Mat how big the world and its wonders were. Calvin had written as much on his Christmas note, when he gifted her with the wonderful contraption and a handful of slides: *The world is a big place, Matty. Here's a good peek at it!*

During his last visit, Calvin had described how he was boarding in a house full of electricity where his writer patron lived: no need for kerosene lamps, with switches that turned on lights above like a wish, a machine that washed his clothes, and hot coils that toasted his bread. And a telephone, of course. If not for the stereoscope where Mat could see so many wonders for herself, she might not have believed his stories of casual magic.

Mat didn't know how long she'd been dreaming of the Palace of Electricity when she heard the thump against her window. A flurry of determined scratching shook her windowpane. She pulled the mask away, startled—and was staring into green-gold eyes that were not human. A bobcat was at her window! The large cat was light reddish brown, with only black spots on his ears and coat to distinguish him from the bricks that camouflaged him. He had climbed up the uneven bricks of the chimney to find her window on the second floor. The bobcat yowled, massive paws scratching against the frame.

Mat gasped. The stereoscope nearly tumbled from her hands.

"Bobby?" she whispered. She froze, not sure. Four months had passed since she'd seen the bobcat kitten she'd raised until it got too big and Mama told Papa to chase him away, and his coat had been more gray than red then. He was far bigger than when she'd found him under a rock ledge and carried him away in her palm. She'd kept him alive with one of Mama's baby bottles. She'd lied to herself and decided his mother was dead—but the truth was, she didn't know if she'd rescued or stolen him.

Heart pounding with anticipation—and a drop of fear, since she wasn't *sure*—Mat cracked her window open. The big cat did the rest, slinking snakelike through a gap that should have been too small. The cat leaped to her shoulders, wrapping around her neck. His fur smelled filthy, like carrion, not like when she'd bathed him in warm water and rose oil. Much bigger claws now raked through her plaited hair to her scalp with such strength that Mat felt her neck crack, and then the cat nibbled at her earlobe with teeth and tongue, nicking her until she bled.

"Stop it, that's too hard!" Mat said, but she was giggling as they tumbled to her bed, rolling in a ball that sometimes put her on top, sometimes the wild cat, their play wrestling so fierce that her bed frame hit the floor. His gravelly purr roared in her ear. As if no time at all had passed!

Mat assessed her injuries, breathless, while Bobby romped through her room in search of mischief, tugging at her desk drawers and swatting savagely at the scarf hanging on her wall. She noted her bleeding earlobe, a bold white scratch across the dark skin of her arm (not bleeding), another on her back (maybe spotting a little). Bobby had forgotten his lessons on gentle play, if he had ever truly learned. Their reunion had overexcited him. The constant scratches were the reason her parents had made her send him away—*You think you're playing games, but that's a wild beast and his nature will always come out,* Papa said. The times Mama had caught him peeing in her kitchen sink, his favorite place to relieve himself, had not helped his case for being a house cat either. Mostly, Mama had been afraid he might hurt one of the babies, which Mat could not say was unreasonable. But she had missed him. Soon after her parents stopped allowing him in the house, he had vanished into the woods.

And now he was back—a fully grown bobcat! She couldn't wait to tell Calvin.

But Papa would tear off a switch if he found Bobby in her room now. Joy quickly turned to panic: how would she get him out of the house? She couldn't hope to hide him. It was a wonder Mama hadn't already called after her to see what the ruckus was. Bobby would have to go back out the way he came, and fast.

Mat went to her window and opened it wide. "Come on, Bobby."

The cat stared, his stumpy tail lashing with irritation at the interruption of their play. Mat almost, *almost* felt a twinge of fright, reminding herself that she did not truly know Bobby anymore, so it might be dangerous to poke and prod him. His eyes brimmed with his history of killing. But she was more afraid of Papa's hickory switch, so she stuck her head out of the window as an example. "See? You gotta go back outside."

Mat's mattress creaked as Bobby stood on all fours, intrigued now.

"You want me to go out there with you? Is that it?"

Mat didn't think Bobby could understand spoken words, not *quite*, but he sprang so quickly that she had to move aside so he could reach the windowsill. Then he just stared at the chimney's descent. Why did cats love climbing up and hate climbing down?

"You go on," Mat said. "I'll meet you outside, alright?"

Bobby made a sound that could have been agreement or cussing.

And so their night's adventure began.

Mat would be expected at the supper table in thirty minutes and had no business going outside to chase after a bobcat, but that didn't stop her from grabbing her Brownie camera—Calvin's Christmas gift from his first year in college—and shoving against Bobby's weight to close her door so he could not follow her into the hall. His massive claws poked under the door. He swiped back and forth, shaking the door, rattling her doorknob.

"*Shhhhh.*"

Mat snuck back downstairs, past the loud kitchen, and out of the house.

Outside, she saw Bobby was staring down from her window. Mat tried to coax him without being loud enough for Mama to hear her from the open kitchen window, or Papa from the barn. Bobby's complaints from her window floated through the woods, halfway between whining and growling. He'd be lucky if Papa didn't come running out with his shotgun.

"Come on down," Mat said. "Stop being a baby."

She remembered a trick from when he was younger: if she pretended to walk away, he might chase her. So, she followed the deer path past Papa's wagon into the woods, walking until her house was out of sight. Sure enough, a twig crackled and Bobby was soon upon her, tangling her legs until she lost her balance, sending her rolling in prickly fir needles. The fall hurt her elbow. Mat held Bobby's mouth away from her face, noticing his sharp yellow teeth, pushing back against the fur of his muscular shoulders. She wondered for the barest instant if Bobby had turned wild after all. But with a playful burr, Bobby jumped away and let Mat rise to her feet again. Now she had a scraped elbow to add to her scratches.

"*No*," Mat said sharply. "You play too rough. Stop it."

Bobby talked back to her in his bobcat language and ran ahead. He didn't stick to the trail, though he never ventured far from it, leaping from bush to bush, sometimes scrambling halfway up a pine tree because he could. Just when she thought he might disappear over the hill, he turned his head to make sure she wasn't falling behind.

"I gotta get dressed for supper. I don't got time to be playin' with you," Mat said.

Bobby ignored her and ran on. Mat stood for a moment and thought it over, noticing how coppery the daylight had become, the sun hanging low in the sky. Then she heard Bobby's familiar call from shivering milkweed a few yards ahead, still close to the path, and nothing could rival the giddiness of seeing him so eager to play. She'd cried for a week straight after he left, and she'd stared at the trees hoping he would come back for nearly a month before she gave up. Calvin had confided to her at Christmas that he might not have survived the wild because he'd been raised by a human hand. And here he was!

She would go home in five minutes. The sun wouldn't fall below the tree line for at least fifteen minutes, so if she started back in five minutes she might make it to the table on time.

Another lie. She knew it even then.

But she needed to capture Bobby in a photograph with her camera! How else would anyone ever believe she'd tamed an honest-to-goodness fully grown bobcat?

Bobby was too quick for her camera. He would need to sit still—*real* still—for her to be able to set up a good shot with her Brownie. Every time she pointed the lens and could make out Bobby's fur in the viewfinder, he was gone before she could click the shutter. Time after time, her viewfinder showed her a tree stump or empty boulder instead.

"Hold still, would you?"

Bobby would not. He raced on with such purpose that she had no choice: she followed.

By the time they reached the first dampness of swamp water turning the soil to mud, Mat realized that Bobby was leading her to the spot where she had found him, a rocky ledge that had given her shade on hot afternoons while he lunged at the tadpoles and water lilies floating just beyond them. It wasn't a cave, exactly, because it was open on both sides, but their secret spot had felt like a castle to her. Papa could walk within five feet of her and never know she was there until he heard her giggles.

Mat was breathless by the time she reached Bobby. True to his camouflage, she had trouble making him out at first, but the sight of him made her grin. Bobby was still at last, his haunches lowered as he chewed on something in the dark. His flanks were in shadow, yet the twilight made his coat shine and his eyes glow like marbles when he gazed up at her. With trembling fingers, Mat pointed her Brownie again, expecting to find he had already leaped away, but Bobby was framed like a painting in a museum. Heart pounding, she pressed the shutter and heard the satisfying *click*. She had her photograph!

She took a step closer to see if she could take an even better photo, when she noticed the poor creature struggling in Brownie's jaw: at first she thought it might be a snake, but it was too broad, and she'd never seen a snake this odd color of slick gray-brown mud. Sometimes it looked like a tube, sometimes flat, and it kept wriggling although Bobby never stopped eating its other half. By the look of it, whatever it was might be two or three feet long. Or it *had* been.

Click. Mat pushed the shutter button again accidentally, startling herself in the same instant she realized she had never seen a creature like it. If it had legs, it might be a weasel. But it didn't look warm-blooded. If not for its size, it might have looked like a . . .

Mat's mouth fell open and she took a step back when her memory formed the word: *leech*. She'd heard her mother and grandmother talk about giant leeches that crawled from the swamp and nested inside babies during the summer. Swamp leeches, people called them. But Mama had never been able to identify anyone who'd ever *seen* one. Was this . . . ?

Mat remembered her camera and raised it again, trying

to see the last of the creature before it disappeared in Bobby's mouth, but the cat's ears had perked up and he'd dropped what was left of it, staring toward the edge of the swamp where he had once played. Bobby growled—not in the playful way he used to with her. Like he meant it. His teeth were fully bared as he scrambled to his feet, charging toward the water. Then came horrific splashing: a sound so loud that it could only be a gator.

"Bobby—no!"

That furious sliver of last daylight gave Mat a good enough view for her to realize that Mat was not tussling with a gator. This creature was also a gray-brown color, with the same slimy skin, but it had long, wiry tendrils that whipped at Bobby's hide, making him yowl.

The mama, Mat thought. Then she turned and ran.

It was dark by the time Mat reached her doorstep.

She'd wasted many minutes lost in the graying woods, unable to see past her tears as she tried to stumble toward the sanctuary of their sturdy oak house. She ran inside and leaned against the door while she pulled the dead bolt Papa had built. She was so glad to be home, her knees were watery with gratitude. The door propped her up while she gasped, shaking with worry for Bobby. And the image of the thing she had seen.

From the doorway, she could see the table where Mama and Papa were already in their seats, holding hands to say grace. Papa's face was stern. Mama's was enraged.

Papa stood up. "Matty! Where were you?"

"Matilda Lydia Powell, you are in a heap of hot water!" Mama said.

Papa walked toward her with the lantern from the table to get a closer look at her face.

"I swear, this child is so spoiled she thinks she can just run off and . . ." Mama was saying, though Papa's face softened as he looked at her. He held up his arm to silence Mama.

"What's happened?" he asked in a tight voice she had only heard once or twice, and only now did she realize it was the way he sounded when he was afraid.

Mat hadn't thought up a story yet, so she didn't know how to answer. What was the point of telling them what she'd seen? Mama would accuse her of making up stories. And what if Papa went hunting for Bobby at the mention of him?

Papa moved his face closer to her, his jaw trembling. "Who hurt you?"

"No one," Mat finally responded. "I saw a gator and I ran off. I tripped and fell."

"So you were off playing by the swamp?" Mama said.

"Yes ma'am."

Papa held the lamp even closer to her face, trying to see any lies in her eyes. He stared at her a long time. When he noticed the camera she was clutching, he seemed to believe her at last. His jaw's trembling stopped, replaced by ironclad anger.

"Shame on you," he said, the words Mat most hated to hear. "Hurry up and go upstairs and get dressed. I've got half a mind to send you to bed without supper."

"That's alright, sir, if that's what I deserve." Mat had lost her appetite.

"Oh, I bet you'd like that," Papa said. "Come right back down to the table proper."

"And you better look like a *young lady*," Mama added.

More hot tears escaped as Mat climbed the stairs, but she hoped Papa hadn't seen.

"Look what you've done!" Mama scolded Papa. "Calling her by that boyish name. Letting her dress any kind of way. She's half wild. No man will know what to do with her!"

Mat waited at the top landing to hear if Papa would say, *Stop worrying so much,* or, *She'll grow out of it,* like he usually did, but Papa was stone silent.

Five minutes of scrubbing in the upstairs sink and the pleated dress from her closet worked a small miracle, wiping away all signs of blood and the creatures outside. Mat took extra care to brush her hair down flat where she'd already sweated out Mama's pressing from last Sunday. Her reflection in the mirror looked like the biggest lie ever told.

Mama did not look her way when Mat sat at the table, said her silent grace, and spooned chicken stew into her bowl. The only one who seemed happy to see her was Harriet, who squealed, "Matty! Matty! Matty!" and gave her a hug from her high chair. Mat made a show of buttering cornbread and breaking it into bite-sized pieces for her, and Harriet squealed some more. Booker was equally delighted to be bouncing on Papa's knee while he ate handfuls of a soft mash from a bowl beside his father's plate. Gazing upon her family—including Calvin's empty seat—made Mat feel the shame Papa had uttered at her like a curse. Mama looked weary enough to fall asleep upright, rubbing her swollen belly. Was it so wrong for Mama to expect her to be more of a helper? Was it fair that Mat spent so much time outside with Papa, leaving Mama to fend for herself with Booker and Harriet?

Mat was opening her mouth to announce an apology when something shook the door.

"What the blazes . . . ?" Papa said. He handed Booker over to Mama and was on his feet, producing his hunting rifle so fast that Mat realized he'd moved it from the closet to be near him, perhaps preparing for trouble when she was late. He took a step toward the door, but she jumped in front of him.

"Papa, no!" she said. "It's only Bobby. I saw him outside. He's come back."

"Is *that* what you were doing out there?" Mama said. "Fooling with that bobcat?"

Another *thump*, and this time it sounded like buckling wood.

"He's back to break down our door?" Papa said. "And steal

our livestock?" He had delighted in Bobby as a kitten, but no love showed in his eyes now.

"Bobby wouldn't do that!" Mat said, then reminded herself that she didn't know the cat anymore. It felt true in her heart, anyway. And she was just glad he was alright.

The door shuddered again and a loud feline screech and growling came from the other side of the house, closer to the kitchen. Papa snapped a look to Mat: they both knew that bobcats did not travel in packs. *That* was Bobby. On the other side of the house.

Which meant it wasn't Bobby at the door. The room felt frigid as Mat's world went askew.

Papa took long strides toward the door and Mat tried to keep pace with him. Her mind fumbled for words to explain the monstrous creature that might have followed her and Bobby from the swamp. "Papa, wait—"

He flung the draperies aside to try to look outside, but it was too dark. A hog squealed from the barn, setting off a cascade of panicked cries.

"He's in the barn now," Papa said.

"That's not Bobby," Mat said. "I swear it isn't, Papa. Be careful! I saw something—"

"Stay here with your Mama."

Mat grabbed Papa's arm with all her strength before he could head outside in ignorance. "Listen to me!" she said, and her tone was so grown that he turned to her. "I saw something by the swamp. Not a bobcat. Bobby was eating some kind of big, ugly leech, and its mama came out of the water, big as a gator. Mean as one too. It was whipping Bobby with these . . . big whiskers? No—tentacles. Thick as ropes. I don't know what it was. But I think it followed me."

"What's she talking about?" Mama asked in a tiny voice, her anger revealed as the fright it truly was. The hogs and sheep in the barn were in a frenzy.

Papa stared down at Mat. "I have no damn idea," he said to Mama. "All of you go hide upstairs—*now*. She's right about one thing: it ain't a bobcat. Someone's after the hogs." He probably thought it was white men from town, and white men from town might not be satisfied with stealing or killing hogs. He was wrong, but whatever that thing was might be just as bad. It might even be worse than jealous white men.

"Be careful, Papa. Please."

"Don't you let no crackers kill you over a hog!" Mama said.

"Go on, I said!" Papa waved to Mama at the table. "Hurry up, Belle!"

He waited until he saw Mama pull herself to her feet, Booker in her arms. Mat ran back to the table to scoop up Harriet so Papa would know he could count on her. Harriet cried in the commotion, clinging so hard to Mat's collar that the lacy fabric chafed her neck.

Papa finally opened the door and peeked outside. She prayed he wouldn't shoot Bobby. But if Papa saw anything, he didn't let on.

"Pull the bolt," he called back to them, and slammed the door behind him.

Tears fell from Mama's eyes, and Mat realized it was all her fault. If she hadn't followed Bobby when she was supposed to be getting ready for supper, the leech monster never would have come after her. Had it tracked her by scent? Or had Bobby led it here?

With a trembling hand, Mat bolted the door while she held Harriet close with her other arm, bouncing her gently. A peek through the curtains only showed Papa running toward the barn before he was out of sight. Mat's heart shook with worry.

"Come up to my room, Mama," she said.

Mama blinked as if she hadn't heard her. Then followed Mat up the stairs.

* * *

Mat pushed her desk against the door to barricade it while Mama opened her closet, still holding tight to Booker. Mama was replaying a bad memory, her face slack with terror while they braced for gunfire and angry voices outside. So far, they only heard Bobby's snarling, sometimes more distant, sometimes very near.

"Tell me again," Mama said, hushed. "What did you see?"

Mat remembered her camera, lifting it from her desk as if Mama could see her evidence captured inside. "I think I took a picture of it. It was big, Mama. And these long . . . whatchacallit . . . *tentacle*s on it. Like an octopus, almost, but it wasn't no octopus. It was the swamp leech's mama! It came after Bobby when he was eating its baby."

Mama's face flickered with relief. Her shoulders sank as she exhaled the breath she'd been holding.

"You know what that thing is, Mama?"

"Shhhh," Mama said, nodding toward Harriet, not wanting to scare her. "Heard stories about swamp leeches. Never seen one, though. Never heard of one big as this."

"But you believe me?"

"I want to, child. Your daddy can hold his own against a beast." Like Papa, Mama was more scared of lynching.

But they hadn't seen the thing. And it dawned on Mat that there might be more than one.

"*Who's there?*" Papa's voice boomed from outside. If there *were* white men in the barn, that thunder in Papa's voice would get him killed.

Scratching came from Mat's window, which she'd closed as soon as they ran into the room. Mama gasped, which set Harriet off crying. Mat turned up her lamp's light, though she already knew before she saw the eyes gleaming on the other side of the glass.

"It's only Bobby. Mama, please let me let him in—I think he's hurt."

Mama backed farther into the closet, bringing both Booker and Harriet with her. She kept the door open only a crack. "Yes, but hurry up," she said. "If you're *sure* it's Bobby."

If Mat had been closer, she would have given Mama a tight hug. Mama casting her complaints aside reminded Mat of when Mama had laughed and daydreamed with her—before the whispers had embarrassed her.

Mat pulled the window an inch, and Bobby did the rest, forcing his body inside. He left a thin streak of blood against the white paint. Two raw stripes in his coat looked like a whip's lashes.

"Come on, it's alright," Mat said, and pulled the window closed behind him.

Bobby jumped on the bed, then off again, pacing the floor. Mat was relieved that he seemed like himself despite the blood. When he padded toward the closet, Mama pulled it shut.

"Keep him away from the babies!" Mama said, her voice slightly muffled, so Mat patted the mattress and Bobby came back toward her. He jumped on the bed and began licking his wounds.

"This is all your fault," Mat said softly to Bobby.

Then the rifle shot came. Mat's heart stuffed her throat.

"Get in here, Matilda!" Mama called in a wire-thin voice.

Yet Mat barely heard her, creeping back to the window to peer outside. Lamplight flickered inside the barn, roaming between the cracks in the wood panels. A second shot flared in the dark like a fireball, making her wince. A high-pitched sound she had never heard before seemed to echo against every tree trunk for miles.

"Goddamn!" she heard Papa rasp faintly. His blasphemy was shocking. "What in the goddamn hell . . . ?"

"Mat!" Mama called from the closet, frantic.

"I'm alright, Mama. I think Papa got it. I'm just trying to see—"

Bobby leaped off the bed, growling low in his throat.

A movement in the dark outside the window made Mat instinctively pull back right before the grass cracked to pieces and flew into her room, a shard scraping her nose. The odd black tendrils lashed into the room, squirming like snakes. The rest of the creature's body was pressed against the top half of the window, which had not broken—the only barrier keeping it out. This thing was bigger than a gator; bigger than the one she'd seen at the swamp. Its skin squeezed across the remaining glass pane as it tried to bulge into the room. The upper pane shivered and cracked.

Bobby pounced, but he whined when a lash caught his ear.

Mat wanted to turn and run for the closet like Mama had said—to be her child instead of her protector. She doubted that Bobby would have fled into the house if he could beat the thing back by himself.

"*Papa—help*!" Mat screamed with all the strength in her lungs.

But she didn't have time to wait for Papa. The beast was already tensing thick tendrils across Bobby's middle while the cat struggled and whined, slashing with his paws. Mat whirled to look for anything that could be used as a weapon, and she remembered the oyster knife in her desk drawer. It wasn't big, yet she kept it sharp. She would have to get in close to try to hurt the thing, but Mat also had to protect her family. And Bobby was her family too.

With a yell, Mat charged with her knife and plunged it toward a tendril, but the slimy flesh snapped away so fast that her blade sank deep into wood. *Damnit*! Sharp pain lanced her forehead and she realized the tendril had touched her, slicing through her skin. If Mama could see from the closet, she would faint. Mat felt ready to faint herself.

Bobby's snarling and the cries of her brother and sister from the closet forced Mat to push aside her horror at her own warm blood. Half-blinded from blood stinging her eyes, Mat fumbled until she felt the knife's handle, tugging to free it. She'd stabbed the wood so hard that she needed two hands for a strong enough grip, and she nearly lost her balance when it came free. This time, instead of trying to hit one of the fast-moving tentacles, Mat stabbed through the crack in the glass, like Papa had taught her when she was hunting: aim for the body's center.

She couldn't see the body well, much less know where its center was, but the creature let out a piercing screech like the one from the barn, so loud that Mat backed away and covered her ears. The tentacles flapped and then retreated, releasing Bobby—but the cat snuck in a ferocious slice with his claws that left one of the odd tentacles severed on her floor.

"Get away from the window!" Papa shouted from outside.

Mat ducked, hooking her arm around Bobby to try to pull him down too—enough to surprise him off-balance. He wriggled free, though thankfully he didn't rake her with his claws.

Another rifle shot. More glass rained into Mat's room. The otherworldly shriek came, and something big fell to the ground outside before it went silent.

"We did it, Bobby," she whispered to the big cat beside her. "And I saved you!"

Bobby bumped his head against hers, knocking her teeth together so hard that she saw sparks, the closest he came to saying, *Thank you.*

When Papa finally agreed that it was safe for her to come outside, Mat understood why no one had ever spotted a leech monster with their own eyes. Papa had covered both corpses with tarp after he shot them, but by dawn the tarp beneath her window had sunk to the soil, with only an oily black spot remaining where the creature had been. It was *gone*, tentacles and all.

The same slick spot was all that remained in the barn.

"But you saw it, Papa? Didn't you?"

In the morning light, their story felt fragile. Since Mama had stayed in the closet, Calvin would never believe her without Papa's corroboration. And who knew how long it would take for her photographs to come back?

"I wouldn't know how to describe it to folks, Matty," Papa confided. "It was so dark in the barn, and it moved so fast. I was hoping to get a better look after daylight."

That was how Mat knew they would not talk about it, not outside of the family. Not ever. Many things happened in Gracetown that no one talked about, or so she had heard. Mama had probably been told stories about swamp leeches by her grandmother and cousins that she'd never bothered to share with Mat.

The new baby came early, two days before Calvin's homecoming. The baby might have died if Miz Effie, the midwife, hadn't quickly unwrapped the umbilical cord from the baby's neck to help her suck her first air from the world. Mama went from screaming to crying with joy, swearing it was her last—again.

Just as Mama had warned, the birth and bleeding had weakened her, so she couldn't stand up to cook and clean and care for Harriet and Booker the way she usually did. Those tasks fell to Mat, of course. So instead of slopping hogs and raking hay and helping Papa fix broken rails in the fence, Mat stirred oatmeal on the stove and washed clothes and played the Victrola for Harriet and Booker, doing silly dances until they squealed with laughter.

Calvin had gained at least ten pounds and looked five years older now, much more a man than a boy. Papa cooked the lamb for supper so well that Mat had two servings although she had promised herself she wouldn't eat any. Calvin asked Mat how she'd gotten the scar across her forehead, and Mat shared a look with Papa and said he wouldn't believe her, so she would wait for her photographs to come back.

It was six weeks before a package from the Eastman Kodak

Company arrived, almost time for Calvin to return to school, and she ripped it open as soon as Papa handed it to her, eager to see what images she had captured.

But all she could see clearly was Bobby, his eyes shining in the dusk light. The shadows beneath the ledge obscured the tiny swamp leech clamped between his jaws. Worse, she must have been too frightened to click the shutter when she'd seen the leech monster, because the last two photos were a horrific blur. And then came a photo of weary Mama smiling with the new baby in her arms.

"Well, will you look at that?" Calvin said, peering over her shoulder. "What a family record! You said you had a special one to show me, and you weren't lying. You could take photographs as a trade one day, you know. Just keep practicing. I'm proud of you, Matty."

A future taking photographs! Mat had never imagined such a notion, and it filled her with a sense of possibility. She might be the first Negro photographer for the *Saturday Evening Post*! Mat swallowed back her bitter disappointment that she had no record of the creatures that had attacked her family, that she and Papa would have to rely on memories that would surely fade with time. She wondered how anyone remembered their own family's faces—the creases, the hairstyles, the *exact* smiles—in the days before photographs.

But photographs, no matter how marvelous they were, did not substitute for life.

When Mama was sleeping, Mat cradled the new baby and stared into her peculiar little face and bright, hungry eyes and thought about the odd creature Bobby had been eating under the ledge. And she imagined how horrible it would be if someone came and stole the new baby away, and how she, too, would track down any creature who hurt her.

In later years, Mat would reflect upon that as her favorite summer of childhood.

* * *

Bobby never visited once while Calvin was there, though he was back at Mat's window two days after her brother left, early in the morning. Even the babies were sleeping, the house silent except for Bobby's fuss. Mat rushed to pull on her overalls and the sturdy boots she had inherited from her brother. She grabbed her Brownie camera and raced outside to join Bobby in the woods washed in the gray dawn.

If she could capture the right image, her career in photography could begin now.

But Bobby, as usual, did not cooperate. He found every shadow and obstruction.

"Would you hold still for once in your life?"

Bobby playfully leaped against her side, pushing himself away with his powerful legs. His claws did not prick her this time, but she could feel the strong tips. Mat swayed and stumbled, relieved that she did not drop her camera and that her bottom landed in soft moss. Bobby licked the top of her head. He was far too close for a good photo now. Unless . . .

Inspiration struck: Mat turned her Brownie's lens toward her face, the viewfinder on the other side. She could not see what image was framed, but the angle *should* be right, shouldn't it? And if the camera could see her face, could it also see Bobby nuzzling her? She didn't know. But she fumbled to reach the button. *Click*.

It might just be a photo of the sky or a tree trunk, for all she knew. Yet maybe she had a keepsake of her and Bobby together. When the cat finally stepped away from her, head upturned because of a dull crack from a tree branch overhead, Mat knew this would be the perfect image. His head was slightly above hers from where she sat, regal, his coat glorious in the rising sun.

"I've finally got you now, Bobby," she said as her camera clicked.

It might be the best photograph she had ever made. Or ever would.

But when Mat blinked, Bobby was gone.

Rumpus Room

"I broke my daughter's arm."

Kat had never said the words aloud. If she'd been able to take responsibility and say to the judge, "I did this," and not, "This bad thing happened," she might be with Yvonne right now. Instead, Yvonne was with Kat's mom in Jacksonville and Kat was in a dimly lit diner off I-95 in Key Largo telling her business to the stranger who'd bought her a Corona Lite. She waited five seconds for him to accuse her of being a child abuser. Instead, he swiveled to face her. Full attention. Gentle gray eyes swept across her face like twin rescue lights.

"Was it an accident?"

Kat nodded.

Oddly, he clinked his bottle against hers. "Accident's an accident. And accidents *do* happen. Don't beat yourself up over it. Believe me, guilt buys you nothing but grief in this world. And there's enough grief to go around. Ain't that right, sister?"

Maybe the beer was going straight to her head on an empty stomach, but she thought it might be the nicest thing anyone had ever said to her. He was the first person who hadn't glared at her after they heard her story—the ER nurse, the caseworker, even her mother, who'd beaten welts into her legs with a belt and called it discipline when she was Yvonne's age. Kat had never spanked Yvonne—*never*. Kat's throat tightened with a threatening sob. She was ready to tell this stranger everything she'd tried to explain to the judge: she'd slipped on the kitchen floor as she was grabbing Yvonne's arm to tell her to *listen*, since Yvonne never listened unless you tapped her shoulder or raised your voice. It was as if her ears didn't work by themselves, as if she needed her skin to hear. So, yes, she'd grabbed her. She'd never denied that. Fine, and maybe she'd been a little irritated at the time. That was true too.

But she hadn't seen the puddle. Ice was always flying wild from the fridge's old ice maker, melting on the floor. So when Kat moved to wrap her palm around her daughter's slim pine branch of an arm, her foot slipped on the water and she fell against Yvonne, pushing her against that cursed cabinet. Then a muffled *snap*, a sound like a physical blow to her own stomach. And Yvonne's screaming. The memory of that snapping bone, that scream, kept Kat on I-95 driving to the ass end of the state talking to strangers in bars and diners—but she couldn't stop hearing her daughter's cry. The scream followed Kat wherever she drove.

This dude didn't know any of that; he probably assumed she was here selling sex. That was probably why he'd sat next to her and bought her a beer. Maybe she'd told him her secret to chase him away so she could drink her beer in peace. But her confession had the opposite effect: he'd turned to face her full-on, not just his mysterious profile beneath a Miami Dolphins baseball cap. She noticed how his pullover matched the cap's aqua-blue just as ZZ Top sang about a well-dressed man on the jukebox. He was at least fifty, the age her father would have been by now. But he looked good down to his snakeskin boots.

He might give her a couple hundred dollars for a good time, and if she weren't broke she might have given him a good time for free. She wanted to make the offer, but she wasn't sure how. She'd never done it for money. And his shiny boots made her think he might be a cop. Was two hundred too much or too little?

While she tried to work out her sales pitch, he said, "You know how to cook?"

In a wild thought, she wondered if he wanted to marry her. It happened in movies, didn't it? Her life had turned into a horror movie for the past month, so maybe it was becoming a different kind of movie now, one with a happier ending.

"I hate cooking," he went on. "But I'm sick of this diner. I've been looking for someone to cook, straighten up. Maybe get groceries once a week. Shit like that. You lookin' for a job? If you are, I'm hiring."

She stared. Somehow, his job offer seemed more bizarre than a spontaneous proposal. "I don't . . . live here. I'm just driving to Key West to—"

"Look for a job?"

He'd figured her out in a glance. She had slept in her car again last night, and she might not have enough gas money to make it to Key West, which was another two hours of driving. And unless he bought her dinner too, she might not eat anything tonight except another package of free saltines from the diner's cracked bowl on the countertop. Maybe he *was* a cop.

He reached for his back pocket, and she was sure he was about to pull out a badge. Fuck. After his pep talk, was he going to try to railroad her for solicitation when she'd never even said it out loud? People in jail hated child abusers.

She raised her hands. "Mister—"

"Easy there," he said with a grin. "We're not all gunslingers down here, sister."

He flipped open his leather wallet, showing her a faded photograph trapped in a plastic sleeve: a man and a girl tall enough to be six or seven, at the beach, faces obscured by the powerful dusk light as they stood beside a boulder. "That's my kid. She died."

Kat had never known anyone who lost a kid. Now every part of this stranger's face—his colorless eyes, his hollowed cheeks, his silver-streaked hair—looked like residual scarring, a mask over the man he had been before his daughter died.

"Drowned a couple years back. Her name was Amber."

Kat finally started to speak, but he held up his hand: *Don't say anything.* He cleared his throat. "All I'm gonna say about that. I can see you're going through something yourself, but as long as your daughter's alive, you'll always have another chance. I've seen enough people in jams with the law to know that someone in your situation needs a job. Something to show the courts. If you need to take some time to get yourself to-gether, save a few dollars . . . I can hire you full-time. Cleaning and cooking. I can't pay more'n a couple hundred a week, but you could live in my rumpus room, so you won't have to blow your pay on rent or food. It's got a separate entrance. Your own key."

Kat had a cosmetology certificate, so she was decent at styl-ing hair, but she'd never been a housekeeper. She also wasn't much of a cook. She didn't even know what a rumpus room was—what kind of old-timey phrase was that, anyway?—and she didn't like the sound of it.

Again, he looked at her like he could see every thought in her head. He grabbed the thin local newspaper on the stool next to his and fanned it across the counter, pointing out the classified ads. "Here," he said. "This is me. Ben Fuller."

He showed her the ad: *HELP WANTED. FULL-TIME HOUSEKEEPER/COOK. MAY LIVE IN.* She took out her phone and texted the number in the ad. And heard his phone ping. He grinned as if her caution pleased him. "It's not a con. And no offense, but—"

"Says anyone about to say something hella offensive."

He winked at her. "You're not my type. And it's not about race—how old are you?"

"Twenty-six."

"Yeah." He downed the last of his beer. Watching him, she

ached for another and wished the ache away. She drank far too much now. "Generation Y, Z, whatever, you're not my type. I just turned sixty. I just hate cooking. And you sounded like you could use—"

"Can I move in tonight?"

That was how Kat came to live in the rumpus room.

Most of the houses on Ben's street were in *Candy Land* colors, lined on the bank of a canal with neon-green water that looked like a Caribbean vacation. The street didn't scream *rich* like on TV, but she knew enough about real estate to guess his house was worth a million dollars despite the Mustang on cement blocks in his carport and chipping brown paint on the walls. The house was tropical style, with an oversized top floor and screened-in wraparound porch. Small solar lights made the row of scrawny palm trees lining the driveway look like a gift.

Kat stood in his gravel driveway to take it in. The sun was moving toward the shadowy end of dusk, more dark than light, and she was at a stranger's house. A one-night stand, paid or unpaid, would have felt less like she was a fool for following this man home. A job that sounded too good to be true was the perfect lure for someone truly desperate. Apparently.

For the first time, she noticed that he was more than a foot taller than she was. A giant.

Ben reached into a large flowerpot on his wood-plank porch and pulled out a key with a Minnie Mouse chain. "Here," he said, dropping the key in her palm. "Don't need you till breakfast. I eat at eight. Rumpus room's in the backyard, under the banyan tree near the canal. Four walls all to yourself. Text if you need anything. You already know the number."

He was right: she wasn't his type. Usually men stared at her chest, yet he'd barely glanced at her before he let himself into his house and closed the door. So much for wondering if he expected her to go inside to keep him company.

His backyard was enough like a jungle that it took her awhile before she saw the yellow paint of a wooden structure about a third the size of a mobile home, a tiny garden house nearly hidden by the hanging tendrils of the banyan tree. A motion light startled her when it snapped on, lighting up the walkway stones of crushed seashells. Then she was at the door, her feet on a thick mat embroidered with *Home Sweet Home* and the image of a cat curled in a ball.

Damn, she *did* like cats. It *would* be sweet to have a place to call home.

Her stomach clenched with certainty that this guy was playing her somehow, but Minnie Mouse let her inside and she flicked on a row of overhead lights. The tiled rumpus room was small and narrow, though the lighting gave it elegance, brightening the hot-pink bedspread on the daybed near the window. The fake marble countertop with a sink and microwave in the corner shined like she was in a five-star hotel. The rumpus room had been arranged with care: bed, two beanbag chairs, a newish TV mounted on the wall, kitchenette, a small table and two chairs, and a door she assumed led to the bathroom. Under the TV, a large basket overflowed with stuffed animals and games like *Jenga* and *Hungry Hungry Hippos*. Cramped but organized.

Then it hit her: a rumpus room was a *playroom*. Kat thought about the man's dead daughter, Amber. Had she played here? Kat imagined she could see Amber's face from the photo, hidden behind bright light. Yvonne would love this little *Alice in Wonderland* room, scattering *Jenga* blocks over the tiles. Kat's throat cinched with an unborn sob. She had never missed any person as much as she missed her daughter. She even missed Amber, a phantom loss nearly close enough to touch as her own.

Kat opened the bathroom door, looking for distraction from the agony of remembering Yvonne's grinning baby teeth. (And her scream when her arm snapped.) The bathroom had a tiled shower stall with a sliding door, cheap-looking toilet, and barely room to stand at the sink. The space smelled musty, even earthy, as if the closed door exiled it to the yard. Humidity clung to the tiles. *Half wild, half tame*, she thought. The rest of the rumpus room was almost enchanting; the bathroom didn't belong. That was what she thought from the very start. Kat stepped back and closed the bathroom door. She tugged on it to make sure the latch had caught so the musty smell would not creep to the back of her throat.

Her stomach growled. The smallish fridge was empty except for a half-gallon bottle of spring water. She was about to text Fuller to see if she could come over to the Big House to make a sandwich when she remembered the freezer. Jackpot! Two full stacks of microwave spaghetti meals and a bag of frozen chicken strips were nestled in old frost. She checked the expiration date on the meals: they were a full year past their best days, but she heated one up anyway and ate it with the plastic fork she found in a packet in the drawer under the sink. It tasted so good that she ate another. And a third. It had been awhile since she'd had food better than a burger.

While she shoved warm pasta into her mouth, Kat flipped through the DVD collection on the shelf under the mounted TV. *Beauty and the Beast* was Yvonne's favorite, so no way she could sit through that. She found a surprise—*Hidden Figures*—and watched it for the first time. Seeing Black women brave enough to fight through the eternal whiteness of NASA in the 1960s gave her the strength to call her mother's number. When the landline phone started warbling, she realized, too late, that it was almost nine thirty. Yvonne was in bed by now.

Five rings. Six. Kat almost hung up.

"Don't you look at the time?"

"I'm sorry, Mom, I . . ." Kat stopped apologizing when she heard Buzz Lightyear's voice booming from the old console TV. "She's still up?"

"She asked for ten more minutes, that's all." Her mother had complained to the judge that Yvonne needed a stricter bedtime, dragging their private disagreements into the courtroom. The hypocrisy raked at Kat, but she didn't want to start a fight. Maybe she wouldn't have to cry herself to sleep for a change.

"Put her on, please."

"I'm tryin' to calm her down for bed. You'll just—"

"*Is that Mommy?*" she heard Yvonne squeal, saying *Mommy* with so much love and longing that Kat's eyesight brightened and dimmed all at once. Tears overflowed.

"See?" Mom said. "Now she's all excited." But Yvonne must have been grabbing for the phone, because the next voice was hers.

"Mommeeeee!" To Kat's ears, it sounded like a plea for help.

"Hey, baby girl," Kat said, stripping sadness from her voice, her superpower. "Are you being good for Grandma?" *And is Grandma being good for you?*

Yvonne told her that she was going to day care—another bit of hypocrisy, since Mom had complained when Kat had to put Yvonne in day care when she had that shitty job at Walmart. Kat wondered if her mother was spanking her too. She would find a way to ask her.

"Guess what! I got my cast off today."

"You *did*?" Kat said, trying to sound excited for her even while she heard the bone snap again, could see the ugly, swollen bruise. Her face was all tears now. She knew she should tell Yvonne how great that was and *I bet that was itching a lot*, but she needed to talk about anything else. Her throat was pinching shut.

"I won't do that again, Mommy," Yvonne said. "I slipped on the floor and my arm broke."

"What's that, baby?" Kat was sure she had heard wrong.

"My foot slipped," Yvonne said. Then she laughed. "*Silly!*"

Was her mother coaching Yvonne? Had the judge called another meeting? Kat blinked and waited for her throat to release the words she had shared with the stranger in the diner: *I'm the one who slipped, not you. I broke your arm.* She was appalled at herself when she didn't.

"That's . . ." She took a breath. "That's *so great* you got your cast off, baby. Nothing like that will ever, ever happen again." That carefree giggle again, like a dream of sudden grace. *WHAT'S WRONG WITH YOU?!* Yvonne had screamed up at her from the floor, eyes wide with agony and surprise as she clutched her parts that Kat had broken. Kat had wailed how sorry she was the entire drive to the hospital, barely able to see the road for her tears, drowning in remorse. It had only been six weeks ago. Was Yvonne burying her inside a happier memory?

"It's late," Mom said in the background. "Go on to your room, Yvonne." *Your room* instead of *Mom's room* sounded deliberate. That room had been Kat's except the seven months she'd lived with Lionel. Yvonne had slept beside Kat in her full-sized bed most of her life.

Yvonne asked for one more minute, but Mom said she was out of time. Kat noticed the predictable annoyance in her mother's voice. If Kat weren't monitoring her, Mom might be threatening to get her belt. Kat tried to say goodbye, though she didn't think Yvonne heard her.

"Where are you, Katrina?" Mom used her full name, embedding more disdain in each syllable. Mom had named her after Hurricane Katrina. Mom had escaped New Orleans a few years before she got pregnant, losing everything she owned, and as far as Kat could figure, Mom had blamed her baby for her troubles. Kat could barely remember a smile from her.

"I'm in Key Largo," Kat said. "I got a job assisting a senior citizen. A place to live. I'll send you money soon." Better than saying she'd moved in with some random guy from a diner.

Mom made a surprised sound she didn't try to disguise. "That right?"

"Yep." Kat filled her lungs and exhaled. "I'm on the right track for the judge."

The silence came in a gale, a disruption of their peace. In silence, they could not ignore the war between them over Yvonne. If Mom was hoping Yvonne would be hers now—a child, at last, who would not remind her of a life destroyed—she was dead wrong. Mom had no idea who she was fucking with. She would get her daughter back. She would never hurt Yvonne again.

"Love you, Mom," Kat said, her voice sweet poison.

"Yeah, you too." When Mom clicked away from the call, Kat was breathing fast, ready to curl up on this tiny new bed to sob—

But the bathroom door was open.

Kat's throat, hot before, went cold. She remembered her care in closing it, yet the door was now wide open, as if it had been propped. The musty odor had already crept into the room, not quite sour enough to notice until she saw the open door.

She stood up straight, the phone forgotten. Vigilant, her eyes went straight to her front door to make sure the bolt lock was still in place. None of the rumpus room's old-fashioned jalousie windows looked big enough for anyone to climb through. Her skin prickled from adrenaline even as her anxious heartbeat slowed. No one else was here.

She walked to the bathroom and flicked on the light, just to check. Foliage was growing so thick against the bathroom's narrow windows that someone might need a chainsaw to get inside—which wasn't a comforting picture. The row of windows was blackened with plant life in the dark. Oddly, again, it seemed that this bathroom was an ancient structure and the rest of the rumpus room was new.

It was fine. She was fine. She swung the errant door on its

silent hinge long enough to postulate a theory: *An object in motion stays in motion. An object at rest might not be at fucking rest.* Panic attacks had been dogging her since Yvonne's injury. Every new place seemed as eager to punish her as her mother, from the rain-slick roads she drove with cramping fingers to the poorly lighted gas stations she rushed away from with her keys fanned out like claws.

To conquer this room, this new life, she would need to conquer the bathroom. This would be just the first of many uncomfortable steps that would take her back to Yvonne, a long march ahead. If this job was legit—and she wouldn't know that until she asked for a fifty-dollar advance tomorrow—no way in hell would she let herself get spooked away from a free place to live, where she could stash away money fast. When she found a second job in town, a night job if she had to, she'd have enough for an apartment near her mother. She could even ask Fuller if she could take hair customers in the rumpus room. As long as she was living in her car, she'd never get Yvonne back.

Fuck this bathroom. Fuck this door. If this door opened on its own all night long, she'd let it fan her to sleep. Just like she'd get used to its primordial odor—not strong, but distinct. Noticeable. A swamp, that was it. The bathroom smelled like a swamp. So be it.

The bathroom looked worse than before, or else she hadn't noticed the soggy brown water stain in the panel of the ceiling over the shower stall. A half dozen gnats were camped out on the mirror, so she swatted them away before she stared at her road-weary face in the light's harsh fluorescent glow. Jesus—her hair was as dry as straw, pulled back into a single frizzy ponytail. The relaxer she'd gotten for her court date was long gone. Her face was spotted with acne from eating so much grease on the road. No wonder Fuller hadn't looked at her the way men usually did, sixty or not. Did she stink too? She sniffed her armpit: not terrible, but not great. She needed a shower.

The stall's grout was spiderwebbed with dark cracks and could use scrubbing, though it looked safe enough to go in barefoot until she could find some bleach. The faucet screamed when she turned it on, so unnaturally human that Kat's body tensed. It was such a perfect mimicry of Yvonne on the kitchen floor that she had to take two deep breaths to shake loose the memory. Rusty water pattered down in a weak stream, swirling brown down the drain, soon turning clear. The water was warm even if it never quite got hot, barely body temperature.

When Kat stepped into the stall and closed her eyes, the tepid water raining on her made her think of blood.

Kat rushed out to try to start Fuller's breakfast by seven, and she found him already outside fishing on the canal bank on the other side of the banyan tree—twenty yards behind the rumpus room. He tossed a bright orange lure on his fishing rod into the water. The canal was wide, more like a river, and he, like his neighbors, had a small aluminum fishing boat roped to a waterlogged wooden stake just beyond small stone steps. Kat walked through the overgrown grass overtaking his yard at the canal bank to reach him. Below, the green-brown water rippled, opaque. She made out a pale flash of a fish skimming beneath the surface.

"Thirty feet deep," he said, not looking at her. "Watch out if you don't swim. The lady next door—nice lady, eighty years old—slipped in and drowned trying to feed the damn ducks." He pointed out a mother duck with a neon-green head and a row of four downy yellow ducklings swimming in a row not far from his fishing line, their gentle wakes blending into one.

Fuller was wearing only an old Pink Floyd concert T-shirt and too-tight swimming trunks, practically a Speedo. His bare, hairy legs startled her, but she kept her eyes at a professional level, toward his face.

"What should I fix you for breakfast?"

He shrugged. "Whatever you can find. Grab some groceries later."

He gave her sixty dollars in cash, not fifty, when she asked for an advance after serving him scrambled eggs, pineapple chunks, and slightly overbrowned toast. She messed up the first batch of coffee she tried with his fancy espresso maker, but he didn't comment on the bitter smell in the house; instead, he complimented her on nailing the cream and sugar just the way he liked. He could probably tell how nervous she was, how much she didn't want to lose this new job. How much she *couldn't* lose it. She was full of nerves, half worried she would make him mad and half worried she would turn him on. She kept a careful distance from him, and she'd worn her most drab sweatshirt so he wouldn't get the wrong idea even by accident. His house, which was large for one person, still felt far too small for the two of them.

Fuller's living room TV was playing Fox News, so his attention was far from her as he answered her questions about where he kept his dish soap and what groceries she should buy him for dinner. After she washed the breakfast dishes by hand to impress him with her attention to detail, he told her to have a look around to get a feel for the house. He never took his eyes away from the lies on his TV, paying her no mind. If she'd pegged him for a Fox News type when they met, she would still be sleeping in the backseat of her car, her stomach rumbling. She would have to quit if he started talking trash about Black people, which Fox News always came around to. Had she fucked up her life so badly that she'd been flung back to 1950? Kat's fist slowly knotted around the three twenties from Fuller as she weighed whether this money might be her last. She'd cross that bridge later, she decided. She'd tell him she didn't want to hear any nonsense from him about race, and that would be that. With a plan, her fingers relaxed.

Fuller's house was over a couple thousand square feet, well-kept for a single guy without a housekeeper. She wondered if he'd been in the military like her ex, Lionel, who was in Germany instead of with her and Yvonne. The books on Fuller's built-in shelves were in perfect descending order of height, mostly biographies and guides for science geeks. Instead of leaving his bedsheets rumpled like she had, he'd tucked the corners tight and made up his massive king-sized bed after he got up. He even rolled up the toothpaste tube on his bathroom counter. For a panicked moment, she wondered how she would keep herself busy in a house that was already neater than anywhere she had lived. She was relieved to find spotted floors that needed mopping and high shelves lightly coated with dust.

She'd explored his bedroom, two bathrooms (neither of which smelled like a swamp), his library, a room that seemed solely for fishing gear and mounted fish, and even his garage before she realized there were no traces of Amber anywhere. Kat had steeled herself to open a door and find his dead little girl's bedroom frozen in time, full of stuffed animals and stolen joy, but she didn't see Amber even in a photo. Fuller didn't have any photographs on display, as if his life had never happened. But people grieved differently. Maybe he wanted to forget his old life, and how could she blame him? If Yvonne had died, she might not be able to stand her photos either. Even trying to imagine that pit of sorrow made a tear needle the corner of her eye.

"I like steaks," he said, handing her an ATM card. "Porterhouse is my go-to. If they don't have that, bring home some rib eyes. But ask the butcher, Manuel. Tell 'im it's for me. And a couple of packs of chicken wings. I like 'em fried."

"What else should go with it?"

Fuller only shrugged, his eyes back on the Fox News demons. "Surprise me."

"What's my spending limit at the store?"

He finally looked at her, eyes blank. A guy living in a

million-dollar house on the water didn't have a spending limit at the grocery store. He didn't use coupons and wait for sales. Kat tried to imagine having an ATM card she would be willing to give to someone she'd just met. Or going for a free-for-all grocery shopping trip with her own worthless card.

Fuller grinned at her. "Go hog wild at Safeway, sister."

With Fox News playing, she didn't like the sound of the word *sister*. It seemed to shade more toward the N-word, and her face burned with a combination of embarrassment and resentment. But she only smiled and said, "Sounds like a plan."

Kat spent almost three hundred dollars on groceries just because she could. Nearly a quarter of what she bought at Safeway was to stock up the rumpus room, including two bottles of her favorite Chardonnay, with a *cork* bottle, price be damned. It was the least she deserved if she had to listen to Fox News all day.

The work didn't take long, even when she was more meticulous about cleaning than she ever had been, sticking her nose close to stubborn spots to make sure they were truly gone. While she was slowly dusting the top built-in bookshelf in Fuller's wood-paneled bedroom, she chuckled to herself at how amused Mom or Lionel would be to see her Mary Poppins act.

"What's funny?" he said, startling her so much that she braced her palm against the wall to keep her balance. She glanced back at him. He looked so earnest with those odd gray eyes that she felt supervised for the first time.

"Me—doing this, that's all. I'm not a neat freak." Kat noticed a bright yellow child's hair clip on the far back of the shelf, behind an old plaque for Citizen Watch. She almost reached for it, but she didn't want to surprise Fuller with a glimpse of Amber, so she kept wiping as if she hadn't seen it. So he *did* have a few memories of his daughter in the house.

His presence simmered beside her, which she might have

mistaken for attraction when she was younger; but she'd learned to recognize it as wariness. Even so, she didn't like him standing behind her in his bedroom, probably staring at her ass.

"Come on down from there 'fore you hurt yourself. You don't strike me as the picture of grace." It sounded more like an order than a suggestion, so Kat stepped down once, twice, three times, until her feet were back on his shiny wood floor. She'd made it to solid ground before she realized he'd held out a genteel hand to help steady her. Lionel *never* would have done that. When she didn't take his hand, Fuller smoothed his hair back instead in a gesture that looked shy.

"Tomorrow morning at five thirty," he said, "you might learn you're great at fly-fishing."

"Oh no, I definitely won't."

"You will if you come fishing with me." Was he joking? He answered the question on her face: "Don't look at me like that. Get over yourself. It's just nice to teach someone." He didn't say it, but she guessed he'd fished with Amber too.

Still . . . nope. *Hell no*, actually. She stepped away from him, shaking her head. He shoved the hand he had offered her into his pocket as if to hide it from sight, stepping away too.

"Be ready to pan-fry some trout tomorrow, then," he said as he turned to leave the room.

"*That* I can do." After she looked up a few recipes on the Internet, anyway.

She cooked him a marbled porterhouse for dinner, a sizzling heap of dead flesh as black as the cast-iron skillet. He said he liked it well done, but it looked charred to her. She only ate a small portion because she liked her steak rare. Fox News came back on after the dishwasher was running and the counters were wiped down, so she hurried to do a quick survey of the house to make sure he would have nothing to complain about before she left for the day.

Upstairs, she met celestial, dying sunlight. His wraparound

bedroom blinds were open, overlooking the waterway and a tangle of palms and tropical trees. As she stood in his open bedroom doorway, she glanced downstairs to make sure he was still hypnotized by his TV. Then she slipped inside his bedroom's wash of golden light, almost like a portal in a science-fiction movie. She would claim she was there to move the little step-ladder she'd left behind. Instead, she carefully climbed the three steps to the highest bookshelf.

She wanted to see the hair clip again. If he asked her what she was doing, she would have no idea what to say. Was it because she missed Yvonne? Did she only want to touch something that had belonged to a child, that might still hold a strand of her hair, even if the child was dead?

But when she looked behind the plaque, the yellow hair clip was gone.

Two nail holes in perfect vertical alignment caught Kat's eye as she turned her key in the rumpus room's doorknob. The holes were at eye level, so obvious she wondered how she hadn't noticed them before. They had been painted over, but indentations in the yellow coat were visible in dim light. She ran her fingers across the holes; her daughter wasn't the only one with a powerful sense of touch. She swept her hand left from the frame to the door, and felt even more faint signs of matching holes just across the crack. And then two more three inches left again. She puzzled over this as she ran her finger back and forth, and her temples tightened as if someone had yanked a band around her head: a door latch. She could almost *see* it through her fingertips: the nails on the door supporting the panel for a bolt lock clear across to the doorframe.

But long gone. Painted over. She stood on the *Home Sweet Home* doormat to mull it over. She took a step away, surveying the door. Her conclusions weren't pretty, just like the image the aligned holes conjured: once upon a time, Fuller had locked this door from the *outside*. Silence enveloped the spot where she stood. No sounds came from leaping catfish in the nearby canal or hungry mosquitoes sniffing her blood.

Kat's heart thrummed. She slipped her hand into her pocket to feel the three neatly folded twenties again, enough gas money to get back on the road. She imagined alternate possibilities for the six mysterious holes, each one slowing her heart a bit more: Christmas wreath. Mezuzah. Some kind of posted sign. Woodpeckers. The holes didn't *have* to be from a lock.

Still, she stayed riveted because she pictured the lock best of all—a bolt pulled across from the outside, shutting in . . . who? Would a parent lock a child inside of the playroom? Was it to keep Amber from wandering to the canal, something any responsible parent might do? Or was it a hint of something she should be very worried about?

"Fuck, fuck, *fuck*."

She would have to ask him. She would have to bring him outside and show him the holes and ask him why they were there.

"And then he might fire you . . . or murder you."

Her whispered worst fear sounded ludicrous. Hilarious, even. Maybe the firing was more likely, but still not great motivation to question her new boss about painted-over holes— which, if she were honest with herself, might not be as perfectly aligned as she first thought, given the places obscured by paint. *Get out of your own goddamn way, Kat,* her mother always said. Was she trying to sabotage her job? Was this like Walmart all over again, where she'd clung to grievances her coworkers didn't notice until she convinced herself the money wasn't worth it? That she should just put up with Mom and live with her until she came up with a better plan for her and Yvonne?

And now look. If she'd kept that job, she might have been promoted by now. And she'd already have an apartment, or at least enough to share an apartment, instead of having to cook and clean for a stranger she wanted to trust but couldn't. Not quite. Maybe not at all.

But Kat let herself back into the rumpus room, latching the lock she suspected might once have been on the other side. She'd closed the bathroom door, but of course it was wide open again, so the smell was more unpleasant now, tickling her nostrils and down into her throat.

A swarm of two dozen gnats circled near the bathroom's jalousie windows, though they were locked tight with no clear holes. And the gnats were everywhere, it turned out, not just near the windows: In the shower stall. On the mirror. The gnats knew it too: the bathroom smelled more like a *bog*, a quiet rot carrying the promise of a feast for creatures who dined on death. Yet the bathroom's rot was active, more alive than dead, as if she might find a hidden heartbeat if she followed the trails of gnats.

But the gnats led nowhere. Maybe they were coming up from the shower drain. Maybe they smelled something in the toilet. Even after a day of cleaning, Kat couldn't rest until she went to work with her newly purchased bleach, scrubbing the shower tiles, the sink, the bathroom floor. Perspiration stung her eyes as she scrubbed in the muggy room. She hated the smell of bleach almost as much as the rot, but even inside the thick chemical scent, the boggy odor crept through. She plunged the toilet brush into the toilet water, irritated, trying to erase the scent at its origins. Where was it coming from?

The answer skittered into sight with a flash of yellow across the rear of the toilet's drain. She fished it out with her gloved hand: a child's hair clip. It was just like the one she'd seen on the bookshelf. Was it Amber's?

Kat was so startled that she dropped it. She pulled it out again and scrubbed it in the sink. The clip was shiny plastic and didn't look at all like it had been stuck in a toilet drain, with no signs of waste or wear. It was identical to the one in the house, a hair clip in the shape of an ice cream cone, pitted to look like a waffle cone. But how was it in the toilet? She had flushed that toilet three or four times since she'd arrived.

With the toilet brush, Kat probed the rear of the drain, poking to dislodge whatever else might be hidden. She felt a tug of resistance when she tried to pull the brush out. It wouldn't budge. What the . . . ?

She yanked, and the brush moved, trailing strings of hair clinging like a squid. Another yank and it came entirely free, the clumped hair limp, dripping across the floor, snakelike.

Kat's arm vibrated with the weight of the hair. The illusion of movement made her let out a strangled yell and drop the toilet brush to the floor. She jumped away from the tangled heap, her knees buckling from the memory of how the hair had *seemed* to move. But there it lay, regular hair after all. Set against the white tiles, the strands spread apart retained a golden hue, only darker where it clumped. Blond hair as silky and thin as a spider's web. (*Good hair*, Mom would say. She was forever praising Yvonne's hair, crediting Lionel's genes.)

The growing army of gnats wheeled above the damp hair on the floor.

Kat was so unnerved that she felt winded, so she leaned on the doorway's frame and laughed at herself. So a hair clip and some hair had come out of the toilet: big fucking deal. Except it *was* a big deal, and she couldn't laugh her way out of knowing it to her marrow. Her laughter was manic, not amused.

She closed the bathroom door, shutting the gnats inside.

Small things had never weighed so heavily on her: The holes outside of her door. The hair. Gnats. She didn't know what they added up to, though she knew she wouldn't be able to get to sleep if she didn't say something to Fuller while looking him straight in the eye.

Solar lights tracked Kat across the walkway, her shadow

marching alongside her, a glimpse of how she would look if she were taller than five three and bigger than a hundred and thirty pounds, closer to Fuller's height and weight. She knocked on Fuller's door without rehearsing. Anything she said aloud to herself would have sounded wrong, so she might as well sound wrong spontaneously. Her hand wound a fist around the hair clip.

Fuller was in shadow from the porch light when he opened his door.

"Can I come in and talk to you for a second? It's about the rumpus room."

"What about it? That's the deal. That's where you sleep."

"I know," she said. "But . . . we have to talk about something."

It was a bold opening, and she had no idea how to follow it up. And why had she just invited herself in instead of insisting that *he* come out? She should have rehearsed. She shouldn't have let her imagination run wild. He turned on his foyer light and made room for her to come in, but she stayed fixed in the doorway so he could not close the door behind her. His face was in full view now, down to the gray hairs in his razor stubble.

"You gonna let all the mosquitoes in?" For the first time, he sounded annoyed.

"I'm sorry. I just . . ." She hadn't planned to give him the hair clip, or even show it to him, but now it was her only reasonable play. Her hand trembled slightly as she displayed it to Fuller under his light.

He didn't hide his surprise. "Where'd you get that?"

"The rumpus room." She stopped short of admitting it had been in the toilet, and she thought better of bringing up the hair. She studied his eyes as he stared.

"That was Amber's," he said quietly. She expected him to reach for it, but he didn't. "Guess she must have dropped it playing out there. I built it for her, you know. That room."

"I figured." She waited for more of the story, though he didn't offer it. "Where's her mom?"

"You tell me," Fuller said, eyes narrowing. He moved closer suddenly, leaning over her to spit outside, over her shoulder. The sharp cinnamon of his chewing gum was in her face, intimate. She also noticed his height again. "Maybe Hollywood? That was the kind of bullshit she always talked about. Big surprise it didn't work out." So close to her ear, the anger in his voice felt more directed at her.

Kat's heart didn't start drumming until he pulled away again, as if she'd only realized in retrospect that he'd moved toward her so unexpectedly. She hadn't even noticed that he was chewing gum. She took a small step back, her heartbeat shaking her ribs.

"So . . ." Was she actually going to ask? "Did that room used to lock from the outside?"

He moved quickly again, this time to lean closer to peer into her eyes, the way she'd won his full attention when she confessed the worst thing she had ever done. "Why?"

"I saw some holes in the wood. They line up like a lock."

"Door's old. Sure. Used to be a shed with a padlock."

"Oh!" She faked a smile, as if backyard sheds and home improvement were her hobby. "So you added the bathroom?"

"Built most of that bathroom myself."

Of course he had. *What did you build it out of, compost and human hair?* But Kat kept that question to herself. Fuller's eyes waited, patient. He still hadn't touched the hair clip; he noticed her noticing.

"Where'd you find that, by the way?" he said. "Exactly?"

Kat hadn't planned to lie, but she did: "Under the bed."

"Oh." He sighed in a shuddery wave, perhaps imagining Amber in the bed Kat was sleeping in now. "Yeah, must've missed it when I cleaned up." His gray eyes misted. "It's hard for me to look at, you know? Would you mind . . . ?" He waved it away from his sight.

Kat slipped the hair clip into her pocket. She wanted to ask about the other one she'd seen in his bedroom—high on a shelf, seemingly hidden—but she couldn't think of a way to make it her business. "I'm sorry to ask, but can I see her picture one more time? Since I found this . . . I just . . . I want to see her better. Does that make sense?"

It *didn't* make sense, not even to her. But Fuller nodded, although he didn't move at first. She watched him thinking it over. Then he sighed and walked away, toward the stairs. She'd expected him to complain or demand a better explanation for prying into his greatest tragedy. The instant he was gone, she wished she could take back her request. What was the point? The longer he was gone, the worse she felt. And the more she wondered if he would come back at all. Or what he was doing out of her sight.

Fuller came back downstairs holding the wallet up high like a prize, his gaze cutting: *You happy now?* He tapped on the banister to keep steady as he swayed down the steps.

He gave her his worn folded leather wallet, and she held the photo close to her face, the way she had stared at the stains on his floor. Even a longer look couldn't make the photo much more coherent because of the bright shroud of backlight, reducing their faces to a duel between radiance and shadow. She barely recognized Fuller in the glare because he had a sparse beard in the photo, and he was so much thinner now. The tattooed tip of a large wing peeked out of his open shirt, probably an eagle like Lionel would get.

She could see a bit more of Amber. Half a smile. An elbow jutting out from her hip with attitude. And long strands of blond hair listing across her shoulders, clamped at the end by a yellow clip. Her hair was the point, Kat realized. She'd wanted to see if it was the same hair . . . *and it was*. The memory of the clump of hair slithered across her arm, leaving goose bumps. The yellow hair clip felt like it was glowing warm in her back pocket.

Kat snapped the wallet shut and handed it back to Fuller. He was looking at the floor, arms folded. "You done?" He sounded more like the tired old man she had painted for Mom.

"Yeah, thanks. Sorry if I upset you."

And, damn it to hell, she actually *was* sorry. Kat felt like a paranoid asshole as she walked back toward the rumpus room and heard Fuller's door close behind her with slightly pointed force—but unease still jittered across her pores. She hesitated when she came face-to-face with the holes on the rumpus room's doorframe again. A breeze whispering through the banyan tree's leaves made her glance toward the canal.

The glow from the neighbor's deck lamp was so strong that she saw the green-headed mama duck skimming across the water in the halo of light. But she was alone. Kat waited to see if the ducklings would come. If the ducklings were gone, that was a bad omen for sure.

Two of the ducklings finally followed, paddling furiously to catch up to their mother.

Thankfully, the bathroom door was still closed.

When she opened it, the air inside was so damp that it breathed rankness across her face, making her blink to clear her eyes. And the linoleum floor was bare. The hair was gone.

Kat might have lost her shit entirely if she hadn't heard so many stories from her grandfather when she was young. Grandpa had grown up in North Florida, in a place called Gracetown, and he'd warned Kat that Gracetown blood ran through her veins, so she could expect unusual events in her life. Kat had taken him at his word, waiting twenty years for dreams that felt like premonitions, or the ability to know other people's thoughts, or conversations with ghosts—but so far, all she had was Amber's missing hair.

And the hair wasn't even missing, it turned out. She followed the hum of the gnats and realized the clump of damp hair was now in the corner behind the door, bunched up. But it was the same hair: it had left a trail of water on the floor.

Kat let out a yell when her phone buzzed in her pocket opposite the hair clip. She closed the bathroom door and leaned against it, not letting herself fully grasp that she was bracing the door so the hair would not get out.

MOM, the caller ID said.

"Yvonne?" Kat said. Often, Mom put Yvonne on the line without speaking first.

But Mom's voice came this time, heavy with disappointment: "It's me, Katrina."

Mom's most common trigger was to call her by the hurricane's name instead of the nickname she preferred, but Kat had bigger problems tonight. "Mom, did Grandpa ever—"

"I wanted you to hear it from me," Mom interrupted, her voice as rote as a recording. "I've decided to petition for permanent custody of Yvonne."

Kat's ears were plugged by a sound like a test pattern squalling inside her head, the first time she had ever felt any of her senses shut down by a surge of emotion. When her ears popped to allow sound in again, Mom was still talking.

". . . not doing this to hurt you. That's the main thing I want you to know. I'm doing this because we both know it's best for Yvonne."

Kat had stopped leaning against the closed door, pacing while she tried to avoid saying anything that might incite her mother. She pinned her lips together so tightly that they hurt.

"You've got nothin' to say?"

Kat's verbal dam broke. "You're not doing this to hurt me? Since when, Mom? You know this would hurt me more than anything in the world. Didn't you hurt me enough? The belt wasn't enough?"

"But I never broke any bones, did I?" she said. "Only one of us can say that."

"Is that why you can't believe it was an accident? You think I'm like you—that I *like* hurting people. You had your chance to be a mom, and you're really bad at it."

"That's funny coming from you. Pot, meet kettle."

If her mother had been standing in the room with her, Kat might have hit her with a pot or a kettle, or both at once. God help her, maybe the rage Mom had planted was too close to the surface sometimes, yet how many times had Mom criticized Kat for "coddling" Yvonne instead of using a belt when she talked back?

Yes, she had messed up—that one time. She'd been mad when she tried to grab Yvonne's arm and she'd tugged so hard that she had thrown herself off-balance. She never would have slipped if not for the water on the floor, so it wasn't a lie to call it an accident. But if she hadn't been irritated, if she hadn't made an explosive movement, it would not have happened.

It was her fault. And Mom knew it.

"Just so you understand?" Kat said, breathing out her rage at both herself and her mother. "Trying to take someone's child away after one mistake—your own daughter's child—is not a normal thing to do. You know who does that? A psychopath does that. I will *never* let her grow up with you."

"If I was so bad, why'd you move back in? Why'd you bring her into my house, Kat?"

The sudden gentleness in Mom's voice, so sincere rather than triumphant as she poked at the ugly truth, scorched Kat's insides. Her mother's last jab laid bare the essence of this betrayal: *You're my mother, that's why. You were all I had.*

"I didn't know the real you until now, Mom."

"Guess I can say the same thing."

Kat ended the call before her mother could hear her wail. On her knees. On the floor. Exactly where Mom wanted her. Or exactly where she belonged. Either her mother was a monster—or she was. Or neither. Or both.

Kat hardly recognized the world enough anymore to judge.

She cried her throat raw, curled on the rumpus room's cold floor. She was lying there when she saw a shadow move from the crack underneath the bathroom door, from one side of the room to the other, toward the shower. The rapid motion made her gasp and sit upright.

Whatever had moved was too big to be the clump of hair, so Kat wasn't surprised to find it where it had been before, still scrunched behind the door. The cloud of gnats circling it had grown to a swarm of thirty or forty, unbothered by Kat's intrusion. But the hair was only hair.

Kat felt an urgent need to touch the hair clip, so she pulled it from her pocket and ran her finger across the dimpled cone. Yes, Yvonne was like her in that way: sometimes she needed to touch or be touched to understand a lesson. Maybe that was what Grandpa had meant about her inheritance. Kat squeezed the hair clip, and her own voice whispered in her ear: *Was it really Bob Fuller in that picture?*

The thought was a blow, knocking her back on her heels. Fuller had looked more different than similar in the photo— she'd only believed it was him because he'd claimed it was, so she'd excused the mismatches, more interested in studying Amber. Did he even have a chest tattoo? She tried to remember seeing him bare-chested, but she didn't think he had. She couldn't compare height, and under that beard the man in the photo might have a very different facial structure. Their body types didn't match at all. Why hadn't she let herself see it?

"What if it isn't him?" she whispered. "What if he stole that picture from you? What if your name isn't even Amber?"

The toilet gurgled.

Kat had already decided she wouldn't spend another night in this rumpus room, and the bathroom was the first place she wanted to leave behind. But her neck moved of its own accord, turning to face the toilet with its lid beckoning, open wide. A few flies buzzed out, joining the horde of gnats.

A thick gray-brown snake was floating in the toilet water, coiled around the drain, a sight so shocking that she sucked in a long breath before she realized it *wasn't* a snake, it was a rope—the braids fraying at the end. Still not good, but at least it might not leap out at her. She breathed motion back into her muscles and took a step closer to the toilet, peering from directly above, almost daring the rope to move.

Fraying strands waved in the water, though it seemed like an ordinary rope—except that nothing was ordinary about a rope crawling through her plumbing when it would have clogged every flush. The rope had not always been there. Maybe, like the hair clip in Fuller's bedroom, it would disappear if she turned her back.

"Why is this here?" she whispered to herself, or probably to Amber.

The rope's thickness seemed familiar, and it took her an instant to remember why: this looked identical to the water-logged rope tying Fuller's rowboat to the wooden stake beside his steps to the canal.

Every instinct screamed at Kat to leave the bathroom, but through the semi-transparent shower door, she glimpsed a large dark spot in the corner of the stall that did not belong. Whatever it was had not been there while she was cleaning. More hair? Frigid dread held her in place for another few breaths before she slid open the shower's door.

The stall still stank of bleach, but in the corner under the faucet a fungus was growing out of a dark crack at the tile's base, as bold as if it had been there all along. *But it hadn't been.* The fungus was at least eight inches tall, the color of caramel, with several thin branches fanned across the shower tiles from the trunk poking out of the hole.

It was impossible. Explanations for the other things she'd seen—including the hair that seemed to have moved—were improbable. But a fungus that grew to that size in only a few minutes could not have happened. Yet, here it was preening for her. Her feet tingled with the memory of standing in the shower stall with naked toes, only inches from this impossible fungus. (At least she *thought* it was a fungus, but how the hell would she know?)

"Son of a bitch," Kat whispered. She wished Grandpa were still alive so she could consult with him on the meaning of such a thing. Kat raked through her memories and landed on his lesson on the difference between a "haint" and an "Abomination," the latter being his word for pure Evil. He'd said she would know if she ever stumbled across a true Abomination because it would turn her hair white and make her bones ache. It would want to hurt her with single-minded purpose, and only incantations and offerings could tear it away from her. Her very soul would tremble, et cetera. (Grandpa had been most prone to talking about haints and Abominations when he'd had a drink, and when he'd been drinking he talked a *lot*. And he went wild with his hickory switch, Mom said, so at least Kat knew where Mom had gotten that tendency from.)

Despite the bathroom's rotten smell, Kat didn't think whatever was nesting here was trying to hurt her. Something was choosing her, that was all. Something wanted to be seen. Grandpa had told her that most haints, unlike Abominations, only craved to be a part of living memory. *Like the way a barking dog only wants you to look out the window too*, he'd said.

Kat took a closer look at the fungus. It looked like a hand. The "thumb" was stubby and short, but the shape hugging the wall looked far too much like a child's hand. Amber's hand? Or was she just seeing what she believed might make sense of it? A hand? A tree? The fungus never moved, though its form was an ever-changing Rorschach to her eyes.

A fat droplet of brown water fell from the showerhead, splattering a mess on the white tile. Then another. Then the faucet screamed and opened up a spray of water with a tinge of green gleaming in the brown—like the canal water. The tepid water soaked her hair, dousing her with the bog smell. Yelling curses, Kat slammed the shower door shut and rushed to scrub her hair with her bath towel. Gnats buzzed around her ears, flitting against her face. Diving into her nose's deep, tender parts. She rubbed her nostrils with both fists to stop their crawling.

What if it *was* an Abomination?

Kat's limbs wobbled from panic as she closed the bathroom door and raced to grab her duffel bag, throwing in the few clothes she'd taken out. She left the two bottles of expensive Chardonnay on the counter, still corked. She might have forgotten a pair of shoes, but she was in such a hurry that she didn't check before she scooped up her handbag and fled the rumpus room.

Outside, she was breathing in gasps as she ran to her car, which was parked alongside Fuller's pickup truck in the wide gravel driveway. She tried to walk lightly across the crushed stones, but the motion lights betrayed her, snapping on with each few steps. *Shit.* She looked up at Fuller's bedroom picture windows, where she could see the light was still on beyond the closed shutters. The shutters didn't move, so she hurried the rest of the way to her car, which was parked closest to the rumpus room.

As soon she was sitting in her old Accord with the soothing *click* of her electronic locks, her panic ebbed. Her fingers were still shaky as she rooted in her handbag for her car keys, praying for them, really, and they answered with their familiar music.

She slid the key into her ignition, but she didn't turn it. Not yet. She didn't want to make a sound. The less panicky she was, without gnats in her nose, the more this felt like she was reliving her last argument with Mom, racing out to her car with her life stuffed in a duffel bag. Running away. As much as she wanted to get away from Bob Fuller and whatever he had birthed in his rumpus room, the sense of unfinished business held her rooted. Her breathing was already fogging her windows, but she saw his upstairs light go off, his house now in darkness. Maybe he was going to bed, so she might not have to worry about him confronting her.

The rumpus room was pale and glowering in the darkness. Kat sat for long minutes waiting to see if the door might open on its own the way the bathroom door had. The hot air inside the car felt charged with anticipation of a dramatic event, though nothing so grand helped guide her. The rhythm of the breeze or the rising and falling chorus of crickets might be trying to tell her something, but what?

The night's excitement had made her abnormally tired, and she hated driving when she was tired. Sixty dollars wouldn't get her gas and a motel room, even a cheap one. Her Accord was twenty years old and the chassis trembled above sixty miles per hour, but the spacious backseat was a decent bed, still lined with her thick pallet of blankets.

"Fuck it," Kat whispered.

Doors still locked, key in her hand, she maneuvered into her backseat to try to go to sleep, curled with her knees to her chest. Her mind rocked from the strange things she had seen, and her questions as she contemplated the photograph that might or might not be Bob Fuller. And a girl who might or might not be named Amber. The only thing she felt for certain was that something had happened to a girl in that rumpus room, probably in that bathroom.

The ghostly clues from the haint, if that's what she was, would not be enough. Where could she find out more about her? She could check a database of missing children in the area for the past few years—maybe there had been an Amber Alert.

Amber Alert.

Amber. Fucking. Alert.

Fuckity fuck fuck. Kat's adrenaline surged, chattering her teeth. Had Fuller chosen that name and shown Kat the photo of a man who looked nothing like him as a sick game, toying with her until he decided to kill her? She'd been so stupid to knock on his door. So stupid to still be here. Every new thought made her more certain that she should drive away.

But it felt too much like leaving another child behind.

The crickets' swell grew louder, and throaty rumbles from bull-frogs rattled the car windows. Kat woke up confused about why she was outside. Her blankets, and the mound of fast food wrappers and empty beer cans on the floor, helped her remember she was in her car again.

And a man was reclined in the front passenger seat.

The seat was angled directly in front of her, with only a foot separating the man's statue-like, shadowed profile from her shocked open mouth. Kat patted the blankets for her keys, her only weapon, and could not find them. Panic swamped her until she noticed the sharp jut of the man's chin, and skin that wasn't just made dark from the night.

It wasn't Fuller. The man sitting in her front seat was Grandpa.

This is a dream, she told herself, until it was obvious. No frog was loud enough to shake a car: that should have been the first clue. And she was wearing footie pajamas from childhood, not the sweatshirt she'd had on when she fell asleep.

Yet, everything about Grandpa looked so real: white hair shaved close to his scalp, his cauliflower battered earlobe, the thin white beard powdering his face. In her dream, Kat could see in the dark, true to her feline namesake, down to the patterns of wrinkles in his blue shirt from the Gracetown Mill where he'd worked. She hadn't dreamed about him since she was thirteen, the night he died. (Now that she thought about it, he'd told her he was dead in her dream before she woke up to learn the news.)

I conjured him, she realized. She had asked for his help—probably for the first time—and he had come. How many other times might he have come to her with answers if she had asked him? In her dream, the rumpus room felt a world away. What mattered more was that she finally had the chance to talk to her grandfather.

"Grandpa," she whispered, but he did not turn to look at her. She didn't want to tug any harder at the dream, so she satisfied herself talking to his unblinking profile. "Why did you hurt Mom so much? Didn't you see she was bleeding from that switch? You hurt her. And she hurt me. And I hurt Yvonne." Speaking the truth came more easily in her dreamworld too.

Grandpa seemed to grow taller, but he was only inhaling for a long sigh, weary and heartsick. "My papa punched me in my ear so hard I lost my hearing," he said. She'd known Grandpa had hearing in only one ear, though she'd never known why. "His daddy got lynched for mouthing off at a white man and Papa wanted to make damn sure I knew my place. I didn't know how to be different, pumpkin."

In the waking world, she would have expected an apology, but hearing him call her *pumpkin* soothed part of that ache. And now he was here to help her learn.

"I think a gator killed that girl, Grandpa." She was talking about Bob Fuller, but somehow her words came out wrong in dream language. "Maybe drowned her in the toilet."

"Unnnh-hnnh," Grandpa said in quiet affirmation. He was smoking his pipe now, the smell of his tobacco filling the car. But his pipe didn't bother her, for once. "They run faster'n people think they do. Gotta always keep your eye on a gator, on land or in the water."

He had given her this same advice when she was a child Amber's age. Maybe a dream was mostly remembering and part wishing. But this dream, like the one she'd had when she was thirteen, felt more like a visit.

"What happened to her? Where is she?" Kat asked.

It seemed for a while that he might not answer. He exhaled a cloud of pipe smoke so thick that it obscured his profile. "You were s'posed to touch the rope," Grandpa said. "You had to touch it to see. That's why she sent it to you."

"Who?"

Grandpa pointed toward the windshield.

The haze parted long enough for her to see a young girl standing at the bank of the canal, beneath the sprawling branches of the banyan tree. She was only a silhouette in the dark, but it was Amber! Kat gasped, yet the surprise was coming from her waking self, not her dreaming self, and the cloud draped everything in white. She couldn't even see Grandpa anymore.

But she heard his voice, crisp and loud and somehow real in her ear: "*Eyes open, Kat.*"

She woke up in time to see Bob Fuller quietly close his front door and check the lock before he walked down his porch steps with a fishing pole. It was still night but closer to dawn, the sky turning gray. She watched through her window propped on her elbows until his motion light clicked on, illuminating her. She dipped low to stay out of his sight as he walked toward his pickup truck. She heard him toss his fishing pole into the other side of the truck's bed.

Her heartbeat rained stones across her head and chest as his footsteps fell on his gravel driveway, closer and closer to the truck's door, three steps, four steps, five. She was parked so close to him, barely a nose or two short of his truck, that if he peeked over his shoulder he might see her. She couldn't risk rattling her beer cans to climb down to the floor, so froze where she was and counted on luck. Seven steps. Eight.

Shouldn't he have reached his door by now?

But his footsteps were moving *away* from his truck. She ventured a peek between the front headrests. He was well lighted as he walked toward the rumpus room, and she took in details about him between ferocious thumps of her heart. He was shirtless, only wearing cargo shorts, holding his key ring ready. His back was to her as he walked toward her front door—the door that had once locked from the outside—so she could not see if he had a tattoo of any kind on his chest. But his back was bare and wiry and looked nothing like the photo once more.

And he had something strapped to his shorts. A holster? No, a sheath for a large knife—a hunting knife. The handle's wooden finish shined. (*We're not all gunslingers down here, sister.*)

Why was he going to her room? Fresh from her dream, she *knew* he was the gator who wanted to eat her, but she tried to tell herself he only wanted to invite her to come fishing again. This seemed less likely the longer he stood in front of her front door in deep contemplation. He swung his hand holding the keys slowly to and fro, though he must've had his fingers clutched around them, because the keys were silent.

Jesus, he was thinking about it. He was considering whether or not he should kill her.

Kat tried to slow her frightened breathing so the fog wouldn't tell him she was in the car. She inhaled for a count of four, held it for four, exhaled a long, slow count of eight, the way she'd learned in her court-ordered anger-management sessions. She did the exercise twice while Fuller did not move, staring at her door like a freak. Her heart stopped punishing her in its fright, its blows less painful. She reminded herself of her advantages: she was in her car, her doors locked. She could move quickly to the front seat and start her engine.

But you didn't test it. What if it won't start?

The horrid thought shattered Kat's false serenity just as Fuller turned around, and she hoped the headrest disguised her as she pressed her head against it for cover. Like Yvonne, she closed her eyes as if she could make him not see her, until she forced them open for a peek: his chest was passing her windshield, in perfect view with a triangle of hair between his nipples.

No tattoo like a wing. No tattoo of any kind.

Now his keys jingled loudly, almost literally in her ear. He climbed on the running board to the pickup's door, and the large wooden knife handle was displayed in her window. Kat kept still and silent by promising herself that she could outrun him if she had to, consoling herself that at least it wasn't a gun. She counted her breaths until he opened his truck's door, and counted them again as his engine came to life, loud as a dragon, and the pickup started rolling out of the driveway. He was looking up at his rearview mirror instead of to his left, or he would have seen her as clearly as she could see him. She watched him roll past her window, not blinking, memorizing his sharp-featured profile to the tip of his nose.

She had gone home with this man.

She had lived in his torture room.

She had run away from Yvonne.

Tears of self-reproach drowned Kat. She was still trembling from anguish and her brush with Fuller when she finally climbed out of the car. Her engine went on fine, she'd learned, so she left it running with the door open as she walked to the canal bank to stand approximately where she had seen Amber in her dream.

The fledgling daylight was mostly gray, but more pinkish bands were emerging, a glimpse of a new morning. The neighbor's solar lamp illuminated the gently rippling waters below, where Fuller's rowboat bobbed. Kat switched on her phone's flashlight for a better look at the rope, which was the same thickness and color as the one floating in the rumpus room's toilet.

You were s'posed to touch the rope, Grandpa had said. But hell no, she would not go back to the rumpus room. The buzzing was so loud from the rear bathroom window that the room must be thick with gnats and flies. The ornery insects bumped against the thin jalousie panes so loudly that she heard pinging and slapping across the glass even from twenty paces. The insects sounded bigger too.

Kat steadied herself with the wooden railing as she climbed down the stone steps toward the aluminum rowboat, which was conspicuously empty. No clues there. But a two-lane bridge beside Fuller's property created a dark nook at the edge of his yard, with a coral ledge wide enough to walk on. She shined her flashlight there and noticed another identical rope tied to a stake pounded into the coral wall, barely visible above the waterline. If the canal water was sometimes higher and sometimes lower, the rope would not always be visible. She was looking at just the right time, maybe. Like Amber wanted her to.

Kat moved gingerly from the steps to the ledge, inching into the darkness. The hair clip still in her back pocket was burning so much that her ass itched (a sign, she supposed, albeit an annoying one), so she kept up her cautious progress despite pebbles scraping beneath her shoes and her fear of falling into the water. She could swim, but not very well.

When she was close enough to the mysterious, slimy rope, she pulled on it—and it only gave slightly. Something heavy was tied to it below. Shining her phone's flashlight into the murky water did no good.

Kat wiped sweat from her eyes with her forearm and checked her phone: 5:48 a.m. Mom would kill her for calling this early, but she pressed *1* in speed dial. Her mother's phone rang.

"Kat?" Mom sounded alarmed. "What is it?"

"I'm alright. Sorry to call so early. I . . ." Where should she even begin?

Mom's concern vanished. "Do you ever look at a clock?"

"Mom, I'm sorry. I'm sorry I ran off. I'm sorry I scared you and Yvonne. I'm sorry I hurt her. I'm sorry about everything."

"It takes more than *sorry* to raise a kid, Katrina. Are you drunk?"

"No. I've stopped drinking." True, she'd just bought two bottles of wine, but she hadn't thought about opening them. "Not for long—but I'll get in a program. I'll get therapy. I'll get another job closer to home. You won't have to take my word for it—you'll see it."

Mom didn't believe her. Her silence made this plain.

"Just please give me one month. Thirty days. Please don't file with the judge."

"I knew saying that would get your attention," Mom said.

"You did, and I completely understand. I didn't give you any choice. I'll do better."

Mom sighed into the phone. "I sure hope so, Kat . . . I . . ." The pause was so long that Kat wondered if she'd been cut off. "I wish I'd done better too."

Kat wanted to tell her about her visit with Grandpa, what he'd revealed about their family curse, but she would save that for later. "I'll drive all day so I can get there. Can I see Yvonne?"

"Of course you can. As long as it's before nine."

Jacksonville was only about a six-hour drive, so she might be able to make it long before dinnertime, if she didn't stop. She might have enough for gas. Nothing would keep her from getting home to her daughter. Nothing—not even her own Abomination—could scare her away.

Kat hadn't realized that she'd nestled her phone between her ear and shoulder so she could grip the rope two-handed. It was heavy and slippery, but not impossibly so. She was slowly raising whatever the rope held, still hidden in the murky pool below.

"I have to go, Mom," Kat whispered, near tears again at the grimness of her task.

"Stop calling me at all hours, hear? I still say you're drunk—"

Kat barely noticed her phone slip loose and clatter to the ledge behind her. She discovered that if she braced her feet against the coral wall, she gained more strength for her pulling, one hand over the other, slowly bringing up whatever Fuller had weighted down in his backyard canal, hidden in plain sight. Another private game.

Through the salty perspiration stinging her eyes, Kat saw the green head of the mama duck swimming just beyond Fuller's boat, webbed feet flurrying to propel her sure motion. Kat took a gasp of air and bunched up the rope to lift it higher, hand over hand. Her palms were scraped raw as she held tight to the waterlogged rope, and something tied to it bumped against the bank beneath her. But she was pulling it out. It was working. Kat gritted her teeth and heaved again. She watched the duck so she would not think about what she might find at the other end, so she would not lose her nerve, so she would not scream from the pain of her burden.

The mama duck swam on, unbothered.

Her ducklings were nowhere in sight.

Migration

Jazmine woke beside her fiancé, Cal, and nearly vomited from his smell. The nausea began with the scents she knew—garlic from the prawns he'd sautéed for dinner, salty-sour underarm musk, oil from his hair follicles. She tried turning away from him in her bed, but she couldn't escape the newer smells, the ones she couldn't name.

Was she pregnant? That thought made her sit up and gasp aloud, but she talked down her panic. She'd been on the patch since college, and it would not have failed her. Besides, the sickness was unlike anything as trite as a pregnancy; it was *deeper*, to her bones. He smelled like . . . boredom. Like gullibility. Like his heart yawned open so wide with sweet, sticky goo that she might drown in his stench.

When they had gone to bed, laughing over jokes she could no longer remember, she was sure she loved him. In a month, she was going to marry this man. *Marry* him! Her stomach flipped, so she cradled her abdomen and pressed her palm to her lips. Something fractured in her—as if she could see herself on a distant shoreline, holding Cal's hand, but she herself was a ship pulling away, gaining speed, trying to outrun a storm.

Whatever she had felt a few hours before, she loathed him now. Her loathing frightened her. Jaz jumped out of bed, not being careful—in fact, *trying* to shake him—though of course he slept on. She gazed at him in the moonlight—his tufts of tight curls, overly sculpted jawline, small signs of flab beneath his chin—and found her fingers wrapped around the base of the brass table lamp. She saw herself lift the lamp high, arm trembling as she tested its weight. Wondered and thrilled at her own shadow against the wall; she was a bad special effect in an old-school monster flick that might have been called *Rise of Gargantua: Spider-Woman from the Deep*.

The shadow looked so right, like seeing her true reflection for the first time. She reveled in herself—the lamp a misshapen extension of her arm, her braids like Medusa's crawling on the wall; she, a grand snapshot of poised violence. Jaz had never felt such delight—could not think of a moment that was even a close second, unless it was escaping Mama and Gracetown in Florida. But her head had not surged with such dizziness then. She hadn't been so giddy she was pissing herself. (Yes, warm moisture dribbled down her bare legs, between her toes.)

Go on and fucking do it already, said a voice in her head.

That voice was supposed to be dead. Expelled.

"Shit," Jaz said, remembering herself. She looked away from her shadow.

And saw that Cal was awake; wide awake, in fact. He was sitting up straight, staring.

"Jaz?" he said. "What are you doing?"

No anger. No judgment. He cocked his head with a spaniel's curiosity. Even concern.

"I need you to get out of here, Cal," she said, "or I'm going to hurt you."

He sat frozen a moment, perhaps believing he was dreaming her. Then he raised his hand and snapped his fingers, loudly. "Jaz? *Jazmine*. Wake up. Snap out of it."

She'd had one sleepwalking incident on Ambien—just one—and now it was his easy answer for everything. All she'd done then was brush her teeth until the bathroom sink overflowed.

He snapped his fingers again like she was a trained dog.

"I'm awake," she said, and smothered a giggle. "Yes, I'm

awake, Cal. Perfectly, wonderfully awake. And I'm going to say this only one more time: You need to get out of here. Or I'm going to hurt you."

He stared, uncomprehending.

She juked the lamp as if to throw it, and that was enough to bring Cal to his feet, sleep wiped from his face. "What the *hell*, Jaz—"

"I'm sick of all of you, Cal—every inch of you. You bore the shit out of me. When you touch me, I shrivel to dust. I can't breathe the stink of you another minute." She had never been so honest with him, or even with herself.

"Where is this coming from?" Still oh-so-calm, as if they should just talk it out. "Boo?"

The *boo* did it, his faux vernacular, like *That's so dope*, which he said to no one but her, as if he hadn't spent his teenage years at a lily-white prep school and done his undergrad in biology at Stanford—trying to find a common language with his scrappy country girl from the Florida bog.

Her loathing turned to a scream, and she hurled the lamp.

The lamp flew. The cord tugged and slowed it before it yanked free, lucky for Cal, though it still sailed with enough force to glance his shoulder and send him back two steps. His feeble little cry was more surprise than pain, but oh! Exquisite. Here was a man who had told her he'd never been in a fight in his golden prep-school world, never been attacked except for polite sparring in martial arts classes. *She* was the first to hurt him, the person he least expected. Even in the room's semidarkness, she savored the ugliness of his lips turned down, his eyes comically wide (*Whatchu doin', Miz Jaz?*), rubbing his sore shoulder as he stepped away.

Dear Lord, was he going to cry? Would he fuck her one last time, through those tears?

"Get your bougie ass out of my house," she said. "Before I claw your eyes out."

He snatched on his dress shirt, climbed into his jeans he'd left on the floor—because his clothes were always, *always* on her floor—and grabbed his phone and keys from the dresser. She could hear his thoughts whirring, trying to figure out where his beloved had gone.

"Jaz, I'm gonna call someone—"

"*That's not my name!*" she bellowed. It wasn't her voice either. The windowpane shook.

The man whose stench swirled like smoke was so startled that he dropped his keys, though he scooped them up again as he took another step toward the open doorway, his wide eyes on her. He backed away, crooning sweet assurances about getting help for her, telling her to stay where she was. When she crouched like a cat and snarled, he slipped out and closed the door. His terrified heartbeat thrummed everywhere, a gentle rain shower over her.

She wanted to touch herself to the sound of his fear and the memory of his cry.

But no time.

He would not go long. He would come back. He was already dialing his phone.

She looked down at her naked flesh. Wouldn't do. She followed the man's example and found clothes to wear, slipped her feet into shoes, the expected rituals.

Then she climbed out the window. The rest of the night, she never fully remembered.

The next thing Jaz knew, she was waking on a dark beach, the pink dawn a ribbon across the sky. Her body was stiff from sleeping on packed sand and stones. Her damp skin and clothes were ice in the morning chill, so she lay in a fetal position with chattering teeth while seagulls fanned out only feet from her on their morning scavenge, ignoring her like driftwood. One seagull wailed loudly, as if to say, *Why?*

Jaz wept, hard. Maybe like never before. She wept until her stomach locked in place, until her shrieking drove the seagulls away. The ocean's morning surf roared back at her, spitting frigid seawater in her face. In Florida, the gulf waters an hour from Gracetown only got cold in the winter. Even the beaches here weren't right.

Weary from weeping as daylight spilled across the cliffs behind her, Jaz sat up and tried to piece together the night. She remembered Cal and the lamp—most of the reason she'd wept. She loved him with new fervor in daylight, but what was next for them? *Yeah, sorry about last night, but I'm cool now.* And Cal wasn't the worst of what had happened last night.

Her memory glimpsed a nightclub, a throbbing dance floor. An alleyway. She heard an echo of a man's strangled scream. Instinct made her look at her disheveled blouse, and she couldn't mistake the faint bloodstain, maybe a handprint, despite whatever effort she'd made to wash the blood away in the surf. She must have gone to the ocean by some instinct, or she wouldn't be so damp. Some part of her had remembered her old lessons about the oceans and cleansing. All she knew was that the blood wasn't hers, because she felt fine.

Better than fine. Except for the thing with Cal and maybe mild hypothermia, she felt fucking amazing.

The low growl behind Jaz startled her, and she was on her feet in a crouch in a blink. A dirty-yellow stray mutt, a shaggy lab mix, had crept within five yards of her, lips quivering as it snarled. The dog was trying to decide its play: attack or flee? It wanted to taste her blood as much as she'd wanted to wash herself in Cal's.

Jaz flexed her fingers, holding her crouch, her head angling, loose. She was not afraid; she was sure the dog could smell death on her.

"Come on, then," she whispered. "Bring it."

The dog cast its eyes down, stepped back once. Twice. With a bark, it turned and ran.

Jaz almost chased it. Almost. Just to see if she could catch it. Then the mood passed and she sagged back down to hug herself.

"It didn't work," she said to the surf and spray. "Goddamn you, Nana—it didn't work."

Since she had just cussed out her dead grandmother, Jaz cried some more.

No one had called it an exorcism. Nana wasn't Catholic, anyway; she'd held no Vatican training, had read from no holy book as she stood over Jaz that night when she was eight. Nana could barely read beyond a sixth-grade level because, well, fuck Jim Crow schools. Back then, you could only go as far in school as your teacher, and Nana's teacher, only a teenager herself, hadn't gone far. Over the years, Jaz had come to believe her grandmother's root work had been as shoddy as her public school education, because whatever she'd done with her prayers and scents and tea hadn't held up.

It happened like this: One day Jaz was feeling fine, her usual eight-year-old self, then she woke up in the middle of the night and poured lighter fluid all over the kitchen floor, trying to set her house on fire while her parents slept. If her father hadn't gotten up to get a midnight piece of lemon pound cake and Jaz had been quicker to figure out the childproof lighter, the Garey household would have been a torch in the night.

But that wasn't the end of it. When Dad had confronted her with *WHAT THE HELL ARE YOU DOING?* Jaz had screamed loudly enough to make him cover his ears, and she'd run at him with a meat cleaver. She'd come within an inch of chopping off his finger on the counter before he wrestled her weapon away, and she raised such a fuss that neighbors called the police.

Jaz didn't remember any of that except for what Mama had told her when she coaxed the story out of her years later, after

Daddy's funeral. What Jaz remembered was sitting in the back of a police car with a flashing blue light that lit up the yard and gardenia bushes in front of her house. And her German shepherd, Scout, barking *at* her, paws smudging the glass as he tried to lunge. And the grown-ups huddling around the police, trying to explain. She could hear Mama say, *There's nothing a hospital can do for her*, so no one had ever tried.

Instead, Mama called Nana and the police let Jaz go, because the Gracetown sheriff's office knew better than to try to meddle in family business better left to Nana.

Jaz had undergone Nana's ceremony, bound to a chair just in case she got any other devilish ideas. (And oh, she had *plenty*, if she could have loosed herself from that chair.) Jaz had seen *The Exorcist* later in life, laughing to herself about the cartoonish inconsistencies. A head spinning all the way around? Please. Levitation? If only.

The movie got the holy water right, at least. Jaz remembered Nana sprinkling holy water on her while she prayed, and although it didn't sting or burn or catch fire, it annoyed the hell out of Jaz, especially when it got into her eye. Then, with more prayers, Nana had sponged her with water that smelled like rum and garlic. She hung a bag of High John the Conqueror root around Jaz's neck. She forced Jaz to drink tea that tasted like dirty toilet water. She lit so many oil lamps with competing scents that Jaz thought—no, *hoped*—Nana would burn the house down herself. At dawn, when Nana proudly instructed Jaz to recite the Lord's Prayer with her while Mama and Daddy stared on with grateful tears, Nana announced she was cleansed. Jaz didn't feel different, though she had lost interest in burning the house down or chopping up her father. And she was glad to go to bed.

Nana gave her a touch-up ceremony when she was sixteen, at Mama's insistence. The second time, the tea had made Jaz throw up, and Nana, barely able to stand by then, said it was the demon being expelled—but sometimes things are exactly what they appear to be, no need to reach for lofty meanings. Whatever was inside of her had said, *Fuck your tea, old woman*; which, coincidentally, had mirrored Jaz's thoughts at the time. No sixteen-year-old has time for constant interrogation about her behavior vis-à-vis possible possession—every bad mood, every cutting glance, every *tsk* of a sucked tooth—so yeah, she'd thought, *Fuck your tea, old lady,* while she spat up her stomach, and it only occurred to her later—*years* later, on the beach—that the voice in her head had not been her own.

Possession came in many forms in Gracetown. On the swamp side of town, among the shotgun houses and shacks still standing after a hundred years, it was no more remarkable to hear reports of possession than a child's bout of pneumonia. Swamp leeches sneaking inside children's beds while they slept were the most common cause, or so Nana had taught, but by the time Jaz left Gracetown, she'd heard at least a dozen origins afflicting residents of all ages: snakebite, a wasp's sting, tainted swamp water, hexes, unclean soil, heartbreak, even bad memories. Nana was rumored to be the best root healer in the county before she died when Jaz was at Howard, so all of the stories had come to Nana's back porch.

Nana also made a bundle from the stories, Jaz came to realize after that day when she was sixteen—it wasn't just her parents bent on blaming a demon for the horrors of life in general. Everyone relied on Nana, and paid her well, to free their loved ones from underworld afflictions—from Pastor James at First Church of Gracetown to Mayor Jackson to the McCormacks, the white family that had owned half the town since slavery.

But why her? Why Jazmine Nicole Garey? She had no reason to think her family's house had been built on haunted ground—though it was doubtful any ground in Gracetown could escape the past's angry haints. She'd gone to church as expected and loved God as well as she could, given that church cut deeply into her Sunday sleeping time.

Why had a demon chosen her?

Nana had no answer for that. Or if she did, she'd taken it to her grave.

It took Jaz two hours to find her car parked haphazardly along the Pacific Coast Highway adjacent to the beach, at the far end of the tourist vista. She'd left the door unlocked and her keys in the ignition, so it was a miracle no one had driven off in it. The road was oddly deserted, as if the world had stopped. Jaz's heart drummed, until she remembered it was a Saturday.

She turned the heater up to the highest setting and warmed her palms, fanning them before the vent. Her cell phone was on the driver's-side floor, also untouched. Cal had left fifteen messages, the most recent only five minutes earlier. And six messages from Trina, who thought she was her best friend and was her only friend that Cal knew how to reach. The only message she listened to was from Mama.

"Call me," was all her message said. "I heard from Calvin. Is that thing acting up again?"

Like the demon was a clog in her drain. Jaz didn't call Mama. Instead, she dialed Calvin's number to put him out of his misery. He picked up right away, breathless.

"Jaz! Are you okay? Where are you—"

"I'm fine. I went to the beach."

"The . . . beach? I called the police. They're here now."

Despite her restored burning love for Cal, she wanted to smack him through the phone. It was just like him not to know *never* to call LAPD on anyone with melanin having a mental moment. "Cal, *damn*. They probably would've shot me!" Then she remembered the reason for her call. "But I'm really fine, baby. I swear. I'm soooo sorry about last night. I took a full dose of Ambien. Never again."

Problem solved. Even the police bought the Ambien bit when she arrived home in an old sweater to cover her blood-stain. She got a stern warning that she should consult her doctor before taking any more sleeping pills.

"Yessir, Officer," Jazmine said sweetly while Cal held her tightly with one arm around her waist, perhaps to prevent sudden movements. Sadly, she realized that Cal's smell still tickled the back of her throat. "Believe me: I never want anything like that to happen again."

But it would. Of course it would.

While Jazmine lay in bed, Cal made a dramatic show of flushing her Ambien down the toilet like she was a music biography. Locked her bedroom windows. Moved blunt and sharp objects from her view, pretending he was straightening up. Please. He would be her jailer, apparently. And he might have aged a decade while she was gone; a spiderweb of new wrinkles framed his eyes.

The wedding was off. Neither of them said it, but both of them knew.

"I never should've left this room," Cal said. "Never should've let you get out. I freaked, Jaz. I was the only one you needed, and I . . . closed the door. I let you out of my sight."

"You wanted to keep me away from the cutlery."

His forced laugh was a huff of air. The new creases by his eyes deepened. "Boo, you know I have to ask . . ." he began. She flinched a bit at *boo*, but it didn't set her off like before. "Do you have a family history with . . . ? I don't know . . . it seemed like so much more than sleepwalking." He sighed. He had brushed his teeth recently, though his breath smelled like a corpse's ass. Jaz wanted to pinch her nostrils shut. "Like . . . a breakdown, a collapse. Like with . . . schizophrenia. Or if not that, some other . . ."

Yes! Jaz stopped listening as Cal went on with his carefully modulated theory. Schizophrenia could trigger voices in your head, breaks with reality. Even the odd odors might be purely neurological. Could it be as simple as an illness she could treat with medication? A brain tumor that might be surgically removed? She'd let herself be fooled by all that Gracetown nonsense of her youth, Nana's mumbo jumbo. Her whole family should have been committed, especially Mama. Maybe that whole godforsaken town.

"Know what?" she said cheerfully. "You're right."

His tight face softened with relief. "Yeah?" He took her hand and held it between his palms, hot as a coal oven. Her skin itched to pull away from his grip.

"Yeah. I'll make an appointment with a shrink. I'll talk to Mama—find out what I can. It happened before, when I was a kid. I don't really remember, though." Best to keep it vague. She slipped her burning hand away, pretending to scratch the back of her neck.

He didn't notice, so thrilled to have an accord without an ultimatum. He was probably pretending to himself that they might still get married. He seemed to feel good about standing by her side. Jaz felt good too. The possibility of schizophrenia brought a holy-ghost kind of euphoria. A promise of salvation.

Then she noticed the plant at her bedside—a mother-in-law's tongue with tall stalks Trina had given her for her birthday two weeks ago with the promise that it was kill-proof. *That thing will live even if you only water it by accident*, Trina had said. Yet the stalks, once green, were curled and brown, a few already littering her nightstand. She never used the term *black thumb* for obvious reasons, but plants had always hated her. Always. At least since she was eight.

"Shit," Cal said. "Almost forgot to call my neighbor to go feed and walk Zora."

With the mention of Zora, Jaz's despair was complete.

Zora, Cal's black Scottish terrier, was the reason she had not moved in with him, although his apartment in Manhattan

Beach was bigger and only blocks from the sand. Zora had hated Jaz from the start—had snapped and growled at her when she first walked through Cal's door, while an aghast Cal had pulled her away by her collar, swearing she had never behaved that way before. They'd both written it off as a pet's natural jealousy. Except it never improved. Same reaction each time. Cal had even brought in a dog trainer, who failed to make a difference. And Cal, unhappily, had made plans to let his sister take Zora when she came back from film school in New York. Damn, he loved that dog.

Jaz had never mentioned how her own childhood dog, Scout, had thumped his head bloody against the sheriff car's window trying to get to her through the glass. And she had conveniently forgotten about her encounter with the stray just that morning, when she'd been certain she could crack that mongrel's neck without breaking a sweat.

Schizophrenia her ass. Nice fantasy while it lasted.

Jaz rolled over, away from Cal. Stared at her plant's dead leaves. "We sure wouldn't want anything to happen to Zora," she said.

She didn't have to look at Cal to know he'd heard her sarcasm. She almost felt bad about how much it must sting. She hoped he wouldn't see her smile.

The weekend was eternal. Without teaching to distract him, Cal hovered and watched. Even when they ventured outside to Starbucks and made one listless trip to Target, she was so preoccupied with good behavior—banishing bad thoughts—that it was no freedom at all. She recited stale lines and pretended to be interested in his talk about politics and superhero movies. Tried to sound hopeful and excited about the appointment she'd made online to see a reputable shrink in Santa Monica. She thought about disappearing in the store's crowd. Or snatching the boy who looked three who had wandered from his mother in the linens aisle while she chatted on her cell phone—because someone needed to teach that bitch a lesson.

Instead, she waited until Monday, when Cal *had* to teach his morning class at UCLA. She was still in bed while he got dressed, pretending to sleep, hoping he wouldn't notice how she was quietly panting as she waited to escape him.

Her duffel bag was packed in the closet. She waited ten minutes to make sure Cal wouldn't come back to check on her, then escaped like a ninja. She hadn't worked out her plan beyond making it to the car, so she turned wherever traffic was clear. Street signs blurred.

Emancipation was dizzying. How had her forebears managed the magnitude of it?

Most of all, she longed to hear screaming. Every crosswalk teemed with people she could mow down; mothers with strollers, pimple-faced boys on skateboards, gawking tourists. Taco stands and donut shops were ripe for her to plow through. The children lining up on the blacktop at the gated elementary school mesmerized her so much that she forgot she was in her car; a symphony of horns sounded behind her. If she'd had an AK with her, she would have sprayed every living thing in sight. (And semiautomatic guns couldn't be that hard to get, could they? Weren't they always in the news?) Oh yes, as Ice Cube had said, it could be a very good day.

As she passed a church with a brick facade and whitewashed dome, she longed for a better relationship with her master. A sense of purpose. Carefully laid-out duties. She wanted to *serve*. But Nana had disrupted her path, so she had never learned how to direct her impulses. Never known to whom she was bound, or why. She was rootless and aimless. Homeless.

No—you're just an Abomination.

Was that her own voice, so small and far away?

Or was it Marcelle Hanley from sixth grade, casting her such a wounded look when Jazmine lied and told the teacher that Marcelle, like the boys in trouble, had been blowing spit-balls? Or Mrs. Jenkins from down the street, who ran out of her house screaming when Jazmine was in the eighth grade and crank-called her to say her autistic son had been hit by a bus af-ter school? Or Professor Franks at Howard, who knew she was lying but could do nothing about it when Jazmine rallied her English classmates to pretend he'd said it was an *open*-book exam? Or Jerrod Kemp from her editing job at that digital rag, whom she'd pretended to like—and even slept with once—so she could erase his precious novel-in-progress he lorded over everyone and wouldn't stop talking about? Or every boyfriend she'd had before Cal, who, in succession, had called her *wack, psychotic,* and a *crazy-ass bitch*?

And she couldn't deny it. She'd tried to make herself into someone new for Cal. She'd thought she could. Except by omis-sion, she had never lied to Cal. Never invited another man into her bed. Never even looked at another dude until—

The other night. At that club.

At a stop sign, Jazmine's fingers seized up on the steering wheel. The streetside Mexican fan palm trees on either side of her seemed to crisscross and blend in her vision, so tall and thin that they looked unearthly, stabbing the sky. No palm trees in Florida grew so tall.

She saw herself back at the dance club: strobe lights in eye-numbing white, red, and green flashes creating snapshots of wanton poses on the dance floor. A boy's face inching closer to her in each window of light. And closer still. Grinning and cocky. Barely twenty-one, unless he had a fake ID. Hollowed cheeks, goth dress. He hovered before her, and she ignored him for a time. The driving bass helped soothe her anger, so she'd forgotten how much she wanted to hurt someone. Then he had ruined it, yelling clumsily in her ear: "Can I get you a drink?" Inside, she was laughing, but she heard herself say yes. She heard herself suggest they stand closer to the exit, away from elbows and careless feet. She heard herself laughing at his jokes. *Got a cigarette? Let's go outside.*

That was all it took to get him to the alley. He'd still been fumbling in his jeans for his lighter when she hit him in the face with the cement block. She'd picked it up with ease, with hardly a thought, and swung it at his nose like Serena Williams. He'd yelled out, and for one shocked moment he'd touched his bloodied face and reached for her blouse, grabbing at her before she could step away. A handprint. Her well-planted kick to his crotch had driven him to the ground. He was unconscious by the time he fell. She'd hit the back of his head twice more, dropped the block when his scalp caved, and gone on her way.

So . . . yeah. *That* had happened. She'd killed some kid, some mother's son.

A sob burbled in Jazmine's throat. She knew she'd hurt someone in her fever that night, but she hadn't remembered how thoroughly dead he was.

When a minivan behind her beeped politely, Jazmine made a right turn to stay nestled on a residential street rather than driving toward Ventura. Another random right. A left. *Away* from people. She needed to be far away from crosswalks, crowded sidewalks, intersections. Jazmine's heartbeat pulsed in her tight fingers on the steering wheel as she drove away from temptation.

The streets grew narrow, signs threatening parking fines and proclaiming cul-de-sacs: *NO THROUGH TRAFFIC.* Above her, the palm trees swayed—fronds whispering above her, perhaps a wind following her. The rustling fronds hissed up and down the tiny street of small houses with dark windows and empty driveways. Jazmine parked at a stop sign. With no other cars to nudge her, she did not move. She thought about calling Cal.

In her rearview mirror, she saw the bicycle approaching from behind. An old woman's bright red skirt flapped as she pedaled, balancing a paper shopping bag on her handlebars. Strands of fine white hair whipped across her brown forehead in the sudden gusts of wind. The bicycle wobbled as the bird-boned woman fought to keep her balance and hold her bag, yet she pedaled on. She was only ten feet behind Jazmine now—closer than she appeared, her mirror reminded her.

A large palm frond dropped across the hood of Jazmine's car with a *thump*.

The old woman gave Jazmine a curious side glance as she pedaled past—she was older than Jazmine had thought, her face a mask of deep wrinkles. The old woman didn't brake or even slow at the stop sign, since Jazmine's was the only car in sight. The stranger pedaled past the intersection toward the next block. Straight ahead.

Jazmine's heartbeat celebrated the rising glee within her. She felt dizzy with it.

"Leave her alone," Jazmine whispered to the empty car. A command.

Another palm frond, a larger one, spiraled to the ground a few feet behind the old woman into the roadway, but the woman didn't turn her head. Good for her. When a storm's coming, you don't stop to count the signs.

Jazmine closed her eyes and reminded herself of all the reasons the old woman was precious: the loves and heartaches she had seen, the children she had suckled at her breast, the tears she had shed for the lost. The whistling palm fronds sang of struggles. A hot tear fell.

Still, Jazmine planted her foot on her accelerator so hard that her tires mewled when her car lurched forward. She opened her eyes in time to see the old woman, at last, turn back over her shoulder—and the slack surprise in her face that turned to an open-mouthed plea before the car's impact crushed her flimsy bicycle and sent her and her red skirt flying. She did fly, at least a few feet, until her bowed head met the taillight of a junk car parked in the adjacent yard. Colorful scarves from her bag rained down.

Fuck your tea, old woman.

The only scream was Jazmine's. She looked away from the mess she'd made and drove on, trembling so much that she could barely navigate her narrow lane. But she had to. She could not be anywhere nearby when someone found the old woman. She'd probably dented her fender.

Just like before, as soon as she'd done the deed, she lost the memory of why. Clawing regret and self-loathing replaced the horrible impulse.

Just like before—she remembered now—she wanted to drown herself in the sea.

The sun was too bright. Jazmine had found her way out of the old woman's neighborhood, back to a major street, and her eyes throbbed in the daylight. She turned at her first opportunity, into the parking lot behind an auto-supply warehouse, hiding between two larger vehicles. She looked around to be sure no one had noticed her.

What could she do? Let a car hit her in traffic? That might be best. Something quick.

Jazmine was working up her nerve to leave her car and walk toward the road when her cell phone chimed on the seat. A video call. She rarely accepted video calls, but she saw the word *Mama*, so she accepted it. Mama was at her usual place at the kitchen table, her phone held so close that Jasmine could only see half of her face, the rest shadowed in bad light.

"Sugar, what's wrong?" Mama said.

Jazmine could only cry.

"Is it Calvin again?"

Jazmine shook her head. "No. Mama, I . . . I—"

"Wait, don't tell me," Mama said. "Not over the phone." Her *Law & Order* addiction made her vigilant. "Just tell me—are you safe?"

The question was ridiculous, but Jazmine nodded. No one was safe, including her.

"Well, you listen here—whatever it is, it's done. It can't be changed. Am I right?"

Jazmine nodded again. She wondered what Mama would say if she told her everything. She might be upset, or she might just say, *Well, it's done, sugar.*

"You get on away from there as fast as you can," Mama said. "I told you living in those big cities would eat you up—all the way in California with no kin. It's not natural. Some things are still better down here. You need to come back home. Right now."

Mama's most familiar refrain electrified Jazmine as if she'd never heard the words, the key to her life's puzzle. Her grief receded, and the day felt right again. She almost forgot the flying red skirt. She no longer felt the need to shield her eyes from the sun.

"Did you hear me, Jazmine?"

"Yes." She almost said, *Yes ma'am.*

"Nana's not here with us anymore, God rest her soul, but there's others in Gracetown who can help you. We'll go talk to Mr. June over at the Handi Mart first. 'Least you can have folks look out for you. Folks who give a damn about you, who knew you before you were born."

Jazmine was nodding again, an acolyte in the presence of a mighty evangelist.

"You grab the first flight—"

"No," Jazmine said. "Not a plane." Instinct told her that she could not trust herself at an airport, on an airplane. She didn't dare.

"Well then, you fill up your car with gas and come on down. Sleep when you're tired, but just keep driving. Don't stop until you get here."

"Okay," Jazmine said.

Why hadn't she seen it herself? Gracetown was both her plague and her keeper. She had grown up in Gracetown, so why couldn't she be reborn there? The drive to Florida would be a couple thousand miles, she calculated. Thirty-three hours on the road, which would take at least two days even with little sleep. But if she kept away from people, didn't drive fast enough to attract unwanted attention, she could do it.

Mama moved her phone to a better angle, and her face was suddenly clear. Full cheeks. Bright, loving eyes. Mama's smile hadn't aged. Jazmine could be eight years old again, for all her mother had changed. Her childhood felt close enough to touch.

She almost told Mama she loved her, but she would say those words in person. Wasn't face-to-face communication best? She might arrive in the dark night and surprise Mama in bed. She might stand over her and watch her sleep, breathing softly in her ear. Smelling her—*really* smelling her.

"I'll see you soon, Mama," was all she said.

Caretaker

TODDLER SURVIVES IN APARTMENT FOR 10 DAYS AFTER MURDER-SUICIDE

GRACETOWN, FL—A Florida toddler, 2-year-old Carson Emory, has been rescued from a Gracetown apartment building after 10 days, apparently left alone after his parents' murder-suicide.

Police report that the child was found clean and well-fed in his crib. In the room across from his, the bodies of his parents, Frank Emory, 35, and Rochelle Emory, 32, had been decomposing behind a closed door. Because of a bedroom window that seemed deliberately left open during the recent cold snap, no other residents in the building realized that the bodies were in the top-floor apartment.

Residents say they never saw anyone enter or leave the apartment. The landlord believed the family was out of town and was collecting their mail.

"The one thing we know for sure is that this child didn't take care of himself," said Gracetown police chief Althea Grant. "Someone was either living there with him or coming in and out of that apartment to feed and dress him, keep him quiet, and make sure those bodies were not found."

Police are baffled by the case, since the mystery care-

taker is not considered a suspect in the deaths: an inves-
tigation has revealed that Rochelle Emory poisoned her
husband, and herself, after she discovered his affair with
a coworker. A suicide note taken into evidence from the
scene matches her handwriting, police report.

Frank Emory taught math at Tallahassee Community
College and Rochelle Emory wrote about magic and rit-
ual in a popular blog called Gracetown's Things Unseen.

Carson Emory, now in foster care, is an only child.
The family's dog is missing. Police would like to talk to
anyone who might have information about who helped
him survive his ordeal.

Because Carson Emory was only two years old, he never knew
what his parents were arguing about. He only knew that Before
his parents spoke to each other in soft voices—not as softly
as they spoke to him, but still softly—and then came the After days when they only spoke in shouts. The worst was when
his mother shouted, because she sounded as if she had tripped
and scraped her skin until she bled. His father's shouts only
sounded angry, the same two words: "Shut up!" (Carson tried
the words on his tongue, "Shut up!" but it made his parents
frown and say, NO, Carson, don't say that, even though his
father said it first.)

Carson practiced several other words he heard from his
parents' arguments on his one-eyed teddy bear, Roscoe: "Stop
it!" and of course, "I hate you!" And then he would apologize
and cuddle his bear to sleep. But as far as he knew, his parents
never apologized when they shouted. And they probably didn't
cuddle, either—though Carson didn't know that for sure, because his crib was in the room across the hall and they always
closed their door at night.

That Night, though, was different. That Night, everything
changed.

It wasn't bad at first: Mama held him in her lap a long time, rocking back and forth with her arms squeezed tight around him, as if nothing and no one could be strong enough to pull him away. Carson liked when Mama squeezed him close; his body's wild, twitching muscles calmed against her skin like she was a warm bath. He especially loved rocking with her when he was tired, his eyelids so heavy. If he ever startled because he thought he was falling, or alone in his crib—he hated being alone in his crib—Mama's rocking told him he'd only imagined it and she would be there forever. Mama wasn't *really* there forever, but that was how it seemed when she held him that way. Of all his memories of Mama, these were the ones he would keep his whole life: She was wearing a red shirt because it was close to Christmas. Her perfume smelled like flowers. Her braid fell forward when she rocked him, tickling his nose.

Not her face. Not her voice, really. Her shirt, her flower smell, her braid. Mama.

And her quiet tears, falling from her nose in raindrops.

"What's wrong?" he'd say, or try to say. It came out more like a whimper.

Mama only sighed and rocked and kissed the top of his head.

Carson would not remember much about his father from that night—he would eventually lose his memory of his father altogether. But he would always remember his dog, Grayboy—a ghost-colored gray terrier who often licked Carson's dinner crumbs from his face, or sometimes snatched food from his hand. Once, Carson tried to get even by stealing Grayboy's food out of his bowl, shoving the bland brown nuggets into his mouth as fast as he could, but Mama had told him, *Stop it!* while Grayboy grinned and laughed at him by wagging his tail.

But Carson loved Grayboy, who would run and catch a ball if Carson threw it. Mama and Daddy got tired of playing fetch, yet Grayboy would run and bring him the ball for hours.

Grayboy was his best friend. Grayboy slept in Carson's room at night to protect him, Daddy said. Grayboy had moved into his room the day they brought him home. They told him the story almost every night.

But not that night. That night, Mama had left him an extra bottle of milk and bag of Goldfish in his crib, patted him on the head with more tears dripping on him in a rain shower, and walked across the hall to her room to close the door. She didn't even say, *Good night,* or, *I love you,* although maybe the rocking in the chair had been another way of saying it.

Daddy never came to him that night at bedtime. Carson never saw either of them again.

In the few seconds between when Mama opened her bedroom door and rushed to shut it again, Carson heard something he hadn't noticed before: moaning. The voice was as low as a grown man's and as helpless as a child's. Carson wondered whose voice that was—and why he hurt so much. And it was Daddy! He was hurt like the little girl Carson had seen bleeding in the ER and Mama had said, *Well, at least you're not hurt THAT bad, huh, Carson?* even though the bump on his head hurt worse than anything in the world.

He wouldn't have had the bump if Daddy hadn't pulled his arm so hard and made him bump his head. And when Mama had said, *How did this happen?* Daddy had told her a lie, saying Carson had been running and tripped. And Carson had started crying because the lie hurt worse than the bump on his head. Mama had looked at him and said, *Honey we've told you,* instead of, *Poor sweet boo,* and Carson had started screaming with rage. And now Daddy was hurting just like he had—maybe even worse.

Carson wondered: *Did I do that to Daddy?*

If he had, he hadn't tried to. That trip to the ER had been days ago, and Daddy had whispered to him that night, *I'm sorry, little man, that won't ever happen again.* That was the first time Carson had seen Daddy cry, when Mama wasn't with them. Carson hadn't thought about Daddy's hard yank again until he heard his soft moaning behind the click of the door.

What Mama said was louder than the moaning, so Carson heard her even after the door was closed: "That's what you get, baby."

That's. What. You. Get. Baby.

Those didn't feel like the right words. She'd called Daddy *baby* like she used to, but Mama's voice had sounded wrong too—as if, just maybe, she were smiling.

"Keep on singing—this is my new favorite song," Mama said, although Carson didn't hear any singing or music. Carson almost, *almost*, heard another moan.

Carson knew something was wrong in his bones, even if he couldn't understand what. But when a long time went by—ten seconds, to him, was a long wait—and he didn't hear Daddy moaning for sure after Mama turned the TV up loud, Carson remembered the second bottle. Mama *never* let him have bottles at bedtime anymore—and he savored the sweet milk, still warm. His tummy was already full from dinner, but he settled against his pillow in his favorite bottle-drinking pose and forgot he had ever heard moaning.

Grayboy whined and paced outside his parents' closed door all night. The door never opened again, even when the sun was shining. Not ever.

In the morning, Carson's diaper was wet and leaking and he was hungry. He emptied the bag of Goldfish all over his mattress. Mama should know he never ate Goldfish for breakfast! And Grayboy was barking, making a racket.

Oh, but Carson was mad. He cried as loudly as he could, shaking the crib bars, until he could not catch his breath. He tore off his sopping diaper and threw it across the room, and it stained the wall. Good. His skin was damp and he was colder than he had ever been, or at least since yesterday. It had been daytime so long, it might already be night soon. Carson's parents had never waited so late to feed him his breakfast and change his diaper.

When Carson was exhausted from crying and Grayboy was finally quiet too, looking sad as he sat in front of his parents' door, Carson decided to go to their room and wake them up.

He had been able to climb out of his crib for a long time, although Mama always said, *No, no, Carson, don't do that.* But he was ready for a big bed without bars; Daddy had promised him one soon. Escaping the bars was easy, really—Carson hoisted himself up in the corner of the crib and balanced himself across the V. Then, hanging on tightly, he carefully swung his legs over until they dangled . . . and then he dropped. He stayed on his feet when they hit the floor.

Grayboy came to him, wagging his tail and licking his face. Grayboy probably wanted to tell him he wasn't supposed to climb out, though Grayboy did plenty he wasn't supposed to. *Plenty.*

Carson ran across the hall to the closed door, already practicing the mean words he would say when he saw them. He reached up for the doorknob . . . and it was locked.

Locked! Carson cried and screamed again, yet Mama and Daddy would not open the door. For the first time, Carson wasn't just mad—he was scared.

In a moment of fear, he almost remembered Daddy's moaning, and Mama's wrong words. But mostly he was scared by the icy cold blowing from underneath their door in a sheet, as if the windows were wide open. *That* definitely wasn't right. Mama often said their rooms were too cold, and she'd thought it would be warmer in Florida.

Grayboy barked again, his nose against the door. Then Grayboy backed up.

Something moved! In the space between the door and the floor, Carson saw a shadow move inside the room. He banged on the door. "Mama!" he yelled.

The shadow grew. At first Carson thought the shadow was two legs, but it had spread until it blocked all of the cold air and light from the room, sealing the door on the other side. The shadow didn't look like a person. Carson couldn't tell exactly *what* it looked like.

Then the shadow spilled beneath the door.

When Carson played in the park, he liked to pour a bucket of water in the dirt until he made mud he could splash in—and the shadow spilling beneath the door looked like *that*, like thick mud, although it was too shiny and dark to be mud. When the shadow reached his toes, Carson realized it was . . . *ants*. So many ants were tangled all over each other that they moved like mud. There were too many ants to count. More ants than he'd imagined in the whole world.

Grayboy barked. But ants don't care about barking.

By the time Carson thought about running away, the ants were already climbing up his legs in a pattern like a candy cane, and all of those tiny little ant legs tickled him so much that he stopped crying and started laughing. Soon his legs were so thick with ants that he looked like he was wearing long pants. If Mama could see, she would say, *Oh my goodness gracious*.

The ants roamed all over him until Carson was wearing ants in a thick coat up to his neck. A thick, *warm* coat. He wondered why he hadn't started wearing ants long ago.

Grayboy came to him and barked sharply in his ear. Carson pushed Grayboy away. Why should Grayboy be the only one with a warm coat?

Carson felt better about everything after he was wearing the ants—once he was no longer cold, he felt better about being hungry and better about being alone. Just . . . better.

And that was only the beginning of Carson's Very Best Time Ever.

When he walked into the living room—when he was wearing the ants, it felt more like *gliding* than walking—*Sesame*

Street was already playing on the TV. He didn't know how he hadn't heard Big Bird when he first woke up. And a bowl of his Froot Loops (his special cereal!) was waiting for him on the table in front of the TV with a spoon. Mama only gave him "sugar cereals" on special days, so he knew Mama couldn't have left it for him. He saw a fly at the edge of his cereal bowl, but it flew away when he swatted at it.

Carson heard a clanking sound from the kitchen. When he looked up, no one was there—although he'd seen a shadow streak across the wall in the blink of an eye.

Grayboy had seen it too. Grayboy barked and ran chasing it, until he was behind the tall counter and Carson couldn't see him anymore.

But Carson heard a yelp.

Grayboy's yelp bothered Carson, yes. Though it was only one. And before Carson could wonder about why Grayboy had made such a sound, the volume on the TV went higher and Big Bird was *dancing* and Carson forgot all about Grayboy for an hour, maybe two.

For the tiniest moment, Carson almost thought he saw Grayboy being dragged across the floor behind him on a bed of ants, but when he turned around for a better look, Grayboy was gone. He *almost* heard his parents' door open and close again.

Carson never saw Grayboy again either. And he began to notice that Mama's plants were all dying and turning brown, then black, until they were the color of the ants. The ants were eating up everything alive they could find. Everything except Carson.

Because he was only two, Carson did not spend much time wondering about the New Way of things—the way the ants kept him warm and made food for him, and even let him float on them like a giant sponge in the bathtub. Sometimes they fanned out on the wall in a shape like a very tall man with a strange, spiky crown on his head. No, not a man—a *thing* with sharp shoulders and a long nose (snout?). These weren't regular ants—the ants were part of something bigger that might even have a name. Sometimes when the ants were wrapped around him in a blanket at night, Carson knew things: the creature was ancient, and lived in the soil, summoned by blood and death and rage to nurture the *for-sa-ken*. The ants had come to take care of him because his parents were gone.

Not *gone*, exactly—Carson knew somehow that they were still in their bedroom, behind the closed door, and something bad had happened to them, but they were in a Better Place now. That was what Daddy had said after his lizard went to sleep. See, Carson had kept a pet lizard in a box near his window and had seen how its belly had stopped breathing and how its face got shrunken and wrinkled after some time. So once in a while he thought of Mama and Daddy *asleep* asleep in their bed, and he missed Grayboy so much, and a great sadness fell over him—something worse than sadness.

But whenever that happened, no matter where he was, he felt the ants come to him, the Caretaker's ant army, and they would rock him back and forth, to and fro—just like Mama.

PART III

The Nayima
Stories

One Day Only

A sound like thunder—if thunder were an army—boomed beneath Nayima's floorboards, and her living room trembled.

Spray lashed the deck outside her glass door. Then the swell of sound retreated across drenched sand below, sucking back the roar as the tide pulled away to marshal its strength.

It was high tide, and a storm might be coming, somewhere beyond the hidden rim of the darkening Pacific she could glimpse through the sheer parted curtains. The ocean swelled beneath her faster than she'd expected, and again the floor tremored. It was like living on a cruise ship, she thought—a ship that never moved or rocked. Rooted.

This apartment was the best place Nayima had ever lived. The best place she ever *would* live, came the silent correction. Maybe the best place, period, now or ever, for anyone. Two years ago, this beachfront apartment might have cost a couple million dollars. She had found it empty and undisturbed, the key not so cleverly hidden beneath a flowerpot beside the door at the top of the wooden beach house steps.

No bodies inside. (Hallelujah!) No rotten food anywhere—or not much, anyway. Maybe the owners had been vegan, because only rice, vegetables, and fruit had gone bad in grocery store packages in the freezer. The fridge had been empty except for a pitcher of water and a six-pack of Corona.

The owners clearly had left Malibu in an orderly fashion. The apartment's furniture was simple and mostly disposable, any metal near the windows rusting slightly from the salt-water air. It must have been a vacation rental, because she'd found a laminated sheet of instructions explaining the electrical wiring, how to work the huge television's remote, and where to find the towels. Of course, no one in Malibu had electricity or working televisions anymore, yet the towels in the linen closet were still there and smelled like that fabric softener with the smiling teddy bear. True hospitality.

The waves crashed the boulders and seawall beneath the apartment again.

"Jesus," Karen complained from the bedroom, "how do you sleep with that racket?"

Nayima closed her eyes. The sound of the ocean might be keeping her alive, making her relish her aliveness. "How do you stay awake?" Nayima called back.

Other people's tastes were a burden. Nayima had invited Karen to move in only two days ago, and already it felt like a mistake. Nayima had spent weeks, sometimes months, craving conversation with another person who would not try to kill or rob her—or report her to the marshals—but after knowing Karen for less than a week, Nayima was tired of her.

Her complaints. Her pessimism.

Her in general.

Nayima asked herself if she would have tried to like Karen more if Karen were a man, or if she herself were a man, but the question felt trite. True, she'd never been in bed with a woman before Karen, but her body liked Karen's warm skin and gentle touch just fine. Karen's sudden kiss was the only reason she'd invited her to move in; otherwise, they might have just kept running into each other on the beach from time to time while they fished and looked for crabs.

To her shock, Karen said she'd never had the vaccine. Another NI—Naturally Immune—was something, anyway. Nayima knew she would have died ten times over by now if she hadn't been immune to the flu, and the same was true of Karen, and probably so for many of the others still finding their way to Malibu. Still, for someone to stride up to you and ask for a kiss was bold, and Nayima had liked the kiss in every way.

Maybe it was the age difference, then. Nayima was only twenty-four, and Karen was forty-five, old enough to be her mother. Or maybe Nayima couldn't just snap her fingers and fall in love, no matter how few candidates were left. Was that it? She was still being picky?

One for the joke file.

Nayima brought out the notebook she'd begun carrying with her after she escaped the chaos in Bakersfield for a change of scenery. She had intended to use it as a journal, though she couldn't make herself chronicle her story, or any stories, about the flu. Instead, she wrote down thoughts that amused her, like she used to in her theater class at Spelman, the first time a teacher had told her she was funny.

It turns out beggars CAN be choosers, Nayima wrote. She drew a circle, two eyes, and a wide O: a surprised face. It made her laugh more loudly than she should have. Even the waves couldn't smother the sound.

Karen came out of the bedroom wearing the white terry-cloth robe the owners had left behind the bathroom door: Nayima's robe. When irritation flashed, Nayima thought about Karen's silhouette in the dusk sun when they'd finally stopped circling each other from a wary distance. The law of the beach—the only law, really—was, *Don't start none, won't be none.*

Karen was Irish-from-Ireland, so her short, spiky hair was carrot orange and her face was permanently sunburned and peeling, no matter how much sunblock she used. But she was strong, and Nayima thought everywhere her strength showed was lovely: steely eyes, a strong jaw, a body of lean muscle.

Karen could haul in fishing nets that were astonishingly heavy. She'd been an airline baggage handler for Delta. Before. Nayima hadn't had time to be anything but a student.

"I wish you wouldn't wear that," Nayima said. "Without asking."

Karen ignored the chide. "I heard you laugh. Were you laughing at me?"

Karen was already reading her notebook over her shoulder and Nayima had too much pride to slam it shut. That, and she wanted Karen to see her jokes. Karen usually said she didn't see the point of jokes; nothing was funny, at least not anymore.

Karen gave a short sigh, pointing at Nayima's last scrawl. "Me?" she said. "Beggars and choosers. I don't get it, really. It's a little mean, isn't it?"

"A little."

"But it made you laugh."

"Obviously I need therapy," Nayima said. *Therapists would be making a killing if they weren't already dead.* She scribbled it down before she forgot.

While Nayima wrote, Karen mulled over the page as if she did not recognize the language. "May I?" she said finally—the way she should have asked about her robe. Without waiting for Nayima's answer, she took the notebook and walked to the love seat, her robe falling open when she sat on folded legs. Nayima watched her face for signs of amusement and saw none. Karen sighed and fidgeted each time the surf roiled beneath the apartment.

"Can we go to the flat I found across the highway?" Karen asked. "You can see the water, but it won't be as loud."

Karen's place was practically a shed, the only one she'd found that didn't stink.

"I already have a place I like," Nayima said.

She had long forgotten how to compromise. She had fought hard for her pleasures and would let go of none of them. If there was a silver lining, as people used to say, she'd learned how to stand up for what she wanted.

"These houses right on the beach are the first place they'll look, Neema." *Neema* might be a nickname, or maybe Karen couldn't remember her actual name. That was how little they knew each other.

"I thought you wanted to move because of the water."

"I can think of a lot of reasons to move. Can't you?"

There. Karen wasn't trying to, but her voice had slipped into Mommy mode. Nayima grinded her teeth. "If you want to sleep somewhere else, you know where to find me, Caitlin."

"Karen," she said. "Not Caitlin."

"Nayima, then. Let's use our actual names."

Gram hadn't raised Nayima to envy or notice blue eyes, but damn if Karen's gray-blue eyes weren't the color of moonlight. Every time Nayima wanted to start a fight, she noticed another aspect of Karen she liked, and this time it was her eyes, even if it was only because they were hers. Nayima wished they were in bed instead of arguing. Her body was waking under Karen's eyes.

"Nayima," Karen said, memorizing her name, her eyes back on the notebook. "I'll get it."

With nothing left to argue about, Nayima was forced to remember the truth of Karen's warning: the marshals would come. She'd driven back southwest to Malibu for the same reasons as everyone else—food, warmth, beauty. Making salt water potable wasn't easy, but it was better than no water at all in the drought regions. She'd hoped she could stop running. She'd hoped maybe this apartment wouldn't just be her *latest* stop, her *best* stop, but her *last* one.

And there were others—not many, but a few. They lived scattered among the beach houses and hillsides, but she had spotted at least ten other people at the pier or on the beach in the three weeks she'd been in Malibu, not counting Karen. She'd chronicled them all in the last page of her notebook, describing her neighbors: a father and two daughters about ten and twelve (she called him Mister Mom, his daughters Flopsy and Mopsy); the Old Man in the Sea who took his rowboat out to fish every day; three rough-looking guys who might be brothers (the Three Stooges); and the Brat Pack, one pimple-faced teenaged boy and two girls, maybe sixteen, who mostly stayed out of sight. There might be more, but on the beach sometimes even with binoculars she couldn't tell if she had seen someone before or if they were new. Like Karen.

The father and daughter moved furtively across the sand in gas masks, always wearing bright blue gloves. They never got close to anyone, so they had survived. Nayima assumed they were not vaccinated—and no way the father and both daughters were immune, if they were related; in any family, maybe *one* would be immune—or one on any street, in any neighborhood. Maybe one or two in each town. A father and two daughters in one family must not have the virus yet.

Good for them. If their blood stayed clean, they might qualify to go to Sacramento. The city had declared itself a separate republic and had electricity, water, crops, livestock. Mister Mom and his kiddos might rejoice if marshals came.

But not Nayima. Not Karen. Not the immune—though they could not be infected, they were carriers, and rumors said carriers who weren't shot ended up in lab cages. Fuck that. If scientists didn't have enough blood from carriers for the vaccines already, one or two more wouldn't help.

Karen was right about the beach apartment they were in: it was in plain sight on the Pacific Coast Highway, so any vehicle driving by might see them without even trying.

Nayima's breath hitched in her throat as her chest tightened, and she could exhale only when the waves crashed beneath her and seemed to knock the blockage free.

The back of her neck tingled. New anxieties, no matter how

big or small, crumbled the wall she'd erected around her memories. The strongest memory charged through: Gram's bloodied pillowcase. A cop had shot Gram to force Nayima to evacuate, knowing she would not leave Gram behind. Nayima could still smell the gunpowder and the blood from his treacherous act of mercy.

Karen closed the notebook and said, "These are good."

Nayima wiped her tears, turning her face away. She did not let herself cry often, or she'd never stop. She wasn't ready to share tears with Karen. "What?"

"These jokes. Not all of them, definitely—but some of them are good."

To prove it, Karen smiled. The sea crashed like cymbals to mark the occasion. Nayima had never seen Karen smile. Gram's blood-soaked pillowcase washed away with the tide.

"Really?" Karen's smile sparked across Nayima's lips too.

Karen read from Nayima's notes in a deadpan: "*I always wanted to move to Malibu, but I had to wait for the prices to drop.*"

"It's the delivery," Nayima said. "When you say it like that—"

"I'm not a comedian, I'm just saying I think it could be funny. To some people."

Some people. That phrase sounded strange, dual plurals in the land of the singular. Nayima noticed faint freckles on Karen's lips and traced them with her fingertip.

"Like . . . if I did a comedy show?" Nayima said, teasing her.

Karen's lips moved closer. "You can do your show for me."

Except for Nayima's kiss from Darryn Stephens, who had surprised her with a declaration of his affection at a house party when she'd been Brandon Paul's date, kissing had mostly felt like an obligatory activity before sex. But kissing Karen was a discovery each time, an exploration. Nayima could kiss Karen for an hour and lose track of time.

They opened the glass sliding door, and the sound of the ocean became a gale. They waded through the sound to the deck's corner bed, which was covered in a thin blanket damp from salt-water spray. The bathrobe fell away. Nayima tasted the salt on Karen's lips, on her neck, on her shoulders.

They were naked in the moonlight, sharp contrasts wherever their skin touched. When Nayima sang out her pleasure, the ocean answered her. Afterward, they lay together, hugging in the chilly breeze. Nayima thought of how warm it must be inland, where she and Gram had lived. She thought of the ghost cities west of them.

"That day on the beach?" Karen said.

They spent all their days on the beach, though only one day mattered. Nayima grinned.

Karen's short-lived smile was gone. Her voice fell to a whisper, a tear creeping from the corner of her eye. "I didn't know . . . I was immune."

A cold ball knotted in Nayima's stomach, but she kept her voice playful. "I was a test? Cool. I don't mind being your guinea pig."

"No, not that," Karen said. "I said to myself, *I'm gonna get it from someone, so it might as well be her—the most beautiful woman left in the world.*"

Only Gram had called her beautiful. She imagined Gram's face—alive, bloodless.

"You could have killed me," Nayima said. "You didn't know anything about me."

"I swear . . . I had no idea about me. I expected . . ."

"A kiss of death?"

"I thought so." In Karen's voice, Nayima heard, *I hoped so.*

Because it was too terrible, she didn't tell Karen the irony: she *had* killed a man by kissing him. A year and three months ago, she'd met a man on State Road 46 outside of Lost Hills, only briefly. She'd fooled herself into imagining a future together. She hadn't come across a survivor in so long that she'd been eager to latch onto him. And she was sure he was immune, like her.

But no. Only six hours later, he was already sick. Throwing up. Because of her.

Kyle. His name had been Kyle. Nayima didn't think of him often, but she owed him remembering his name. She had leaned over him in the dark, giggling with mischief after he'd asked her, so politely, to stay away. She had kissed him—killed him—in his sleep.

Was Kyle the one standing between her and Karen? Who made her itch to flee? Karen and all of Malibu felt like nothing but a mirage.

The surf's mighty hiss buried the rest of their unspoken words.

By morning, Nayima was using her neatest handwriting to make her flyer, page after page of repetitive motion, all caps for clarity. Her sweaty hands were sticky inside her gloves, but she didn't want the paper to spread the flu. Whatever she touched might turn to dust.

ONE DAY ONLY
COMEDY SHOW!!!
FREE WATER
PIER AT PCH
DAWN—FRIDAY

It was Wednesday, so people had two days to hear about the show. Maybe their seaside hamlet would be stable for two more days. Sleeping beside Karen, hearing her breathing between the swells, Nayima'd had a premonition: they should grab their backpacks and leave Malibu. Too many people were coming, and the word would spread. Mister Mom might already have sent out an alarm. Then they would be invaded by marshals looking for carriers to punish for the end of the world.

But Karen had said that *some people* would find her jokes funny. And if that was true, why not give them a show? She'd always wanted to try stand-up comedy, and this was her only chance.

She might give someone their last laugh.

"Free *water*?" Karen said, reading her flyer. As if Nayima had promised the moon.

"I could purify a few cups. There's only about ten."

"You don't know that for sure," Karen said. "People are hiding. Besides, no one will take water from you. They don't know you. They won't go near you. I wouldn't take it. You make your own water, or it's an unopened bottle. That's it. Think like one of *them*."

Karen was in her mommy mode again. She was insufferable sometimes. Nayima wasn't going to cross off *free water* from every page in her stack. Or deny someone who might not have time to desalinate it themselves.

Nayima made fresh water every day, more than she needed: slowly boiling a covered pot of water with a glass in the center on her deck firepit, allowing the freshly condensed water to drip into the glass, or simply leaving bowls and glasses wrapped in plastic in the sun. The kitchen cabinet had been full of bowls and glasses to use. Not everyone had that, or even knew how to ensure the water you had was safe to drink. She herself had learned how long ago at camp.

"I'm bringing the water," Nayima said. "It's my show."

Silence. Nayima braced for what she knew Karen wanted to say: *They won't come. Don't expect them to come.* A quiet plea.

Karen's shitty attitude again.

Nayima figured the others wouldn't come—they were all fugitives, whether it was from the flu or from flu-hunters, and fugitives did not gather on the bones of the world to take in a show. Hell, either she or Karen—or both of them—might not make it back to the apartment. Yet hearing it from Karen infuriated her.

Nayima snatched up her pages and stood up to pack her backpack: her Glock, her key, and the plastic box of thumbtacks she'd found in the kitchen drawer—at least a hundred—with heads in the soft pastel colors of Easter eggs. As an afterthought, she packed a hammer; water bottles, beef jerky, and an extra pair of sneakers were always inside her pack, just in case.

"I'm coming with you," Karen said. "We're not supposed to go out alone, remember?"

That had been Karen's rule, not Nayima's, and probably served Karen more. If trouble came, Nayima might not have time to slow down and see after Karen, which she told Karen with a look. Nayima had made her no promises of heroics and she didn't expect heroics in return, though Karen's hangdog eyes wanted to stay with her always. Karen might kill or die for her.

Why did that simple *caring* repel her so much?

"Come on, then," Nayima said. "Post office first."

The post office closest to her apartment was a twenty-minute walk on the Pacific Coast Highway, in a small roadside strip mall modeled after a frontier town, with wood facades and old-fashioned lettering. Most of the other storefronts' windows were broken or partially burned out, but the post office was still in good shape even though the door was unlocked. Most people weren't looking for anything the post office had to offer—except announcements and notices.

The daykeeper had come and gone. On the door, Nayima found the newest sign tacked into the wood: the day, date, and year stenciled in bright red paint. Someone spent time and care spray-painting each sign and came every morning to post a new one. Beside it, an older paper flyer flapped in the breeze, from weeks or months before: *SURVIVORS—REPORT TO SACRAMENTO FOR TESTING & VACCINE,* above an eagle crest proclaiming, *REPUBLIC OF SACRAMENTO AUTHORITY.*

Nayima chuckled every time she saw the sign. Traveling four hundred miles on the 5 was easier said than done, even if you had a car and gas. And *AUTHORITY* was a stretch. The daykeeper, whoever they were, had more authority in Malibu.

Also, the sign had implied fine print: if you tested positive for antibodies, you were a carrier. And no carrier in her right mind would report to anyone.

Another older sign read: *CERTIFIED VACCINATIONS!!!!* At her feet lay the litter of old vaccine needle packs from a long-ago drop or visit from Sacramento. At one time, more survivors had lived here. Like Karen, they had stayed hidden and missed the worst of the plague. Karen had said she'd heard helicopters and megaphones about six months before, but she'd thought she had dreamed them. And she had been afraid to show herself.

Nayima didn't go inside the post office to see the bulletin board, which she already knew was crammed with index cards and paper scraps from long ago, people searching for loved ones or trying to pass on news of the plague. She doubted that there had been many reunions. Instead, Nayima tacked her flyer beside Sacramento's, struggling to drive the tack into the sturdy wood. She should have brought nails, she realized. But four pretty little tacks would hold it in place for a couple of days.

Nayima stepped back and assessed the flyer, only wishing she had included her name. Still, the simple proclamation felt like her finest moment since the flu began. Even Karen exhaled a *hnh* sound as if to say: *Okay, I get it now.*

One Day Only. Three words evoked excitement. Joy, even. What was that name of that baseball movie with the line, *If you build it, they will come*? And even if they didn't come, the sign was hopeful. Maybe hope could be contagious.

Karen moved closer as if to hug her.

"No," Nayima said. "Someone might notice." She couldn't help glancing around to see if anyone was nearby. The only movement was from seagulls wheeling toward the surf.

"So what? There's a vaccine," Karen said.

"I bet none of these people have seen a vaccine," Nayima said. "That's still just a myth until there's a better supply line. Trust me, they'd just assume we're carriers who don't give a damn about getting infected. It's a quick way to draw a bullet."

"You have so many reasons," Karen murmured.

"Reasons for what?"

"That I should go piss off. I just want to celebrate a leaflet."

Kyle had tried to keep Nayima away from him too; maybe she had learned the habit from him. But if she stayed with Karen, the woman would get killed or caught one day. Karen wasn't careful enough. She'd been too spoiled in her Ventura County hideaway, so far from the bigger cities and the roads. Everyone Karen knew was dead too, though she still had no fucking idea.

"Every morning, I half expect you to be gone," Karen said. "Is that the way it'll be? You'll be a phantom in the night? Like I dreamed you?"

Probably, Nayima thought. "I don't know," she said.

"I would have loved you even in the real world."

Nayima looked at her, startled. Only Gram had loved her, and her best friend Shanice, and her cousins in Baldwin Hills. No one else. She had dated and fucked, but she had never *made love* before the flu. Karen looked lovely in that moment, her face framed against a palm tree and the clear morning sky the color of a postcard. Nayima could imagine how she looked to Karen's eyes: like a future. The beauty in Malibu was a lie.

"*This* is the real world," Nayima said. "Get used to that before you start using words like *love*."

The light left Karen's eyes before Nayima turned away.

Even at the end of the world, everyone wanted to come to Malibu.

The Pacific Coast Highway was clogged. That was Malibu's greatest drawback—still. Nayima had visited Malibu with friends on spring break in her senior year of high school, when most of her friends had been white and thought vacations were for skiing and surfing. As novice drivers they had felt they were taking their lives into their hands when trying to master the manic traffic on the PCH. No one slowed down for almost any reason, driving as if they would live forever.

Now, cars snaked up and down in both directions as far as the eye could see, bumpers almost locked together. Most of them were coffins with a view, and too many of the windows were open, but the sea air had long ago washed away the odor, accelerating decomposition so that the sight of near-skeletal drivers and passengers was far worse than the smell.

Nayima and Karen grew hushed as they crossed the PCH back toward the pier, past the proud parents of honor roll students and US Marines and those who'd had Babies on Board. The sight of a child's remains still strapped into a car seat had haunted Nayima's dreams for two nights, so she never let her eyes wander, focusing on the rusting hoods and bumpers instead. A few of the cars' windows were spray-painted over, someone's valiant attempt at neighborhood beautification.

But maybe it was only fitting that they could never escape the dead.

The whitewashed structures lining either side of the Malibu Pier entrance made Nayima think of a Moorish castle, except for a tacky blue sign above that once had glowed in neon:

MALIBU SPORT FISHING PIER
LIVE BAIT & CHARTER BOATS

She surveyed the area, deciding she would do her stand-up act closer to the sidewalk rather than on the pier itself. She would build a stage just far enough away from the road that the corpses in the stalled cars wouldn't ruin her act, yet far enough from the ocean that her voice wouldn't be washed away in the waves.

So much to think about. So much planning to do.

Working on her own now, Karen used the sole of her shoe to tack a flyer to a wooden bus bench advertising a law office. She and Karen had found a steady pace together as they walked up and down the highway, so they had posted all but two of the flyers by the time they reached the pier itself. No matter. She would come back and post more flyers the next day.

A sudden motion from the pier shocked her. The Old Man in the Sea was shuffling toward them with a bucket in one knobby hand and a fishing rod over his shoulder. His face was nearly hidden in the tangle of his white hair and wild beard. Nayima wondered if he had any other clothes except his tattered fisherman's raincoat.

He wasn't wearing a dust mask, so he slowed when he saw them, changed the angle of his approach through the walkway. Karen followed Nayima's lead and backed away from him, giving him a wide passage—which turned out to be a good thing, because a mighty stink of unwashed skin and clothes walked with him. He hesitated, as though wondering if they might try to steal his catch.

Nayima pointed to the sign. "I'm doing a comedy show," she said. "Right here, in two days. I hope you'll come."

He shuffled to the sign on the bus bench and read it a long time, as if it were more than just a few words. Then he turned to look at her, assessing her. Judging by his sour face, he found her unfit for the task.

"George Carlin," he said.

She'd heard of George Carlin, though she'd never seen his act. "Kind of like that, I guess," she said. "Except—"

"Richard Pryor," he interrupted.

She *knew* Richard Pryor. One of her few memories of her father was when he'd come over three or four times the summer when she was sixteen, and with nothing else to talk about, he'd put on a Richard Pryor stand-up DVD, turning the volume lower and lower until they could barely hear it because Gram was in the next room. Then he'd gone back to the Philippines, where he was stationed in the army. Nayima wondered how the Philippines had fared with the plague.

"Pryor's a lot to live up to, but I'll do my best," Nayima said. She remembered Pryor's routine after he went to the hospital for freebasing, and the one after his heart attack, and wondered what he would have said about the apocalypse.

"She's very funny," Karen assured the old man.

He scowled at Nayima, then at Karen, then back at Nayima. Both of them were wearing masks and gloves, but Nayima felt naked, as if he could see the antibodies in their blood. As if he knew what she had done to Kyle.

"More vaccine's coming," he said. "Radio said so."

They both thanked the Lord above. Nayima felt a sting in her eyes as she summoned tears that would look like joy. Her theater classes had not been wasted like Gram had said they would be.

"Did the radio say when?" Nayima asked, trying to sound eager instead of terrified. She did not have a radio; she'd broken it on the way to Malibu. Also, there were no batteries in her apartment—she'd looked—so a radio wouldn't do her any good.

He shrugged and began walking on with his fish. He swung one stiff leg, his gait uneven. Water from his bucket splashed. His bare feet were gray with grime, toenails blackened.

"Free water!" Nayima called after him. "Tell your . . ." She almost said *friends*. "You know . . . other people."

He kept walking without looking back. "Jerry Seinfeld!" he said, like an epithet.

She would have to bring up her joke game to get this withered old grouch to laugh, especially if he was comparing her to comedy legends. How was that even fair?

"Well, shit," Karen said, once he was out of earshot. "What happens to . . . us?"

"I'm not gonna stick around to find out," Nayima said.

I, not *we*.

Not *us*.

Nayima did not sleep that night.

Karen had said they should leave Malibu by morning, and now Nayima understood the meaning of the phrase *The show must go on*. While Karen sobbed in the bedroom, Nayima worked by candlelight at the living room table to write more flyers, even though she knew she should be writing more jokes. She wanted to prove herself, yet there was no point in honing her material if no one would hear about her show. She doubted the old fisherman would tell anyone to come. And if he showed up, he'd be a heckler for sure.

Nayima finished the entire ream of paper: a stack of two hundred. She hadn't been so excited about a project since years before the plague. Maybe ever.

By the end of the next day, Malibu was Nayimatown. Her flyers were everywhere; clamped beneath windshield wipers on empty cars, tacked to telephone poles, pinned beneath rocks atop the giant beach boulders. She'd remembered every spot where she'd seen Mister Mom or the Three Stooges or the Brat Pack, where anyone might be likely to go. While she placed the flyers, she ran over her act in her mind. She might not have a notebook one day, so she would need to be able to rely on her memory.

Karen did not hang flyers with her the second day. She was packing.

Nayima was always packed. She wore her world on her back.

On the day of the show, Nayima set out with her backpack before a hint of daylight. She did not want to see the apartment in sunlight, or she might come back. She locked the door and kicked the key down over the railing to the sand below so she would not be tempted to return. The tide would bury the key or sweep it away.

Karen followed her, but neither of them spoke. They were each carrying a plastic crate that would serve as Nayima's stage, to give her a small height advantage, a touch of grandness. The surf's music followed them, coaxing tears from Nayima. She would miss the ocean wherever she went next. Karen had a backpack too—with far too much inside. Karen was already breathing hard under the weight of her pack. She would not last. They had been walking for fifteen minutes before Nayima realized her tears might be for Karen.

"Let me take your crate," Nayima said. "I can carry both."

She knew Karen had only offered to carry one of the crates to be useful to her. Nayima had sterilized extra water bottles for the audience, so her backpack was much heavier too.

"You were right," Karen said, "I packed too much."

"It's okay."

Karen's sigh was more a silent wail. "Nothing is okay, Nayima."

"I mean don't worry about it now. When we get there, decide what to leave behind."

She saw Kyle's slack, sleeping lips like a photograph. *I'm sorry*, she whispered to him. She had to leave Kyle behind too if she was going to make room for Karen. Or anyone.

Now that the day had arrived, she almost hoped no one would come see the show. She and Karen needed the extra water for themselves. Karen had been honest about what she thought, and at great cost. Honesty was the greatest treasure left; maybe the only one that mattered.

"I'll try not to be like this all the time," Nayima said. "I can be better."

"Me too," Karen said.

Nayima's heart sped with the rising tide, as if it were wind pushing her. As soon as the show was over, if there was a show at all, she would search the driveways and parking lots for a working car with keys. Maybe she could get one to start. She'd once found a PT Cruiser that had driven her straight to paradise, and maybe she could find a vehicle that would let her go there again.

They could.

The skyline shone in the barest pink, just enough to show the silhouette of the pier's sign ahead. And below it . . . vague shadows. Movement. Or was that her imagination?

"Someone's there," Karen said. She sounded happy, but Nayima's chest cinched with ice.

Silently, Nayima held out her arm to stop Karen's quickening pace. She gestured to the side, and they crouched behind a dumpster on the side of an old surf shop. Karen groaned from the weight of her pack.

As the light grew, Nayima recognized the Old Man in the Sea. He had brought a folding chair and was already sitting, dressed as he'd been the day before.

"Holy shit," Nayima said. "He came."

Karen clasped her shoulder and shook her. "Aren't those the kids and their dad? Check it out. Over by the sign?"

The father and his two children looked elephantine in silhouette because they were wearing gas masks, but they were ten yards from the old man, keeping distance even from each other. Four! Four was a good crowd, half of the town's remaining population.

Though two were kids—she would have to keep her act clean.

Since no marshals were in sight, she and Karen resumed their walk to the pier. She chose a spot a few yards away from the old man's chair, far closer to the PCH than she'd planned, but she didn't want to ask him to move. She would do her routine without looking at the cars.

Nayima felt shy beneath the strangers' stares, under the weight of what they needed and her promises to them. She opened her backpack and stood ten water bottles upright, fighting common sense that told her to keep them.

"Here's the free water," she announced. "It's desalinated, but go on and boil it. I boiled the bottles too, but you can use gloves."

When Nayima stepped back, no one stepped forward for the water. Good.

She measured the space in the center of the pier's walkway to set up her crates. While Karen offered her a hand to steady herself, Nayima climbed up and tested her balance with one foot on each. The crates were not quite even, rocking her like she was surfing.

Nayima wished the sun rose in the west, but the dawn sky was growing bright with resolve, washing everything in pink and lilac like the colors of her thumbtacks.

"We're up here!" she heard Karen shout out behind her, motioning to someone from farther down the pier. Nayima hoped Karen had sense enough not to be hailing marshals.

"There's, like, six more of them," Karen told her, excited.

Two members of the Brat Pack had come in dust masks and blue gloves, a new young couple who looked carefree in beach clothes and light jackets. Most of the faces were new: a brown man with three women of different hues, all of them taller than he, all four of them hiding their faces behind clean, colorful scarves. Their clothes were clean too. Someone was wearing perfume, even.

"Are you from Sacramento?" one of the women asked, hopeful inside her purple scarf.

Nayima shook her head. She repeated her spiel about the free water, so the woman in the purple scarf walked up to take a bottle in her gloved hands. She motioned to Nayima, asking if she could take two, and Nayima nodded. The woman offered one bottle to the old fisherman, and he shook his head, waving her away. He was not wearing gloves.

Nayima counted: twelve people had gathered in Malibu! She had not been in the company of so many others in more than a year, almost since the plague began.

"It's great to be here!" Nayima proclaimed.

The crowd, stone silent before she'd spoken, transformed into a rousing amen corner. The old man was already smiling. Their clapping was muted by their gloves.

Nayima was so shocked by their response that she almost forgot her first joke. She'd planned to open with the one Karen liked about Malibu prices going down, but it felt wrong now, especially with the car tombs in view. Why were most of her jokes about the lost?

She blurted: "I went swimming in the ocean the other day— my friend said, *Aren't you afraid of the sharks?* I said, *No, I'm only afraid of the lifeguards.*"

She'd rushed it. Her delivery had been bland.

But their laughter nearly rocked Nayima from her unsteady crates. The bearded man laughed so loudly that the approaching tide could not smother him. He pointed at her, head turned over his shoulder to be sure everyone knew she was there. Farther back, the children squealed and tugged at each other, until their father separated them. Most of them applauded.

Nayima told every joke she could think of, every joke she had ever known. She raised her voice until she was hoarse so everyone would hear her punch lines. Their smiles were hidden, and sometimes the waves drowned them out, yet she saw laughing in their eyes. She luxuriated in so many eyes. Especially Karen's—staring at her as if she were the goddess Yemayah rising from the sea.

Nayima smiled at Karen, her hand over her heart to say: *I love you*. She didn't know if it was true yet, or if loving was even possible anymore, but Karen deserved to be loved as much as these strangers deserved to laugh. As much as these children deserved a childhood. As much as they all deserved a memory without claws.

Nayima did not stop her show—not at first—even when she heard the faraway *chop-chop-chop* sound of helicopters and saw the swarm of black dots advancing in the morning sky.

Attachment Disorder

Republic of California
Carrier Territories
2062

The news of death came in the snake of black smoke from the southeast. The horse ranch.

Nayima knew what the smoke meant, so she didn't jump on her bike to race fifteen miles through scrub brush and remains of what had once been vineyards to inspect whatever was left of the ranch. She didn't even wake Lottie, since Lottie was allowed to sleep late on Sundays. A deal was a deal, and rest would not come easily to any of them after today.

Refusing to hurry, she gathered everything she wanted to keep and checked the packed contents of her backpack. Her old Glock—fully loaded—and shells. Extra shoes, protein capsules, water-purifying packs, yellowing Rand McNally paper maps of Central California she'd found in an old toolbox in her house's shed, cleansing wipes, and underwear. She shoved her hololens in her hoodie pocket and zipped it. Raul would see the smoke on his monitor soon, if he hadn't already, and he would investigate. And then he would call with the bad news.

Nayima waited for Raul's call from the creaky rocking chair on her front porch, beside her wooden butter churn, presumably handcrafted forty or fifty years ago. She guessed the churn, like the rocker, had been more of a prop for the previous owners, who no doubt had bought their butter packaged from the shell of a grocery store that had once done business a few miles down the road. But Lottie had arrived from the lab-coats in Sacramento with a taste for butter, so Nayima had learned how to make it for her.

Beyond the porch, Nayima had uncovered her hoverbike, which rested beneath the house's awning, gleaming in metallic black like the officious police vehicle it had once been. The hoverbike and Glock were Nayima's world; the house was just where she slept.

She knew she should run with Lottie for her sake, or at least try to, but even that certainty did not move her from her post on the porch, binoculars in one hand and Glock in the other.

If she heard engines, it was already too late. If she saw drones, it was too late.

Let them come, then. She had met this moment so many times before: During the evacuation, when Gram was too sick from cancer to move despite police orders. Hiding in abandoned buildings from the infected who were enraged by the resistance of the well. Then, after the sick were long gone, hiding in bushes and abandoned cars and even an old mine, once, from the survivors hunting down carriers. Each time, she had thought: *Let them come.*

When the hololens shivered in her pocket, Nayima slipped it on the way Gram had worn her reading glasses, near the edge of her nose so she could also see her bike, the road, the thirsty brush, the graying, empty sky. The holoscreen glared on and flickered, appearing above her fence line. Raul looked a decade older since she'd seen him last weekend. His feed wasn't flickering from that distance; he was standing in a haze of smoke. He was calling from the burning ranch Lizette and Dimitri had shared before Dimitri died after a fall from a newly broken mare six months before.

Someone might follow Raul now. Fool! The fire was probably a trap, singling out the weakest first, the oldest, the solitary, to draw out the rest. But was she any less foolish, waiting on her porch for them to come?

Raul's voice was smoke-roughened: "Lizette's gone. All the horses burned. Dios mío."

Nayima felt sharp grief for the horses. Half a dozen beautiful creatures, gone. Senseless.

Lizette and Dimitri had made the choice to live alone, just as she had. Their years in lab cages had taught them to cherish every choice, and to make the freest ones. Researchers had learned a generation ago that burning did not cure the plague, only the vaccine from antibodies in their veins. And the plague did not infect horses, which was why so many ran wild in the valley between Nayima's house and Lizette's ranch. Lizette and Dimitri had started collecting horses when they realized how many were dying for lack of food and water in the wild, maybe to make up for lost human lives.

No, the plague had not been their fault. But they had carried it.

"This didn't have to happen," Raul said. He sounded enraged rather than sad, though she understood. Just last weekend, at the group dinner, he'd told her and Lizette they needed to move to the compound, at least until they all decided what to do next. *Until we all decide*, he'd said, as if everyone's agreement was assured. Raul still hadn't figured out that they would never all agree: Nayima would always dissent. Always. She would never move back to Sacramento, no matter how pretty the promises. Lizette would not have either.

She hoped Lizette had the chance to kill herself before the fire. They had talked about it, of course, when they'd met at the ranch for meals every other Tuesday, far from the compound the others foolishly called El Nuevo Mundo. Who would shoot whom. Where the poisons were. Nayima had once uttered her plan aloud, and even Lottie had not flinched: *I'll shoot Lottie. Then I'll shoot myself.* How had Lizette managed with Dimitri gone?

"I'll come for you both now," Raul said.

"No. Go protect the others."

"Come quickly." He wanted to say *ahora*, an order. Instead, he trained his feed so she could see the blackened, smoking ruins of Lizette's front porch, a wretched mirror of her own. Nayima closed her eyes. Lizette's corpse lay inside, and Nayima had seen enough corpses.

"Entiendo," she assured him. "I'll come."

"Quickly, Nayima." The others had assigned Raul as their alpha because he was the only one with the health and youth for the job, yet his bossiness burned her ears. Still, they were under attack, so she couldn't let her temper flame over something as petty as sentence structure and tone of voice. "I had to call the marshals. They'll be there too. Lo siento."

Of course he'd called the marshals.

"Te quiero," Raul said. His voice broke, a contagion.

"Me too."

"You know you should have left before now, Nayima. Keep her safe."

"Fuck off. You know I will."

She blinked hard, held the dark for two seconds. Heard the connection snap away. When she opened her eyes again, Raul and the smoky ruins were gone, with only her bike in sight. They had even killed the horses. That wasn't robbers, or vandals. The Cleaners had found them. And the marshals were waiting.

Nayima had shaken off the habit of fear, though she was scared now. Scared and sixty-six, with bad knees and hips. And a failing brain, hacked by either age or her chips, or likely both. She was an old woman now, the same age Gram had been when she died. *Lottie Powell Houston,* she recited silently. *Born December 9, 1948, died sixty-six years later, when the rest of the world met the plague.* Gram, with her usual good planning, had gotten out just in time.

"Who was that?" Lottie stuck her head out of the window, her dark hair's ringlets tangled from sleep. "Who were you talking to?"

"Raul," Nayima said, adding as she saw Lottie's face light up at her father's name: "Cleaners got to the ranch. We have to go." She pointed toward the smoke plume, watched Lottie's eyes moon in shock. Lottie had called them Uncle Lizzy and Uncle Dimi. Gram would have softened her words with *pumpkin* or *darling*, but gentle words gagged in Nayima's mouth. She hoped Lottie wouldn't start crying.

"Why are you just sitting there?" the girl wailed. Lottie was only eleven, but she was long grown. She left the window, running back to grab the bag Nayima had packed with her, feet pounding across the floorboards.

That's my girl, Nayima thought, but hated thinking it.

Lottie *wasn't* her girl. She never had been. And she certainly would not be after today.

A movement in the eastern sky caught her eye, and Nayima's finger tightened on the Glock's trigger until she saw it was a hawk, bigger than a drone. Some drones were so small they looked like insects, though most were the size of smaller birds. Her heart was pulsing so hard that her veins prickled to her toes. Only a hawk.

They would run. If the Cleaners were organized, they would have been here by now. Their plan, probably, was to follow Raul back to El Nuevo Mundo, where they could kill all twelve of them at once.

"Hurry up!" Nayima said, rocking forward to gain her balance so she could stand.

She and Lottie could make it to El Nuevo Mundo before the Cleaners, undetected. Maybe these assholes didn't know where she lived yet, or they were saving her and Lottie for last. Or maybe the fire was only Sacramento's ploy to try to scare them off their land. Maybe.

On her feet, Nayima noticed she was frozen in place. The Glock seemed easier.

She wasn't afraid to die, but living scared the hell out of her. Especially with Lottie.

You've got this, pumpkin, she heard Gram whisper behind her right ear. Her voice was so clear, Nayima nearly gasped.

Then came the more familiar genderless voice behind her left ear, also inside her head. Nayima had named the chip's voice Sonia. *"Your blood pressure and heart rate are unusually high. Please report to HealthHost immediately to have your chip replaced for more thorough care. You are—"* A long pause, a different, deeper voice—*"six months."* Then, Sonia's voice again: *". . . overdue for your chip replacement. This is in violation of Carrier Codes six through ten under the Articles of Reconciliation . . ."*

Nayima heard the tedious message several times a day. The threat in the word *violation* had worried her the first time, but not after six months. She used the music of Sonia's dying sing-song to move her feet one after the other across her dusty soil to the hoverbike.

Gram's voice, though, was newer. The first time she heard it, Nayima had dropped the bowl she was holding and ruined the dinner she'd fussed over for Lottie. She was almost sure the voice was triggered by her chip somehow. She was forgetting more things all the time, though going senile didn't mean you heard voices. Could be a malfunction, or could be prodding for service, the way her gadgets used to get buggy when it was time to spend money for upgrades.

Hell no, she wouldn't let them open her up again. She would take Lottie to live with Raul the way he'd always wanted her to, but she wasn't going back to Sacramento. Never. No matter how many voices she heard, or whose.

As Nayima prepared to swing her leg over her hoverbike's saddle, she noticed the woman standing fifty yards from her, at the closed gate. The woman was wearing a short, pale-blue hospital gown, her silver hair in neat cornrows, her skin nearly blending with the soil. Nayima would know Gram anywhere. Dead or alive.

"*You may now be experiencing visual and auditory hallucinations,*" Sonia said.

"No shit," Nayima said.

Lottie bounded outside with her pack and her doll, meeting Nayima's eyes with defiance. They had talked about this: no toys. Toys were a distraction and easily dropped for tracking.

"Leave it," Nayima said.

"No. I tied a rope to her—see?" True enough, Lottie had tied twine thoroughly around the doll's torso, knotted at several points, and after two feet the twine bound the doll to her own waist. She had wasted time tying herself to a doll.

Nayima took one last gaze at the space where she had lived for nearly ten years, the government's reparations after her long imprisonment. She felt nothing: she saw only drought-ravaged soil and cracked walls and flaking paint and dusty windows where she had so often sat sentry. Yet she felt a pang when she saw her black cat, Tango, watching from the window. If Tango had been a dog, she might have brought him too. She'd named her black cats Tango since she was a girl, as if the same cat had followed her to the end of the world.

"Go leave the door open. Let the cat out," Nayima said.

"Why?"

"We're not coming back. Don't waste time asking."

Lottie looked at her closely, as if to see if her face matched the sorrow of her words; she was convinced enough to run back to the porch without more questions. Lottie flung the door open and hurried back toward the hoverbike to board behind Nayima, her eyes high on the smoky sky, cradling her doll like an infant. Tango bounded out of the house, finally free to rejoin his wild brothers. The house would be overtaken by cats. Nayima almost liked that idea.

She jabbed in her passcode on the console, pressed the power button when it glowed blue. Like her chip, like *her*, the bike was an old model in need of upgrades. But it could still hit sixty miles per hour and hover a steady foot high. She'd clocked and measured the bike just two days before. As soon as Raul mentioned he'd seen it advertised at the bazaar, Nayima had insisted he buy it for her.

The bike pitched forward, Nayima's hand a bit too heavy on the accelerator before she braked abruptly, testing her reflexes and the bike's mood. Lottie tightened her arms around her and pressed herself into Nayima's back as it bobbed. Hugs did not come easily to them, so Nayima noticed Lottie's grip and weight and warmth in a way that made her too sad to think.

You've got this, pumpkin. Go on, now, Gram said. Sure enough, Gram was still standing at the gate, waving her on like they were at a racing track. The back of her hospital gown billowed, showing her bare, sagging buttocks that looked more and more like Nayima's.

"Thanks for not shooting me, Mama," Lottie said.

Lottie had not called her *Mama* in nearly a year. At first, Lottie had forbidden it. The word *Mama* cut through her bones. Mamas left you. That's what Mamas did. Gram was standing at the gate to remind her.

"Don't thank me yet."

Nayima squeezed the accelerator. The hoverbike flew.

The day Nayima's mother packed and moved away, she'd told Nayima her sad story: how she'd married her Spelman English professor at twenty-two; he'd been twenty years older and divorced and she worried he would be in his sixties when she was only in her forties—but she told herself she would worry when the time came. Then he'd died of a heart attack only five years later, when Nayima was four.

"And sweetheart," Mama had told Nayima that day as she packed her powder-blue suitcase, so matter-of-fact, "I wasn't ready."

Wasn't ready to be a widow. Wasn't ready to be a mother. Wasn't ready.

Nayima had been dreaming about her mother more often since the memo from Sacramento came two weeks ago. Gram hadn't expected to be raising a child again, and Nayima had resented Mama mostly for Gram's sake. It wasn't fair to drop a child in someone's lap out of the blue. Just like with Lottie. And like Mama, Nayima wasn't ready.

Nayima used to tell herself, *She's not from my body,* as if this would make it easier if—no, *when*—she and Lottie were separated. But Lottie was Priscilla Houston's granddaughter, and Lottie Powell Sears's great-granddaughter, and she was Nayima's offspring with Raul, even if Lottie had been mixed in a tube and gestated in an artificial womb. Even if she and Raul hadn't known Lottie existed until she was four.

Lottie was the only living offspring of two carriers, dreamed into creation in a lab. And Lottie had tested clean of the antibodies since birth, so the lab-coats had no use for pricking and prodding her. After four years, the bureaucrats in Sacramento had let her go—to her biological parents.

Nayima had always known it was too good to be true. All of it.

From the time she'd first learned of Reconciliation, she'd known it couldn't be the freedom promised: two hundred acres, a private home, and no more medical experiments. Then, the caveats: the cranial trackers and HealthHost chips and rationed water were a different kind of cage. And they had sent Lottie seven years ago—yet another means of control. The memo from Sacramento had not surprised her. She was just surprised that it had taken so long.

Although you are of course lawfully entitled to your property under Reconciliation, we are alarmed at the growing number of extremist organizations with an agenda to harm you, primarily a group that calls itself Cleaners. The perimeters have faced constant skirmishes in the past two years, with daily protests and increasing casualties.

Additionally, a growing number of citizens, many of whom are first-generation survivors, now believe it is too great a public safety hazard to allow Carriers to remain unsupervised, for fear that the virus might mutate and grow impervious to the vaccine we have manufactured based on your service to our research. Although it is well documented that there is no longer scientific basis for this fear, it is nonetheless driving extremist activity. For this reason, we have created a living area for Carriers that will give you much greater access to the amenities available in the city and increased security to protect you from those who wrongfully blame you for the Doomsday Virus.

Once you see the scope of the vision—a neighborhood modeled on the world of your youth—we believe you will find the proposed living quarters much more comfortable, especially as your age advances. Please see the photos on the next page.

Fuck the photos.

Was it better to die free? Or to keep on living, even if living would mean going back to the zookeepers in Sacramento? Lottie would have to decide for herself. She could die free with Nayima, or be a prisoner with Raul. Lottie wasn't a carrier; she might have a chance for a life in Sacramento.

Nayima would let Lottie decide at El Nuevo Mundo.

* * *

She could make it in an hour if she took the abandoned high-way and cut across the prairie the last five miles, her typical route, but Nayima decided to avoid open spaces. She went fif-teen minutes out of her way to the untended almond groves that gave cover and didn't make her such an obvious target for drones. *You're still wearing a tracker, dumbass*, she reminded herself, though the Cleaners wouldn't have access to Sacra-mento's tracking data. Probably. Unless there was a breach. Or burning the ranch had been a change of tactics.

Nayima was fairly good on the bike, considering she'd only had it for a few months, yet the speed taxed her reflexes around boulders and broken trees, and her joints ached as she held on to her grips. The grips were pressure-sensitive, which made the bike's movement herky-jerky, sometimes shifting Lottie's weight behind her, forcing the girl to tighten her arms, viselike.

A tree trunk appeared from nowhere, almost a hallucina-tion, taller than a foot. Nayima steered around it so violently that Lottie gasped when the rear panel nicked it. The bike swayed right with their weight, like a horse trying to throw them. Nayima was sure they would both fall. Then the bike was upright, lurching forward, and they were both still on board.

You're going too fast, Gram said.

Sonia joined in: "*Your heart rate is dangerously accelerated. This rate has not been recorded in . . . seven . . . years. Please rest immediately until your heart rate returns to normal.*"

Nayima had disabled her chip's regular updates long ago through her HealthHost account, but apparently her prefer-ences were glitchy now too.

The girl whimpered.

"It's okay, Lottie." The lie stuck in Nayima's throat and burned her face. But Lottie wasn't yet strong enough to pilot the bike herself, and she would do neither of them any good if she panicked.

It's okay, Gram echoed to her.

For a long while, forty minutes, then an hour, it *was* okay. Nayima found her speed at a brisk fifty-two mph on a deer trail through the rows, and the engine ran as smooth as glass. The gaps widened between the trees, fewer obstacles. She caught herself thinking how pretty it was, how she wished her land was greener. (Right. *Her* land.) She was admiring the beauty when she saw the man-made red color in the corner of her eye, and she made a wide circle with the bike to double back and see what it was.

"What?" Lottie said.

"*Shhhh.*" Nayima's voice whispered barely above the bike's hiss. She leaned to peer down, Lottie still tugging on her. "Let me loose," Nayima said, and when she was free she bent down low enough to see it: an aluminum wrapper of some kind, maybe for food, maybe for something else. But *shiny*. New.

"What is it?" Lottie asked.

"I don't know yet."

Nayima set her hololens to *Telephoto* and scanned the grove ahead. She looked a long time, lingering on gray twigs and brown bark, pulling out, zooming closer. A dark rabbit hopped behind a log. The colors seemed right.

But no. *Blue.* Someone was wearing navy-blue pants, their knee propped up from behind a tree, mostly hidden. Tan hiking boots. A large man sat not even thirty yards ahead of them. Two more legs in gray sweatpants strode across her vision before she could pull back to see his fuller figure, but that meant there were at least two. Behind the trees just ahead of them, only fifteen minutes from El Nuevo Mundo.

No one was allowed in Carrier Territories except marshals, who would be bad enough, but these men weren't in uniform. They were not marshals.

"*Your heart rate is increasing,*" Sonia said. "*Please rest to reduce your heart rate.*"

It's okay, pumpkin, Gram said.

"Someone's there," Nayima said quietly.

"It's not—?"

"No one we know." Raul was the youngest carrier at fifty-nine. Nayima was younger than most at sixty-six. No one at El Nuevo Mundo walked with that young man's stride.

The bike sputtered a little too loudly, dipping an inch and then rising. Hoverbikes always wanted to be moving forward. Nayima steered left, back the way they'd come another thirty yards, then rounded toward two fallen pines crossed to provide the most shelter, big enough to stash the bike behind them and Lottie in the gap between them.

The bike dropped and rolled to a stop as its wheels descended, a racket over the almond hulls and pine needles. They both exhaled, relieved, when it came to a silent stop. For a moment, they only breathed together.

"Let's go home," Lottie finally whispered.

Lottie raised her hand: *Hush*. She wanted to call Raul so he could warn the others, but these men might have signal trackers. Maybe their earlier call had already been intercepted. Maybe that was why the men were here. She was just lucky they hadn't heard the hoverbike's approach.

Lottie scowled at Nayima from the shelter, realizing that Nayima meant to leave her. She was a lovely child. That had been hard from the start: the fresh prettiness of her ancestral face. Harder with Lottie's new tears.

"I have to see who's there," Nayima whispered.

"Let's just go back."

Nayima shook her head. She couldn't go back to waiting. She had probably been planning to leave since her HealthHost chip tried to lure her back to the lab. Since Sacramento's lies about a safer haven. Her days of running were over.

"I have to deal with this." Nayima handed Lottie her hololens, although she hated to part with it, just like she hated to leave the bike. "Check the time: if I'm not back in an hour—"

"An *hour*?"

"—or if someone comes, you hear more engines, call Raul. But only if I don't return. *Only* if someone comes. Our calls aren't private, hear? Calling is a last resort."

Lottie nodded, her eyes so wide and frightened that Nayima was sure she would call Raul as soon as Nayima turned her back. She wasn't even sure Lottie shouldn't. She would just have to find those men without the hololens.

"Are they gonna kill you?" Lottie asked, tears in her voice.

"They might. Or I might kill them first."

Lottie's face and eyes became stone. Nayima had bequeathed stone to her daughter if nothing else. Her daughter. *Her* daughter. Nayima almost changed her mind. Maybe Lottie was right: maybe they should go back to their house. Back to the smoke and the butter churn.

"I'll be back," she said instead. They both knew it was a ridiculous promise, and Nayima knew it was a temporary promise at best.

Lottie's stone softened to skin and tears again. "I love you, Mama."

Nayima wanted to say, *Don't*. "Me too." *Pumpkin*. "Now, stay hidden."

Nayima took a few steps away, turned back to survey Lottie's hiding place: you had to look closely to see her brown face against the dead bark, in the shadows. Lottie still clasped her doll to her chest like a breathing thing, and Nayima was glad she'd brought company. The bike's black tail wasn't as well hidden as she'd hoped, though it was still hard to see at ten yards.

If she had to, she would shoot the men, or die trying.

Then she would come back to Lottie.

Nayima's right hip seemed to scrape its socket with each step, and before long she was limping. Her knees and ankles popped, angry. She stepped into a rabbit hole covered in pine needles and nearly lost her balance, falling against a spindly tree. Pain shot up from her toes to the back of her neck. *Damn.* She searched for a sturdy walking stick, stripping a fallen branch.

Better. Much better. Gram had walked with a cane. Nothing to it. She moved purposefully, raised her feet high to avoid rustling, stepped gently as rainfall. But the woods were disorienting, especially woods as regimented as these: every tree trunk identical to the one she'd just passed. She had spent so many years surrounded by concrete or scrub brush that she did not know the language of trees. She had a compass, yet she didn't want to veer even a few steps toward where she'd seen the men. She needed to walk a straight line.

"*Your blood pressure is rising dramatically,*" Sonia said. "*Please take your medication.*"

Slow down, pumpkin, Gram said. *Slow and steady. This is the way.*

Ahead, Gram was waving as she had at the house's front gate. She was in her nurse's uniform now, her hair salt-and-pepper instead of the silver she'd worn on her deathbed. Gram had retired from Pomona Valley Hospital only two years before she got sick. No matter how many steps Nayima took, she got no closer to Gram. And although Gram vanished from time to time, she mostly stayed in sight, pointing out the path.

"Gram, they fucked up my head," Nayima huffed. "They fucked up my everything."

I know, baby. But they didn't break you.

Then Gram was gone, and Nayima wavered in her footsteps. She confused the trees again. *Oh!* Gram was standing on top of a tall boulder wearing her purple Sunday best with her ostrich-feather hat. Overdressed as usual. Her white pumps glowed, a beacon. Gram waved and pointed: the red wrapper she'd seen was still there, gleaming in its shaft of sunlight.

"*You are experiencing hallucinations*," Sonia said. "*Please have your HealthHost chip serviced immediately to avoid further neural interference.*"

Nayima had hardly taken ten steps away from the wrapper when she heard a man's voice ahead, unconcerned about being heard. She stood as straight and still as a pine to try to make out the words, but her ears were foam.

Breathe, Nayima, Gram said.

Nayima took a deep breath, held it—felt her heart's thudding and icy-hot blood rushing in her veins—and exhaled through her mouth the way she had in the days of her yoga class at the strip mall in the land of the dead. The sky wheeled overhead, then it righted itself as she breathed. She hadn't been this afraid in a long time.

She plunged her walking stick into the hard soil, a silent spear, and walked forward in the trees' shadows, correcting her course to the burr of the stranger's voice.

". . . those horses. There's herds all over out there, but they could only torch the ones inside the gate . . ."

Nayima's anger made lightning seem to split the sky, sharpening her senses. The man still sounded muffled, although he might be only five yards from her. She hadn't understood him sooner because his mouth was covered with some kind of mask. Only a fanatic or a fool would be wearing a mask on a day this hot, with no one in sight, still two miles out from El Nuevo Mundo. No marshals or soldiers wore masks in Carrier Territories. Not anymore. Carriers' blood had wiped out the virus as mightily as it had spread it.

Only fanatics would wear masks. Only fanatics would slaughter horses.

Nayima's index finger felt numb from hugging the trigger. She walked like a cat from tree to tree, one step to the next. She could smell tobacco vapor light in the air. Close.

". . . Well, tell them to hurry the fuck up," the voice said, as if it were in her ear like Gram's. But it wasn't. She was sure of that. This voice was real.

Nayima peeked past a thick tree trunk, and there he was: his back to her in a black jacket, gray sweatpants, a hunting rifle slung across his shoulder. He was on a hololens, poking absently at his backpack on the ground with a twig. He had probably been waiting a long time. He seemed impatient. He had forgotten to never stop watching.

An easy shot. Too easy. But where was the other one?

There he is, baby, Gram said.

At an angle ahead, two o'clock, ten yards, the man in the navy-blue pants was pissing against a tree in a steady stream. He was wearing his backpack. His rifle was at arm's length, standing just clear of his stream.

"*Your respiration is increasing*," Sonia said. "*To avoid hyperventilation, take deep, even breaths. Rest or seek a medical professional.*"

She was a good shot. Shooting had been her hobby since Reconciliation, no matter how expensive the bullets were. Cans. Bottles. Old tires. Rabbits and squirrels, sometimes, like Gram used to hunt when she was a girl in Gadsden County, Florida. Nayima had a split second to choose: which man could reach his rifle sooner? She almost spent too much time pondering it. The pissing man was shaking off.

Her excitement made her crack a twig, and the one with the hololens was about to turn when she fired into the back of his head. He fell forward. The gunshot exploded in the woods, hunching the pissing man's shoulders. He didn't have time to zip up before he reached for his rifle, and he couldn't raise his rifle before Nayima's first shot grazed his shoulder and backed him up a step, then her second and third shots riddled his chest. He gasped a long breath inside his plastic contagion mask—the way Gram had gasped when her pain stole her breath—and dropped to his knees while he stared with bewilderment. Nayima imagined what he saw: an old gray-haired Black woman with a walking stick, face brittle, eyes bright. This was not the person he had expected to kill him today, if he'd even bothered to imagine that he might die.

The walking stick trembled in Nayima's unsteady hand.

"*You are losing consciousness*," Sonia said.

"No, no," Nayima said, then—

When she woke, the silence startled her. The gunshots were fresh in her ears, though no birds were flapping in the leaves, no creatures scurrying for safety. The gunshots were long gone. Panicked, she checked the men she'd killed. One still lay before her as she'd seen him last, shaggy hair covering his face. The other had fallen forward onto the ground, pants still unbuckled, his ass crack pale white. She had never seen their faces.

The dead man's hololens chimed so loudly beneath him that it must have been set to *Urgent*. That was what had made her stir: a chime. Someone was calling. But no one had come yet.

"*You have had a fainting episode. Please lie still and call for medical assistance*."

Nayima's right side ached, especially her neck. She ignored the shooting pain as she braced with her walking stick, and the trunk's firm weight helped her stand. Dizzyness came and subsided.

If not for Gram waving to her from the rows of almond trees behind her, Nayima might have lost her way back to Lottie.

Lottie let out a gasp when bushes shuddered at her arrival, but her face quickly brightened. She leaped out to wrap her arms around Nayima, nearly pulling her off-balance.

"I heard gunshots!" Lottie said, tearful. "I wanted to call Papa, but I was afraid to."

Nayima knew the rest: Lottie had thought, for that instant, she might be alone. The girl was still shaking against her, so Nayima held her more tightly.

"I'm here," Nayima said. "Mama's here."

"Those men . . . ?"

"They're gone now."

Nayima hoped she would never forget the look on Lottie's face then, relief and adoration, the purest moment between them. But she had no time to savor it.

"Pumpkin, I have to give you a choice," Nayima said. "I was planning on asking you later, but you need to decide now."

Lottie watched her with Gram's eyes, the slant of Mama's nose—waiting.

"If we ride on to El Nuevo Mundo to meet Raul, there will be marshals there too—to protect us." She practically spat out the word *protect*. Probably her biggest lie yet.

"Protect us from men like those up there?"

"Yes."

"They'll guard us at El Nuevo Mundo?"

"The government wants us to move to a special place built for us."

All joy left Lottie's eyes. "Go back?" She had only been four when she'd been sent to Nayima, yet that was old enough to remember what it was like to live in a cage, even if hers had plexiglass instead of bars.

"Right now, you and me, we're free," Nayima said. "A little bit free, anyway. We both have trackers in our heads. Sacramento can find us. But if we stay in the Carrier Territories, we can find somewhere else to live. Fend for ourselves. Until they come for us. That's the difference. Either we'll go to them or they'll come to us. But I don't know when. And even before the marshals come, more men like the ones who burned the ranch might come. Or those up there I just left."

Lottie was mulling it over with renewed tears. She didn't like the choices. "Will Papa stay with us?"

Nayima shook her head. "You know your papa. He'll go to

Sacramento with the others. That's what he'll want for you too. He'll think it's safer there. Especially after today."

"No he won't. He'll want to be with—"

"You know your papa," Nayima said again, and Lottie did, so she was silent. "Now, there's something else . . ."

Lottie waited, agonized.

"I have a faulty health chip," Nayima said. "I'm having hallucinations—seeing people who aren't there. Hearing voices."

She expected greater alarm from Lottie, saw none. "Like who?"

"Like . . . Gram."

"My great-gramma?" *My* great-gramma. Lottie had claimed her. She knew Gram from Nayima's stories. Lottie had been so proud when she'd finally been given a name instead of a specimen number. "Do you see her right now?"

Nayima scanned the area back toward El Nuevo Mundo. No sign of Gram. Then she looked back the other way—the way they'd come—and found Gram sitting against the trunk of a tree about twenty-five yards back, still in her nurse's uniform. Waiting.

"Yes," Nayima said. She pointed. "There. Under the tree?"

Lottie craned to follow Nayima's pointing finger. "I don't see her."

"I'm the only one who sees her. My chip is scrambling my brain. It's like a trick to get me to go back to a doctor. To let them go back inside my head. And I'm old, Lottie. My body is slow. I don't know how well I can protect you."

Lottie shivered and took Nayima's hand like a parent would. "Does she scare you?"

"No." Maybe the Gram hallucination was a window to her unconscious. Maybe that was how Gram had helped her find the men. "She shows me things I already know, deep down."

Lottie scrunched her face in the sun, considering the weight of everything she'd heard. "Mama . . ." she finally said, "I don't wanna go with the marshals."

"*You heart rate is accelerating*," Sonia said. As if Nayima didn't already know.

"Me neither, Lottie."

"You killed the bad people."

"Not all of them. More might come for us."

"But the marshals might catch them?"

"Yes," Nayima said. "I'm gonna call Raul as soon as we finish talking, so they might."

In the distance, Gram stood up and wiped dust from what she used to call her derrière. She walked to the middle of the deer trail, watching them. Still waiting.

"I wanna go home," Lottie said, certain. "Papa will come stay with us."

Raul would be livid. He might try to take Lottie by force. But Raul would be the least of their problems if they went back to their house.

"Are you sure?" Nayima said. "We won't be safe back there."

"I just wanna be with you."

How had Mama done it? How had she packed that suitcase and sat Nayima down on the bed with that cigarette hanging from her mouth to tell her she was leaving? More than sixty years later, Nayima still didn't understand it. She couldn't leave Lottie even if it meant they might both die together.

Nayima stared down the path between the groves at Gram, expecting to see her wave, some gesture to show her opinion, but Gram was only standing in the path with her arms at her side, staring on. Then Gram turned away.

Walking back toward home.

PART IV

Future Shock

Ghost Ship

"One last thing," Nandi said in Zulu, not English, at the dock, so Florida knew she didn't want to be overheard by crewmen or waiting passengers. "I'll need you to carry this box to your cabin. Open it *promptly*. And carry it with *both* hands, please. I've paid for your rations on board, so no need for these."

Then Nandi had whisked the packs of cookies from Florida's hands—the sweets Florida had been collecting for weeks and had shepherded so carefully past security, tolerating insulting questions (*Don't you think you're big enough?*)—and in their place had given her a frightfully heavy box, at least seven or eight k, decorated with warning arrows and stickers, also in Zulu: *Carry Upright*. Who knew how long she would be stuck carrying it? Why couldn't Nandi have sent this to the cargo bay with the rest of Florida's deliveries like any other passenger?

Now Florida understood why she was being sent on her Pilgrimage by sea, a recreation of her long-ago ancestors' Middle Passage, rather than a hyperflight that could have taken her to New York in only two hours. Even a sixteen-hour jitney plane would be so much faster than a ship, and the price would be less than Nandi's new ostrich-feather hat. Ships could be beset by pirates and rough seas and seemed primitive even to Florida's unpampered sensibilities. The true advantage, for Nandi, was that flight security was stricter. Why would anyone bother to blow up a passenger ship?

Florida was now a smuggler. Diamonds or banned tech or who knew what Nandi sent on the ships with her couriers when she offered Pilgrimages: passage to the States for a year. Florida had never imagined Nandi would choose her, the way she professed she couldn't do without her; the passage alone was more than a month each way. Florida was also surprised that Nandi would risk her on a smuggling trip—the penalty for almost any infraction on a US-bound ship was being cast overboard. Theft. Assault. Even vandalism. The orientation had been very clear: passengers had a 5 percent voyage fail rate! But here she was, and Nandi had been brazen enough to set her package in Florida's hands in front of witnesses, begging for inspection. (Though Nandi had gotten it past security herself as far as the dock, at least; wealth and standing had true advantages.)

"I don't see how you eat that poison," Nandi said, in English this time. She slid Florida's cookies into her pocket. "It's just like a USian to eat for pleasure. Don't get spoiled already."

Nandi did not say goodbye, never mind that she had raised Florida since she was eight, in a way—if obtaining ownership of a child through her dead mothers' labor contracts constituted rearing. Nandi seemed to want to touch her, though she only gave Florida a knowing smile, bowed her short-shaved silver head at her, and pivoted toward the shore to return to her domed palace. Florida watched her feather hat floating away above the crowds.

For the first time in her life, Florida was among only strangers. *Wealthy* strangers, based on their colorful coats. Wealthy *USian* strangers. Florida's clothing was shades of dirty white: grays and tans and browns. Worker fashion. Now she would have to put up with stares from USians who were returning home after safari. Florida had never seen so many USians collected in one place. They were loud, shouting to be heard over each other. They wore mountains of soft clothing. All were eager to go home, happy and smiling, except when they saw her. Noticing brown or black skin was a favorite sport in the States, so most stared at her. Fine with her. Most of the Aggie campus in South Africa was made up of African American expats, so this was the first time Florida had noticed her skin in as long as she could remember. She hadn't reached the States yet and she was *Black* again. And in a sea of whites.

Racism still thrived in other parts of South Africa, she had heard, but the New Azania Campus of Naidoo Industries, as it was called—made up of agricultural engineers and workers—was a world unto itself. Privilege and prospects had everything to do with contracts and little to do with skin color. Nandi herself was proof: darker than Florida by shades and too much wealthier to even compute. Nandi's father had built New Azania, buying up once-prized drought-ravaged lands near Cape Town to experiment with bioengineering. This rising need for workers and scientists in South Africa had coincided with the Purging in the States, with millions of nonwhites driven beyond the US borders to avoid prison or police executions in their homes.

But "freedom," Florida's mothers had learned, was only earned by release from service contracts. And the debts they had accrued over the years had not been nearly enough to repay Naidoo, so they had died penniless, much like the sharecroppers of their forebears. So many others in New Azania, like Florida, were trapped by the decisions of others, trying to save for liberation, or passage back to the States out of nostalgia for familiar accents and home soil—even if it was a land that did not want them, winnowing down the population to whites remaking the storied multicultural nation in their own pale image.

And here they were, sneering at her. The USians were returning to their world of dominion. They did not like Florida. And she did not like them.

"There's a story, ya know," Florida said in her best USian accent. "About a ghost ship. Bet they didn't tell you there's a ghost ship floating out at sea, full of rotting bodies. Maybe we'll pass right by?" It was half a truth, but she felt like an actress. Such liberation! To speak whatever was in her mind, unafraid of docked rations. And it was so amusing the way their smiles faded. At least they stopped staring at her. And crowded her less. And let her pass.

But her improved mood didn't last long as she remembered the cookies Nandi had taken from her. She would not be free of Nandi even at sea. Nandi would control every bite she ate.

All Florida had wanted in exchange for forty days of boredom and peril on the ship was a sweet taste on her tongue every day, something to look forward to. Now she would not have that. All that waited ahead of her was time. And risk.

Shovel it, then. She would not return to Africa. She had a year to either escape or plot a way to earn a living on the dying lands for which her mothers had named her. Her older mother had been a biologist, the younger an engineer, neither of them treated much better than slaves from the time they had set foot on the New Azania campus. Both dead of red lung by the age of forty. (Red lung: as if chemical poisoning were a demonic dust.) No, that would not be Florida's fate. She had avoided red lung in Nandi's well-ventilated dome and labs, but she intended to wrest more from life than healthy lungs.

She had found a way to escape, her mothers' dream for her.

The mysterious delivery in her hands was her chance.

On the US-bound ship, a passenger cruiser called, predictably, *Whistling Dixie,* Florida learned the meaning of the orange tag she wore around her neck. The uniformed greeter at the portal was covered in facial hair except for sharp, watching eyes, even hairy across the bridge of his nose. Florida had never seen anyone so hairy.

"Huh—slow down, you!" Hairball said, and Florida thought she would have her package confiscated. Instead, Hairball flicked at her tag. "Orange cabins are helpers' quarters. Not this way—*that* way."

The entrance forked. *This way* was gleaming and satiny, with conveyor seats and trays of water for the lighthearted crowds. *That way* was gloom and poor lighting, with no offerings except a long walk down a narrow corridor.

"But . . . I'm a passenger, not a worker," Nandi said. "I have a private cabin."

Hairball sneered. "Yah—like anyone else would fit with you! Keep moving."

Of course. How could she have expected Nandi to pay for even second-class passage? She'd probably gladly acquiesced to the racial segregation that had become the norm in the United States again.

Florida tried to prepare herself, but the cabin that matched the color and number hanging from her neck was still worse than she'd imagined. She'd hoped for at least a sponge bed, picture window, a chair and desk where she might enjoy the solitude that had been impossible for her in New Azania. She'd rolled her eyes through most of the orientation, believing only the privileged were susceptible to anxiety caused by boredom. More than a month with no concerns but (mostly) her own? No constant summoning? Yet the cabin was hardly bigger than a closet, with a thin pallet that would barely contain her, a retracting sheet of metal as a "desk," and no window. *No window*! No way to see the ocean. It looked more like a prison cell. And she saw no comfortable space for the box. Florida let out a frustrated shriek. Her neighbor tapped the wall, complaining already.

Florida was about to pound back when her box . . . *thunked*. Something inside shifted, scrabbling. Florida remembered Nandi's last instructions: to open the box right away. Whatever was inside was either growing or—

"Oh, please don't let it be . . ."

Yes. It was *alive*. Florida knew that before she pressed her thumb to the lock pad Nandi had configured for her, and it was confirmed when she saw a spray of thin gray fur, a white belly, lashing tail, rounded ears, large eyes, sharp teeth. And claws. The creature slashed at her, raking Florida's right ear, drawing blood. Florida cried out as the creature leaped from the box and desperately sought to hide, wobbly from the trank Nandi must have given it. It fell to its side, disoriented, paws scratching the metallic floor.

"So, by now you've seen the favor I need from you."

Nandi's hologram appeared from a pinprick of projection light on the box, projected so convincingly across the pallet in her purple robe that Florida wondered if it was a live feed. But no, the 3D hologram was recorded—Nandi's eyes were looking in the wrong direction, toward the door.

"You kaffir," Florida said to the projection, wishing so badly that Nandi could hear the banned word from history that she loathed. Florida touched her ear, felt the dampness of blood. Not too much, but still. It stung.

"Don't be angry. Anger is the meal of fools. Nelson Mandela said that."

"You liar. He never said that." Florida hated the way Nandi recited supposed quotations from Nelson Mandela, usually about industry and obedience. Florida had been twelve when she learned through research that Mandela had said *none* of the things Nandi claimed.

Cursing out the hologram was therapeutic, clearing her head. Anger melted, replaced by terror. Florida had smuggled a *live* creature aboard a USian ship! If she got found out, she would be expelled like a stowaway, thrown into the ocean. The orientation had been specific.

"The first thing you should know: it's mute. No voice box. So have no fear of discovery. If you are smart—and I've told you many times, Florida, you are *very* smart—you'll have no trouble keeping it hidden for the voyage. The tranquilizer is under the flap. You'll also find a sedative mist: it's safe for both of you . . . but conserve it, only use it at night. You have a long journey ahead. Keep that same box for storage and use it when you arrive."

The States, Florida reminded herself. This was all so she could go to the States to wade in the Atlantic off the shores of whatever areas had not flooded in the state of Florida. USians avoided the sun most of the day because of UV, but there would be beaches.

"I paid for double rations. One is for you, the other for your charge. You must play with it several times a day—they grow aggressive when they're bored. Actually, so do you—you'll be good company for each other. The crystals beneath the flap will help disintegrate the waste for easy disposal. You'll receive delivery instructions when you land. You must deliver it personally. This breed is from Naidoo Labs, so it will be the first of its type in the States. You're a pioneer! Once you deliver it, I will deposit a full 2 percent of its price in your account."

A one-of-a-kind animal delivery would fetch a hot fee. Two percent might be significant. Not worth dying over, but it might clear her debt. Was Nandi setting her free?

Nandi's voice turned hard: "Needless to say . . . if any harm should come to this animal, if it is injured in any way, you will be sent back to suffer severe consequences."

"I'm not an animal handler, you—you—stain on two continents."

What did she know about animals? Pets were rare in the Aggie districts because of lack of space and long working hours. Naidoo Life Systems specialized in biotech to help humans adapt to environmental shifts—and Nandi's personal hobby was the genetic manipulation of animals. One of her experiments apparently had gone right. But Florida was far from an expert.

The little creature was already on its feet, sniffing the door. Searching for an escape. They were alike after all.

"Is this a cat?" she asked the hologram, forgetting Nandi was not on the other end. She had read about cats, although this animal's face seemed too narrow, the ears too big.

"Be very careful, my little tsotsi. This is dangerous work. But you will be fine."

The hologram pixelated and vanished. One-time play.

Florida faced the creature, whose mouth was frantically miming a memory of speech. Florida saw the shaved neck, the fading scar, and realized Nandi had surgically removed the animal's voice box instead of finding the right stew of genetics to silence it. Had she done the cutting herself, too proud to consult anyone else with her plan? Florida rubbed her ear, wondering why Nandi hadn't removed its claws too.

Tentative, Florida reached her hand out. The creature's face crinkled to pure loathing, baring its sharp teeth. Was it trying to spit at her? *That* was unpleasant.

"You listen to me," Florida told the cat. "We're stuck together. You don't like me, I don't like you. But neither of us wants to get thrown overboard, so don't be afraid of me."

Already, secretly, she felt herself becoming glad. The cabin was disappointing, and now she would have amusement, or at least chores. What Mandela had said about industry was true—it sharpened the mind as well as passing the time. (He had not said it, but she had learned inspiration from the quote before she realized Nandi had made it up. Same difference.)

She lifted the flaps in the box and found the supplies, including a powder marked as food. Once Florida hydrated it, the powder turned a gray-white color, thickish liquid in texture. The creature made a silent motion with its mouth and ran for the dish, licking greedily.

Good. Feeding it was the first step. Keeping it alive.

Florida realized she needed to give the animal a name.

The name she chose was Burden.

The first few days were horrid.

Florida was so worried about discovery that she did not dare leave her cabin, more awful confinement. Sleep, too, was difficult, because each sound the creature made in its endless investigations of the cabin woke her. She used far too much of the sedative mist on both of them those first days, inhaling calm so she could stop their racing hearts.

"This is new for both of us," she said to Burden. Instinct told her to speak gently, since she preferred soft talk herself, and soon Burden was sleeping against her, a warm mound at the small of her back. She began to understand why someone would want a pet, even if she would *never* understand why an USian would want a pet transported from a lab.

When Florida was ready to explore the ship, she chose her destinations carefully according to the map she had memorized. Whenever she left her cabin, she made sure no one saw the tiny paw trying to force its way out, and that the door was securely closed, locked. The other travelers housed on her corridor were USians and held themselves above her although they were helpers too. They clung to imaginary distinctions when on this floor where they all had nothing. In New Azania, at least, the distinctions were real and not imagined: you were either growing richer by controlling the bio systems, or you were hired labor. Little in between. But fine. She would not make friends. Fewer people to explain herself to.

She heard the din of laughter and conversation before the elevator deposited her at the first observation deck. A polite alarm sounded when she tried to pass through the door, and her badge flashed orange. Lower Observation was for black badges only, she remembered. A separate elevator took her to Upper Observation.

And there she sat, with nothing but the ocean all around her, the frivolous USians below. They had plush seating and silly gaming, but she had the most unhindered view of the sea and its undulating white crests. She felt as if the watery void hugged her, somehow.

Florida tried to feel excitement for approaching the nation she had heard so much about but felt only growing dread: The US might mean discovery. The US meant uncertainty. Even if she weren't discovered, the US meant even worse discrimination. If only she could stay in this place, this one time, between destinations, with no responsibilities except the care of Burden. If she could perfect a constant state of leaving. Maybe that was what had happened with the ghost ship, she thought. Maybe the passengers and crew had chosen the journey over their destination.

Florida had learned about the ghost ship during her research when Nandi told her she was being sent out to sea. She'd seen reports that the official 5 percent passenger failure rate was a lie—the actual failure rate was much higher. Ships had vanished more than once, never heard from again. Florida scoured the blue-black waves around her for her ship's twin floating somewhere off course, its comms disabled and useless. A passenger ship would have enough rations for years. What reward might she win for spotting the lost ship?

"Hey there!" a deep voice said behind her, terrifying her. The authoritarian ring made her assume it was a crew officer, perhaps one who had discovered Burden in her absence. But she turned and saw only another passenger, this one with thickly knotted black hair in braids, rocking slightly off-balance from what might be some form of intoxication. Or . . . happiness?

The hair-laden passenger grinned straight, lovely teeth at her. "My name's Lesedi. You look so grim. The trip just started."

Florida sneezed, standing up to exit the observation level. Her sinuses had been irritated since the trip began, and now she was allergic to company. Standing so quickly made her dizzy.

"I am . . . Florida." It was rare, so rare, to share a name with a stranger. Her full, proper name was Florida of Naidoo Life Systems, but Florida did not want to say so. That was not a proper name, anyway.

"I come here every day. This—" Lesedi said, signaling the ocean, "is what I asked to come for. Here I am. On a ship. It's worth putting up with my mistress."

"Your what?"

"My . . ." The woman paused, as if embarrassed. "The woman who hired me. From New York."

"You call her *mistress*? And . . . do you also have a *master*?"

"Only on this ship. It's a pretty easy job, since everything they need is here. I don't care what they want to be called." Florida must have looked appalled despite her efforts, because Lesedi said, "What do you call *your* employer?"

"To her face?" Florida responded. They both laughed, which turned into a sneeze for Florida. She sneezed into her arm. "At first, before I knew better, I called her *Mother*. She was 'raising' me, or at least training me at the Aggie camp. I was young. Now I call her Nandi."

"Well, you can't call an employer by their first name in the States," Lesedi scolded. "Don't let anyone hear you."

"You've been there?"

"I've heard stories from my cousin. She told me not to come, but . . ." Lesedi indicated the ocean again, "how could I miss this? Saltwater air. No noise. No trash."

Florida had seen a trash mountain through her binoculars, though she decided not to mention it. Trash was everywhere. "Will your employer send you back home?"

"No, I'm only a ship's valet. I'll have to work and save up. But I'm not worried. I'm a good worker. The States will suffocate you only if it's all you've ever known."

Florida wasn't sure about that.

"So . . . is it true . . . ?" Lesedi began.

"What?"

"That Aggies . . . the Blacks who came from the States to work . . . you're like slaves?"

"Who said that?"

"My mistress said I'm lucky I'm not a slave like the Aggies. With a long-term contract."

Florida felt more anger than she would have expected, but only because of the sting of truth. Her mothers had said the same thing before they died. "That's insulting."

"No offense meant, I just . . ."

Now Florida felt tears to accompany her anger. She turned her face away to hide them. "It was good to meet you, but I have a headache. I need to go."

Florida hurried away, sneezing again, yet with every step she regretted her emotional response and hoped she would see Lesedi again. She already missed having a human to talk to.

As she left, she heard Lesedi sneeze behind her.

Florida would not see Lesedi again before the power failure.

Just a blip, a flicker, a slight browning of the corridor lights, and then the reliable hum of the auxiliary rod and the ship's cabins were fully powered again.

The cabin's minor anomaly happened in the middle of Florida's sleep cycle—she'd been sleeping longer than usual because she hadn't felt well for a couple of days. The outage made little sound except ambient noises she had learned to sleep through. She did not wake to see her cabin's holo-clock flicker off and on, from blue to red and then back to blue, or hear her toilet automatically refresh, or hear her door hiss open the same way all of the C-wing cabin doors did at 01:18 a.m. Passenger 77-C, Florida of Naidoo Life Systems, heard none of this.

But Burden heard.

Burden stared with fascination as the lights floating on the wall flickered off, then on. Motion was rare in this lifeless cage. Burden was immediately upright, ready to spring!—when a *whishing* sound made his back arch.

No giant challenging predator: it was Door! Retreating!

Any mammal primarily derived from Felis silvestris catus, no matter the cosmetic genetic variations, would be drawn to the scent of newness in the open space that had once been Door. Burden crept from the pallet, senses alert, moving quietly so Big would not be disturbed. Burden could still smell the trap Big had hidden under the floor.

Burden had not been feeling well for a few days, but now the creature's limbs felt wild and strong. He stepped free just as Door *shooshed* closed again.

Florida's first waking instinct, always—*Where's Burden?* And for the first time the animal did not turn up on the pallet or in any of its favorite hiding places in nooks and shadows. She knew he was gone at a glance, her heart pounding, yet she searched anyway. She scoured places that defied reason and logic, tears blinding her. (She would never learn of the power failure. She would convince herself she might have opened her door in the night because of the strength of her sleep supplements from Nandi.)

Soon—door securely locked behind her, just in case—she moved her search to the corridor. To the elevator. To the observation deck. She was noticed everywhere she went, but she could not afford to care about staring. However unlikely, in her mind she saw herself sweeping the animal under her clothes undetected, scurrying back to her room.

But she could not find Burden anywhere. *No, no, no, no, no.* The horror stayed glued to her thoughts. The impossibility of it alone! *Why?* Why, why, why?

She cursed herself when she remembered to check the supply/transport box Nandi had given her for a tracking device, and naturally she found one nestled beneath the waste crystals. Her hands shook as she powered it. So much time wasted!

The device displayed a three-dimensional rendering of the ship, though no signal from Burden's tracker. Had someone thrown him overboard? She backed the tracker's control several hours, to the point when Burden was still in her cabin. She found it, zoomed the image to isolate the Stacks. No movement of the white dot at first. Sleeping in her quarters.

Then—rapid motion down the corridor. Florida gasped. She slipped in her corneal lenses to view the tracker privately, then followed the white dot that raced around the corner ahead of her. She chased it, as if Burden was still close enough to catch. Florida could not fit into the vent beside the tube, but she rode the elevator down another level to match the dot's motion.

Yet the elevator door would not open for her. Black card level only. Florida's heart raced as she watched the dot make its way along a corridor beyond the sealed entrance. What to do?

Then, abruptly, the dot stopped moving. Florida held her breath. The tracking dot stayed fixed for a time, then . . . it was inside one of the black-level cabins. It remained there one hour on the tracker's timer. Two hours. No motion. Then the tracker's dot vanished. Gone.

Florida scurried out of the passageway when she heard approaching voices. She did not want to be seen where she did not belong if Burden had been discovered. Had a passenger or crew member found the animal right away and expelled it? But how? Not from the cabin, certainly. The tracker had not moved beyond the passenger floors. No—someone had found Burden and realized his value. *Someone had disabled the tracker.*

It was all clear to her. These were USians: they treasured pets. Of *course* someone would hide the unusual-looking cat. But had they scoured the chip for information about its owner? Did the tracker lead back to her cabin as surely as it led away? Had Nandi been so careless?

Back in her cabin, Florida wept until her face was burning and raw, until her eyelids were acid. She did not eat. She sat frozen on her pallet, waiting to be accused. Waiting to be stripped and thrown into the ocean to feed the sharks. She calculated scenarios again and again, and she came to the same answer: she would die. Any passenger might have smuggled the engineered cat on board, but a simple investigation would point toward Florida—the Aggie.

She longed to talk to Nandi, but even if Nandi were willing to pay the comms fee (Nandi could afford virtually anything she liked, yet was famously stingy with expenses for Florida, as her cabin attested), Florida could not hope their communication would be private. Even if she were to risk it, what could Nandi advise her to do except get the animal back and to cease communications?

Her fear spurred a coughing fit. Florida coughed until she was doubled over. Until her lungs pinched and she could barely draw a breath.

Florida did not remember her mothers. Nandi had washed away their memory, claiming it was to erase the trauma (Florida had later found the record of her watching her mother claw her chest to breathe as she died), but in an odd way Nandi wanted to be the only mother Florida had known even if she did not mother her. Naidoo Life Systems had been Florida's home—she'd been trained in genetic food engineering since she was old enough to read.

Florida was convinced Nandi cared about her, or Nandi would have left her to sleep in the lab quarters with her cohort. Nandi was not cruel. She had only developed a cool amorality that Florida had decided might be necessary when the stakes were life and the future of the planet. Earth was sustaining its last generations, unless science engineered radical breakthroughs to fight the changing climate with its droughts, floods, and food scarcity. Though sometimes radical breakthroughs bore questionable methods. Nandi was not cruel at heart, but by trade.

Still, sending the animal with Florida had been cruel, even unintentionally. What Nandi believed was deep "trust" in Florida's wits was only her willingness to throw her away. It had also been hubris, which meant that Nandi might have made other mistakes. Because Florida did not remember losing her mothers, this was the worst moment of her life. She could not confront the other passengers to claim ownership. She could not arrive in the States without the animal. And at any moment, because of another passenger's whim, carelessness, or spite, she could be pulled from her cabin and expelled. She was helpless and silent.

After a good rest, her cough went away. She also realized she'd been tolerating a small, constant headache for days, but that, too, was gone. No one had questioned her about Burden. Perhaps the other passenger was as frightened of discovery as she was—that was best.

More than a week after Burden vanished, Florida ventured to the observation deck to try to find Lesedi, but she was not there. No one was in Upper Observation with her, and only two or three USians were in the vast space below, without abandon, games, or laughter. Just sitting and staring out to sea, transfixed. One, she noticed, was quietly sobbing.

The sound of crying made Florida miss Burden. Florida had been learning to manage the fear and problems Burden had brought, and now she slept alone. A pet was a companion if you were lonely. She giggled, remembering how Burden had whipped and chased its tail. Then she sobbed too, her body unfamiliar with laughter. She studied the ocean again. Now, so much vastness did not feel like a hug, more like a tomb. A place to get lost from memory. She searched, anxious for movement, for any sign of the ghost ship floating rudderless.

Was there a face staring from somewhere else, looking for her too?

Quick research told her where to find Lesedi's cabin. Florida had no Burden to rush back to now. They might be friends now. They might love each other now. They might be family now.

Florida knocked. Waited. Knocked again, more loudly. Waved to the door's camera.

Finally, Florida's video monitor flared on. Lesedi's hair was covered with a scarf of deep, dazzling red. So much brightness! Florida's face became a smile—

—and a sick knowing stole it from her. Lesedi was ill. Her eyes were bloodshot, her skin dry and flaking. She was lying down, had been ill for some time. For how long?

"Florida," Lesedi said with a smile in her voice, though not on her face. Her throat was parched. "I've wanted to reach you, but I can barely lift my head."

A horror was swallowing her. "What's happened?"

"I've caught something. A lot of us have. You should stay away. People are dying."

Florida almost, *almost*, remembered her mother's gasps.

"What do you mean? No one told me."

"It's disarray—I'm telling you, a *lot* of people are sick. On the crew too. It comes so fast. And they don't send medicine to our wing. But I hear it's not curing them. The only working elevator is to Upper Observation. We're sealed off." She heaved for a breath, weary from the telling.

Florida had not tried to go anywhere except Upper Observation since Burden left. Everything she needed was in her cabin, including enough flavorless food packets for a month.

"I was sick too," Florida said. "I'm better now."

Lesedi took a long breath and shook her head. "Then you're the first I've heard. No one survives. The ship is—" she took a long breath, "quarantined."

"What does that mean?"

"It means . . . we're infectious, so they isolate—"

"I know what *quarantined* means. What does it mean for us on the ship?"

"Think and you already know," Lesedi said. "They leave us to die. Leave us *here*."

The 5 percent passenger failure rate was a 5 percent *ship* failure rate. Of course.

"But . . . the ship costs too much. The passengers, with so much money—"

"Tomorrow's problem," Lesedi said. "We all agreed to . . . the terms. They salvage the ships down the line. When they figure out what caused the . . . plague. It's happened before. My cousin warned me about getting sick on a ship."

A plague, and maybe not the first. So there *was* another ship floating on the route between Africa and the States. Perhaps more than one.

"I just hoped . . ." Lesedi said, and heaved to breathe, ". . . it wouldn't be mine. Yeah?"

"Yes," Florida said. "I hoped that too."

"I was excited to see New York."

Florida wanted to tell her everything: about how her employer had forced her to smuggle in Burden, and how Burden had scratched her, and how she had gotten sick. Since she was an Aggie, perhaps, her body had fought off the illness. But maybe Nandi had carelessly released a contagion with her smuggled goods: a living creature was never mere cargo. And maybe Florida had spread the illness. USians were not Aggies who had been raised on supplements, so their immune systems could not fight. All because Nandi thought she was so clever.

Florida wanted to tell it all, and not telling might have felt like dying if Lesedi had not been dying before her eyes.

"When I come back," Florida said, "get up and let me in."

* * *

Florida was healthy, so she had brought only a light health pack in addition to her supplements. The Mother's Cure Nandi had made up for her was meant as a general curative for infections or viruses specific to travel. Florida had been saving it for a serious illness, so she hadn't considered squandering it over a headache and fatigue. Once the overnight coughing passed, she'd been fine. (In fact, she'd attributed some of her illness to the stress of losing Burden. She'd finished off the sedative already.)

Now Florida took a dose of Mother's Cure to cleanse her blood of any remaining infection. With time, she could factor in whatever virus Burden had been carrying to perhaps create a better antidote, but Mother's Cure might save Lesedi. Might save any of the other survivors.

But Lesedi first.

Lesedi was so dehydrated, Florida was almost too late. For the first hour, Florida was convinced Lesedi would die in her arms, a new kind of void ready to swallow her. For the first time in memory, she prayed.

The days passed slowly, so slowly, and Lesedi did not improve. Though she had lived longer than the rest, it seemed. No matter how much Florida made a racket with banging and screaming or endlessly trying to open comms from Lesedi's cabin, or her cabin, or a call box on the wall, no one answered.

Was it contempt? Or were they all gone? From time to time, she thought she saw sudden movement, or heard a clatter, and called out for Burden. But the cat never came. Nandi's failed lab experiment was probably long dead too.

With time, Florida overrode the codes to open the C wing so she could explore. She reached the black-level observation deck—empty, by now—the dining hall (the smell told her not to investigate), the rations stations (all, apparently, in good working order and well stocked). She brought food and water to Lesedi's cabin.

Florida hoped it was a sign of good things to come, though it was a ragged hope in a ship crammed with the dead. The smell was not too bad yet because the cabin doors were sealed, but she would have to start throwing the carcasses overboard, one at a time.

Florida cleaned Lesedi's waste as she had cleaned Burden's. She bathed Lesedi. She sang her the shards of long-ago songs, making up the words she had forgotten. Lesedi's needs were so great that the Mother's Cure was quickly depleted, but she was smiling at Florida now. Lesedi seemed, maybe, to be getting better. At least then she would not be so alone.

While Lesedi slept, Florida went to the observation deck—the luxurious one with comfortable seating and beverage dispensers that still worked, not the workers' deck where now-dead crewmen had tried to confine her.

She spent hours staring at the vast, empty sea, the captain of her own ghost ship.

Shopping Day

Only powders and canned foods were left in the pantry by shopping day, so Aisha's lunch for Mom was a mystery stew of flavors tastier than it had any right to be. She'd saved a turkey neck bone, and the meat slipped from the bone. Mom's tired face brightened after she took her first bite, and she smiled at Aisha over her raised spoon. Even Darnell and Rita slurped from their bowls with appreciation, emptying them fast. Two hours of prep and cooking, gone in a few greedy gulps. The twins put down their empty bowls, knowing better than to ask for more, although they were staring at Mom with longing as she ate at her usual measured pace. If you didn't remind her, Mom sometimes hardly ate at all.

"Who wants this last piece?" Mom said from habit, but Aisha insisted that she eat every bite. The twins glared at her in silent protest, though even at eight years old they understood that she needed her meal because it was dangerous to go outside. They had friends and neighbors who had never come home from shopping day. By living carefully, Mom had gone a full month without needing to shop, and they were low on everything now. Most of all, the twins needed albuterol for their asthma. She could barter for groceries with the neighbors, but medicine was precious and meant biking to the distribution lots.

"If I'm not back by six o'clock," Mom said, "you know what to do."

The protocol was this: The curfew was enforced at six, so the only ones out were robbers and soldiers. Each night, they made sure their windows and doors were boarded tight. Aisha had to inspect every inch, looking for weaknesses and imperfections. The only way they had survived in their ruined neighborhood for so long after most other people had left was by being careful. If Mom was ever gone for six hours without word, that meant Aisha had to tell the twins to grab their backpacks and they would use their last credits to board a train. All reports said the camps were worse than the cities, so she would try to find her aunt in Jacksonville if she had to leave Atlanta. She was still only sixteen, yet she might pass for eighteen: unclaimed minors were sent to children's camps. She and the twins might be separated! That *couldn't* happen.

"This is the last time," Mom promised, wrapping her head with the scarf that protected her scalp from the sun's vicious midday heat. "Once I get the meds, we'll go. Sadie says Jacksonville is getting better. Flooding's gone down."

Aisha tried to pretend this was only an ordinary shopping trip as she hugged her mother goodbye, although she had known for two years that every hug could be their last. She wished her mother's old Smith & Wesson had bullets and was more than just a prop. But they had to choose medicine over ammo, and medicine cost most of all.

With her mother gone, Aisha mapped out the day so she wouldn't make herself sick with worry: for the first hour, she would practice the piano. For the second hour, she would give the twins their thirty-minute lessons one at a time. For the third hour, she would find any scraps she could fix for dinner. Her plans kept her mind on her fingers, on the arpeggios, on the scales she was trying to teach her younger sister and brother, on the boiling water on the stove. She did not check the news because the news would only make her anxious.

Only if Mom is late, she told herself. *I'll only check then.*

Up until the instant the digital clock changed from 5:49 to 5:50, Aisha expected her to come panting through the door. Once, Mom had come back at 5:47—her latest *ever*!—and Aisha had paced the entire time, so she had not allowed herself to worry again. When 5:50 came, it was a betrayal of her trust—and then terror flooded her veins with ice.

All three of them sat in silence staring at the clock until 5:55. Darnell and Rita had given up childish habits like squirming at the table, since they were always grateful for food—*any* food. And they all knew the clock meant Mom was running out of time.

"We have to start locking up," Darnell said. "That's the rule."

"Five more minutes," Aisha said.

The twins looked at each other like they were parents and she was a wayward child. Rita didn't say anything, though tears shimmered in her eyes. Aisha didn't know if Rita was more worried about Mom's safety or afraid that robbers or soldiers would come to their door. Rita looked ready to sprint from her seat, her meal forgotten.

"Trust me—we have time," Aisha said. "She's just a little held up. She's pedaling full speed right now with her bag of surprises. Close your eyes and you'll see her."

Saying it aloud made it seem true. With her eyes closed for ten seconds, Aisha saw her mother's timeworn sneakers pedaling furiously. The twins closed their eyes too and looked noticeably relieved, so much that Darnell stirred at his plate and took another bite. Under the table, Aisha checked her phone for news and saw the alert right away: their street was being relocated tonight. The relocations had been taking place in communities bordering theirs, but somehow they had been spared . . . until now. The government wanted to keep track of survivors, and forced relocation was the new state law in most of the neighborhoods still harboring a few people.

Three thuds landed on the door as soon as Aisha saw the bulletin. She caught her breath.

"Aisha!" a man's voice called. "Open up! Hurry!"

It was only their neighbor, Devon. He was from Jamaica and had been visiting family in the US when the trouble started. Now his family was dead and only he and his wife, the visitors, were left. He was wild-eyed when she opened the door.

"Your mom back?" Devon asked.

Aisha couldn't lie. Her face must have said it all.

He cursed. "She stopped by before she left and said to look out for you. Come with us now. Everyone has to leave the building. They have tear gas."

As if in confirmation, Aisha heard a not-too-distant sound like a small explosion: soldiers were launching tear gas into a neighboring building.

"But where are they taking us?" Aisha said. "How can we let Mom know?"

"They'll give us trackers," he said. "That's their story anyway."

Another boom outside, and the sound of screams this time. Darnell and Rita jumped up from the table and huddled together in the corner by the stove. They were crying now.

Devon's wife, Nia, pushed into the apartment in a cloud of coconut oil she used for her dreadlocks. She must have had a year's supply, Aisha thought—her mind was looking for anything else to think about, so she fixed her attention on the salt-and-pepper locs that grew down her neighbor's back. She tried not to see the desperation in the woman's eyes. Desperation . . . and something new. And dangerous.

"Why are we still talking?" Nia said. "Get your things! We'll claim you."

Aisha wanted to hear it as a generous offer, that a neighbor was willing to vouch for them to keep them together, which was what Mom said mattered most—but Aisha's head was shaking.

Something felt wrong. "*No*," she said. "She'll be here any minute. She's on her way!"

Devon took Aisha's shoulders and shook her hard, as if to knock thoughts from her head. "It's almost six, girl! You're talking nonsense. They've picked her up by now."

Aisha's eyes didn't soften to signal that she understood, so he hissed with irritation and rushed into the kitchen, grabbing Rita by one arm and Darnell by the other. The twins wailed.

"Stop it!" Aisha said. "Let them go!"

Nia, who was oh-so-gentle and had fixed them endless plates of spicy jerk chicken back when chickens were plentiful, tugged on Aisha to keep her from interfering. "You don't understand! This is what she wanted—we *promised* to look after you. Everyone loses people, Aisha! *Everyone.* But you'll have each other! You'll have *us*."

Devon was so strong that he had heaved one twin under his left arm and one under his right like potato sacks, and no amount of wriggling could free them. They screamed.

"Come with us or not," Devon said, his voice strained from their weight. His steps were slightly staggered, but he bumped past the table to make his way to the door. Rita wailed anew when her knee hit the tabletop. A dish clattered to the floor.

"Stop it—you're hurting them!" Aisha said.

"He's saving them, child," Nia said. "Can't you see that? Do you want them in a camp?"

As another tear-gas bomb exploded, this one close enough to smell the bitter chemicals, Aisha thought she *did* understand. When Mom always said, *You know what to do*, this was what she meant—the hard thing. The unspeakable was what she must do. Everyone lost people, just like Nia said. Their lives in this tiny, forgotten apartment had been a dream that ended long ago. They simply hadn't known it yet.

"Wait," Aisha said, her throat nearly sealed with a sob. "I'll get the bags."

As soon as she spoke the words, Mom was standing in the open doorway like she'd been conjured. Her scarf was gone, her hair mussed. Sweat dappled her shirt. But her shopping duffel was slung across her shoulder, bulging with necessities. Aisha stared for long seconds to make sure Mom wasn't only her imagination, and then Rita and Darnell were calling for her. Slowly, Devon lowered them to their feet. He did not seem happy to see her.

"What's going on?" Mom said, her voice even, not angry. Mom defused conflicts, she never exacerbated them. That was another way she had kept them all alive. She had once talked a robber out of hurting them with kindness in her voice and an apple.

"Relocation," Nia said. "You told us if it ever happened . . ."

"We were just doing what's right," Devon said.

Then Aisha remembered that families with children got extra food credits, and she wondered if her neighbors had come for selfish reasons. Stories said that sometimes people bought and sold children they had "saved" from the camps. Aisha stared into Devon's eyes to try to see the truth, but he looked away.

"Glad you made it back," he said, his voice soft. "We were worried."

Mom might have been wondering the same thing about their motives, yet she always hid her worries behind a smile. "Thank you," she said. When they didn't leave immediately, Mom repeated herself: "Thank you so much."

Devon and Nia looked at each other, as if trying to reach a decision. Then Devon took a step toward the door. "Of course," he said. "Neighbors look out for neighbors."

As soon as they were gone, the door shut and locked tight behind them, they all hugged Mom and could smell her visit outside: the sweat on her skin and smoke in her hair. They hugged so tightly that they could feel each other's hearts beating in their breasts.

"The inhalers?" Rita said. Her wheezing was more obvious now that she'd had so much excitement.

"Yes, I got everything. Now you grab your bags." Mom lowered herself to eye level to talk to the twins in a voice as if she were about to tell a grand fairy tale, with a pose on one knee that Aisha thought she might remember most about her mother for the rest of her life.

"We're together now," Mom said. "Let's see what's next."

As always, Mom pretended to smile.

The Biographer

The Biographer arrived much sooner than Olivia expected. The young woman on her doorstep that morning was wearing a wool coat too threadbare for the snowy trek up the hill to Olivia's house—which was fashioned after a castle with its pale stone facade and a half-frozen moat filled with koi. The stranger was breathless after climbing so many steps, but Olivia hesitated before opening her door.

She wouldn't have expected a Biographer so early, which seemed counter to the strict protocols Biographers were famous for. Through the viewfinder, the stranger had a studious look but was also much younger than any Biographer she'd heard about, maybe in her midtwenties, so Olivia at first thought she might be only another of the faithful on a sojourn to say she had met her face-to-face. Usually these people were harmless, though one could never be too careful about opening one's door.

Then the young woman held out the golden envelope and crimson seal for a clear view on her security camera. Olivia had heard about the "golden appointments," as they were sometimes called tongue in cheek, but it looked the way it had been described in rumors. The envelope reminded her of a story her mother had told her from her youth involving golden tickets, but Olivia could not remember the story or author because it was from Before, as if a wildfire had consumed her childhood. Everyone had the same experience if they had been born before the Plagues, yet it still made her feel tainted and empty at times—like now, facing a Biographer at her door and having so little to say. And far too early to say it.

"Olivia Burns," the young woman announced. "Congratulations—you have been assigned a Biographer. Now your story will be told."

Olivia hadn't had her wake-up tea yet, so it was hard to feel celebratory. She had turned only sixty on her last birthday and had fully recovered from her bout with the virus, so this encounter had the markings of a bureaucratic error. But she wouldn't make the young woman wait outside in the cold, so she pushed the wall panel button to unlock her door, which slid open on a silent track, letting in a bracing smack of cold air across her face although she was several yards from the doorway.

Before entering, the young woman ceremoniously fitted herself with a snug medical mask covering her nose and mouth in skintight fiber designed to better display facial features. Second Skin, they called it. The mask created a bizarre flattening effect across her features, especially her mouth, though Olivia could still make out the nub of the woman's nose, rounded like hers. She'd heard that Biographers were assigned subjects who were similar to help create rapport. And it was true—the young woman's brown skin, windswept corkscrew hair, and old-fashioned round-frame eyeglasses reminded her of herself at that age, which seemed both long ago and as if she could find that youthful face in her own mirror.

"A mask isn't necessary," Olivia said. "Wear it if you prefer, of course. But my house is sanitized. And I've long recovered. I can swab and show you my med file—"

"Not necessary," the woman said. "Oh—!" She tripped slightly on the small step into the house, and the large plastic box she was carrying slipped from her arms, scattering files and photographs on the stone foyer floor. Olivia bent over to try to assist her, but that made the woman hiss and wave her away, so Olivia took a step back and watched her collect her research, all of it protected in plastic sleeves. She glimpsed a photograph of herself on the set of her most famous film, *Sick*, that she had not seen before. She only saw the image in a glance; her face looked oddly contorted, and the image filled her with unease. Before she could ask for a better look, the Biographer had deftly refiled it in the box.

"I apologize for my clumsiness," the Biographer said. "Please rest assured that the story of your life will be treated with my utmost care and respect."

"Yes, about that . . ." Olivia said. "Aren't you early?"

"I'm sorry about the hour. I tried to time it—"

"No, not just that . . ." Olivia twirled, her arms raised like a phoenix's wings in her bathrobe. "I'm perfectly healthy. I've recovered. Remember that old quote by Mark Twain . . . ?" From the way the Biographer's eyebrows lowered, she seemed to have no idea who Mark Twain was. "The point is, I'm not dying. So you're a bit early. I'm sure I have three or four good films left in me."

The Biographer smiled, a misshapen leer beneath her tight mask. "That's just a misconception, Master Burns. We—"

"Dear God, *Master*? Please call me Olivia."

"Of course . . . Olivia . . ." The woman said her name as if it were an unfamiliar language. "Especially for someone of your stature, the Academy of Biographers believes that it's best to get an early start to create the most thorough scholarship."

Damnit. So she wouldn't be able to send this young woman away and enjoy a quiet cup of tea before getting back to work on her script after all. She had never heard of anyone sending a Biographer away, especially not so soon.

"I'm sorry, so . . . how does this work? Obviously, this is my first time."

"I'll be staying with you for a short while," the Biographer said. "I'll go back down the hill now and get my bag. I had to be sure I would find you. This will surprise you . . . but sometimes people hide from us."

It didn't surprise Olivia at all, if only because of the disruption. She almost protested that she didn't have a guest room, but the size of her house would have called her a liar. Truthfully, she had never explored some of the rooms on the third floor. The Biographer would have to sleep up there with the dust and tarps that had probably been there since the original owners died of Plague forty years before. And how long was "a short while," anyway? Olivia had hoped to finish her shooting script within the week.

"What's your name?" Olivia said.

"I'm sorry, but too personal a relationship between Biographer and subject can taint the scholarship. You can make up a name for me, if that makes you feel more comfortable."

Olivia resisted the urge to roll her eyes. The stories of the ridiculous protocols were true. "Fine. Go get your things. I'll fix you a cup of tea."

"No, please," the Biographer said. "It's our honor, and a requirement, that we cook for you and serve you during our stay. If you just give me a minute . . . I'll fix the tea for *you*. I know just how you like it."

Olivia Burns would have been an unlikely candidate for a Biographer if not for pure luck—if *luck* was the right word for her dystopian film about an oncoming global plague (which she had only meant as a metaphor for climate change and bigotry) that unfolded almost exactly the way her film had predicted it.

Sick had been her first project out of film school, funded by an arts grant her academic mentor had told her about after she started sleeping with him. The grant had been minimal, with most of the shoot taking place on deserted shrubland in the Mojave desert. The ten-day shoot had been miserable, between the heat, failing camera equipment, and a temperamental crew unaccustomed to hauling their own gear. The cast was so small that she'd had to play one of the parts herself—Cassie, who was so traumatized by the loss of her family in the fictitious plague that she rarely spoke a word (which was the best fit for her limited acting ability).

Sick's release hardly had the hallmarks of any kind of classic. Despite her grant, she'd spent her last money in postproduction and struggled to find a distributor. Finally, she'd thrown it on the Internet at the mercy of fate. At the time, she'd considered the film a failure: too "arty," too pedantic, too grim. But it survived the Plagues. She'd kept her physical copies pristine alongside her water and food supplies even during the worst times. It also didn't hurt that she was one of the few filmmakers who survived the first Plague years.

Sick hadn't made her a profit—but it made her a prophetess.

And that, it turned out, was a story worth telling.

Olivia's throat tickled with a cough while the Biographer was outside retrieving her bag, so she quickly flicked the inside of her cheek with a swab from her foyer drawer and was relieved when the pleasant tone signaled she was still free of the virus. But the cough was hard to kick—some patients had spasmodic coughing the rest of their lives even after the virus was gone. Olivia, however, was lucky. She'd coughed until her ribs hurt for the first week, yet the new serums were deft at fighting back against infection. Researchers had not vanquished it completely—and probably never would, the Cabinet of Science confessed—but the current virus's destruction bore little resemblance to the early days from decades before, when Plague had changed the face of the world. "It isn't just here to kill us," her main character, Sadie, had said in *Sick*. "It's also here to set us free." (Her friend Lakisha, who had played Sadie, complained on the set that the dialogue was too on-the-nose, but Olivia had insisted on keeping the line. Couldn't even death be considered a kind of freedom?)

Olivia couldn't have known then that those words would later be enshrined at the base of statues in her own image at the Survival Monuments in London, Dubai, New York, Tokyo, and Mexico City. She would never have believed how close the Plagues would have brought humankind to extinction, and that so much would be different in the After, including an indie film-maker's ascension to dizzying heights of esteem. When she'd learned through the Art Authority that she would receive a life-time stipend and this castle on a hill, she'd laughed herself to tears.

For all her riches, she had only six wayward cats to keep her company. And now this strange Biographer who would not even reveal her name.

"Life is a mystery every day," Sadie had said in *Sick*.

Maybe her dialogue *was* bland and on-the-nose. But that didn't mean it wasn't also true.

"One lesson we learned from the Plague," the Biographer said when she returned and had served Olivia a mug of perfectly brewed chai, "is that each human life is a miracle worth chronicling."

The sentiment was lovely, so Olivia decided not to bring up the obvious fact that less than a quarter of the population could expect to be assigned a Biographer, by her estimate. Clearly, most lives were deemed far less miraculous than others. Still, it was a clear improvement over the old times, when biographies had been written by chance by obsessed scholars acting independently and filled with bias, not organized through an academy with training and a creed.

It also amused Olivia to hear her Biographer use the word *we*, since this youngster had clearly been born long after the worst Plague years. She had grown up in the new world and had seen few glimpses of the old one: the wars and senseless fires that had swallowed so many libraries, museums, and treasures.

"So how does this work?" Olivia said when the last of her tea had cooled and the Biographer had run out of platitudes. Their long silence had veered beyond awkward to troubling. They were sitting across from each other at Olivia's vast dining room table, which had chairs for eight—ironic, considering that she entertained only rarely.

"Ah!" the Biographer said. "I observe you. That's the core of all biography."

"Observe me doing what?"

"Whatever you would ordinarily be doing."

"As in . . . finishing my script?"

The Biographer smiled, that horrid grin again. "That would be my honor, of course."

Olivia was relieved, quick to rise to her feet. She felt a cough try to rise in her throat, but she suppressed it for the sake of politeness. And she certainly didn't want to give her Biographer the impression that she was frail at sixty, when the observation would be enshrined into history.

The Biographer rose as well, mirroring her motions, a tablet computer ready in her hands. "I'll be right behind you."

In her office, Olivia suffered impulses to squirm in her straight-back chair with this young woman perched in her window seat five yards away, watching her like an owl. Occasionally, the Biographer whispered an observation into her recorder, scattering Olivia's thoughts although she couldn't make out what she was saying—or especially because she couldn't. The *clack-clack-clack* of her retro-styled typewriter usually chased away sounds unrelated to her stories, but she could not unremember the presence of someone chronicling her every move. She glanced up and found the woman taking a photograph of her. Olivia chastised herself for not dressing in day clothes instead of staying in her bathrobe. She had lived alone for too long. History would remember her as a lunatic hermit who didn't practice basic daily rituals.

This would not work. Not at all.

"I write better when I'm by myself," Olivia said after ninety minutes of struggle.

"Oh!" The Biographer sounded more surprised than disappointed. "Of course. I'll make my way around your kitchen and start working on your lunch. But may I ask one question?"

"Ask away." The sooner she started her interviews, the sooner this woman would go.

"That typewriter. I've read that you have an attachment to it because your father used an antique IBM Selectric when you were young, from 1987, I believe. But you had a manual one built, modeled on one from 1939."

They were statements, not questions, though Olivia guessed what she was asking. "When I was a young woman in my late twenties, I went for long periods without a home, without electricity or solar panels. An old typewriter I found in an abandoned warehouse helped save my life. Writing was always the way I felt most alive, even when I was surrounded by death. When I didn't have paper, I typed on the back pages of flyers and posters I found hanging on the walls."

"Do you still have any of the old manuscripts from that time?"

Olivia felt a physical flash of pain in her chest as she remembered the fire that had devoured the subway station where she'd lived for six months with her typewriter—deliberately set by police, as far as she knew. She still had a burn on her shoulder blade from her narrow escape. Even the memory of losing her typewriter and its fruit wearied her.

"No," she said. "All that's lost now. I was barely able to save a copy of my film."

"What were those scripts about?"

"The same thing most of my stories are about," Olivia said. "Surviving."

It then occured to Olivia that the Biographer took frenzied notes during her observations, and didn't use her recorder or take any notes when Olivia was mining such difficult memories. Shouldn't her personal history be the lifeblood of her biography?

"Did you get all of that?" Olivia prompted.

The Biographer nodded, tapping her temple. "Yes. I'll remember." She noted Olivia's puzzled stare with a huff of impatience. "You're confused."

"A bit."

"So here it is in small bites, Master . . ." Despite the artificially respectful moniker, the Biographer's tone was so condescending that Olivia flinched against her chair. This arrogant little bitch. When she'd been this woman's age, she'd been trapping squirrels and wild hares for food in the woods, and a man with snowy dreadlocks who looked eighty had taught her how to tan rabbit hides to make them into warm vests. Surviving in ways she could not imagine.

". . . You need to understand that we're not journalists. These won't be interviews. And you're a storyteller, so we can't have you telling your own story, can we? That's an *auto*biography— completely your right, but unregulated, as you know."

Tradition or not, Olivia came close to telling her to get the hell out of her house. The words tickled her tongue. Instead, she said, "*You* asked *me* about the typewriter."

"And thank you very much for your answer. That was lovely. I promise it was."

I promise it was. Olivia couldn't suppress the cough she hid behind her palm. What a bad actress this woman was! Or worse—she couldn't be bothered to try to hide the disdain nestled beneath the surface of her professed admiration.

"I'll make you some honey lemon tea for that cough." The unpleasant young woman gave a bland curtsy before she turned toward the door.

* * *

Time passed slowly with the Biographer in her house. Olivia was usually restless in her sleep before dawn, eager to begin her days at her typewriter, but now she wanted to linger on her silk sheets, avoiding the strange girl as long as she could.

First, the Biographer was dirty. Olivia had barely noticed the crud under the woman's fingernails when she first served her tea because of whatever long trek she had made. But by the second and third days, it was clear that she did not change her clothes or bathe. Her blouse grew so rumpled that she must be sleeping in her clothes too. She had also taken to walking barefoot, and the soles of her feet looked like they had been painted black. The unmistakable odor of unwashed skin was baking from her more strongly each hour, making Olivia's throat pinch shut when the woman leaned over her to serve her meals at the table.

And the food! The meals she fixed felt like food for the infirm: soups, mashes of indistinct vegetables, dry toast, apple sauce. When Olivia complained that she was feeding her like a patient, the Biographer only gave her the placid smile that was her substitute for interaction. Olivia got up late the second night to cook herself the foods she craved from her freezer, only to find that her lamb cubes, chicken breasts, and caramel-chunk ice cream had been removed. When she asked the Biographer why she had moved her food without permission, the grubby young woman gave her a blank stare and insisted she had never seen the food.

"How long will you be staying?" Olivia finally asked on the third day.

"Not much longer." As vague as possible. As usual.

"Is there an average stay for a Biographer?"

The woman shrugged. "The duties sometimes take more time, sometimes less."

THE WISHING POOL AND OTHER STORIES

Duty was a strong word, Olivia thought, since all the woman seemed to do was sit staring at her, or chronicle the books on her shelves, or cook her another mess of a meal. (On that note, at least Olivia was losing weight.) Her cats avoided the stranger, so she rarely even got feline comfort since the Biographer's arrival. The kitties stayed hidden at night, when Olivia was sure she could hear the Biographer walking aimlessly through the house, occasionally bumping into things. One night she broke a ceramic bowl, waking Olivia after midnight, and left the pieces at the foot of the stairs, almost as if she hoped Olivia would trip over the ruins of her life. No apology. No explanation. Olivia didn't have the energy for a confrontation, so she threw the bowl away herself. She noticed that the trash can outside of her kitchen door was overflowing with other items from the house—many of them old and rarely used, but still. The nerve!

Telling the Biographer not to touch her things was of no use. The woman smiled and nodded after every correction, then carried on exactly, if not worse, than before.

By the fourth day, Olivia was so frustrated that she researched Biographer protocols on her computer—because she was sure this woman must be in violation of several. The Academy of Biographers had a website with an official seal picturing an old-fashioned fountain pen inside a wreath, though the site did not have a way for nonmembers to access any of its files, or even a welcome message, so she gave up on finding official accounts. She found plenty of complaints elsewhere online about the caste system declaring some people worthy of biographies and not others, and a few rogue biography organizations boasting more egalitarian goals and "happy endings for all," but the long threads (many of them heavily redacted) offered no information about sanctioned Biographers and how to be rid of one.

Olivia was a bit disappointed in herself that she had never taken notice of the quiet controversies around Biographers, since she had never believed such matters affected her—and wasn't that so much of what was wrong in the world? Weren't lack of empathy and apathy a big part of the reason the Plagues had taken hold with such unrelenting might? Hadn't that, in fact, been a big part of her inspiration for *Sick*?

On the fourth night, while the Biographer was warbling an unrecognizable song at the top of her lungs while she clanked pots and pans together in the kitchen, Olivia noticed that the woman's file box was unlocked, a glimmer from one of the plastic sleeves peeking through. Olivia quickly opened the box and pulled up the sleeves one by one: many held photographs, some held documents and letters.

The first photo was from the set of *Sick*, capturing a moment Olivia had nearly forgotten: that day the pressure of long hours and little money had caused her to scream at her best friend, Lakisha, her face so contorted with rage that she was barely recognizable. *Dear Lord!* Lakisha was long dead—nearly everyone of her generation was—and Olivia hoped the Biographer had interviewed people who knew her truer nature as mild, even shy. Sleeve after sleeve painted a less flattering portrait of her, from overdue water bills to discarded manuscript pages she thought she had destroyed to the deluded letter from her mentor blaming her for his destroyed marriage because of their three-month affair. She had only been nineteen, and he was a grown man of forty! Again, Olivia was sure she had burned the letter as soon as she read it . . . but somehow the Biographer had it in her files. One photo was just mounds of ash and charred walls. But in the center—

Oliva gasped. Her old typewriter! This was her subway station shelter after it had burned.

Her fingers were trembling, so she slammed the file box of horrors shut. Why was the Biographer only cataloging her worst moments? Her biggest failures? Her sharpest pain? Her most deeply buried shame?

"Are you alright?" the Biographer asked.

Olivia didn't know how long the woman had been standing behind her, but surely she'd seen Olivia rifling through her files. Though Olivia didn't really care about being caught.

"Have you started my biography?" she said. "I'd like to see a few pages. I don't like the direction it seems to be taking—"

The Biographer barked out a laugh so loud that she covered her mouth with both hands. Tears of glee peeked from her eyelids. "Subjects can't read their biographies!" she said, muffled. And laughed some more.

A new shame overtook Olivia: She had never read a biography, she realized. Not once. She had seen biography sections in the National Library behind golden doors, yet she had never been curious enough to apply to read one. How could that be? *Everyone* has a story.

"You look a bit pale to me, Lakisha," the Biographer said. "I'll bring you some tea."

"You know damn well my name isn't Lakisha," Olivia responded.

The Biographer's eyes seemed to dance with glee at irritating her. "Oh, that's right. Lakisha was your best friend since childhood. She was the best part of your film, you know. It's a shame the way you treated her."

"I want you to leave," Olivia said, fighting back tears. Her friendship with Lakisha had never had the time to recover from the trials of the movie shoot, a regret she had smothered over the years. "This match isn't working. I'll ask the Academy for another Biographer."

The woman ignored her, turning back toward the kitchen. Olivia noticed a thin veil of smoke through the kitchen doorway. She coughed, a reflex. Whatever was burning did not smell like food. More like . . . papers?

"That's a nasty cough!" the Biographer called. "Your hacking has been worrying me."

"That's ridiculous. I can count on one hand how many times

I've coughed since you've been here," Olivia said. "And you're burning something in my kitchen. Anyone would cough."

By the time the Biographer returned with a cup of tea that smelled like mint—at least she could brew good tea—Olivia had calmed down by reminding herself that all things came to an end. The Biographer might not leave today, but one day she would. And then this horrible ordeal would be over.

The tea was sweeter than usual, though Olivia didn't complain. Unlike the meals the Biographer served her, at least her tea had something like flavor.

As usual, the Biographer sat across from her watching her.

"Let's keep things pleasant between us," Olivia said to break the silence. "I'm sure the Academy was exercising wisdom when it chose you."

"Not at all," the woman replied. "I was the only one willing."

Her staring eyes were more unnerving than usual now. Olivia had only taken three sips of tea, but she put the mug down on her table. Her coasters were gone. The Biographer had left at least half a dozen faded rings in her good oak from tea mugs and glasses since she arrived, so the tabletop was already ruined.

"I'm going upstairs to do some writing," Olivia said. "I'll need to be alone."

"Still trying to write on the typewriter your father gave you?"

Olivia attempted to stand up, but an alarming wave of dizziness rocked her back. "I've told you . . . my father always used an electric typewriter. He didn't give it to me . . ."

"Are you sure?" the Biographer said. "That's not how I remember it."

In fact, Olivia suddenly *wasn't* sure. Sitting still didn't soothe her dizzy spell, and her mind was reeling, unmoored. Whose typewriter had it been? Was the smoke in her house from the subway fire? Had she ever lived at all? Her mind fumbled to answer the simplest questions.

"You did something to my tea," Olivia said, finally understanding. "You drugged me."

The Biographer stood up and walked to Olivia, squatting to meet her at eye level. When the woman removed her mask, Olivia was shocked at how wrinkled her face had grown underneath, unless it was only her imagination—or was she looking into a mirror?

"It's against the rules . . ." the Biographer whispered, "but I like you, Olivia, so I'll give you a preview of your biography. You have faithfully used your long-dead father's typewriter, which survived the Plagues . . ."

"That's . . . not true. I had it made—"

". . . and you might have had three or four more films left in you, but you got sick."

"I'm not . . . sick," Olivia said, though she had to gasp to draw the air for speech. "I recovered. I had a . . . mild case. That was . . . weeks ago."

The Biographer was so close that her stench clogged Olivia's nostrils. "You were cut down by the very Plague you prophesied in your film."

"Why . . . are you doing this?" Olivia choked. The room was dimming.

The Biographer leaned closer to her ear, her breath hot and putrid. "Why do you think?"

Olivia knew the answer. She heard herself laugh even as her lungs cinched, starving for oxygen. She reveled in one last marvel of irony and tragedy, a fiction more true than reality, the escape from her suffering. She opened her mouth and coaxed out what her Biographer would accurately chronicle as her last words: "It's a good story."

The Biographer squeezed Olivia's damp, cooling hand between two dirt-crusted palms. "I shouldn't say this, but it's one of the best we've written."

Oh yes, it was good. Someone might even venture past the

golden doors to read it one day. Olivia almost smiled before she—and her untold stories—slept in her Biographer's arms.

Acknowledgments

I have to start with home. My parents, John Dorsey Due, Jr. (who is eighty-eight as of this writing) and the late Patricia Stephens Due, always encouraged my dream to be a writer and never pressured me to follow in their paths. And their paths were *mighty*—they are both in the Florida Civil Rights Hall of Fame. I feel blessed daily that my parents believed that progress was important in all forms—including the arts. If they had discouraged me, I might never have become a writer. I also want to thank my sisters, Johnita Due and Lydia Due Greisz, for being the lifelong friends our mother truly wanted us to be.

Also, thank you to my husband of nearly twenty-five years, Steven Barnes, who has been my most precious collaborator in every way—as a partner, as a coparent, and as a creator. We collaborate on screenplays more often than prose, but his spirit and feedback are present in almost everything I write. I'm also so thrilled to still be sharing a home with our eighteen-year-old son Jason, who has taught me so much as he strides toward adulthood. While my stepdaughter Nicki lives on her own now, she is still very much a part of our home.

I must also thank my oldest friends: Luchina Fisher, Olympia Duhart, Craig Shemin, and Kathryn Larrabee. You keep me young at heart.

Also, thanks to Johnny Temple at Akashic Books for bringing this project to life. And many thanks to the editors at the publications listed below who solicited stories from me and encouraged me to continue my practice of writing short stories, my first love, while I was in the various storms of life. This collection would not exist without them.

Some of the stories in this volume were originally published elsewhere. "The Wishing Pool" was published in 2021 by *Uncanny Magazine*, and was showcased on *LeVar Burton Reads;* "Haint in the Window" was published in 2022 in the anthology *South Central Noir,* edited by Gary Phillips; "Incident at Bear Creek Lodge" was published in 2022 in the anthology *Other Terrors*, edited by Vince A. Liaguno and Rena Mason; "Thursday Night Shift" was published in March 2018 in *Dark Discoveries;* "Last Stop on Route 9" was published in January 2021 in *Nightmare;* "Suppertime" was published in 2023 in the anthology *New Suns 2*, edited by Nisi Shawl; "Migration" was published in November 2016 in *Nightmare;* "Caretaker" was published in 2019 in *Fangoria;* "One Day Only" was published in 2019 in the anthology *Wastelands: The New Apocalypse*, edited by John Joseph Adams; "Attachment Disorder" was published in 2019 in the anthology *A People's Future of the United States*, coedited by John Joseph Adams and Victor LaValle; "Ghost Ship" was published in 2022 in the anthology *Africa Risen*, coedited by Sheree Renée Thomas, Oghenechovwe Donald Ekpeki, and Zelda Knight; "Shopping Day" was published in 2020 in the Serial Box anthology *How We Live Now;* "Return to Bear Creek Lodge" was published in 2023 in the anthology *Christmas and Other Horrors*, edited by Ellen Datlow; "Dancing" was published in the 2023 anthology *A Darker Shade of Noir: New Stories of Body Horror by Women Writers*, edited by Joyce Carol Oates.